# Pra

"Be prepared to get [...] searched, and sumpt[...] writes with her whole heart and soul. I adored *The French Kitchen*."
—Kate Thompson, author of *The Little Wartime Library*

"In *The French Kitchen*, award-winning author Kristy Cambron weaves multiple characters and storylines into a tapestry of secrets, betrayals, and redemption. Full of mouthwatering culinary scenes and peppered with several appearances from famed chef Julia Child, who worked in intelligence during World War II, this story of spies and lovers zips between the coast of northern France during the war and Paris in the early 1950s as a former American intelligence operative desperately searches for answers about a loved one lost during the war—and in the process, finds the possibility of love where she least expects it. Delicious!"
—Kristin Harmel, *New York Times* bestselling author of *The Stolen Life of Colette Marceau*

"Kristy Cambron has long delighted readers with her richly textured tales of epic historical episodes and the intimate, intricate workings of the human heart. In her latest work, *The British Booksellers*, Cambron delivers yet again, with her powerful punch of assiduous research and skillful, lush storytelling. Sweeping across generations and both World Wars, this is a luminous ode to the soul's deep and indelible yearning for love, hope, and truth."
—Allison Pataki, *New York Times* bestselling author of *Finding Margaret Fuller*

"With pitch-perfect prose and impeccable research, Kristy Cambron brings to life the Forgotten Blitz bombings of World War II—and shines a light on the ways in which we find hope in even the darkest moments. A testament to bravery, loss, and the power story has to unite us, *The British Booksellers* will steal readers' hearts. This stunning novel is a poignant reminder of the indomitable nature of the human spirit and the enduring power of true love. Five huge stars!"

—Kristy Woodson Harvey, *New York Times* bestselling author of *The Summer of Songbirds*

"From page one, the dynamic, endearing characters in *The British Booksellers* stole my heart. Kristy Cambron is an assured storyteller, weaving together dual periods and complex family structures with ease. Fans of *Downton Abbey* will adore *The British Booksellers*."

—Erika Robuck, national bestselling author of *Sisters of Night and Fog*

"Set in the English countryside and spanning two wars, Kristy Cambron's latest, *The British Booksellers*, is a beautiful and enlightening novel that captures the lost love and youthful dreams of two unlikely soulmates, Charlotte and Amos. Full of longing and sprinkled with literary gems, I was completely swept away with this enchanting tale."

—Nicola Harrison, author of *Hotel Laguna*

"Impeccably researched and highly inspirational, *The Italian Ballerina* shows the complex political and human plight of those fighting for freedom in World War II Italy and how personal sacrifice and daring can have an impact on generations to come. Cambron uses her considerable talents as a writer of historical fiction to bring to life a large cast of characters scattered across the globe in several different time periods, each of the 'good guys' someone we would be honoured to call a friend. An uplifting tale that educates, energizes, and comforts the reader. I was captivated from its enigmatic, action-packed beginning to its most wonderfully satisfying end."

—Natalie Jenner, author of the international bestseller *The Jane Austen Society* and *The Bloomsbury Girls*

"Incredibly researched and emotionally evocative, Cambron—once again—takes us into the depths of war as well as to the heights of love, bravery, sacrifice, and devotion. I thoroughly enjoyed every moment within this story and must warn readers—you'll completely lose your heart to young Calla. Enjoy!"

—Katherine Reay, bestselling author of *The Printed Letter Bookshop* and *The London House*, for *The Italian Ballerina*

"With rare insight and remarkable finesse, Cambron excavates the forgotten fragments of history and crafts them into a sweeping masterpiece. Encompassing decades and inspired by a true story of extraordinary audacity, *The Italian Ballerina* explores how the ripples of the past merge with the present and reminds us of the capacity of ordinary individuals to rise against darkness and leave a legacy that outlasts their generation. Intricate and transportive, soaring and deeply resonant, this is Cambron at her finest."

—Amanda Barratt, Christy Award–winning author of *The White Rose Resists*

"Gripping and atmospheric, *The Italian Ballerina* explores the collective, intercontinental strength and struggle of those brave men and women who stood up against injustice to end the horrors of World War II. Cambron centers her story on civilians transformed to heroes—the prima ballerina turned nurse, the farmer turned medic, the small child turned pillar of strength, the soccer star turned caretaker—and readers are reminded that there are no small parts in this life. Though Cambron shines a spotlight on the vileness of hatred and war, she equally illuminates and emphasizes the way an 'ordinary' gift, if used, can be a lifeline to hope for generations. Awash with vivid characters and exceptionally well-researched, *The Italian Ballerina* is an outstanding work of historical fiction."

—Joy Callaway, international bestselling author of *The Grand Design*

"Poignant and inspirational, *The Italian Ballerina* captured my heart and wouldn't let go. Told in a non-linear style, the stories of Court and Julia in the past and Delaney in the present are woven into the life of Calla, a little Jewish girl caught in the horrors of World War II. Cambron's extensive research is evident, but it is the individual journeys of the characters that make this book special."

—Robin Lee Hatcher, Christy Award–winning
author of *I'll Be Seeing You*

"Based on true events, this exquisite tale impresses with its historical and emotional authenticity. Historical fiction fans won't want to miss this."

—*Publishers Weekly*, starred review,
for *The Paris Dressmaker*

"Told with precise details of the Nazi occupation of Paris, the story moves swiftly along, alternating between Lila's story and Sandrine's. The pacing is good, the characters entirely believable, and the revelations of the French underground's workings are fascinating."

—Historical Novel Society
for *The Paris Dressmaker*

"In the timeless fashion of Chanel, Ricci, and Dior, Cambron delivers another masterpiece in *The Paris Dressmaker*. Penned with unimaginable heartache, unforgettable romance, and cheering defiance against the oppression the Nazis inflicted on Paris, readers will be swept away into a story where battle-scarred good at last rings victory over evil. *Tres magnifique*."

—J'nell Ciesielski, author of *The Socialite*

"Kristy Cambron's masterful skill at weaving historical detail into a compelling story graces every page of *The Paris Dressmaker*. A thoroughly satisfying blend of memorable characters, evocative writing, and wartime drama that seamlessly transports you to the City of Light at its most desperate hour. Well done!"

—Susan Meissner, bestselling author
of *The Nature of Fragile Things*

"Enchanting and mesmerizing! *Castle on the Rise* enters an alluring land and time with a tale to be treasured."

—Patti Callahan, *New York Times* bestselling
author of *Becoming Mrs. Lewis*

"Cambron's lithe prose pulls together past and present, and her attention to historical detail grounds the narrative to the last breathtaking moments."

—*Publishers Weekly*, starred review,
for *The Illusionist's Apprentice*

"Prepare to be amazed by *The Illusionist's Apprentice*. This novel will have your pulse pounding and your mind racing to keep up with reversals, betrayals, and surprises from the first page to the last."

—Greer Macallister, bestselling author of
*The Magician's Lie* and *Girl in Disguise*

"With rich descriptions, attention to detail, mesmerizing characters, and an understated current of faith, this work evokes writers such as Kim Vogel Sawyer, Francine Rivers, and Sara Gruen."

—*Library Journal*, starred review, for *The Ringmaster's Wife*

# The
# FRENCH
# KITCHEN

*The*

# FRENCH
# KITCHEN

—— A NOVEL ——

## KRISTY CAMBRON

THOMAS NELSON
*Since 1798*

*The French Kitchen*

Copyright © 2025 Kristy Cambron

All rights reserved. No portion of this book may be reproduced, stored in a retrieval system, or transmitted in any form or by any means—electronic, mechanical, photocopy, recording, scanning, or other—except for brief quotations in critical reviews or articles, without the prior written permission of the publisher.

Published in Nashville, Tennessee, by Thomas Nelson. Thomas Nelson is a registered trademark of HarperCollins Christian Publishing, Inc.

Published in association with the Gardner Literary Agency.

Thomas Nelson titles may be purchased in bulk for educational, business, fundraising, or sales promotional use. For information, please email SpecialMarkets@ ThomasNelson.com.

Publisher's Note: This novel is a work of fiction. Names, characters, places, and incidents are either products of the author's imagination or used fictitiously. All characters are fictional, and any similarity to people living or dead is purely coincidental.

ISBN 978-1-4003-4527-4 (epub)
ISBN 978-1-4003-4526-7 (TP)
ISBN 978-1-4003-4528-1 (audio download)

*Printed in the United States of America*

25 26 27 28 29 LBC 5 4 3 2 1

**For Julia:**
*who taught the world to cook
but showed us so much more about
how to truly live*

 

**And for Anne:**
*who taught me to believe
anything is possible*

Well, all I know is this—nothing you ever learn is really wasted, and will sometime be used.

—JULIA CHILD

# PROLOGUE

24 December 1943
Château du Broutel
Rue, France

What would a French glamour girl wear to stash weapons in the dead of winter besides a haute couture gown? Kat Harris wished she knew.

She couldn't recall that instruction during the years of her mother trying to turn her into a Boston debutante before the war. Nor in the mere weeks of field operative training she'd received before landing in France. Neither could have prepared her for this—attending a lavish holiday soirée in an eighteenth-century château swarming with the Nazi elite, and now having to squeeze her emerald ball gown under a workman's canvas coat and trek through the woods in a pair of gumboots, all before the next dance.

Snowflakes had just begun to drift on the wind. A crescent moon offered slivers of light on the forest floor as Kat darted up the rise to the south edge of the forty-acre estate. She paused at the tree line— breaths racking in and out under a bodice that was cinched tight— and stole a glance over her shoulder to check the bramble-lined road that cut through the heart of the woods.

All lay still except the whistle of wind through skeleton trees and the mad thumping of the heart in her chest.

The empty road should have been fortuitous; night was nothing if not a subverter's ally. Yet instinct warned with a pit in her stomach: *Don't take the stillness for granted.*

In occupied France you lived by your wits or died the moment you abandoned them. She'd have to hold fast to them now, even if the box truck with the faded fish market emblem that ought to have been idling just off the road . . . wasn't. And two members of their team who should be accounted for . . . weren't.

Kat peered through the shadows and spotted the ghostly outline against the ridge.

*There it is—the fence.*

Their Maquis contact with the Resistance should have already slipped through. And if Xandre had done so, he'd have left a path of clipped barbwire tines, just enough for Kat to squeeze over and under, then follow. That was, if the pulse of deadly electricity had been cut.

Though signs posted nearby screamed *Danger!* and *High Voltage!* in both French and German, the wire lacked the telltale pulse of an active current. Kat gathered her hem before she could think better of it and slipped her leg over the lowest rung. Once through, she hurried toward the rendezvous point—the old groundskeeper's *gîte* left abandoned in the woods.

A stone wall surrounded the structure that mimicked the Baroque style of the grand château over the rise. She hastened through the rusty gate (mercifully left unlocked), around the gîte's brick-and-stone side (moonlight showing it painted over by years of patina and grit), then eased to the back, where understory grew wild and a bower of ash trees sprouted from the cracks of a toppled stone wall. She clung to the shadows, watching and waiting until certain it was safe.

Snow dusted the top of the mansard roof, making it appear more like a ghost castle from a children's fairy tale than an abandoned outbuilding that could be useful. But this place was forgotten. Isolated. And, as their team had noted, had adequate cover from the fence line and a village road conveniently tucked behind. Though it was a pity the war saw a once-grand structure now left to ruin, neglect and lack of Vichy police patrols ensured it could be useful again.

For *them*.

A figure's movement caught her eye—Xandre.

The Maquis contact appeared in the same state livery he'd worn in the château ballroom, but with an overcoat and a snow-speckled flatcap and wielding a shovel that reflected moonlight with each pierce into the ground. Wooden crates were stacked three-high against the rock wall behind him. And still others waited for their turn to be unloaded from a nearby turnip cart.

*Why is he burying the weapons?*

*And why there?*

Kat scanned the rock wall. Then the grove. The road in the distance . . .

They ought to have gone to the row of horse chestnuts at the far end, which stretched high above the crumbling side wall. The trees had shed their autumn color weeks before, blanketing the ground with leaves of ochre and rust. And soon, a layer of snow. If they had to hide the weapons, it was the best place—where the ground was soft and dig marks would be easier for their contacts to find.

"Célène!"

The whisper-shout of her cover name snapped Kat's attention back to the hollow. Having spotted her, Xandre leaned the shovel against the crates and crossed over to her place hidden in the trees.

"How did you, uh . . . get here so fast?" Winded and with breaths clouding on air, he was clearly stunned she'd managed to make such good time on the lengthy trek from the château.

"I ran."

"You mean you ran all that way?"

"It doesn't matter." She shook her head, then, with her heart in her throat, dared ask, "So? What happened? Where is Dominique?"

"He's safe." Xandre tipped the brim of his cap off his brow and offered a cocky smirk toward the crates. "He got the weapons out—every single crate—from the rail lines. As you can see."

"Then where is he? And Henri? I looked for the fish market truck, but there's no sign of it. They should have been here long before now."

"Must have been held up. No mind—turns out mere rumors of electrified fencing make those Nazi underlings think they do not need to patrol the whole of the château grounds. That gives us all the time we need."

"But you made this sound urgent or I wouldn't have come! I left the Vichy police captain on the dance floor. And I can't hope to make it back now before the Nazi minister's toast. The captain will know something is not right when I don't return on time."

The shock of what she'd just realized rebounded through her thoughts.

"My cover will be blown . . ."

"*C'est vrai*. But we cannot help that now. We'll have to use their ignorance against them. Even the Vichy police do not know of this place set so far back in the woods."

Of course that wasn't true. Kat had learned of the hidden road and abandoned groundskeeper's gîte from the Vichy captain himself. She'd stood in that very hollow once. Had found solace there in moments of desperation. And could only pray the captain didn't remember it as she did. And that once it was discovered the weapons were gone, he wouldn't realize the Maquis were cashing in on the lack of patrols in this place.

"So you're burying the weapons until Henri can retrieve them?"

"Right. And by the time the Vichy police learn they're missing, he'll have put weapons in the hands of the Resistance up and down the coast. And we will be long gone."

"Fine. We're here together now. Let's just get the rest of the crates unloaded." She bounded out, lest they waste time.

"*Attendez!*" Xandre called behind, his plea to wait tracking at her heels.

Kat rounded crates with swastikas emblazoned on their sides to find there was a hole—hastily dug. And not concealing crates of small arms but bearing a mound of dirt and a woolen blanket that just exposed the polished surface of . . .

*Jackboots?*

The telltale dead weight of a pair of midnight-blue trousers and Vichy uniform boots stared back from the hole between them.

A shiver nearly cut her in two. Bodies never remained hidden. Those of Nazi soldiers or Vichy police, even less so. A skeptical eye was all that was needed to generate public displays of the Nazi execution machine—one whiff of resistance in the air coupled with a uniform who didn't make roll call, and it could be disastrous.

"What have you done?" she breathed out on a ragged whisper.

"What we must do to survive." Xandre yanked the blanket back into place against the reaching fingers of the wind, covering the boots in a bid to urge them on.

"You think I'm squeamish about a body? *Now?*" In the field you saw what you saw, and numbingly often. But this? The ramifications could be severe. Again.

When Xandre refused to look at her, Kat shoved him off-balance, enough to thump him on his backside in the snow. And when he rose, in one fierce motion she curled a fist around his lapel and yanked—*hard*. Enough that he was forced to meet her square in the eye.

They hadn't time for this, but she couldn't afford not to do it either.

"Answer me! What did you do?"

"*D'accord! D'accord* . . . I had no choice," he countered, the excuse swift over a stunned chuckle. And far too easy, as if he was amused that she'd thrown a tantrum over decisions in the field.

"That's not good enough. We are not to get involved by force. *You know this!*" she bit out on a steel whisper, yanking his lapel again in a challenge with her eyes piercing his. "This operation is for subversion only—to coordinate retrieval of the weapons. To report who we see from inside that château. And if necessary, only as a last resort, to use deadly force to do it. You have thrown this entire operation in jeopardy and left the very lives of our team in question, including mine!"

He paused, as if calculating. "And yet our body count was blown ages ago."

She shook her head, vehemently. "That's not fair."

"*Non.* But it is truth. Every Resistance fighter puts their life on the line. We know the risks. And because of what we do, these weapons will allow the Maquis to overthrow this estate—to take this country back. If the day comes for France to rise, there will be no need to look back on what we had to do today to defeat evil tomorrow."

"You would repay evil for evil then? At any cost?"

"If I have to, *oui.*" Xandre snapped out of her grip, brushing off the front of his coat as he leveled a challenging stare back at her.

"Look at you. So high and mighty when you know you're prepared to kill a man just as easily as I. A policeman came over the rise for a smoke and caught me along the road. I could not hide the crates. So it was this or we were dead. And the weapons were gone."

"But the Vichy police will notice he is missing! It is not a question of what is easy but what is right. They will punish innocent civilians because of this. Do you not recall what happened just months ago—how many they executed in the village square? Even those the authorities knew had nothing to do with the Resistance. It was simply to stoke terror and keep neighbor reporting neighbor. And I won't stand by and watch it happen again."

"This one will not be missed. Not like that." Searching her face, Xandre's features softened along with his voice. "What was I to do, *hmm?* You were coming to meet me here. Do not punish me for following the captain's order."

"Which was?"

"Why, to protect you, of course." He continued staring back, punctuating the sharpness of his accusation like she should have expected it. "You didn't know you're his pet? What do I care if they execute some old men or women in the village if it saves me in the end? So I will do whatever I have to, even if it is to keep an eye on the Vichy captain's girlfriend."

Kat stumbled back, horrified. "Do not ever say that to me again. We'll hide the weapons. Bury the officer. And then I'll meet the captain back in the ballroom to report who is in attendance at the party, just as we planned. But after this night, you will leave Château du Broutel. Do you understand? And if I find you here again, I swear I'll break every rule of lethal force to prevent you from ever returning."

She'd gritted her teeth on the last words. And would have fought him further, had a sharp sound not cut the night.

The bark of a deep-chested dog echoed through the trees, freezing them both in place.

Their breathing forming clouds, they listened. Again and again, the bark drew nearer. Xandre motioned his chin over the rise as a beam of light appeared, moving against the sky and silhouetting lacy patterns of trees atop the ridge.

"Looks like you were wrong, Célène. There's a first time for everything." He tapped his wristwatch and mouthed, *"The patrols."*

How could that be? Kat had never been wrong in the field. Not like this. She'd been so certain the patrols wouldn't come for them. But the beam of torchlight cutting over the rise didn't lie.

She grabbed up the shovel leaning against the crates and stabbed the mound of frozen dirt with its tip. "Let's just get this done and get out of here."

The Maquis contact didn't argue this time. Xandre forgot wounded pride and, instead, turned as if to muscle the rest of the crates into stacks behind her.

If only that were true.

If only she was not wrong again.

And if only subversion were that simple. The next sound Kat heard was death—the click of a Luger trigger aimed at the back of her head.

# CHAPTER 1

12 May 1943
502 Washington Street
Boston, Massachusetts

*W*ake up, Kat . . . wake up.

Kat jolted awake, the warning of tiny *ping-pings* of metal hitting the concrete floor. She blinked but held still against the sagging pea-striped sofa at the back of her family's auto refurbishment garage, still palming the volume of Alfred de Musset poems that lay next to her on the cushion.

At the time, she'd told herself she'd only read a few pages and take a twenty-minute nap after. Chase that with a pot of strong chicory brew, and then she'd tinker under the hood of the silver Zephyr V-12 the rest of the night. How had she let hours pass? The tone arm on the Philco glowed through the dark from its corner shelf, and the soothing sounds of Glenn Miller's orchestra had long since been replaced by the ceaseless hum of static.

Realization hit and Kat shot up from behind the behemoth Zephyr parked in the center of the garage with its hood open as though it intended to swallow her whole. A lock of deep chestnut hair slid down over her shoulder as she stretched to peer around the metal beast. She tucked the unruly waves behind her ear—an unfashionably long style, but one she kept so she could knot it at her nape when bent over the hood of an auto.

Glancing toward the side door facing the armory, she looked to the blackout fabric that normally blocked the view of the dry goods establishment across the street. But the curtains were parted—the street behind them still, the night sky an inky black. Not at all how she'd left them.

Could she have dreamed it? Or imagined the noise, hoping to catch phantom thieves who weren't really there?

Another distant *ping-ping-ping* sounded.

Kat froze, head angled to listen with her good ear.

The faint sounds of a grunt and a curse followed as the thief continued puttering in the dark. And with it, fury combusted in Kat's middle.

*Oh no you don't.*

The last time their shop had been turned over, they'd lost more than a month's wages and every good set of tools they owned. The war put parts at a premium; it would take ages to replace the stolen items—if ever. The only reason her late father's prized Philco hadn't gone with the rest was that Kat had interrupted the thieves and they'd scampered off, leaving the radio sitting in the center of the garage floor like a present left behind. After that, she was convinced the expensive model would be too tempting for the thieves not to try again, and she vowed to sit up in the garage every night if it meant saving it a second time.

Kat cast her book aside and scanned the floor around her, then swiped up the nearest thing that could serve as a weapon—the Clayton & Lambert blowtorch with the brass bell jar and fiery tip that when lit would ensure she'd be taken seriously. Fisting the wood handle in a white-knuckle hold, she shook the bell container.

*Blast.* No gas left.

It would have to threaten as a bludgeon instead.

Slipping down to the floor, Kat padded forward with her shoulder pinned to the Zephyr's whitewall tires, the blowtorch raised high. When she cleared the left quarter panel, the doorway opened up to the half-moon linoleum counter curving around the front of the shop with aisles of auto parts and mountainous stacks of white-wall tires lit by the glow from the industrial desk lamp in the corner.

And there he was—the rotten thief.

This one stood, his back to her in a tuxedo and . . . shiny wing-tip oxfords? This must be the best-dressed thief ever. The neatest too. He rifled through drawers like his sleeves were on fire yet made an attempt to tidy one before moving on to the next. And odd, but he knelt to pick something up from the floor like he had no concern for the Philco. Nor with the cash drawer, which since the first robbery, Kat was devout to empty and lock in the office wall safe each night behind great-granddad's portrait.

"Stop!" Kat blasted, the blowtorch raised like a baseball bat ready to swing for the fences at Fenway. "Or I swear you'll wish you'd cho-sen another garage when you're picking your teeth up off the floor."

The thief obeyed. And went rigid as he stood with hands arrested at his sides.

Breathless and with her middle hitching like a clock wound too tight, Kat ordered, firmly, "Now turn around—*slow*."

The man did as commanded. Turning. With one step of the wing tips. Then two. And . . . was he laughing?

"I should have known you'd be here, Kat, haunting these walls."

"Gav!" Kat lowered the torch when she could finally make out his face. "You fool," she blasted through shaky breaths, and hunched over, palming the knees of her denim coveralls. "I could have killed you, you know."

There stood Gavin, her kid brother who was only a year younger but not a kid by a long shot now. He stared back with his usual boyish grin, as if incredulous that Kat had come out swinging. Everyone knew obligation came first to her—full stop. And though their aunt and uncle now owned the shop and weren't as miffed as she about the stolen goods—there was a war on after all, they'd said, and times were hard for everyone—Kat would fight tooth and nail if it meant protecting what their father had worked to build all his life.

Standing again, Kat took in every six feet plus that was Gavin.

When was the last time she'd seen him? When he'd come home for the Christmas holidays? He must have grown another inch, maybe two, since he'd started law school; his lean frame towered over her medium height now. He stood before her, disheveled in a tux and dangling bow tie no less, like he'd slipped out from another highbrow party to stumble across the railroad tracks to downtown. Dark chocolate waves that matched Kat's hue were longer now and fell over his forehead, drifting down to mask the trademark Harris eyes. His were a cool blue like hers, but not as icy—a tick darker. And often stormy, like they could be open and honest yet still hold back something of a secret if they wanted.

And they seemed to want to now.

"I always said you have ice water running through your veins. You'd have knocked me flat without batting an eyelash."

"I can't say." A hitch, extra breath, and she added, "I was thinking about my lashes just then."

"What would you have done if it wasn't me? Burglars can be dangerous, you know."

Kat squared her shoulders to him. "So can a woman who thinks she's about to lose her late father's prized possession. I suppose I'd have acted first and apologized later."

"Apologize? You? Never. That'd be too much like giving in." He chuckled. And she grimaced, because they both knew Gavin could read her better than anyone. And hated any reminder that she might need someone to know her that well, even if it was her kid brother. "Are you at least going to put that thing down?"

"Fine." Kat set the blowtorch on the linoleum counter with an echo against the high ceiling and wall of blacked-out windows facing

Washington Street. She looked down at the tile at his feet and bent to pick up the hex-head screws scattered around them.

"What are you doing here, Gavin? Besides making a mess?"

"I was looking for you. Since you didn't come home."

She flipped her wrist to check the time. "So you thought you'd pick the lock on this door at three o'clock in the morning? You couldn't just knock? I'd have let you in."

He glanced at the side door, something dawning as she stood and placed the box of screws on the counter. "How did you know I picked the lock?"

Kat offered her little brother a cool gaze. "No broken glass. Masking tape is split at the top of the frame. And the curtains are parted when I left them drawn."

"You actually taped the door? You really should consider becoming a police investigator. At least then you'd get paid a decent wage."

"And what outfit would hire a woman?"

"Much the fools, them." Gavin looked to the dark abyss at the back of the garage. Then with a softer tone, he said, "Even if you didn't hear me come in. You fell asleep on the sofa again, didn't you? Not safe, Kat."

"What if I did? Who else will keep an eye on this place?"

"Or an ear?"

Hostility clawed at her insides at the implication that she had a disability that would always mean she couldn't do what others could. Not fully. And it amounted to more than being deaf in one ear since birth; it was symptomatic of everything she wasn't in all the days since then.

But Gavin had never looked at her like the unpolished, unladylike, and very unmarried society misfit their mother saw in her. He shrugged it off when Kat didn't fit in at deb balls or skipped out on their *maman* and stepfather's swanky parties, perhaps thinking she'd rather be tucked under the hood of an auto at the shop. (She would.) Or reading her books. (She did.) All Kat could do now was hope his doubting look was just a concerned brother worrying she'd tested her limits again and, had things gone south, what that might have caused.

He spoke clearly and slowly even now, keeping eye contact so Kat could match what she did hear with their childhood trick of lip-reading to fill in the gaps of what she couldn't hear.

"Look, I meant what I said. I was worried when you didn't show at the party."

She broke eye contact and shrugged, turning to tidy the open drawer. "You know Maman's parties aren't my thing."

"No. They're not. But I wonder sometimes if you spend so much time here because you actually enjoy it, or you're just hiding out from your family."

Crossing her arms over her chest, Kat turned to challenge him as she closed the drawer with her hip—putting up a little defense and wanting him to know it. "I didn't show at the party, so you thought you'd come here and rummage through the shop. Why?"

"I didn't have a choice. I need something."

"Don't tell me. You're home because you've drained your funds at the billiards tables again and they finally cut you off because of it."

"You mean Maman and her husband?"

Yes. Kat supposed she did. And sighed at her own long-standing distance from a man who just happened to have more gold than Midas yet actually seemed nice in the almost decade and a half he'd been their stepfather. And the French-born mother who'd left their pops scandalized when she'd had their marriage dissolved, busted up their young family, and promptly married another man—a decorated military colonel from old Boston money, at that.

Kat still hadn't forgiven her for breaking Pops' heart. He might have died in an auto accident on icy roads a year ago; that was no one's fault. But the light had dimmed in his eyes long before that. And that was Maman's doing.

"Please tell me you're not here for money." Kat noted the whiff of liquor that tinged the air when he moved. "Not when we're doing all we can just to keep the lights on. And this place doesn't give us two nickels to rub together otherwise."

"I would never ask for money."

"Then what?"

"I need the—" Gavin stopped short, sighed, and ran a wary hand through his hair, resting his palm at the base of his neck like he was thinking his answer through. "I need the compass, Kat."

"The compass." Her brow flinched, in that spot between her eyes that tended to crease on its own when the rare something managed to take her by surprise. "You mean that ruddy old thing we used as kids when traipsing in the woods?"

He stepped forward, eager yet sheepish in the same heartbeat. "Yeah. I turned over the house looking for it. Last place I thought it could be was here."

What was this? Embarrassment? Guilt? Surely not after all this time.

Gavin didn't own a reluctant bone in his body. He was all athleticism and sun-kissed smiles and finding pleasure in his life of leisure, down to the Beacon Hill mansion their stepdaddy owned and the plain sailing and lobster boils hosted at their beachfront home in the summers. And while their maman had moved up-up-up the social ladder of Boston proper with Gavin and her fabulously wealthy new husband, Kat had spent her teen years among lug nuts and spare tires and the ghost of a father who couldn't seem to remember how to be anything but broken.

"Yes. I have it," she confirmed on a humorless smirk, still not understanding. "But I'm not convinced it even works. When we used to sneak out at night and meet in our tree house behind Pops' brownstone, you followed the path of streets you knew instead of the arrow on some antique that probably would have pointed the wrong way."

"Maybe only I knew how to use it."

Kat crossed the counter to the baby-blue Frigidaire tucked in the kitchenette nook. She dragged a spindle chair over and stepped up, feeling around in the dark for the old Waitt & Bond cigar box she'd wedged behind the unit. With the shop having been turned over, she wasn't taking chances with losing what she had left of their young years, even if nothing held particular value except to her.

"That still doesn't explain why you'd want that old thing when Lou could buy you anything in the Sears and Roebuck catalog. Ten times over."

"He's a good man, no matter what you say. But even then, I'd never ask him for a favor. Not for this."

When her fingertips grazed the side of the box, Kat pulled it free and stepped down to the floor. "What does that mean?"

He glanced at her bare feet and smiled wide. "No shoes again?"

Kat shrugged and turned her attention to the pair of used sneakers with rippled soles tossed in the corner. "I heard through a friend that the MIT track team had an extra pair of Tracksters, and I handed over most of my savings to buy them secondhand. Even if the coach couldn't understand what a girl could want with shoes that weren't kitten heels. 'It's not feminine,' he said. Turns out they're too big, made for a man's feet. But I can still avoid blisters if I run with rags stuffed in the toes."

Gavin nodded, as if not surprised. "Yet you still got them to give you a pair."

"I had to try them, didn't I?" Kat flipped open the cigar box lid to search for the compass buried with the other treasures inside. She found the old brass Testrite and held it out, trying not to think of all the whys behind the request. "Here. Take it. Even if you still haven't answered my question."

Gavin did, albeit with a hint of reluctance, and turned it over in his palm like it was the first time he'd ever set eyes on it. "Kat, if I could explain . . ."

"You have your reasons." She closed the cigar box and brought it to her chest, folding her arms over the red-and-black Blackstone logo like a shield. "And I accept them. That's what works between us."

"You don't even want to know where I'm going?"

"Of course I do. But I know if you want to tell me, you will. It's as simple as that."

"And if I want to but can't?"

Kat leaned in, glaring. "If it's one of those girls from the country club parties you frequent . . . If you've gotten one of them in trouble, I swear I'll box your ears. And then I'll really let you have it for being *le roi des cons.*"

"The king of idiots, *hmm?*" He gave a weak smile at the child-hood tease, then stared down at his wing tips. And the humor faded again, just that fast. "You still have that French edge to your voice, you know. From the summers we spent in Maman's country home. Running wild through lavender fields and flying over ancient stone walls like we were invincible. Those Lille estate owners didn't know what to make of us little Yanks, did they?"

She swallowed hard.

Memories of their childhood summers spent in France? This wasn't like Gavin to revisit yesterdays. Nor like her to allow emotion to creep in when he did.

*"Don't look back."* That's what Kat had whispered in his ear when she'd hugged her little brother goodbye at the courthouse all those years ago. And it had been their mantra ever since. When they'd been separated. When Maman had remarried. When the bills piled up and Pops' shop always seemed a whisker from going under. When Pops had died and left Kat to face the future alone.

And when the darkness of a new war stretched its long fingers across the Atlantic to their American streets and homes and hearts and stole sons with it, Kat had to suppress the sick feeling in her middle that this might mean war had finally found them.

"Gav? What's wrong?"

He slipped a hand in his trouser pocket, tucking the compass

away with it. "I'm going away for a while. A sailing trip with friends."
When Kat stepped up to interject, he caught her with a soft palm to
the shoulder. "And no—Maman doesn't know. Not all of it anyway.
I'd like to keep it that way for now. I'm of age, so this is my decision."

"And what." Her voice broke, the syllable coming out more a
squeak than a word. Kat cleared her throat, trying again. "What decision is that?"

Decisions—their weight had the ability to sink or save the heart.
Trouble was, you never knew which road you'd chosen at the beginning. It was not unlike Gavin at ten years old, when the choice was
put to each child as to which parent they'd live with. He'd been too
young. Too headstrong and wild with the pursuit of whatever glossy
object flashed in front of his eyes to know better. Of course he'd been
drawn in by their stepfather's gilded mansion and the dock with the
shiny new sailboat. What child wouldn't?

Maman had thought Kat would choose the same life of privilege
with the best finishing school and designer gowns, of garden parties
and summer homes, and assurances that they'd find her the perfect
marriage match from one of the wealthiest "old money" families
in Boston. But when eleven-year-old Kat had stared into Pops' eyes
from across the judge's chambers, after he first lost his vast auto-
manufacturing business with only the autobody shop left and, soon
after, lost his family, she saw the depths of hurt in those Harris
blues so bottomless he might drown. In that instant she chose her
father's survival. And with the one-word answer that sounded like a
curse, she'd uttered: *"Pops."*

In one breath, Kat had lost her mother. And in the next, lost
Gavin too.

Brother and sister had grown up miles away but a chasm apart.
With genuine affection but still with wildly different lenses through
which to look at the world. And not even an old compass that tried
its rickety best could bridge the divide from denim coveralls to the
gin-soaked tuxedo that stood before her now.

"There's only one reason I can think of for young men to disappear in the night. And it's not to hop a boat to Pleasure Island. At least not in the middle of a war."

He stood tall. And firm. Looking older and far too unyielding for his twenty-four years when he gave a heavy sigh. "No. It's not."

"What about law school?"

"That's . . . on hold for a while."

She paused, considering. Trying to calm her breathing. This wasn't a garden party; it was war. And now two bloody years in for the Americans, there seemed no end in sight. What did he mean by hinting he now had a part in it?

"What will I say to them? After you're gone, I mean."

"I'll send a letter explaining it all once I'm settled. Should only be a few days—a week at most." Gavin reached out then, arms enveloping Kat without the slightest breath of warning. He held on for long seconds, only breaking the silence to whisper into her good ear, "I have to do this, Kat. You have to let me go."

"I know."

A lump formed in her throat and she fought against it, battling to do the thing she'd always been best at—pushing emotion out of the equation until all that was left was the comforting strength of resilience. But for the iron will she'd always prized within her, Kat couldn't bear the thought of letting the moment pass without submitting to it. Even if she surrendered her independence for a moment between them.

"You'll write to me?" she whispered, squeezing him tighter with the cigar box of their childhood treasures anchored between them.

"Of course. I'm not sure from where, but as soon as I land for basic—" He stopped before saying more, then whispered, "Take care of Maman and Lou, okay? And yourself. I love you, sis."

Kat bit her lip. "Me too."

Gavin let go. Just that quick. And stepped back, like emotion was threatening to make him a fool as much as she.

"I ought to go. I'm on the milk train tomorrow."

"I could drive you—"

"No." He spoke with a heaviness that said he needed space. "A walk through the Commons might do me good."

"Right. Of course. Go." Kat gave a firm nod. Just once. And that was that, as he looked back over the counter and the stacks of papers still there and she used the seconds to push back tears that threatened to show themselves before him.

"Don't worry. I'll clean it up. You were never here."

He offered a ghost of a grin and shook his head. "I was never here."

The Philco hummed its static melody in the background as Gavin slipped through the side door into the shadows of Washington Street. She stood in the open door and watched him jog away like he bore the weight of the world on those tall shoulders, yet the breeze that tossed the wild waves at his brow and flipped the sides of his tuxedo jacket could have knocked him over.

"And don't come sneaking around in the middle of the night again, okay?" she called after him. "I'll light the blowtorch next time."

Still hugging the cigar box, Kat watched as Gavin half turned, gave a salute, and disappeared into the night.

That memory fixed itself in Kat's mind as she stood there for long seconds after. Watching the empty street. The lampposts and neon signs doused so only the lines of buildings cut jagged shapes into the sky. With bare feet pressed into the rough concrete sidewalk, and the cool spring breeze tossing her hair about her shoulders. And Kat held her breath so long she hadn't even realized it, until she finally exhaled—long and low.

Once she had his letters, she'd be able to breathe again.

*Really* breathe.

Like a fool, Kat believed it. And clung to the thought of that silly compass guiding Gavin home. No matter how far away his bravado might take him, no matter how many miles separated them or how long it took, he always came back. She pinned her hopes on that one truth for the longest time.

Until . . . the letters never arrived.

∽

9 August 1951
1 Rue du Château
Le Crotoy, France

The telegram burned in her pocket as Kat climbed the front steps and lifted the brass knocker on the cottage door.

*Tap, tap, tap.*

In some ways this place was just as she'd remembered it, with vines climbing three-story stone walls and a miniature spire kissing the clouds, leaded-glass windows overlooking a lonely stretch of beach, and the sea roiling with foam and waves in stormy shades of blue. But the perimeter fence was new. As were the shuttered windows and empty flower boxes. This place was as tucked away from the world as its owner had kept it during the war. And now, eight years after she'd last seen it, the seaside hideaway was even more isolated than the memory she'd fixed in her mind.

Wind flapped her azure tea-length skirt against her legs as Kat waited and used the blade of her hand to block the sun reflecting off the windows. After no response, she pounded her fist against the wood, this time in a series of short knocks that hollowed to thuds on the other side.

"Bonjour?" Kat peeked in the oval window by the door and its gauzy white curtains behind the glass. The edge shimmied; he was there, all right. But he generally avoided society, as the villagers had been quick to note, if they knew of the gentleman at all.

She'd have to press a little.

"I know you're there, Captain. I've already inquired in the village," she charged, her French snappy as she crossed her arms over her chest and tapped her toe in the event he was watching. "Very well. I'm perfectly content to wait."

Kat jumped back a half step at the sound of bolts unlocking from the inside.

The door cracked. She held her breath and wrestled wild, shoulder-length locks back from the wind blowing them into her view. All at once light cut the darkness and there he stood.

*Heavens—it really is him.*

Her heart quickened.

*Captain Fontaine . . . After all this time.*

There was the same towering frame. The brow creased in scrutiny. (He had no humor to spare, apparently, to find her on his doorstep.) Several days' growth shadowed his jaw, the ebony color still matching his crown, but the years had now gently flecked it with gray. White oxford shirtsleeves were ironed with a sharp crease. (As always for the military-minded man he'd once been.) And yet, despite the attempt at a gruff exterior, he appeared somehow unchanged. That was in his eyes—soft, gold-rimmed, and given to a calm and careful manner that even still she'd not been able to forget.

Kat drew in a steadying breath. "Captain?"

"You are mistaken, miss. There is no captain here. Good day," he bit back with the thick French accent she remembered, and moved to shut the door in her face.

She caught it, wedging her ballet flat between its weathered wood and the doorjamb. "Rumors would contradict that point. I can go back to the village and inquire again, but I fear that would be an even bigger waste of your time. And mine."

He didn't refute the logic but instead gave a little sigh of frustration.

Finally able to breathe, Kat stared up at him. And willing herself to be brave, she prepared to utter what she'd rehearsed the entire train ride from Paris.

"Gérard," she whispered his name this time, then drew in a steadying breath. "It's *me*. Célène."

"I know who you are."

"What a relief we can skip the pleasantries then. I go by my name now—Kathryn Harris. Or just Kat. But I suppose you must already know that."

The exhale after all that felt good.

He wouldn't say one way or the other, just kept his brow fixed on Kat like she was a puzzle to be worked out. "What do you want?"

"Well, for starters, I've come a long way. May I at least come in?"

Arguing with her must have seemed more trouble than it was worth as he left the door ajar and retreated to the safety of the shadows in the hall.

Closing the door behind her, Kat was flooded with relief that the inside of the cottage wasn't what she might have guessed while standing on the outside. Recluse or not, the captain had kept the front room cared for in tidy simplicity. Books neatly lined the shelves near a stone hearth not yet needed for the season. A brass lamp glowed on a low table nearby, flanked by a modern dove-gray sofa. Unlike her maman's mantel in Boston, there were no personal touches here— just an oversize framed photo of a stormy beach hanging over the fireplace and a tabletop wireless on the sideboard against the wall that pulsed with melodic classical music set at a low hum.

The end of the hall opened to the spacious kitchen, its vaults and a thick-beamed ceiling just as she remembered it. And blessedly awash in sunlight from beach-facing leaded glass windows.

The captain turned, waiting to talk until Kat could read his lips along with his words. Seemed he'd remembered that little detail about her. Or if he hadn't known it then, he seemed to now.

"What do they say about me?"

She took a seat at the weathered farmhouse table and crossed her legs at the ankles, watching as he filled a kettle for tea. "Who?"

"The village. You said you inquired."

"I did. I suppose I wanted to know if the rumors were true—that the former police captain lived here. And if so, was there danger of him acting aggressively toward trespassers."

"Yet you chose to trespass anyway?"

"I suppose I did. Even when they all told a similar tale. If they'd even heard of the captain—many haven't, because this cottage sat empty for years after the war. But it seems he's returned to France. And is rumored to be rich as Croesus, yet chooses to remain holed up in this seaside cottage and rarely engages with anyone. Nor leaves his property. Though I'm not certain I believe that. I'd say it's rather that no one actually sees when you leave."

"You think I do?"

"Oh, I know you do."

"Just as blunt as I remember." He seemed to like that Kat knew him well enough to guess correctly and looked like he battled the ghost of a smile on his profile because of it. "And it's my name I also go by now—Gérard. I believe I told you that once."

He paused, as if to let it sink in. Or to see her reaction. She gave none, even if somehow it suited him. Even as he continued.

"And even if no one cares what I do, why would I wish to leave this cottage?"

*Touché.*

This sun-drenched space was warm. Spacious yet somehow cozy. And unpretentious, with the melody of waves ticking time outside and soft music drifting down the hall. Gérard moved about the room with a quiet confidence in much the same way he had the first day they'd met. Save for this time, his shepherd, Bella, wasn't tooling around at his knees with each step. That broke something in Kat's heart now to realize it seemed he'd lost the four-legged companion along the way and had never replaced her.

He was in this idyllic place quite alone.

"Where did you go for so many years, after the war?"

"I thought the village said I never leave this property," he countered, seeming with ease.

"And I said I know you do. But very well, if you value your solitude. I'll drop it in favor of getting down to business. I brought this." Kat cleared her throat and took the telegram from the pocket of her frock, then flattened it on the tabletop to slide across to the edge closest to him. "I trust it's familiar. After all, you sent it to me."

Gérard stilled his hand on the kettle as he glanced over his shoulder, then stepped up to the table. Scanned the missive. And dropped it again just as fast, not even watching it flutter to the tabletop before he turned back to the stove.

But . . . he didn't deny it either.

While that might have been a tell under normal circumstances, it wasn't for this man. In all the time they'd known each other, he said what he meant and always meant what he said. That made the thoughts he didn't voice what most interested her now.

"So?"

Kat leaned in, tapping her index finger to the telegram with authority. "So . . . you sent this to my family's Boston home. As it concerns my late brother, I thought that warranted a face-to-face meeting. And before you ask—yes. I did come all this way for a telegram. Even to you. And even after all these years. What I want to know is, where is Gavin?"

"I'm sorry." The apology was flat enough that not a soul would believe it genuine. "You've wasted your time."

"But it says, 'G is alive.'" She qualified, not willing to let him off the hook. Not when she'd dropped everything to board a cross-ocean steamer and trek off the beaten path to his door. "And it was sent from Rue, the closest commune to this cottage."

"Was it?"

"It says so right there. And there is no one left who would have sent this to me but you. If this telegram is true—if my brother is alive somewhere in France—you had to expect I'd be on the next boat to find out. So you can't be surprised to find me sitting in your kitchen."

"Kat . . ." He stopped, maybe because it was the first time he'd used her real name? It sounded about as foreign coming from his lips, she guessed, as it was for her to hear it spoken by them. "Some things ought to be left alone. If the war taught us anything, it's to try our best to get past it and make a new life for ourselves."

She glanced around, finding everything about his life at the cottage standing in stark contradiction to his own words. "You can't believe that."

"I assure you I do."

It was Kat's turn to feel a crease in her brow, his apathy cutting deeper than she thought it could. When he didn't elaborate, she pinched finger and thumb to the bridge of her nose. "Am I to understand you're telling me to simply . . . forget my brother? Not to seek answers for why someone dear to me went missing? And to ignore this little bribe you used to get me on a boat, when I still don't know why?"

"Non. What I mean is, you might be in for more pain than you realize. When a person starts digging for answers, they have to be prepared for it to change everything. And rarely can they bear the reality of what they find. I'm simply trying to spare you that."

"Good thing I'm not the kind of girl who needs to be spared. And that doesn't sway me in the least. I've waited long enough for answers. If they won't come to me, then it's time I start chasing them down. That's why I'm here. I want the truth of where my brother is."

"I don't know where he is. I wish I did."

No satisfaction accompanied the answer, even if everything in those eyes said he was genuine in it. "And I wish I didn't believe you, but I do. So I have a proposal. I think we can help one another."

Gérard ticked his head to one side. "How?"

"I've followed reports of the prosecutions in France. You've thus far escaped arrest by the Courts of Justice. But with ongoing public outcry and the stark increase in the government seeking reprisals against those who collaborated during the war—"

"I was *not* a collaborator." He took an automatic step forward, like he was ready to fight any government official who'd dare claim differently.

"That may be true, but it doesn't change the fact that many still believe it. And that prosecution could yet be in your future. So I've come to strike a deal. You know France. You have the connections in Paris I need to help me find my brother." Emotion caught in her throat, though she tried to hide it. "Or at least to find out what happened to him. My maman and stepfather were left devastated by his loss. They searched for a time, using my stepfather's connections in Washington, DC. And when that came up empty, they made some sort of peace with Gavin's loss. I thought I had too. But this telegram changes everything. And I won't spend another dime of their money just to hurt them all over again. Any agreement we make would have to remain confidential between us."

"I see. You received a telegram. You want money. And heard I have it?"

She shook her head. "Non. I want answers. I just need help finding them. And forgive me this—you said I was blunt—but I need my mother off my back while I do."

Considering, he gave a slight nod. "I don't know how me helping you financially would accomplish that, but fair enough. What do I get in return for my investment?"

"I offer my family's connections, if there's any influence we can leverage with the French government. And my sworn eyewitness testimony, if need be, to protect you from prosecution here." To sweeten the deal, Kat added, "It could spare you a long prison sentence, if not save your life."

Gérard doubted her, of course, with a tiny flicker of something that flashed in his eyes as he pulled out a chair and settled across the table from her. After long seconds, he sighed and asked, "Why would you care about standing up for me—the enemy?"

"Are you the enemy? Because despite what happened during the war, I believe I know the truth about you. Or am I mistaken in what happened the day of the executions? Do you deny what I witnessed of your character in the village at Rue, when you could have turned me over to the Reich but didn't?"

She was taking a calculated risk bringing up that horrible day.

If anything Kat had learned in the mire of war could be proven true, it was in the earnestness of the moments they'd shared. When every loyalty around Kat was in question . . . when war made death so callous and unmerciful yet so common . . . when they were forced into the gut-wrenching reality of witnessing the worst of humanity right in front of their eyes . . . Gérard could have turned her over to the Vichy police. He'd learned she was working with the Resistance. Yet he'd shielded her. Comforted her. Saved her even, when he was duty bound by his uniform to have done the opposite.

Regardless of the reasons why, Kat couldn't let go of that. It was all she had left to make what she'd come to say plausible.

"I don't deny a single thing I said or did that day."

"That's what I thought." Kat nodded, knowing.

She didn't trust him. Not fully. Such trust would never be offered. But Kat could tolerate his version of truth and a telegram to stir her spirit again as long as they led to one end. That was enough for now, even if the tricky part was still ahead of her.

*Deep breath.*

*And don't mince words . . .*

"Then the way I see it, there's only one solution. Gérard Fontaine, I'm here to ask you to marry me."

# CHAPTER 2

12 June 1943
Château du Broutel
Rue, France

*Stupide!*

Scolding herself, Chef Manon Altier could think of only two certainties in that instant: Their new kitchen maid had been set to arrive before teatime but never showed. And Manon had been so distracted by the high stakes of this, she'd curdled her béchamel.

On a normal day this was nothing; she'd have simply started again.

*Unsalted butter, flour, salt, pepper, and nutmeg in a pan . . .*

Manon could whisk a roux in her sleep; it was the backbone of any French chef's arsenal. But by committing the cardinal sin of allowing her mind to wander beyond the confines of their kitchen to every what-if scenario of a missing field agent masquerading as a maid, she'd added cold milk and shocked the binding agent into a mess of abhorrent lumps. With the remaining entrée of Comté-and-smoked *jambon feuilletés* needing a good twenty-five minutes baking time to turn the puff pastry a rich golden brown, the ornate clock positioned high on the kitchen wall warned they now had scarcely more than twenty.

*This at least can still be saved.*

Yanking a copper saucepan from its hook over the chef's block,

Manon moved to the stove in the immense stone-framed alcove. Breathing deeply, lifting her chin, and keeping her calm as a leader must in the kitchen—and in this blasted war for that matter—she poured fresh milk in the pan to start mending.

Minor nuisances of this sort were common in the kitchen. Seized chocolate, broken emulsions, split crème au beurre . . . even ovens that wouldn't draw or razor-sharp cutlery that sliced unfortunate fingertips. Redeeming a curdled béchamel was simply a matter of skill and experience conquering frayed nerves. Manon would warm some fresh milk. Dribble it in. Whisk until her elbow caught fire and the lumps would be smoothed out. Then she'd pack the remaining puff pastries, forgo the intricate leaf design she'd planned to edge the tops in favor of a simple plait, brush them with egg wash, and pop them in the ovens with a prayer.

But the other—the missing maid? That was far more to contend with.

They managed supply shortages, made rations stretch, and dealt with black-market finds that had been promised good but nearly always soured, if they arrived at all. Air raids pummeled. Menus were forced to change at the last possible instant. And her kitchen staff had to routinely subvert the enemy living under the same roof. Yet what they produced *was* French cuisine, even though they had to fight to create it. And while she didn't doubt the skill she'd acquired from top-notch instruction before the war, Manon had to remind herself that with a skeleton staff, being in the middle of a war offered no foray into the majestic world of the culinary arts.

Tonight they simply cooked.

As chef of the grand Château du Broutel, she knew this precarious position well. And the absence of nearly all the remaining roles in a *brigade de cuisine*—and a kitchen maid who'd created more angst with her absence—meant Manon was forced to serve as their *chef de tournant* this night, or the multiskilled expert who could step into any role. That she was a woman in this position added another layer of complexity to the delicate balance they must hold at all times.

In occupied France women did not work, let alone manage a kitchen at a fine château. French women obeyed, submitted, and endured. They had babies. They were to bolster the republic with their domestic pursuits and show their dedication to victory through the heroism of gardening, sewing, birthing, and baking, all with little to no provisions with which to do so—a very Nazi-assigned position administered by France's new puppet régime. And though innumerable risks existed with taking on a new maid who brought Resistance connections, if anyone was perfectly placed to do so, Manon was.

Here she was invisible.

An unattached woman of only twenty-five years but still with a renowned history of culinary work in Paris and abroad. The proficiency of her skills had won her the role. And a war that had taken almost every able-bodied man to fight somewhere ensured she went unnoticed in it. Her pert nose was almost always bent over a saucepan. The lines around her emerald eyes and firm mouth chose not to give way to a smile. *Ever.* And her deep auburn locks were so often tucked under her *toque blanche,* that no one even considered it was a fiery woman who ran La Marquise de Longvilliers' château kitchen. It seemed the Reich rats who occupied the estate could overlook the owner and his wife putting a woman in the post if no one actually saw her, and if the food placed before them was exquisite French cuisine.

"Chef!"

Frédéric bounded down the servants' staircase, the footman nearly careening with the pâtissier moving by at the bottom. Valens was balancing the tray carrying his citron tarts to plate with pistachio crème and fresh raspberries on the far side of the kitchen. The pastry chef was startled but sure, and though he was the oldest on her staff, his tall frame remained an oak in the center of the kitchen as the boy skirted around him.

*"Je suis désolé!"* Frédéric apologized, just missing a collision as he ran toward Manon. "Chef! Chef!"

Too young to fight, too old for the nursery, and jittery as a fish lost on land, Frédéric was the lad left to help Manon serve a traditional seven-course meal at the Reich's regional headquarters, and in a dining hall that sported more *litzen* than Germany's homeland. Thank Providence she still had Valens. They'd worked together in the Ritz kitchen in Paris before the war, and he remained her most trusted confidant—and the last family she had—now that they were years into it. Manon knew when she woke each morning that if they survived this war, it might well be because of his steady support.

Manon did not look up, opting to remain focused on her whisk as she addressed the young footman. "Calm yourself, *s'il vous plaît.*"

Chastised, the lad halted before her, sucked in a series of what were probably meant to be composing breaths, and ran a finger along the inside of his celluloid livery collar to stop it from choking him before continuing.

"Oui, Chef. Je suis désolé."

*Oh no.* That was not done.

"Do not apologize in my kitchen." Manon stared up, sharp, and waited a few long seconds for her instruction to hit its mark. When she was confident it had, she added, "We simply do the work. Do it with precision. And make no excuses. Do you understand?"

"Of course, Chef."

*"Bien."* She turned back to her whisk and pan. "Now, what do you need?"

*"Où est les hors d'oeuvres? La soupe?* The butler is frantic for the first courses. The guests have been seated for"—he checked the clock on the wall and gulped like he'd just swallowed a mouth full of mud—"more than five minutes now."

*Yes, yes. I know. Our dear butler keeps his times holy too.*

"The first courses are plated." Manon pointed to the round-top servants' door at the back of the kitchen with one hand, still whisking with the other. "You'll find pâté en croûte and smoked salmon canapés garnished with lemon, dill, and capers on the butcher block. And the soup crocks are in the larder to keep cool."

"I'll fetch them." Frédéric maintained his self-control as he marched around the corner but yanked a kitchen porter's collar as he passed and tugged him along. Manon had a pretty fair idea the lads bounded across the parquet floor once they were out of sight when she heard shoes stomping tile. He returned a moment later, carrying a silver tray with rows of chilled vichyssoise in pristine porcelain crocks in his gloved hands, then moved by as if to rush up the servants' staircase.

"Wait! We must finish."

Manon left the whisk in the pan, knowing she had enough time to dash the garnish across the tops of each crock before the milk could think about burning. She turned, fetched the toasted sourdough baguettes with piped pesto roquette she'd prepared ahead of time, and handed them to Frédéric.

"One each," she directed and moved to the wooden block, giving an expert chop to chives for the soup tops. "Serve the first two courses with elegance but serve slowly. *Le poisson* is almost ready. But after the fish, we require additional time for the first entrée course to bake. Do you understand?"

"Shouldn't the new kitchen maid have done this already? Where is she anyway?"

Valens perked up at the question, giving Manon a sidelong glance from his post. She could feel his energy shift from stoic to disquieted, his graying profile piqued even from across the kitchen. The mechanical manner of her work always the best cover she had, Manon discarded the statement with a flick of her wrist and focused on rolling the blade through the mound of chives on the chopping block.

"I haven't time to fret over a tardy kitchen maid."

Frédéric shrugged. "The trains must have been held back again. Our overlords do relish their security checks."

*Chop. Chop. Chop.* Manon slid the knife blade under the pile of green confetti, lifting it into her palm. "What has that to do with us? We have a dinner to serve." She added the splash of vibrant color to the creamy soup tops, then thrust a tray of canapés into a passing footman's hands. The other she handed off to Frédéric, the waves of vichyssoise just rising to the rims of the bowls' fluted edges but blessedly not spilling over.

"Off you go. And remember: chin up. Serve with slow elegance, oui? I trust you to give us enough time to perfect the next courses before they must be presented."

Valens waited for the footmen to disappear up the stairs. When they'd gone, he did as Manon expected and marched across the kitchen—those soft brown eyes seeking her face the instant he'd squeezed in at her side.

"What has it to do with us?"

"What?" she replied, her attention too focused on the task of whisking to fool anybody.

Valens stilled her hand with a graze of fingertips to her wrist, asking for her attention. When she finally looked up at him, his eyes met hers with concern—so familiar now, it might have been paternal. He glanced at the empty stairs again. "You said, 'What has it to do with us?' It is everything, non?"

Manon parted her lips to respond, but no reply came.

How she wished to say all the things that marched through her mind in an endless parade day after day. If the maid had been caught or—heaven help the poor girl—tortured, were they discovered? Were the Wehrmacht merely waiting for the seventh course to be served before they stormed down to the kitchens and arrested them all? Would she and Valens be dragged into the night, hauled up against the château's stone wall, and bullets planted in their skulls? Or worse, would they, too, be tortured into giving up the names of the Maquis contacts and the poor citizens who'd helped them?

Who could one trust in times like these?

The château walls had eyes. And the kitchen's ears were always listening; they must have a care. Valens knew this because he'd approached under the guise of helping to pack the remaining pastry parcels to get into the ovens and now stood side by side with Manon, keeping his voice steady but low.

With furtive glances, Manon surveyed the corners of the kitchen occupied by staff the Germans had forced in: Franz, their sous-chef, serving as both their *boucher*—meat butcher, and *poissonnier*—fish chef—that night was bent over a marble counter, plating the last of his sautéed scallop and sole creations for the next course. Helmut, the bright young *saucier* with the sharp wit but terrible eyesight, could not serve in the Reich's ranks as a soldier, but he could be quite useful in the kitchen even with jam jar–thick spectacles. He had finished his savory accompaniments to whip a fresh raspberry mousse for the dessert course. Madame Larue was a burly, leather-faced Frenchwoman whose origin and loyalties were as yet unknown, save for that she had worked for the château's mistress for many years and seemed to brighten only by a kind word from La Marquise de Longvilliers. The dishwasher faithfully scrubbed the copper pots and pans to a shine and polished silver throughout the course of each day without so much as two words to anyone.

"What is it?" Valens whispered, while expertly crimping seams and brushing a layer of egg wash on the pastry plaits along the edges.

"That's just it," she whispered back, combining the last of the jambon to the remaining béchamel mixture. "I don't know. The maid was to arrive at midday, but she never showed."

He glanced at the clock first, then on instinct looked to the blacked-out windows and the world of night they knew lay beyond them.

"There has been no word?"

Manon gave a slight shake of her head, whispering, "None. I was told to expect a skilled maid who can cook and bake beyond reproach. I'd been assured this one would be exactly what we need.

And she has already passed a Gestapo check. Why would they go to those lengths if not to ensure she arrived safely?"

They both knew what that meant—their Maquis contact had gone to considerable effort to supply a replacement for the last maid who'd left, this one with appropriate skill. And with a convincing backstory and forged identification papers to match, it would be easier to slip her in where she could be useful right away.

"That is all I know. But I fear the worst . . ." When her voice trailed off, too worried to speculate further, Valens nodded.

All it took during war was for someone not to arrive as expected, and the brutal outcome was more than likely they were deported, dead, or both. Neighbors reported neighbors now, decrying the smallest infraction—or none at all—as disloyal to their authoritarian government. Offenders were dragged off as they walked down the street. Homes were raided in the dead of night. Or worse yet, those even suspected of consorting with an enemy of the Reich ceased to exist. They were simply there one day, gone the next. Like a ghost that vanished with the morning fog. Neighbors walked quickly past empty houses after that, as if the same fate were catching.

Strangers were at an even more chilling disadvantage. Anyone popping up in a new town could be a spy, a turncoat, a threat . . . And they were subjected to scrutiny or torture as the enemy gripped with a tighter squeeze on their control.

Like all in Europe, they were not immune to witnessing the horrors of unexplained and immediate death. Yet Valens still declared, with a tiny measure of hope flickering in his eyes, "I will send a message."

"So we're to just wait?"

"That is all we can do. But in the meantime? I believe we should spit in your lovely béchamel." He smiled then—just a hint, as if comrades ought to be careful in exchanging anything that sparked of joy in their broken world, lest they be cast in a suspicious light. "Then get this entrée into the ovens."

"And prepare ourselves for the inevitable."

"What would that be?"

Manon slid the tray of pastry parcels into the oven and hoped beyond hope they came out a crisp golden brown. With a sigh—for war had made cold beasts of them all—she added a heart heavy, "Célène is dead. And the clock is ticking to find her replacement."

# CHAPTER 3

10 July 1943
90 Mount Vernon Street
Boston, Massachusetts

They lived well—*very well.*

Kat had to admit that as she drove Pops' old rust-hued Ford AA tow truck across the city and slowed its roll when Maman and Lou Sullivan's four-story Greek Revival came into view.

Even though it was supposed to be her home now too, the pristine maple tree–lined street, the soaring brick exterior, and the stately neighborhood that opened up to row houses on Acorn Street and led to the opulence of Beacon Hill all remained foreign. And since Kat spent most nights sleeping in the back room of the auto-body garage instead of in the professionally decorated bedroom her mother kept for her, the mansion had become the cold reminder of a home in which Kat would never fully belong.

Threading her vehicle to the back of the row houses, Kat was shooed unwittingly into a valet line where chauffeurs opened luxury auto doors and men in military uniforms and ladies in sparkling gowns and white mink filed out on their arms, then flowed up to the hostess's door.

*Oh no.*

*Why is it on the one night a girl attempts to drop by her estranged maman's mansion that there must be the fête of the century there to greet her?*

Stealing a quick peek in the rearview mirror, Kat checked the pop of cherry red she'd swept over her pout. It was neat enough, even if wearing the splash of color did make her reflection seem a bit unrecognizable. Tiny pearl studs Kat had slipped in her lobes on the way out the door winked back at her now. And she'd twisted her long hair into a semi-passable updo. Thank goodness for those little necessary touches now—along with the belted Kitty Foyle frock Kat had tugged out from the no-man's-land in the back of her closet and pressed with a cool iron. Maman should be satisfied. And while Kat couldn't hope to blend in with the finery filtering into the mansion, at least she wouldn't be a complete fool like if she'd arrived in her usual fashion of a plain blouse and grease-stained dungarees.

A parking valet approached. The tow truck's engine coughed as the tuxedo-clad gentleman fought to open the driver's side door. Its rusty hinge cried out, grating metal to metal against the trill of summer cicadas in the magnolia trees.

"Good evening, ma'am." The valet cleared his throat over the awkwardness and offered a blessed supportive smile with a valet ticket and then a gloved hand to help her step down.

"Good evening." Kat took the ticket. Then his hand. And raised her chin a little higher with an *I belong here* air before whispering, "The clutch sticks. You'll want to give it a good pump or it'll die on you."

"Very good, ma'am."

*Good luck to us both.*

Hanging brass lanterns should have lit the way along the garden wall. But it wasn't just London that had endured blackouts during their Blitz; Boston was overseen by its own version of Britain's enthusiastic Air Raid Precautions wardens, which meant the lanterns lay cold and partygoers wove through a shadowed courtyard. The gatehouse and garden trellises overflowed with New England aster and blush summer roses and led to what Maman called the "grand" entrance—the double doors with half-moon overhang and classic columns that welcomed guests into Geneviève Sullivan's society world.

Once inside, the first things to hit Kat were the heat. The noise. The heady scent of Chanel No. 5 floating on air. And how she didn't recognize one face in the crowd.

Chattering guests, tinkling champagne flutes, and windows shuttered in the midst of an unseasonably warm night were a toxic combination. Diamond-frosted ladies wore red-lipped smiles and victory rolls in their hair. Gentlemen sipped from crystal tumblers. Eyed the gams on the gals with calf-baring skirts. And mingled with the crème de la crème of Boston society who had come out in droves to whatever this month's gathering was.

Kat wove through the maze of smoke and smiles in the marble entry, past tuxedo-clad waiters with trays of caviar canapés, raspberry entremets, and champagne bubbling gold in the light. The usual talk in between sips was of business and Boston brokerages. Money and marriages. And snippets of high-society gossip tossed in for good measure.

Then there was the *other*—the war news.

Whether it came from *Newsreel* footage that preempted the latest Cagney film or newspaper headlines, words like *Midway* and *Dutch Harbor* had become part of every American's stream of consciousness. And places like Corregidor, Kerch Peninsula, and the Coral Sea had suddenly become pins on a map. The primary conversation in Maman's home would always be high society, but the war was never too far off topic when uniforms were intermingling in the crowd.

Kat scanned the formal parlor with its impressive rust-brick fireplace flanked by floor-to-ceiling windows and blackout shades covered by luscious gold curtains that belied the darkness outside.

Lou's prized swordfish lorded over the space like it was pointing the way through the gourmet kitchen to the back door. Tiffany Favrile art glass vases boasted punch-pink peonies from the garden, adding a splash of color as side table adornments in the room. Gold- and silver-etched frames prettied the mantel in an artful line—enough to boast of the Sullivan family but not too many to appear cluttered in a row house that had been decorated to a fine, expensive pitch.

Drawn, Kat moved to the images.

There was the usual—a wedding photo of Maman and the much taller Lou in a gilded frame in the center. Another of them in white-tie dress at a star-studded event with the governor. There was one that must have been a proud moment for Maman: Kat lost in a sea of ivory gowns at her last deb ball in 1937. And then a series of framed snapshots of Gavin at his graduation. Gavin raising the first-place cup at a polo match. Gavin and Lou on the eighteenth green, with lively smiles and driving irons slung over their shoulders. And at the end of the line, the most heart-wrenching image: Gavin standing in front of his graduation gift—a forty-foot sailboat—his arm swimming around their mother's petite shoulders, and hamming to the camera with his typical grin.

Kat traced an index finger over the glass.

There had been such a void without him these last weeks. With no letters. No news, save for heartbreaking reports of mounting American casualties overseas. No way to make it through each day without the nagging fear that a government telegram would arrive on their doorstep. And with every photograph that showed off her brother's intrepid spirit, she missed Gavin even more. His wild optimism. The adventure in his smile. And the way he was always loyal to the great loves of his life: his sailboat and his family.

She had to look away or tears would sting her eyes.

"Oh! *Qu'est-ce que c'est?*"

A singsong cry in a French accent rose from the connecting parlor just as a half-moon of cocktail dresses huddled around a sleek baby grand piano parted like a split sea. Maman emerged in a glittering black gown with an ivory gardenia tucked in a twist of deep chestnut hair nobly streaked with gray.

Kat prepared herself—dabbing under the row of bottom lashes and straightening her posture just in time—as Maman wove her way through the crowd and met her half-delighted yet half-disappointed at the same time.

"Kathryn, is that you?"

"Hello, Maman."

"I was greeting our guests, and whom do I see? My pretty girl." *Kiss, kiss.* The faint scents of jasmine and vanilla enveloped Kat as each cheek received a sweet peck on air, the way the French did it. And the way her maman greeted everyone, from blood relative to the upscale milliner down the lane. "I thought perhaps you did not remember the date"—she paused, as if the words pained her to speak aloud—"and were going to remain at that auto establishment you frequent."

"You mean Pops' garage?"

"But of course you put the date in your diary, because here you are." Geneviève gazed down at her daughter's dress. And Kat tried to laugh off the look of displeasure that washed over Maman's face. An expert at manipulation, Maman pivoted by painting a smooth smile on her lips. "My dear, when was the last time you considered your wardrobe? Indigo is a winter hue. It's not right for you."

From Gavin's haunting smile on the mantel to a tipsy pianist who'd sat at the baby grand and was now belting out a drunken version of Benny Goodman's "After You've Gone," to a sleek Frenchwoman with a permanent air of disappointment when it came to her only daughter . . . every second proved more overwhelming than the first. To breathe. To think. And certainly too much to come up with a reply to something so trivial as choosing the correct hue to complement one's complexion.

"I . . . I'm sorry." Kat raised her voice over the burgeoning music. "What date?"

"This is our anniversary soirée, of course. You know Lou loves his parties. And he'll be so delighted to see you!" She ignored the impropriety of shouting across the gargantuan space and called out randomly, "Lou? Lou? Look who's here!"

Geneviève stopped midsentence and exclaimed, *"Charles, darling!"* when a silver-haired man behind oversize ebony resin spectacles, an ivory silk tucker, and pomade glistening in the chandelier light bent to kiss her cheeks. Kat heard him exclaim something about the fabulous party and how they'd do lunch soon when the weather cooled down, for he couldn't "bear lobster thermidor in this dreadful summer heat."

Kat took a breath to scan the wide parlor, to see if she noticed any of Gavin's friends on the guest list. Maybe she could find out if any had heard from him.

Instead, she spotted her stepfather's tan-skinned and snow-white crown.

Lou's slender frame was backed into a corner with a gentleman in wire-rimmed spectacles, an ordinary face, and a plain black suit. Lou swirled amber liquid in the bottom of a tumbler, nodded to the conversation, and took a deep swill. If she didn't know better, Kat would have guessed this was another one of Lou's surreptitious business deals, given that the men seemed to blend in with the oversize potted plant off to the side. Or perhaps something else? It was difficult to tell from this far away, but Lou seemed . . . tired. Weary? Even a little somber?

"That was Charles Dover," Maman said, drawing her back. She gave an artful tip to one brow as if Kat should be impressed. "Fashion editor from New York. He works side by side with Edna Woolman Chase, you know."

That name must have meant something, though Kat wasn't sure what. "I can't say I know her."

"Of course you do. You've just forgotten. Editor in chief of *Vogue* magazine? You met her here two—no, three Christmases ago." Geneviève squeezed her shoulder, as if a little pinch could force her daughter to recall memories of the things her mother found of the utmost importance. "Anyway, Charles is here for the summer. With his niece. You remember Mimi Dover." She pointed to the petite blonde with the dangerous curves and Betty Grable smile standing in the center of a gaggle of suits.

*Here it comes . . .*

"What a lovely young lady she's become. Rumor is, she's to inherit a hefty trust fund." Giving credit to her intuition as a debutante of notice, Mimi glanced in their direction and gave a light wave to their hostess. "You two were friends once, weren't you?"

"When we were girls, yes. We still are, I believe."

"*Hmm.* She used to be sweet on your brother, wasn't she?"

The conversation would soon be drowning in another matchmaking scheme if Kat didn't shift tracks fast, and to something she actually did want to discuss.

"Who is Lou talking to?"

"Oh, that man. Always chatting with a senator for this, a congressman for that. I can't begin to keep all the names straight. If it's discussion about that cad Wild Bill Donovan, it'll mean another trip to DC, I'm sure." She waved the notion off like she was swatting at a bumblebee at a family picnic, then drew Kat away with an elegant gloved forearm hooked through her elbow. "You'll have to say hello to Lou later. Now come, come . . . I've gobs of people for you to meet."

Kat dropped her voice to a whisper. "Maman, I don't wish to be rude, but I need to speak with you. Can't we go somewhere private?"

"Ah, I know what this is about."

"You do?"

Maman gave a brave smile, ignoring Kat with a gentle pat to the hand. "Of course. But do not worry about your dress. The guests will overlook it if they know you're with me." A waiter waltzed by with a tray of champagne. Geneviève grabbed one for herself and tried to force another into Kat's hand. "Here—Dom Pérignon. Lou brings it out for every party. Cannot let it go to waste."

*That's it.* Kat refused the outstretched flute and, instead, tugged her maman by the elbow into the first place she could think of with a door that closed.

Lou's library was as pristine as the party was full.

Built-ins gave three walls a backdrop of white, the shelves immaculate with floor-to-ceiling books. On the other, golf trophies glinted in a golden row on a shelf behind an oversize walnut desk. Dueling wingbacks flanked the fireplace, with burgundy leather shining in the light from the hall. Hanging swords and a framed tapestry of the Sullivan coat of arms hung above the mantel, along with a brass wall sconce illuminating a crest with crown, gilding, and dancing red lions.

Kat clicked the double doors closed and moved to the desk lamp. In the wash of light she could see Maman's air change from breezy and blush-cheeked to tight-lipped and dour in a blink. Her mother stared back, a champagne flute gripped in each hand, like a caged animal desperate to escape.

"What is this, Kathryn? My guests—"

"Your guests can wait. Have you heard from Gavin?" Kat took a step forward. Hopeful. And willing to meet in the middle if necessary. She'd already decided by coming here this night that she'd endure whatever criticism, whatever disappointment, whatever blind distaste her mother offered, if it produced answers in the end.

"I need to know if he's written to you. A letter. Postcard. Or made a telephone call. Anything."

"Oh, you know Gavin." Maman let out an uneven laugh and set the flute Kat had refused on the edge of the desk to sip Dom Pérignon from the other. "That boy never will be tied down. It is not like him to remember to write a postcard, let alone buy a stamp to post it."

*Okay . . . no letters for you either.*

*This could be bad.*

"So, you're saying he's made no contact at all?"

"Whyever would he? Gavin has gone sailing for the summer. With the Martin boy and a couple of others. I cannot remember their names. But you know how it is. For boys to have their adventures when they are young. I didn't see any harm in letting him go."

*The Martin boy . . .*

Kat's heart sank.

Maman couldn't know that Gavin's best friend, Allan Martin, had signed up. Months ago he'd wandered into the shop and asked Kat to order a set of top-of-the-line Goodyears for his widowed mother, knowing she would have no idea which snow tires to purchase for her new Cadillac. He'd ordered them. Paid in advance for both tires and service. Hugged Kat, and that was it. Allan shipped out for the navy the next week.

Like Gavin. And so many others.

"Gavin is sailing with Allan Martin . . . in the middle of a war?"

Maman smirked. "As he said. You've known the Martins since you were a little girl. And Allan was always interested in you. Before you stopped attending social events, that is. I always thought you and he would, well, you know."

"We were only ever friends." She sighed at having to repeat the same verses each time they met. "And I'm not going to marry just so you can see my name in the society column. I'm happy as I am."

Geneviève slammed her flute down on the desk with such fury, Kat half expected the crystal to shatter.

"What is the matter with you, Kathryn? I do not deserve this. Not when all Lou and I have done is offer you a proper place in society. Do you know how many young women would envy the opportunities you so easily shun?"

"I was just being honest—"

"Oh, honest? Let us tell the truth then. Who paid for your years at Wellesley? It was I who convinced Lou that college was a sound investment so you could meet someone. Instead, you receive a piece of paper that says you speak French, Russian, German, Latin . . . What good is it now?" She made a *pfft* sound and flicked her wrist on air, like to educate a marriageable woman was a passing whimsy.

"There was a little more to college than that."

"Who secured you invitations to every important party in this city? Who ordered you custom gowns to wear in the same room with Carnegies, Cabots, and Vanderbilts? And now, you fritter away your days at some garage with no husband." Without warning, she snatched Kat's hand and thrust her oil-stained fingernails into the lamplight. "How dare you show up to our home like this, to embarrass us in front of our friends?"

All Kat could think was how she'd known this would happen. Yet for the hope of learning any news about Gavin, she'd convinced herself that things might be different—Maman might join the human race and be reasonable for once.

"I'm sorry I'm such a disappointment to you," Kat whispered, then drew in a deep, calming breath. She'd need the anchor for what was to come. "But that's not why I'm here. I only came to confirm where Gavin has gone. And now I know for certain he's not sailing."

For the first time Geneviève looked like she'd managed to fall from her high horse back to earth and earnestly took in what Kat had said—the last part anyway. "What are you saying? That my son lied to us? He would not do that to his maman."

"I don't know if he lied. But I have reason to believe Gavin signed up for military service. That's why we've not heard from him."

Maman sank her fingernails into the edge of Lou's desk like a frightened cat. "How do you know this?"

"Gavin came to the shop one night. Weeks back. He asked me not to say anything but seemed to imply he'd write when he landed in basic training and would tell you then. But I haven't received a single letter. And I'm concerned."

With a frantic shift, her maman began tugging at Lou's desk drawers in search of something but not finding it.

"Maman?"

She gave a ferocious tug to the bottom drawer when it caught and wouldn't open. "Oh, that man. Lou keeps fresh hankies in here. And now this drawer is sticking when I need one?"

"Is it locked?" Kat swept over to her side of the desk. And when Maman swayed on her feet, Kat braced her at the elbow and led her to one of Lou's leather wingbacks, then helped her to sit.

"I didn't come here to embarrass you. I didn't even know you had a party tonight. I just needed to find out if Gavin's reached out at all."

"I told Gavin not to do this!"

Kat swallowed hard. "You told him not to do what?"

"This! He said he needed to go fight for his country. To stop Hitler or some such nonsense. But we agreed—he is needed here. He could study the law. And with Lou's connections in Washington, he could secure Gavin a position of diplomacy to aid the war effort at home. My husband is a decorated war hero, for heaven's sake! But now this? After all the favors he called in to prevent Gavin's number coming up?"

Geneviève pounded an angry fist on the chair's clawed-wood armrest, then anchored her forehead against her palm to cradle the weight of her shaking head. "That foolish, foolish boy . . ."

The last words were drawn out on a guttural wail. So much so that Kat looked to the closed double doors when a knock sounded on the wood and smoky air and noise emerged as Lou poked his head in through the crack.

"Everything all right in here?"

Her stepfather slipped in, his face curious but brightening when he rounded the wingback and spotted Kat.

Lou came over, and she half rose to receive a genuine welcome kiss to her cheek. "Kathryn? How lovely to see you at one of our parties again."

Despite the misfortune of her mother's choices, Kat had to admit his manner was far warmer than any Maman offered. And without children of his own, Kat and Gavin were it—as much his children as any parent could claim. It was hard not to feel affection for this man who loved their mother, no matter how much her heart might feel it as disloyalty to Pops' memory.

"Hello, Lou." Kat tipped her brow in apology. Maman's tears would ensure there was no easy explanation. "I'm sorry . . . We . . ."

"What's this now?" Lou knelt. Took a folded hanky from his pocket and offered it to his wife.

"You see? He knows what I need before I speak it." Geneviève accepted the linen square with a shaky hand and dabbed under her eyes as she mumbled, "Surely there is something you can do to stop this?"

"Stop what, lamb?" he cooed.

"You are a colonel in the United States Army. Didn't you say they assured you Gavin would not have to go? Well, now we need your influence again to undo this mess."

"He's gone." Lou sighed, giving a slight nod of understanding as Maman cried like a kitten that had spilled its cream. "I see."

Kat bit her bottom lip and nodded back.

"Yes, he's gone! And I don't care what that boy thinks he wants. Do you hear what FDR says in those silly fireside chats? Talking about sacrifice—the mission and duty it is of every man to defend his country. But Gavin is a *boy*."

"He is a boy with his own mind. Always has been."

*See? Even Lou understands. Why can't you?*

Kat didn't want to—couldn't bear to let Gavin go either. But at the very least, the three people on earth who cared about him more than any other should be able to put their own fears aside and let him go, shouldn't they? Countless mothers and sisters and fiancées and wives were in the same plight and all trying to muddle through a war with their shoulders back and chins held high until their men marched home.

"Our generation remembers the first war," Geneviève argued, her tears subsiding in favor of indignation. "*We* do not need to be instructed in sacrifice. Nor do we need to offer up sons to the altar of another foreign war, like we did the last time. You understand, Lou. You told me yourself you would never be the same after the Great War claimed both of your older brothers. You lost your entire family out of that. I may have been born in France, but I am American now. And even I can see far enough across the ocean to remember what it was like when war destroyed our world the first time."

"Of course. I see it too. This war should end for the good of all. And I would do anything in my power to bring our son home—"

"Then do it. Bring our son home." Geneviève cut in, blinking through the long seconds Lou did not answer. Then with a confident nod, she shot to her feet. Smoothed her sparkling gown. And as Lou stood at her side, she jabbed the hanky back into his hand.

"Non. Come, Lou." She snapped her fingers at her husband. "We will not simply accept this. The governor is here. And at least one of those congressmen you know. We will find them this instant. And you will fix this. Or else telephone Donovan in the morning. That director of yours can clean up this mess even if you can't."

Kat watched, numb, as Geneviève painted her smile back in place, flung the library doors open, and disappeared into the party once again. Lou patted Kat's wrist and, with a supportive half smile, told her he'd go do battle with her maman.

Hovering in the library doorway, Kat found it hard to know whether to stay or go as she watched her stepfather follow his wife into the fray. She wouldn't be dressed down by her sharp-tongued maman again, that was sure. And she wasn't certain she could fake her own smile and cross the room to greet the blooming flower that was Mimi Dover either. But it didn't feel right to go back and hide at the auto garage. Not now. Not when, somewhere deep within her, Kat had the horrible, sinking feeling her brother might have bitten off far more than he could ever chew. And if she lost him too . . . what was left?

"*Ahem.*"

Someone cleared his throat next to her. Kat glanced over, a wave of surprise that it was the man from Lou's acquaintance.

Up close, he appeared mid-forties. Unassuming in a rumpled suit instead of a tuxedo like everyone else. With thinning blond hair and a tan line on his finger from an absent wedding ring—must be a story there. And with a surprising layer of interest in deep brown eyes behind wire-rimmed spectacles that seemed to show compassion as much as knowing for the heated exchange he'd just witnessed. Or surely heard.

"My apologies, sir. My mother is as predictable as these parties are stifling. But you are a guest, so I probably shouldn't say that."

"I never mind the truth being spoken. I much prefer it, in fact. Tell me, are you Kat Harris?"

Never one to give up information too easily, she blinked back at him. Then tipped her chin a little higher. "Who's asking?"

"That's what he said you'd say." He chuckled. Then, as if satisfied, he slipped an ivory card from his inside jacket pocket and handed it to her in one smooth move. With a tip of an invisible hat, he offered, "Good evening, miss. It's been a pleasure."

One side was blank. Kat flipped to the other and found **Brewer Fountain. Monday. Noon** typed in bold block letters.

Breath stolen, Kat looked up again.

"Who told you I'd—?"

She scanned the entryway, Mimi, the scads of guests surrounded by smoky air, and found . . . no one. The mysterious man with spectacles and kind eyes had faded into the party throng. Now all that remained was a card in her hand, a wayward invitation, and far more questions than she possessed when she first walked through the mansion door.

*c⁓*

31 *December 1951*
92 Avenue d'Iéna
Paris, France

This was Paris after all, so there must be pink champagne. Pity there was also a flat of *les riches* waiting for Kat to choke on it.

In all of two seconds she and Gérard had appeared as the bride and groom at the salon's magnificent double doors, and behind the tuxedos and red-lipped smiles sipping cocktails, all the knives were out . . .

*For her.*

A hush subdued chatter as all eyes fixed on them.

Few of this crowd had been at their Boston wedding. It was the crème de la crème of postwar Paris who'd gathered for the New Year's wedding party in Kat and Gérard's new home—a lavish corner flat in the 16th Arrondissement that doubled as her husband's wedding gift to her.

Not unlike the soirées Maman used to host before the end of the war, guests formed little packs hemmed in by cigarette smoke, ivory coffered ceilings and Baroque-blue walls, and floor-to-ceiling windows that had miraculously survived the occupation unscathed. They picked from trays with saffron and shallot hors d'oeuvres topped by generous spoonfuls of Prunier's or dessert offerings with flawless pistachio and rose petit fours. Conversation lingered on whether the Marshall Plan would ever be effective or if the Communists really would invade Western Europe. The more cautious debated what in the world 1952 would bring.

Behind the placid veneer, however, Kat had to consider what fueled the stares.

Even to her they were a puzzling pair.

Gérard once again became the enigmatic French aristo of old

prewar money. Though speculation was discreet, he was still re-membered to have been a tad too friendly with the Nazi régime and, by some miracle, had thus far avoided prosecution. And she—Kathryn "Kat" Harris—was his new expat bride with a tentative smile and chestnut crown set against a raspberry silk cocktail dress, who seemed to be the one under intense scrutiny. After all, she'd swooped in and sealed a marriage to the wealthiest bachelor in Paris when it was whispered her stepdaddy had his own fortune in the States. And that seemed to make more than a few enemies out of the unattached ladies who registered frosty glares every time the new four-carat Argyle diamond on her finger caught the light and erupted in rose-hued sparkles.

Kat leaned into Gérard's side, caught the woodsy scent of his aftershave as she raised up to whisper in his ear. "When you said you should present your wife to society, I never dreamed that meant all of Paris in the same room."

He smiled in profile, surveying the glittering guests all the way to the back of the salon, where French doors led to a grand balcony and the imposing view of the Arc de Triomphe beyond.

"*Hmm.* Some could still be on holiday. Saint-Tropez can be seduc-tive this time of year, you know."

"I'm completely serious. Was this the way to be introduced? A society wedding in Boston. Our Paris wedding party tonight. A room full of names I'll never remember. And all staring like they don't need any more time in which to decide how much they loathe the bride."

"Don't worry about that."

"Whyever not?"

"It's not taken long for me to go from recluse to slipping back into Paris society. But this crowd is predictable if anything. As soon as they see the dollar signs attached to a name, you're back in the club. With verve." His expression changed, the thin veil of humor fading in a blink. "Besides, if they loathe anyone it will be me."

"I may have to quote you on that one day."

"Be my guest, Chérie. As long as you remember, this was all your idea."

How could Kat forget that whirlwind? She'd come to find him over the summer and posed the ridiculous plan that they marry—in name only, of course, and each for their own gains. That was followed by Kat making multiple trips to France that autumn to make plans. And Maman's insistence on a lavish Boston wedding before Christmas. By New Year's Eve they were here, celebrating with his Paris crowd this marriage that by all accounts only had to appear real to be accepted.

But he'd called her Chérie . . .

*Darling.*

And grazed the small of her back with fingertips just above the low waist of her asymmetrical gown. Kat drew in a sharp breath—whether from the unexpected butterfly's touch of warmth or the reminder of what they must do at this party was a toss-up.

"Remember," he whispered next to her good ear. "No fear, or they'll eat us alive. We have to look married."

"We *are* married."

"Touché." Gérard shouldn't have laughed but did, a soft chuckle that only she could hear. "I meant that just like the last time we waltzed into a ballroom chock-full of the enemy, we will be the portrait of a couple interested only in each other. And no one will be the wiser."

"As opposed to the truth of what we really are?"

"Everyone hides, Kat. And what we can't hide, we exploit. *We* are society tonight. The room will remember our names, and that's all that matters now. Come on." He slipped his arm around her waist, gave a gentle squeeze at her side to nudge her forward with him. "We have work to do."

One of Gérard's great talents was to surmise the true nature of any room with glaring accuracy. It was the first impression Kat remembered of him when they'd been thrown together during the war: He missed no detail, no matter how trivial. And now, years after the war ended, Gérard gave that same delving précis to the *real* Paris in the room—not the preening peacocks the gathering appeared to be.

With a nod to a cool blonde in ice blue surrounded by tuxedos and nursing a cig, he remarked, "Chic but broke. I'll let you guess her remaining assets with which to ensnare a husband." Of the couple conspiring by the fireplace: "Stuffy and entitled. But devious. I'd cross them long before they cross you." Then on to old money. New money. No money left but hiding it. (The scandal of it all.) Married for love. Married for lust. Married for sheer survival during the war. And married now for any other reason and miserable . . . Between the façades and the truth was a maze of a Paris crowd Kat still hadn't ironed out. And at this rate, wasn't sure she ever would. Or to which category their marriage belonged.

"A cozy bunch. All your friends?"

"I thought Mimi was your friend, remember? Quite the stroke of luck she joined you in France as your travel companion up until the wedding and then stayed on after." Gérard tipped his shoulders in a shrug. "But I guess you could say *friend* is a relative term. Especially these days."

"You mean in Paris."

"I mean anywhere."

The line of sight that had Gérard so easily assess the room did that thing again—his gaze drifted off to another place, and he seemed to look beyond the sparkling reflection of the patio doors into the dark Paris night beyond.

"They will love you," he offered and, noticing how the guests watched them, lifted her hand to press a lingering kiss to her wrist. "Trust me. Now smile. The socialite du jour is headed this way."

Gérard squeezed her hand and let it go, then perused the party far more at ease than Kat did when playing the room. It was plain to see: These were not her people. Not like they could be his. Except for maybe Mimi, whose rekindled friendship had become a surprise comfort these last years after the war.

"Is that my Kitty-Kat?" Mimi enveloped Kat in a hug that felt more like she was grasping for a lifeline than offering the warmth of an actual greeting. "You look fabulous, my dear! *Très chic.*"

"Bonjour, Mimi. You too."

The socialite wore glamorous white silk with a bevy of black pin-dots, a cinched wasp waist, and a boatneck collar that just tipped the sculpted blonde curls cascading off her porcelain shoulder. It was evident that after her own whirlwind wedding, Mimi had taken in every ounce of couture Paris had to offer.

"I'd say congratulations, but I'm already making bets on which of the shrews in the room tries to one-up your nuptials." Mimi tapped her chin with a gloved index finger, thinking aloud as she scanned the salon. Then she glanced over the ruching on Kat's right shoulder. "Even if they can't hope to win with your killer ensemble. Wait—is this from the Dior spring collection? How dare you arrive here more chic than me!"

"Is it Dior?" Funny, but Kat hadn't a clue.

She'd asked Gérard's secretary to purchase a cocktail dress for the wedding party, with specifications on the length and asymmetrical bodice to cover the scars on her right shoulder but with little else by way of expectations. It arrived within a day. Had fit. And that was that. The raspberry silk wasn't her style at all, but it was Paris style and Gérard noted that's what mattered.

Lucky for her, Mimi didn't wait for an answer. She sipped pink champagne, gossiped behind a gloved hand, and gave the giddy impression of an essential society guide with just the right amount of innocent stardust in her eyes.

"You've arrived in this salon to save us. And not a moment too soon," Mimi whispered, with a wink to a garçon and his tray of bubbly. She lifted a flute and passed it to Kat. "Here. The room looks friendlier if you drink fast."

Kat took a tiny swallow. Only to placate her friend. She couldn't afford anything impairing her tonight, not if they were going to accomplish what they'd set out to. "So? Where is this Léo I've heard so much about? I'm beginning to wonder if your new husband exists but in letters."

Mimi looped an arm through Kat's elbow with the familiarity of old friends.

"Oh, my husband exists. You know I was never going to have one of those big society weddings. Elopement is much more my style." She rose on tiptoes to scan the crowd through curls of rising smoke. "He's probably stopped to schmooze the minister of industry and his wife. There's some legal matter he's angling a quick fix for. You know how those things can be. *Ah*, there he is—"

She pointed to a man, who except for Gérard, was average height to the gentlemen in the room. Laughter shook his broad shoulders and tossed a crown of thick, golden hair he'd wrangled into a tight part. He displayed enough charisma, it seemed, that he could have guests gathered around him enthralled at whatever he'd said.

Kat's midsection fluttered.

Too much hinged on tonight. And Gérard had told her that Mimi's husband was the reason why. They were to greet him. Befriend him. And through her companionship with Mimi, Kat was to find out everything she could of this Léo—including what information he might have about Gavin's disappearance during the war.

Something about him having connections they needed . . .

"Léo needs to convince that man to lift building restrictions or whatnot so he can make a boatload of money. I said Daddy would give us another loan. But, well, that husband of mine wants to do this on his own. He thinks if he can prop up some old château in the north, we can sell it for a pretty penny and it will be enough to set us up in Paris without my family's help. To fit in here, you need *serious* money. And the right connections. Seems your darling Gérard has both. That makes your wedding party a business venture as much as anything, I'm afraid."

"I'm glad we could help."

"*Chéri?*" Mimi called out to her husband and waved him over. He raised a finger to hold her off, until she stomped her kitten heel in mock defiance. "This is a wedding party, remember? Come meet the bride."

Léo excused himself, then turned to greet his wife's friend with eyes that smiled at the corners. Until they tempered—with a challenge?—when they landed on Kat. And hid what must have been roaring through his mind a million miles an hour to see her standing before him.

Just as it was for her.

In that instant everything Kat and Gérard had planned began a steady crumble. She looked up. Scanned the room. Felt her eyes sting from the smoke. And had to temper her breathing through the desperation to try to find her husband through the crowd.

"My dear husband, this is the bride." Mimi swept her arm around Kat's waist and gave a pert side hug, shaking her from her stupor. "My Kat—Kathryn Fontaine. From summers in Boston and Christmas at Cape Cod. We've been friends since we were children. I knew her and her brother before the war."

Kat's heart squeezed at the mention of Gavin. And maybe Mimi's did too, because she paused for a breath and offered Kat something of an off-kilter smile. "But now that we're both here in Paris, I get to call her my dearest friend in all the world."

Recovering quicker than Kat, Léo was genteel. Unshaken. And far too smooth when he offered, "*Enchanté.* My wife speaks of little else these days than her kindred spirit from Boston."

He bowed his head as one would when meeting his wife's dear friend for the first time. Only this wasn't the first time. It was a lifetime away from a château in Northern France and the posh parties of Paris after it. And new spouses who hadn't a clue the extent of the history that had just exploded in the room.

In that instant, every memory of that Christmas so long ago came flooding back. He was Xandre. She was Célène. And what was done in the woods that night had made her vow never to set eyes on him again. And if she did, Kat feared she'd be forced to finish what they'd started all those years ago.

# CHAPTER 4

11 *July 1943*
Fort-Mahon-Plage
Baie de Somme, France

The fisherman's cottage was nestled atop a treed rise beyond the dunes, where its weathered stone and thatched roof waved to England from across the sea.

Unlike the stretch of tranquil beach that spanned the larger fishing harbor to the south, the road to reach this place was rocky and narrow off the dunes and hemmed in by a thick forest of pines, accessible by a flight of hastily set rock steps. Manon had not visited here before, but Valens had given strict instructions where to stow her bicycle and to wait for the signal before she trekked up the rise.

She hung back behind the wind-battered shed just beyond sight from the village road. The wind roiled as storm clouds gathered over the water, carrying the first speckles of rain as she chewed her lip and scanned the horizon, from the stretch of sand touching the sea and up to the ridge above the pines. And finally exhaled when a steady stream of smoke began its rise over the treetops.

Heavy black smoke was the invitation, meaning Valens' contact, Henri, must be there.

After tucking her hair under a sage paisley scarf, Manon secured it with a loose knot at her collar. Then she rolled her bicycle into the old shed to stow it—lest the invaluable item be purloined in times like these.

Having left it in a shadowed spot behind weathered crates and fishing whatnots left over from past years, she stepped back out onto the road. Clouds of smoke continued billowing from the tiny smokestack, and wind kicked off the Channel punished as she climbed the rise to a rough, salt-stained door. She pounded her fist on it as instructed, in three clear-as-a-bell knocks.

"Have you lemon sole for sale today?"

After a pause at the code she'd shouted, the door cracked.

Light from inside cast upon a man's face . . . who was *not* Henri.

The Maquis contact was supposed to be sturdy but gruff. Experienced and *sérieux*. Manon had been told Henri had a thickset frame, sharp nose, and salt-and-pepper hair at the temples tucked under a flatcap emblazoned by a red poppy on the raised side. The man before her was considerably younger—more her age than Henri's. But weathered, too, from the sun. His beard was unruly, his deep brown hair tipped with highlights that curled over the tops of his ears, and light eyes that looked as though they used to smile once but, like hers, did not so often now. He'd rolled his cabled sweater sleeves up to his elbows, revealing bronzed skin to match his face, no doubt from dragging waterlogged nets into fishing boats all day.

"I brought this." Manon held up the treasure of an unopened tin of Compagnie Coloniale tea from her trench coat pocket. "And extra payment for fish."

After seeing she'd come alone, the man opened the door wider.

"*Viens ici.*"

Manon obeyed, stepping in.

He bolted the door behind them with a resounding click. The rifle she hadn't known he'd gripped behind the door, he now slung over his shoulder, the leather strap crosswise over his chest. Manon untied the scarf from her neck and pulled it off as he swept by, then slipped the kerchief into her pocket as her eyes adjusted to the light.

The cottage was unobtrusive and humble for its purpose as a Resistance safe house. Simple stone walls held the aroma of pine mingled with the scent of the sea, and the hint of burnt rubber lingered as leftover evidence of what had caused the black smoke rising from the chimney. Drips of rain counted time from rustic beams outlining the ceiling. A hearth housed a roaring fire that had kept the smoke alive, where a spit and cast-iron pot bubbled over hungry flames.

The man turned broad shoulders away and gathered papers and maps, what looked like brass nautical tools, and books that had been butterflied in piles over the center of a dining table. Manon used the seconds to peek into the shadows beyond the edge of a quilt tacked against the wall like a curtain, though she could make out nothing sure through the darkness.

Trying to sound steady, and only mildly interested, she inquired, "Where is Henri?"

"Out. I am Dominique Moreau. I work with Henri at the market stall in the village. He's asked me to look after his cottage while he is away." He bundled the last of the wares into a crate and swept behind the curtain, leaving her alone with the tea tin gripped in nervous hands.

A rifle slung over a man's chest was normal for times like these. But for a woman to step into a cottage alone with an as-yet-unknown caretaker . . . that's where her experience with subversion fizzled. Manon was not prepared to calculate in a situation such as this. Whether she ought to trust this man as an associate of Valens. Whether they were, in fact, alone in the cottage—and if they were, what that could mean. She could not even judge whether to find comfort or concern in the fact he kept his weapon so close.

"We do not often see visitors," Monsieur Moreau said when he returned empty-armed save for the rifle, which he leaned in the corner within reaching distance of the stove. "But if you're here for lemon sole, that must mean you've come from Château du Broutel?"

Without realizing it, Manon exhaled the breath that had been wound tight within her.

"Oui. By delivery truck. And I cycled the rest of the way from the village."

"Here." As if knowing, he pulled out a dining chair nearest the fireplace and patted the back for her to sit. "A gale is moving in. And these dunes do not care that it's supposed to be summer. You must be chilled to the bone."

"I think I am." She held out the tea tin.

"Merci." He accepted it with a nod of thanks, then inclined his head toward the bubbling cast-iron pot. "We've tea now. And fresh clams for a fisherman's stew. It's unremarkable by the château's standards, I'm sure. But it's yours if you wish."

Manon shook her head, always cautious yet somehow unable to hold fast to wariness of this stranger. If tea and stew were topics to be trusted, and the fact he knew of their code to offer any assurance, then it was a welcome respite not to have to stand guard for once as she always must while in the château kitchen.

"Just tea then."

"Like Henri? I've not met him yet but was told he prefers it with tipple." Manon pointed to the jug on a high shelf within reach of the tiny stove. "The calvados."

"Is that what Valens calls the ripe paint stripper Henri drinks? The Maquis supplies it to the locals, and I'm afraid that brew has become Henri's one solace on bitter-cold nights." Monsieur Moreau chuckled under his breath. "Non, merci. I'm not sure I could stomach any more of that or roasted corn water for as long as I live. What will the world be like when we have all the tea we want and cream in our coffee again? The stuff of dreams, non?"

"The Boche couldn't drink all the tea we had when they first took over the château. But the supply dwindles now as regular rail deliveries are becoming scarce. I set some aside when we have it, just in case. And I'm glad to bring it. Though I was not expecting to have to deliver it so soon."

All jesting about rationed tea set aside, he nodded. Thoughtfully. As if he understood better than she might expect.

"You are the chef." He noted rather than asked her title and grasped a tea towel to lift a boiling kettle from the stove. "Henri warned me someone might come from the château while he was away. Though I admit, I did not think it would be you. I was told to expect Valens?"

"Oui. He is our pâtissier. But . . . he is ill."

Monsieur Moreau kept his back to her but paused, as if thinking some undefined thing through. "You are worried for him?"

"He will be well soon, I'm sure. But I wanted to be the one to speak with Henri, in person this time."

"And will you speak with me instead?" He poured hot water from the kettle into mismatched cups and reached for the tea parcel to let the leaves steep. "Because I was the one who received Valens' missive about the missing maid. We hoped she'd have turned up by now."

"She hasn't."

"And if what Valens said about that is true, then events are . . . concerning."

Of course they were.

Whenever someone who was supposed to appear somewhere in wartime simply vanished, as in Célène's case, it set teeth on edge. More and more Reich soldiers arrived at the château by the day, and all morose from their battles at the front. It was rumored the tide was turning against them. And with each of the vehicles emblazoned with a swastika that rolled up the winding gravel lane to the château and emptied another high-ranking official on their doorstep, it meant caution was heightened. Risk exponentially increased. And they were all on tenterhooks from dawn until dusk. One never knew who listened in on private conversations, followed you on an innocent walk to the village, or suspected subversion was afoot when you left for a fisherman's cottage along the shore—even when it was.

"Why did you not come before now?"

Manon shook her head. "I daren't. The Vichy police are always watching. There has been a rumor in the château that some of the highest-ranking officials in the Reich may soon take a holiday there."

She noted his reaction to that—a tiny raise of the chin in a little tell that said he wasn't surprised to hear this but rather was interested in how she knew of it too.

"If that is true, never have we had a better opportunity for you and Valens to funnel critical information back to the Resistance."

"Oui, but we've also not seen this level of security. Not ever. The Reich has even brought in members of the Gestapo, who we've not seen much at all here. They've also employed extra Police Nationale to patrol the grounds, and the nearby village in Rue, round the clock. I couldn't take a chance to leave before today or else risk being detained on the road. Not until I had a legitimate reason for venturing this far."

"The Boche don't strike me as particularly worried about justification when they detain someone."

"Not as a rule, no. But their deliveries are bound by orders from above. And that can be quite useful to us." Manon reached down to her sock and removed a folded missive she'd tucked there, then offered it to him. "These are the new patrol times around the château. Along with expected rail delivery dates for the next few weeks."

He opened the paper and scanned the list inside. "What will be in those deliveries?"

"Standard foodstuffs to plan dinner parties. And wine."

"Wine?" His eyes flashed. "What about weapons?"

Manon shook her head. "I don't know beyond that. Though I caution you, arrangements could change at any moment, so I would not set your watch by them. And though I was told to inquire after lemon sole so you'd recognize me, we actually could use the fish. Whatever you have for a dinner party on Wednesday."

"Let me guess. You need fish because you spoiled your supply?" He placed a steaming cup in front of her, then settled in the chair opposite to warm his hands around a cup of his own.

"How did you know that?"

"Henri laughed about it for days, when Valens told him how their chef managed to outwit the Reich officers by pricking the tinned fish so it would turn. Clever."

"We did. The mackerel went first. Then the sardines and prawns not long after. She lowered her head a touch to hide an irreverent smile. "In terrible fashion I might add. The officers were furious, thinking the soldiers unloading the train cars had so mishandled the crates that they'd dented the tins and spoiled the goods. We're still trying to air out the larder. And those soldiers are now walking in their sleep on the dreaded night patrols as reprimand."

"Serves them right, the devils." His unmasked grin said anything being spoiled for their enemy's benefit was as cheering a thought for him as it was for her. The glimpse of amusement shared across the table lasted for a long second between them, until it was hidden again behind the lip of his cup when he took a sip of tea.

"I don't know if I can help." He sighed into the next words. "But I'll try. Fish is a given. What else do you need?"

"A replacement. And as quickly as possible, before the Nazi authorities place kitchen staff of *their* choosing—which would only add risk to those working under me. I could actually use someone who could step in and assist as *chef de tournant*. There's so much more we could do with that arrangement."

He leaned back in the chair, its wood old but too damp to creak with his weight.

"Right. Say that again, but pretend I know nothing about how a French kitchen operates."

"The chef de tournant works as a sort of swing chef who can step in at any station where we're understaffed. One would expect them to be able to cook and bake, butcher, sauté, prepare desserts or sauces—whatever we need done with both accuracy and skill."

"The one who was supposed to arrive could cook. And bake. She could speak multiple languages and apparently was a crack shot. She was to drop into Lyon, meet with Allied agents there, and they would deliver her to your château. This SOE agent was a virtual unicorn were Baker Street to tell it. And we can't find you another ace at the drop of a hat. These things take time."

"If she was indeed to arrive from Lyon, then where is she now?"

"I'd say either in a jail cell with the GFP blowtorching the skin off her feet or already buried with cyanide coating her dental work."

"What is the GFP?"

"Geheime Feldpolizei—their street police. Nazi thugs in plain clothes moonlighting as Gestapo here in France." He exhaled low and stared past her for a moment, where flames danced on the hearth. "Either way, God be with her. We're of no help to her now."

No need to go on.

Manon had seen and heard enough to know how this worked. Either the GFP disposed of suspected spies on the spot, or before they could begin their brutal interrogation, the agent would bite down on an emergency capsule of potassium cyanide and be dead within seconds, thus preventing giving anything away in torture.

She pitied the poor agent, whoever the woman was. And if they could not find an answer for her whereabouts, any loved ones back in England would always wonder what had happened to their girl. That seemed even more tragic than a self-sacrificing death.

"How long do we wait for a replacement?"

He shook his head, as if the answer was matter-of-fact. "I cannot answer that."

"Why? Henri gave an anticipated date to Valens before."

"Things are different now." Monsieur Moreau rubbed a palm at the base of his neck, then sighed as he turned his cup back and forth in a semicircle against the table. "Look, we had our contact wire the Brits as soon as we received your message. They were working on it with the Yanks last we knew. But now there are certain . . . complications, and we've had to go radio silent—for them as well as for us. It's not as easy as putting an advertisement in *The Times*, you know. These things must be managed delicately. I hate to be the bearer of bad news, but we have no choice except to wait until they contact us."

"Managing delicately sounds controlled for a fisherman who's bound by the sea's moods, if you don't mind me saying so."

"I won't argue with that."

The man was both well-spoken and appeared educated for a laborer who spent his days avoiding home-brewed calvados and wrangling fish from the sea. Books were stacked on every free surface. His French was impeccable. And the colloquial dialect of the Normandy coast, spot-on. But just then there was the tiniest glimpse of something otherworldly about him, as if he'd dropped from a far-off place and decided a crumbling cottage on the dunes was simply the place to wait out a war.

And though Manon was an accomplished chef who pilfered tins of the Reich's goods in order to trade for favors, the man sitting across the table couldn't have guessed her true identity any more than she could place his.

Careful was one thing; clever was another. It seemed he'd offer as little as necessary in order to keep them both safe, which she appreciated. But only to a point. He was being cagey. And they both knew it.

Manon leaned forward, elbows on the table. "You might as well spit it out."

He nearly spit something all right—his tea, while covering a choke at her frank delivery. "Pardon?"

"Whatever it is you're not saying. I'm here now, so please do me the courtesy of dropping the veil. And stop pretending you're some high-and-mighty operative who's so far above the rest of us when we've been here under this blasted occupation for years, and this is the first time I've set eyes on you. We know France. And we know the château. Try to offer the courtesy of treating us as equals."

He tapped an index finger against the handle of his cup. "Am I to understand you're calling me a . . . snob?"

"I'm not sure that word should apply in wartime."

"You might be surprised," he countered.

Drawing his brows in, he pinched his forehead in the center like that little spark of moxie was quite unexpected but not altogether unwelcome. He tempered his smile so it only lasted a breath before being replaced by seriousness again.

"The Vichy police captain has been to see us." When Manon gasped and shot a glance around the space that seemed as unassuming for a safe house as one could be, he raised a hand to calm her. "Not here. But to the village square. In Rue. He came to our stall at the fish market three days ago."

"You don't mean Captain Fontaine, of the Police Nationale? The one who lords it over security at the château?"

"The very one."

Manon tried not to cross paths with the captain often—only when a large shipment was to be delivered and the Nazi officials ordered Vichy police to inspect the trucks. Nevertheless, the man was a formidable presence on the grounds. His orders were sharp, smart, and followed without question. And on the occasions he had shown up in her kitchen, Manon had worked on the fringes so she stayed out of his eyeshot. It was best to keep the façade of invisibility with anyone of rank. She doubted the man could pick her out of a lineup had his life depended on it.

Still, Manon swallowed hard and dug her nails under the lip of the worn wood table, managing the nervous tension that surged through her body. "What did he want?"

"To buy fish."

"Fish . . ."

"Oui. He'd heard we run the market stall in the village and that we sometimes supply private orders outside of what's set apart for the local authorities. So he came to inquire about regular deliveries."

"You mean the head of château security, the Vichy captain for the Reich's regional headquarters, came out of his way to talk to you about buying goods on the . . . *marché noir?* Instead of sending a messenger?"

It didn't seem Monsieur Moreau missed the irony of a black-market meeting either, but still he shook his head.

"Non. He's requested a regular shipment to the château. Something about streamlining what comes in and goes out from the château grounds. But since you're the head chef, I'd expect he'll discuss this with you as soon as he has the opportunity. And when he does . . ." He tipped his brows to give her a pointed look beneath them. "I, uh, wouldn't let him know you find it an insult to have a man usurp your authority in the kitchen. At least not right away."

Somehow he'd guessed right; war or no war, it was her post.

Manon swirled the tea in her cup, again trying not to seem as interested as she was, with her gut feeding on fear inside. "Did he inquire about my kitchen—or my staff?"

"Non. You and your staff are in no danger. But I don't believe the captain is a man accustomed to letting anyone run errands for him. He's a bachelor. Lives alone. My contacts tell me he stays at the château for days on end to manage security during the big events. And he travels to his home the moment the last guest leaves. Every time."

"That is true."

"I gather he'll ask his own questions as he has them, so best be prepared for that. And try to forget he carries out orders from the most formidable evil on earth, day in and day out."

*The most formidable evil on earth . . .*

The words struck like a dagger through the chest.

Yes, she knew of their evil. All too well.

Manon understood their barbarism with every nerve ending in her body and every breath she drew into her lungs. With every memory of the French men and women who were blown to bits on the outskirts of Paris when the Germans first rolled their panzers in to invade the city streets. She recognized it with every blitz bomb and bullet and beautiful soul they'd wiped from the earth, without justification or certainly without mercy. And now with each beat of her heart in the hellish landscape that was Northern France, Manon wished nothing more than to seek vengeance for that evil—both against the soulless puppeteers of the Reich and of Frenchmen who would do their bidding.

"Chef?"

"*Hmm?*" she snapped back with her title spoken.

Wind pounded the shuttered windows, and Manon was reminded again just where she was. It was not the summer of 1940. It was not a bombed Paris flat crumbling in front of her again. This time the horror was only in her mind. She might have been sleepwalking through the last three years as a hollowed-out ghost in a château kitchen, but realizing she was sitting in the fisherman's cottage had reignited the memories she kept so close yet fought so hard to keep at bay.

"Are you well?" Monsieur Moreau shifted his gaze down, trying to coax her from staring at the tabletop. Only then did Manon realize she'd gripped her teacup so tightly, her knuckles had gone white and her fingertips were numb to its warmth.

"Oui." She released her hold and set the teacup back on the table like priceless porcelain. Then cleared her throat over the embarrassment. "Please do send word when you have our replacement. And I would appreciate a delivery of fish before the next dinner party so I have corroboration for my outing today."

"You shall have it."

He rose when she did, awkwardly pushing his chair back with a scrape against the stone floor and a measure of surprise on his face.

He must have seen her hands shaking. Noticed the words tripping off her tongue. And beheld the dead giveaway of a blush she could feel burning like fire on her cheeks. But he seemed unsure of what to do and, instead, grabbed up the rifle as she moved, following behind her to the door.

"Henri and I will arrive with a delivery for your next dinner, if that will suffice. Can you notify the guards at the gate so they'll let us through?"

"You've been through a Gestapo check, then?"

Deadpanning, he answered, "As far as they know we have."

"Of course. Anything else?"

He pointed to the paper she'd handed him. "This rail shipment from the West scheduled to arrive at the château—can you ensure we have access to it?"

She swallowed hard. "Why?"

"We've been waiting for this. And have good reason to believe it will include wine—Sancerre. Several crates of it. But there will be one with a smudge on the wood. Noticeable, right under the swastika stamped on the side. If you see this, I need your clumsiest staff member to carry it in. I need them to carry it, drop it, and shatter what's inside."

Poor Frédéric—the lad came to mind right away. "I have someone who can do the job. Don't worry. I'll tell Valens and we'll see it done."

"You don't want to know why?"

"Non. It's probably better if I do not. So if there is nothing else, I'll bid you good day, monsieur. And wish you safe travels in your deliveries."

Giving the man any glimpse into her moment of remembrance felt like an intrusion. Though he'd done nothing wrong, it was a private moment. One Manon never wished to share or been able to, not even with Valens, who was family to her. And though war made odd compatriots out of strangers—setting mismatched cups together at the same secluded fisherman's cottage table—the only thing that felt natural was to run.

Run and not look back.

"Chef?" he asked from behind.

"Oui?" Manon stopped, turned, and found too late he'd been on her heels when she nearly careened with her palms to his chest.

"You dropped this." He held sage silk in a calloused palm.

"Oh . . . *merci*. I hadn't realized I dropped it."

Instinctively patting her pocket where she'd put it, then raising her palm to the plaits coiled at her nape, she brushed the space where the silk would have held her auburn locks safe against the wind.

"It's Dominique." He offered the ghost of a smile—something real with the name, though she knew it likely wasn't his. He probably had many names. And who knew how many pretty faces lined up to receive them. "Monsieur Moreau sounds so formal, even for a snobby fisherman."

"Very well, Dominique." Manon took the kerchief, shoved it in her trench pocket, and whispered "Merci" again as she turned, finding herself stuck fiddling with the uncooperative bolt on the door. "Oh, how do you . . . ?"

"It sticks." Dominique was at her side in a breath and reached up, slow as if not to startle her, and moved the bolt aside with one experienced flick. "There."

He raised the butt of the rifle to his shoulder and waited.

Manon guessed the pause was so she'd look at him. Or share her name in kind. And even with her hand on the door latch and her feet ready to run, something told her the invitation was genuine. She was struck by what she hadn't felt for so long in their war-torn world, save for when working alongside Valens: unyielding kindness. A lack of judgment, perhaps, for her stricken state. Or a measure of patience that said somehow, in the depths of eyes that matched the stormy sea just off the dunes outside, before her stood a stranger no more.

They might never meet again. But in this moment, Dominique was telling her they'd part friends. That somehow humanity had managed to win this round of the terrible game of war because two might choose to defy it.

"You understand, I can't let you go unless I've checked that it's safe."

"Oui. Of course," she breathed out, shaken but covering.

Dominique cracked the door and scanned the ridge to the road as Manon changed her mind—needing something to busy her shaking hands—and retied her kerchief over her hair, waiting for the signal to go.

In a fleeting instant he nodded her through. She stepped over the threshold from the warmth of the cottage into the Channel's bitter gale, as if the whole world was growing angrier around them.

"Come again, Chef?" he called, edging the door closer to the frame. "If you have need of us, smoke will rise here each time the storm clouds roll in."

Manon took a first step against the stones but, on a split-second whim, turned to look over her shoulder and called, "Manon!"

"What?" he shouted back, holding a palm cupped around his ear.

"My name. It's Manon. And you know where to find me should you need a good meal, or spoiling our overlords' provisions." Offering a rare smile in return, she held back errant whisps of hair from blinding her face and shouted over the wind, "Might as well tell you—I'm an expert at both."

# CHAPTER 5

12 July 1943
Freedom Trail
Boston, Massachusetts

Another sweltering day hit in the midst of an unseasonably steamy summer. Preferring the cool of dewy grass and a lingering haze over the trails, Kat had stepped out for a running jog before the sun rose and baked off the moisture.

She'd worked in the auto shop through the busy morning hours. Tried not to stalk the clock until lunch. And stepped out into the sunshine a good hour earlier than noted on the card she'd received at the party.

After a serious debate with herself about whether she should actually show up, and a long, winding trek to surveil the streets bordering Boston Common, curiosity won the battle, and Kat finally settled on an empty bench in front of Brewer Fountain.

It was safe—there she could see the walking paths leading to and from the fountain. Women had taken Roosevelt's victory gardens scheme to heart and were tilling vegetable rows in the green. And while most were focused on their surroundings as the Brewer Fountain's impressive bronze sculptures depicting Greek mythological figures of Neptune and his wife stood guard, Kat could keep an eye on the traffic that swept along the corner of Park and Tremont Streets at the same time. And on the pricey Ford Super Deluxe she'd noted was idling not far off, with its windows curiously rolled up on what was a sweltering day.

Ladies strolled past her bench, pushing buggies under the speckled bower of sun and shade from the Common's famed old English elms. Mothers tilled and traded gossip in little groups, looking up every now and then at little ones splashing hands in the fountain and reminding them not to soil the housewives on the home fronts' repurposed summer wardrobes. A group of young lads lauded toy sailboats in mismatched races along the surface of the water, turning them in circles and watching as they capsized under the fountain's spray. And children played hopscotch and jacks on the paved surface, not even noticing the eerie accompaniment of gas mask bags strapped tightly over their tiny shoulders or war bond posters plastered on nearby buildings shouting, "Make Every Pay-Day Bond-Day!"

Kat checked her watch again. Then glanced, eyes only, over at the Ford Deluxe across the way.

*Noon. He's late.*

Being the pragmatic woman she was, Kat decided she'd give Mr. Spectacles five minutes to show before she tore up his card and tossed it in the nearest trash bin. And if that auto kept its tires stilled on the road in front of her, she just might stay longer than five minutes, if only to satisfy her mounting curiosity.

An earsplitting shout followed by a thunderous splash drew Kat's attention from scanning the park for the man's face. The commotion didn't appear serious, thank heaven—just a young officer in USAAF dress drenched from head to toe, and his officer's hat floating away as he splashed through the fountain on his hands and knees.

From reading bystanders' lips, Kat could tell he'd just knelt to ask his sweetheart to marry him, only to trip over a sailboat-carrying lad who'd run by and promptly flipped the ring—luxurious little velvet box and all—into the water's depths.

Within seconds the mishap engaged the entire corner of the

park to help him in his plight. The would-be fiancée was shouting and waving a bouquet of lilacs with such fervor that petals
rained down on the water's surface. The mothers dropped spades
and hand hoes and rushed to help. One consoled the young lady
through her tears, and the others directed where the lad ought to
push sailboats out of the way as they swore they saw a diamond
sparkle under the waves.

Kat couldn't help smiling at the innocent chaos and raised a hand
to her mouth as cover. It was, after all, a dear scene, even for the
Laurel and Hardy look of the thing. And the proposal proved entirely
romantic because the officer continued wading through the water in
a frenzy and hadn't even noticed his girl had already shouted "Yes!"
several times.

"*Wo hast du das gelernt?*" A voice cut into Kat's thoughts from
behind, asking, "Where did you learn that?"

Save for her professors and a handful of fellow students at
Wellesley, Kat hadn't heard actual German spoken aloud for ages.
And certainly not in any corner of a public park on a random
Monday.

The man from the party slipped onto the bench next to her.

Saying nothing right away, he watched the scene too. He was
wearing a casual striped shirt rolled at the forearms, a light beige
trilby shadowing wire-rimmed spectacles, and chestnut trousers
with oxfords that, even for their worn state, still owned an impressive shine. Crossing one leg over the other, he tapped a folded newspaper against his knee and waited.

"*Befürchten Sie nicht, als deutscher Spion abgestempelt zu werden?*"
Kat parroted back that he ought to be worried someone would label
him a German spy if he spoke that language out in the open. And
then added, "*Où ai-je appris à faire quoi?*" in French, saying, "Where
did I learn to do what?" to make an equal point.

"You read lips." He nodded to the scene. "You were trying your
best not to laugh at that over there."

"It's easy enough to make out. Even those children can see what happened."

"But you didn't just see, did you? You *know* what they said."

Kat didn't deny the random skill, just folded her hands in her lap as they watched a policeman approach and help muscle the young officer from the fountain.

"Care to enlighten me?"

"If you insist. The moms forgot birthday cake for the children. Though who'd want it baked with saccharine and the government's new initiative to push powdered eggs? The copper over there cut short his lunch from the street vendor to come over and save the day. And far be it from me to ignore a young airman who's both willing to rescue a botched proposal and fight for his country. I haven't decided which is more heroic, that he waded through the fountain or that he was on time for his meeting."

"I am late, yes." The man nodded as though unoffended, which was good. Whatever this game of wits was he'd started, he seemed content to let it keep rolling. He took a pack of Lucky Strikes from his shirt pocket, lit one, and took a lazy draw. "At least I was in time to see what will become a charming story for the grandkiddies one day."

"And even after following me for an hour before you sat down."

He cleared his throat. "Did I?"

"Yes. You stayed pretty close on my tail all the way from the garage. Down Washington Street. To Trenton. Then Park. Now here. And you weren't exactly trying to hide it." Kat pointed out the Ford Deluxe. Then tipped her chin toward the corner shop on Trenton Street. "I saw you behind me in the reflection of the bookshop window display."

"Ah. So you weren't that interested in purchasing a copy of *The Moon Is Down*."

"Already read it. Not one of Steinbeck's best, even if it is still selling. But that's beside the point. You obviously know me. So? Who are you, and why are you following me around?"

"Henry Wharton Birch."

Kat scoffed. *Who were these people?* "You're joking."

"Something funny?"

"You don't think that's a little too on the nose, Mr. Birch?" When he didn't waver, she laughed, adding, "James Fenimore Cooper's *The Spy.* The main character, Henry Wharton, who's sentenced to hang as a British spy? Is that what you want me to believe, that you're some kind of secret government operative?"

"You tell me. And you can drop the 'Mister.'"

"Fine, Birch." Kat glanced down at his ring finger. "What does your wife think of your job?"

A little crinkle formed at the corner of his eye, giving away that he was amused at her response. He blew smoke in the air, watching the women tilling the gardens as he chose his words. "My wife is proud that her husband is a junior vacuum cleaner salesman for Hoover."

"Junior?"

"Commonality makes anything more believable. But like you, Kathryn Elisabette Harris, we all have roles to play. Yours is to fix automobiles, pleasure-run in the Common in the mornings, and read everything you can get your hands on—especially the books that are still selling. Though I admit I was surprised to learn that extends to comics."

Kat swallowed hard at the fact he knew how and where she spent her mornings and her days stacking comics in the auto shop waiting area.

"Do you know how many children read comics while the parents have their autos fitted for new tires? I could open a bookshop with the volume of *Superman* and *Wonder Woman* left behind."

"It may not be a bookshop, but I am here to offer you a job."

"I already have a job."

"Yes. You do. But aren't you weary of spending your days wrestling lug nuts and selling spare tires? Or stacking comics? Surely you want to use what you learned in your years at Wellesley for a higher purpose." Birch tossed his cig to the ground, grinding it under his heel. He gestured toward the kids at play again on the green, their gas mask satchels bobbing up and down as they ran. "What if you could do something more than buy war bonds on a mechanic's salary? What if you could contribute something important to this war? For your country. For *them*."

"Okay. For argument's sake, let's say you've caught my attention. What is it you want?"

"You have a specified set of skills, Miss Harris, that if I'm frank, we just don't see every day. The United States government is overseeing a subversive operation that is just now growing out of its infancy. And it is those skills that can be useful to us and that I have particular interest in. There is a post on my team, and forgive me for stating it, but the others don't want me to fill it with a woman."

Not a complete surprise, except perhaps for his part in it. "But you do?"

"Not just any woman. I want to fill it with *you*."

A summer breeze drifted between them then, catching a lock of hair from the pin curls at Kat's nape to dance on the wind. She swept it back, pulling it behind her ear as she considered, watching the engaged couple walk off, the airman's uniformed arm slung over his girl's shoulder as she admired her freshly washed ring, and he preening like a peacock with each soppy step.

"Who is 'we'?"

"We?"

"You said, 'skills that *we* don't see every day.' I saw you and my stepfather cozied up in conversation at the party. Did he put you up to this?"

"No. If I've learned anything in my years of working with the man, Colonel Sullivan would fight like mad to keep his children out of this war. He'd give up his own life in order to—of that I am certain. His inquiries were on a different matter."

"What matter?"

"Nothing to trouble you with. But I can assure you, he is not a party to this particular opportunity. Nor should he be."

"Then who is?"

Henry's attention drifted to the car traffic scooting by. He took off his trilby, turned it over in his hands as the breeze toyed with the pomade on his neatly combed, thinning part. Then he turned to look her in the eyes.

"Your brother."

A thousand questions flew through Kat's mind, sparking every inch of her body with instant electricity. If Birch was playing a betting game—following her across the city, appearing late to a meeting he'd set, and letting her know in no uncertain terms that he'd researched every last detail about her—he'd just laid a royal flush on the table.

Whether she won the hand or not, Kat couldn't care.

Not now.

She stared straight back into those eyes, searching for the rim of kindness she swore she'd witnessed there during the party. Kat fought to keep her hands from knotting in her lap in a dead give-away of reaction, even as she demanded his full attention.

"You know where my brother is?"

"No," Birch confirmed, honestly it seemed. Then paused before continuing. "But Gavin is why I'm here."

"Are you with the army?" He shook his head. "The navy then?"

No, again.

"I want you to know, Gavin came to us. And because he is Colonel Sullivan's son—"

"Stepson," she muttered, the tangle of insinuations building to a fever pitch in her mind.

"Yes. Knowing that, I'd never have recruited him. But this was Gavin's choice. And it turns out he came to us at the right time. He had exactly what we needed to move forward in a critical operation."

"And I'm about to move forward with screaming to attract that horde of mothers or that overly helpful copper over there if you don't start giving me answers. *Now*. Or this meeting is over."

"I'll give you all the answers you're looking for, Kat. But you don't want to hear them from me. Not really."

"What does that mean?"

Birch replaced his hat, stood, and, on a dime, turned as though to walk away.

Fury rose within Kat, so she shot to her feet too. She'd worn heels and a silly dress that day—a floral print in dusty blue, knowing she couldn't walk through Boston Commons in oil-stained dungarees without receiving staunch disapproval from the masses of pedestrians she'd pass on the way. It would be nearly impossible to chase him down should he get away, but she'd make a scene if she had to. The skirt billowed against her calves, tossing in the breeze as she caught Birch by the shirtsleeve at the elbow and dug in for dear life.

"Tell me where my brother is." He turned, and Kat stared at the man. No games now; she'd show him stone in her eyes and a rigid determination in her stance. And if he even dared to walk away, she'd follow him to the Deluxe and chase the car to the end of the street—to the ends of the earth, even—to get the answers he'd so casually dangled in front of her like a carrot on a string.

"I wish I could." He nodded. Just once, as if accepting something. Then handed her the folded newspaper. "I'll need your answer by Thursday morning. If not, this offer won't be extended again. But I hope you'll consider it from Gavin, if not from me."

Birch turned, strolling away like he hadn't a care in the world, and tipped his hat to the gaggle of gardeners and the copper as he drifted away under the elms. And soon slipped into the Deluxe's passenger-side door.

Kat watched the sedan drive off.

She waited mere breaths before she fell back onto the bench and with shaking hands unfolded the newspaper. Inside lay an ivory envelope tucked between the headlines of the war in France, with one word, *Kat*, scrawled in Gavin's unmistakable hand. She slipped her index finger under the lip of the seal and tore it open. Then turned the envelope over.

A brass key slid into her palm, followed by a heavy card stock note.

While it didn't hold an explanation, the note was from Gavin. She pored over every word . . . every letter . . . every drop of beautiful ink . . . and soon, every tear-splotched inch on the page. And if she wished it, he promised answers with the name of a hotel, a summons to appear at eight o'clock sharp on Thursday morning, and a key to room 12 on the ground floor, signing it with a simple but potent: *Don't look back.—Gav*

$\sim$

*31 December 1951*
92 Avenue d'Iéna
Paris, France

"Your name is Kat? Is that true or . . . ?"

The man she knew as Xandre all those years ago stood before her now, goading with whispers when Mimi had stepped aside to greet another member of the Paris posh society who'd happened by.

"It's Mrs. Kathryn Fontaine," Kat bit back, but with a smooth smile.

"*Hmm.* I can see it. You never looked much like a Célène anyway." He snapped his fingers at a garçon to bring his tray of cocktails over. The waiter obeyed, and Xandre lifted a tumbler from its sterling silver face. "So, how is it you ended up here, alive, and married to the enemy?"

"I could ask you a similar question."

Though he bore deeper creases at his eyes and brow, was clean-shaven with hair slicked down in a sharp part, and had donned a tuxedo far too posh to have been mistaken for the village recruit he used to be, Xandre hadn't changed all that much since those long ago days when they'd crossed paths at the château. Not enough to think he wouldn't add a cat-and-mouse edge to everything he said.

"Oh, you mean Mimi? Oui. Marriage can become quite the opportunity, non?"

Kat refused to be taken in, though her insides churned with warning. She shifted back on her heels, giving an extra measure of breathing space between them. "I think you meant to say, 'Congratulations.'"

"Of course. That's exactly what I meant. I wish many years of happiness to you both." Xandre noticed her discomfort enough to step forward and close the space again. "So? Is he?"

"Is who what?"

"Your groom. An enemy. At least of the new France." Xandre took a deep swill, letting the ice hit his lips after draining the last bit of amber liquid. "Could be lucrative to know the truth."

Kat wasn't certain why, but she still searched the salon until she found Gérard's tall form. A woman in her midyears with a peacock-blue, curve-hugging dress held him in conversation near the fireplace. He laughed at something she'd said, offering a flash of amusement that took over his face as he answered. And didn't seem to notice the bride who was wishing, however slightly, that he might look up and meet her gaze.

"That's what everyone is saying. Not to his face, of course. But more and more collaborators are being prosecuted by the day. Even Madame Auclair over there, who seems to have your groom so transfixed . . . Her husband has a prominent position at the Courts of

Justice and a towering stack of debts to go with it. And the influence to do something about it if they learn what he's hiding. I'd wager it wouldn't take much to buy his cooperation."

"Who says my husband is hiding anything?"

"I haven't decided yet whether he is or isn't."

"You are the last person qualified to accuse someone of collaboration." Kat inclined her head a little lower, dropping her voice so only Xandre could hear as she gritted through her smile. "Only a rat would play both sides while he waits to see which sewer he'd like most to swim in. Perhaps you should scurry back to yours."

He smiled over the rim of his tumbler, as if some challenge had been laid down. And tried like wildfire, it seemed, not to enjoy the bite she took out of him.

"That right there." He pointed his index finger at her from the side of his glass. "I've missed that fire. And I have to admit, I had no idea the dominoes that would fall when you took up with the Vichy captain again and you two popped up in Paris, with your little heiress friend in tow. And then your dear husband managed to track me down here. I should have been annoyed, but look where we now spend our holidays. So everyone wins, eh?"

Kat eyed him, staring daggers through to his back collar. "What did you just say?"

"I knew I should have expected your husband to pay me a visit when he learned I was in Paris—" When her gaze shot to Gérard's tall form again without thinking, Xandre laughed on a dramatic *tsk tsk tsk* and crossed his arms over his chest. "Oh, I see. He didn't tell you? Seems the groom has some explaining to do. That, or he'll be sleeping out here on the settee tonight."

It might be the only point Kat ever agreed to when it came to Xandre's point of view. When she and Gérard had brokered their deal, the telegram was the spark. Or the hope that Gavin was alive somewhere. And it had nothing to do with dragging innocents like

Mimi down into the fray. What Kat couldn't understand was, when her husband had worked out that this devil was somehow in the mix, why he'd not come to her with that information.

For now? She'd play Xandre's game.

But later, when she was alone again with Gérard, all bets were off.

"What did I miss, my darlings?" Mimi slipped into the scene, her blood-orange cocktail between them bright as her smile. She pulled a swizzle stick from her glass, pressed her lips around a Maraschino cherry on the end, and popped it into her mouth.

"Your husband was just offering his congratulations."

"Oh, he was . . ." Mimi beamed and leaned in so her skirt pressed up against her husband's side. She dotted a sweet peck to his cheek. "Always the gentleman, this one. Just think, Kat—if you hadn't met your groom, I wouldn't have come to France with you and met my own. Aren't I lucky to have found my love all the way across the sea? And in Paris, no less."

"That's right. Here . . . in Paris. Of all places in the world for fate to step in." Kat forced a smile at them both.

He'd married Mimi. And though her friend was pretty as a peach in summer and innocent as a dove, far be it for Kat to think that union or his presence in Paris at all was mere coincidence. Mimi Dover was petite. Young. And owned a trust fund that ensured she was too flirtatious and naïve for anybody's good—least of all her new husband's.

That Gérard was a part of it and hadn't let her in on their past associations was the biggest tell; his character had not and would not change.

"That reminds me, Kitty-Kat. Since you're living here now, there's someone you simply must meet." Mimi hooked her arm around Kat's elbow, then handed her cocktail glass to Xandre. She tugged Kat toward the other side of the grand salon. "You'll watch that for me, won't you, darling?"

"Of course." Xandre tipped back the last of his wife's cocktail and faded into the throngs of the party, Kat watching him dissolve behind haute couture dresses and tuxedos as Mimi tugged her in the opposite direction.

"Oh! I see you two have already met," Mimi chimed when she stopped at the fireplace by Madame Auclair, who seemed genuinely annoyed that their conversation was interrupted, and Gérard, who did and said nothing, save for to reach over and slip an arm around Kat's waist with a fake besotted smile. "This is Madame Évelyne Auclair. Évelyne? The is Gérard's beautiful bride—Kat Fontaine. From Boston. And the sparkling new addition to our little Parisian society!"

Kat greeted the woman, whose icy reception said whatever this society was, it surely did not want or need another member. Nor did the woman appreciate being pulled from whatever private confidence she'd been sharing with Gérard.

How many layers of mystery would be peeled back in a single night?

"I'm sorry . . . what society?"

"Don't you remember, silly?" Mimi gave Kat a playful slap to her gloved wrist. "The upscale eating society. There was a gentlemen's dining club, *Club des* something or other—" She flicked her wrist on air, memory fleeting, it seemed, as fast as the French words to describe it. "Anyway, their wives got together and formed Le Cercle des Gourmettes some years back, before the war. It was a society to sample the best of French cuisine as good as or better than the men. Sadly, it has disbanded. But now that a couple of the former members are graduates from Le Cordon Bleu, there is talk of starting a bona fide cooking society from the group. I told you about it in my last letter. You said you'd come with me when you two finally settled in Paris."

"Did I?"

In all honesty Kat couldn't remember a snit of what she'd said in the last six months. Between declaring "I do" before all of Boston society, saying good night to Gérard when he went to his own room on their wedding night, waking alone and with the weight of a massive ring on her finger every morning since with no idea what she was doing married, and now with Xandre being tossed in the mix . . . Kat had just been trying to keep her head above water, even up until that very moment. It made no sense she'd remember some trifle of society gossip Mimi had shared, even if she'd wanted to.

"It did slip my mind." Kat tried her noble best to keep the conversation from backing her into a corner she couldn't get out of. "But oughtn't we wait until Paris is back on her feet to do anything?"

"Nonsense. You wrote something once about the beauty and art of French cooking. Truly, I was inspired. And now there is the perfect opportunity for us to learn how to prepare French cuisine. And more importantly, to present *you* to society. Évelyne here is our *la reine de Paris*." Mimi gestured to the ice queen. "See? My *français* is miles better after a little practice. One of our mutual acquaintances, a Mrs. Martha Gibson, has inquired about cooking classes. Others have done the same. And here we are. But you'll come, won't you, Kat? Oh, say you will. You know I'm *une catastrophe* in the kitchen. I'll die without a friend there. From a grease fire, food poisoning, or both."

Desperate, Kat looked up at Gérard, his strong profile next to her. *Save me?* she willed, begging him with her eyes as Mimi continued her self-deprecating chatter. *Say something. Anything to get me out of this . . .*

"She'd love to."

Gérard's acceptance dropped like a stone through water.

"I would?"

He squeezed Kat's waist in a little shimmy that said to play along, no matter how she wished not to.

"What do you think, love?" he whispered into her good ear, nudging again. "Is this something you'd like to do?"

"It seems I can't say no," Kat said, blazing a smile that said her new mission in life was nothing if not to learn to sauté in the French way. "Shall I have our secretary telephone yours to make plans?"

"I must pose it to the instructors, of course. It will be their decision as to whom we shall admit. But oui—this is *très bien*." Évelyne tipped her chin up, the air of superiority something she didn't mind showing to Kat before turning to Gérard's handsome visage and continuing with velvet dripping off her tongue. "I have no doubt once they hear of your wife's charm and beauty, they will accept your bride as one of our distinguished number."

"See? I told you!" Mimi winked at Gérard, seeming quite delighted with herself for having arranged a first social outing for his bride.

*Darling Mimi.* Her friend had missed every bit of the ice that had just frozen the air from Évelyne to Kat. Or from Kat to Gérard and back again. And the little distraction of her husband's thumb rubbing the small of her back—the touch burning through the fabric of her dress enough to pull her back to him.

He met Kat's eyes for the first time since they'd walked through the salon doors and tipped up his brow ever so slightly, asking her if she'd play along.

"Merci, ladies." Kat agreed, though he'd have to offer more than a pressing gaze and a few sweet words to expect her to hold to it. She fixed her eyes on her husband, and with a straight-shot air of confidence, she added, "I look forward to all that is ahead."

"Of course you do. I'll set a luncheon to discuss it, soon as we're able," Mimi answered. "And just wait until you meet the instructors, Kat. You'll love them."

Gérard cut her off with an assured, "She will. But if you don't mind, right now I should like to dance with my wife." He lifted Kat's hand and pressed a kiss to it, pulling her along with a soft, "Honor me?"

Between the mixed signals from Gérard, outright ire from Évelyne, Mimi's bubbling air, and the ghost of Xandre drifting back across their paths, Kat's life had become a minefield of risk. She wasn't sure of anything just then, even as Gérard gathered her in his arms to create a dance floor in the center of the salon. But the one thing she did know: It would take considerable effort not to let on that these instructors would be teaching a former sous-chef at the Château du Broutel how to boil an egg.

"*Mai oui!* You must meet Julia Child." Mimi beamed in a chorus of smiles as the bride and groom took to the dance floor. And lifting another Paris-pink cocktail from a passing tray, she held it up in a toast. "She's not unlike our happy couple tonight—truly one of a kind."

# CHAPTER 6

*14 July 1943*
Château du Broutel
Rue, France

A muted thumping woke Manon to a sweat-drenched panic in her sheets. Blinking through the darkness, she sat up, fought to slow her breathing, and swept long auburn locks over her shoulder to get cool air on her neck.

Always, it was the same dream . . .

The running.

The futility.

Shattered hope and the terror that plagued her with the brutal sights and sounds of the Nazis' advance on Paris. Even though it was years ago, she could close her eyes in sleep and be back there in a flash.

Guttural screams and the whistle of bombs drew her back to the outskirts of the city that wasn't supposed to be bombed. Yet she could still see bodies falling. Feel the panic as she ran, her feet dodging fallen brick and stone in the streets around her home. And would swear she could taste the plaster dust floating on air as she ran toward the block of flats with thick black smoke billowing from its center.

She clamped a palm over her sob now, fearful she'd cry out in the dark.

"Chef?" Another knuckle-knock this time, soft and low.

"I'm awake," she called back, shaky, and reached over to flick the lamp switch by the bed.

The chamber was awash in a soft glow, the light illuminating sterile service quarters with a hefty wooden armoire built in, the bureau with her basin and pitcher, and an empty iron-frame bed beside Manon where the new maid ought to have slept. A window cutout had a deep ledge and blackout fabric pulled taut against the brass hook on the wall, giving no indication of day or night from the attic-level room. But the clock by the bed now warned she'd somehow managed to sleep past the five o'clock hour, and despite Manon's need to find her bearings, a bustling kitchen would not wait for the breakfast preparations.

It was always the same when the memories overtook her.

The surge of anger would follow upon waking—enough to catapult her from the mattress and keep her going at a breakneck pace in the kitchen all day. Valens had told her they'd get revenge on their captors. They'd flee Paris. Go north. And secure a placement in a kitchen, somewhere they could be useful in subversion through their work.

Feeding rage had worked for a while.

But when night came, with the clock ticking and memories creeping closer through the darkness . . . it would all start again. Those Paris days at the start of the war were so vivid, so all-encompassing, so shattering that Manon had little power to prevent them from stalking through her dreams. Even now, three years later, she must wrestle with wondering what might have happened had Valens not pulled her back from the edge of the street the day the Nazis swarmed Paris.

Oblivion had seemed so close she could almost touch it . . .

"Chef?" Valens' voice was more urgent now on the other side of the door, and he rapped again.

"I know," Manon called, though with an uneven voice. Trying to cover, she added a steadier, "The soldiers' breakfast. I shall be right down."

"Non. Delivery trucks are here, Manon." He paused, his voice deadly serious. "Men are unloading fish now. In the courtyard."

*That's right.*

*Tonight's dinner . . . and Dominique's promise to deliver fish.*

Deliveries arrived to the kitchen service door on the regular.

Fresh produce was trucked in from nearby farms. Wine deliveries came from Loire Valley vineyards in the west. Even some delicacies found their way north on the rail lines from Paris, if they weren't hit by Resistance raids along the way. It was a fortunate day when milk and butter were delivered from farmers close by, even if those little luxuries were becoming scarcer. But, of course, this one delivery was different. Her visit to the dunes meant everything must tick like clockwork when the fishermen arrived at their door, especially with the hawk-eyed Captain Fontaine as overseer for the lot.

But this would be the first château delivery for Henri and Dominique. She'd have to be present.

"I understand." Then remembering Dominique's request, Manon called to the door. "Do have Frédéric come at once, *s'il te plaît.*"

"I've seen to it. He's downstairs, already dressed in his livery."

"Merci," she mumbled and waited until the sound of his footsteps trailed down the hall. Pulling the long gold chain and wedding band from under the neckline of her slip, Manon pressed it in a delicate kiss to her lips—the terrors put off again until bed.

Now, she must work.

Manon bounded from the bed, flung open the doors of the armoire that took up the wall opposite, and yanked out her chef's whites. After a flurry of washing her body and face in icy water from the pitcher and basin on the bureau, she donned the service skirt required of women, her double-breasted chef's jacket, her "mended many times over stockings," and serviceable shoes, then twisted her hair up in a plait under her toque blanche.

After one last check in the mirror to see all was tidy, she fled down to the kitchen. The scent of fish didn't hit her at the bottom of the service stairs—a good sign. There should only be the slightest hint of the sea about the air, but no true fish odor if the catch was fresh. She stalked across the kitchen, giving orders along the way, to Frédéric and the other staff readying the service trays that would soon carry the officers' breakfast upstairs.

The bustle continued through the open door to the cobblestone courtyard, and the backs of two workmen unloading crates outside the open door of a box truck.

A man turned, crate in his arms, and froze for a breath when his eyes landed on her. "Bonjour, Chef." Dominique nodded, tipping the edge of his flatcap in a warm but still respectful greeting that would be believed of indifferent strangers.

Manon hadn't realized until that instant what it felt like to have a friend. Or at the very least, to know someone was on your side. It was a comfort to have Dominique there, his eyes doing their level best not to smile back like they'd met in the cottage days before. It was a relief, even if just to stand in the same space for a breath and remember you and your ally toiled toward a similar goal.

And that you'd both survived to wake on another day in it.

"We've brought a delivery of lemon sole. Care to have a look?"

"Oui. I want to ensure this is fresh." Manon came over, pretending to check a line on Dominique's clipboard.

When he edged the crate in at her side, she glanced over her shoulder. Captain Fontaine was on the spot again, the morning sun shining down on his impeccably starched and ironed Police Nationale uniform while engaged in conversation with a younger man she hadn't seen before. The gentleman with the salt-and-pepper hair under the poppy-emblazed hat was there; this was surely Valens' contact, Henri, who'd just been brought on to begin making regular deliveries at the château. He moved about in the back of the truck, saying nothing. Just hoisting crates and stacking them for unloading at the edge of the tailgate.

She inclined her head to Dominique, mouthing a soft, "You are early."

"You did not think I would take a chance of being late, did you?" he whispered, then took a crowbar and cranked the lid off the top crate to show the catch. "Not when the captain requested regular shipments to the château. I need him to believe he's in charge."

"Is that so?"

"Under your authority in the kitchen, of course." His eyes sparkled, just a bit, at the secret between them. "Your catch, Chef."

Owing to its name, the fish had its typical lemonlike shape rather than an actual citrus taste. But when sautéed, it offered a light and sweet flavor that paired well with the officers' favorite Sancerre—a sauvignon white that, though like liquid gold in wartime, was frequently shipped in from the Loire Valley.

She checked the fish eyes: not cloudy. The scent was clean. And their scales, firm. This catch was fresh, as if it just swam to the surface and jumped in a boat. It would have had to just been caught.

"Did you . . . ?" Manon stared up, sure she was unable to hide the surprise that must have washed over her face. "But these are fresh. Too fresh to have been even from yesterday."

"Wasn't tired. Henri returned last night, and I dragged him out on the water. We've had it on ice until this morning."

"Is that him then?" She looked to the man loading crate after crate in his waxed fishmonger's apron.

"Henri?" Dominique called, pointing to her. "This is the chef. She will be accepting our deliveries from now on."

Henri paused just long enough to give her a respectful, "Chef" and tip his hat, then went back to work without another word.

"I owe you a great debt. This will bring high marks at dinner."

"There is no debt, Chef. This is our job now, according to the captain. For security purposes, he wants the same men tasked for each delivery. And we are to notify him if there is the slightest change." Dominique paused, shifted his view to the younger man with the captain, his smile a little bright for their war-torn state. "Henri has brought a Monsieur Ferron as part of our number. He'll be assisting with deliveries that come in from the rails as well."

"And why is he not . . . ?"

"In uniform? Off fighting somewhere? No doubt that is what you were thinking and the captain is asking. But he'll explain it. He favors talking, that one. A little too much."

"I see."

"And you are wondering about me, then? Why I do not wear a uniform?"

"Non—of course not."

"I have a medical exemption. But as Pétain's government demands, I wish to serve the people of France in any way I can." Without warning, Dominique brushed his hand against hers, the warmth of his fingertips slipping a folded scrap of paper into her palm. Then he whispered, "For Valens."

Manon drew in a deep breath, nodded, and concealed the paper under the top layer of fish before she replaced the crate lid.

Dominique nodded back, accepting her silent thanks before saying louder for the benefit of all in the courtyard, "So, the fish. *C'est bon?*"

"Oui. You can stack the crates over there by the door." Manon nodded, ticking something off on the clipboard as she took a step back. She motioned to another stack of crates, those Henri was unloading from the truck tailgate. "And what is this?"

"Wine. A new rail shipment." He tipped his eyebrows up in a knowing gesture to their aforementioned plan. "The soldiers received it at the gate, and we said we'd bring it up—save them the trouble."

"More wine? *Bon.*"

*This is it . . .*
*Time to put on the show.*

"Frédéric?" she called to the boy, who snapped to attention in the kitchen and skirted through the door to the courtyard.

He inclined his head in an at-your-service bow. "Oui, Chef?"

"Help these men bring the wine in. And show them where to store it in the cool part of the cellar."

"Right away."

Ever in charge over any operations under his watch, Captain Fontaine snapped at the new deliveryman. "You heard Chef." He thrust the papers at Monsieur Ferron. "Help with the wine. *Maintenant!* And you will report to me for instructions before you leave."

The man took the orders in stride, pocketed his papers, and jumped into action without delay.

"Chef." He addressed her as he rushed over. He lifted one of the wine crates, just so Manon could make out a wide smudge under the Reich logo stamped on the side. "I am Monsieur Ferron—Xandre. And will be pleased to make deliveries for you."

"*Excusez-moi—*" she started, desperate to grab the crate. But seeing the same thing Manon had, Valens cut in to assist.

"Allow me to help you, monsieur." Valens muscled the crate from the man's arms with a respectful air, so as not to take it as an affront that he was overstepping. He handed it off to Frédéric, saying, "Take this. And we will show them into the cellar."

Though he didn't appear able to handle much, bless him.

Valens' face was still gaunt, and the circles under his eyes belied the illness that had kept him from visiting the dunes. It was not the first time Manon noticed, but his chef's coat was swimming on his frame. Though they had ration coupons while the Reich officers did not, she knew all of her staff to be fed. Still, Valens offered a sure grip and quick steps that seemed to win the silent approval of the captain's watchful eye, even if he was still poorly.

"We'll manage this, Chef." Valens hoisted another wine crate in his arms and started on his way. "You have more important things to do."

Manon nodded to him, watching as he and Xandre disappeared through the doorway to the kitchen. And poor Frédéric followed, having not a clue what scheme awaited him on the way to the wine cellar.

Dominique held Manon's gaze then, seconds only, waiting together until a crash resounded against the parquet floor. She jumped a little, knowing what would happen yet still feeling those tiny pinpricks of anxiousness until it did.

"Chef!" Captain Fontaine shouted from the edge of the courtyard, that royal blue uniform now striding past her as he stalked to the kitchen door. "Can you not keep your staff from destroying all of our provisions?"

"It seems you have to go," Dominique whispered.

"Oui. I think I'd better. If only to protect poor Frédéric from the captain's wrath."

"We hope to see you soon, Chef." He half turned on his way to close the truck doors and, with a fleeting smile, looked to the clear, cloudless sky overhead. "Does it look like rain?"

# CHAPTER 7

15 July 1943
61 Exeter Street
Boston, Massachusetts

The GM "Old Look" transit bus lumbered along, ushering un-
named passengers down a road to nowhere.

By high summer, gasoline rationing had been in full swing for
a year. Travelers had flocked to the rails, and civilian travel was dis-
couraged soon after in favor of catering to those in wartime service.
None of that was an issue for the US government, as Kat had been
shimmied from an auto to a train and onto a bus that, by the feel of
repeated wheel-bumps under her seat, was struggling to pass along
a rugged country road.

The thirty-five-footer was able to accommodate some forty-five
people by Kat's estimate, but with alternating seats unbolted and
removed from the floor, occupants could not sit next to one another.
The handful on this journey sat silent behind windows blacked out
from the inside. From the instant Kat had slipped the key in the lock
and let herself into room 12 at Boston's storied Hotel Lenox, she'd
stepped into a world like this—flipped on end.

A sealed envelope had been laid upon a made bed, with typeset
instructions inside: Don the wedding band provided. Cut her hair—
scissors were in the nightstand drawer. Change into the navy suit
and simple tam hanging in the wardrobe. Gather cut hair in the

shopping bag hanging on the back of the en suite door, and along with every possession she'd brought, hide the lot under the mattress. Then wait until the clock ticked fifteen minutes past the hour, at which time Kat should place the key on the nightstand and leave.

If she chose to do this—whatever *this* was—there was a fifteen-minute window to decide. By then Kat would exit through the hotel lobby carrying only an over-the-shoulder envelope satchel with a compact, cigarette case, and identification inside for Mrs. Betty Prior of 31 Noble Lane in Baltimore. She'd climb into the back seat of a black Packard 120 auto . . . and leave her whole world behind.

Best Kat could guess, the Packard had a heavy steel frame, the feel of the model V-8, and the rumble of 120 horsepower, making the auto faster than average when it pulled away from the curb. Knowing the specs ought to have helped keep her bearings with windows blacked out, even noting each turn to memorize a street map. But once Kat was deposited at a train station and handed a ticket to board, the auto sped off and she had no choice but to lose the ability to track how far she'd go.

They were leaving Boston.

For where exactly . . . she hadn't a clue.

An eyes-only glance around the transit bus now confirmed what Birch had told her—that he'd wanted her for a job that others did not favor filling with a woman. Unsurprisingly, the rest of the recruits were men. Some slept. Others sat quietly, keeping to themselves with trilbies tilted down. Still others stared ahead into the screen that separated a wooden driver from the ambivalent passengers behind. No one spoke or made eye contact, favoring instead the heady calm of silence before they came to their final destination—and their new wartime life.

The bus halted to a stop on singing brakes.

Without warning, doors banged open. Sunlight streamed in. And a man in a suit appeared, popping up the steps to stand next to the driver's seat with an issued bark: "Everyone off!"

The suit was about a minute older than Kat, if that. And looked far too green and a shade too thin to be any kind of threat, especially to a couple of the recruits whose "borrowed" clothes didn't seem to fit properly over their muscular frames. They obeyed, however, perhaps owing to their recruiting meeting being a mite more informative than hers.

Kat stood as men filed past. Then pulled the leather satchel strap over her shoulder as they exited single file.

"Where are we going?"

"Out. *Now*," the suit gritted back.

Not nearly a good enough order for her to follow. Kat stood firm, demanding this time, "I'm not going anywhere until you tell me what this is."

The suit marched back and grabbed her by the tender spot of her arm just below the shoulder, fusing a grip that dug nails into the skin through her gaberdine suit. She gasped inside, from shock and a little wince of pain, but gave no indication on the surface that he'd rattled her.

Kat followed along as he tugged her to the doors.

Being manhandled by an underling in a suit certainly wasn't what she'd signed up for. And if cutting her hair and a blind transfer from three types of transportation wasn't enough, it seemed a step too far to allow a man to put his hands on her. Not if she was giving up everything to step through the door into this government-sanctioned world. And if yanking an insubordinate off the bus was making a point that the recruits weren't to ask questions, Kat refused to let it be the only woman of the lot to be made the example.

She played subservient until they'd just stepped off the lip of the last step.

Without warning, Kat lunged her weight and delivered a fierce elbow to the kid's side, knocking the wind out of him and throwing him off balance. And when he stumbled into the transit bus, it gave Kat the seconds she needed to wrangle free, pull out the hotel scissors she'd slipped in her satchel, and heave the open blade against the vein pulsing in his neck.

The kid had a sidearm. But it was just that—at his side. That made surprise her ally as they stood, like rams with horns locked together, each betting the other wouldn't go through with winning whatever game it was they'd started.

"Your name, miss?"

Kat stared in his eyes. Saw the mix of disbelief veiled by arrogance and guessed he was trying to save face that a woman had in any way bested him. She answered with a cool, "It's Mrs. Betty Prior, thank you."

He shifted his gaze to the hand holding the shears against his throat. "You're particular for a secretary."

"A secretary?" She scoffed. "Certainly not."

"You are if the name on my clipboard is right. You're here amongst future field agents with the Office of Strategic Services, Mrs. Prior. And making a poor first impression of who will process their future OSS field reports isn't the way to go about it in your first minute here."

"Everyone calm down, please. Mrs. Prior is with me." A voice sounded from behind, loud, but with the same smooth tone that had spoken German to her on the bench in the Common.

"Good day, Mr. Birch," Kat tossed over her shoulder, still staring at the kid and holding firm in her grip with the makeshift weapon just ready to nick his Adam's apple.

"Would you mind, Mrs. Prior, to let my pianist go?"

"Pianist?"

"It's a fancy title for a wire operator. And while they could be a dime a dozen here in the States, they do hold particular value for us in the field. That's where I'll need this one."

"I see. But if this is the way the United States government treats all of your new employees, I might have reservations about accepting this job."

"Not as a rule, no. But our intake team knows to do a sweep of pockets when recruits board. I suppose Jeffrey here hasn't seen a satchel on the bus before—a mistake he isn't likely to make again. Not even for a secretary." Birch paused, then with a sharp retort, added, "Go on, Jeffrey. About your work to process these men."

At the invitation to defuse, Kat stepped back. She nearly pocketed the scissors but thought better of it at Jeffrey's scowl and lowered them in a closed fist at her side instead. And for the first time, she looked around at the recruits left gaping.

Pinched brows and tepid stares appeared horrified by such an undignified display, so much so that the men turned away as Jeffrey adjusted his shirt and tie. Kat stood in the blazing sun, her heart still about to thump clean out of her chest as he issued a sharp glare before marching off and snapping instructions at the men to follow.

Sweat trickled down the back of her neck. Birds chirped in the distance, from the thick mass of trees on all sides. And she drank in calming breaths while she surveyed the vast blue sky above them, clean air, and the relief that followed as she watched the horde of recruits disappear over the rise.

Heavily forested and hemmed in by mountains, it was some sort of campground. And more like a place to hike through the woods, like she and Gavin had enjoyed as kids, than a government training facility. Though a reverberating *boom* sounded somewhere in the background and then another, the telltale sounds of weapons firing signaled that the trees must hold a depth of US military secrets after all.

Birch paused, looking her over. "Your hair's uneven."

"And is looking like a starlet a requirement for this job?"

"You'll find no Gildas here. It was merely an observation." Birch placed his hat back on his head to shield his eyes from the sun. "But you'll want it seen to before you show up in the office."

"There's an office out here? Where are we?"

"We call it 'The Farm.' Government land outside Baltimore. And

a breeding ground for the Office of Strategic Services—OSS to those
in the ranks. This is where we bring the best and brightest in the
nation to be trained for communications and subversive operations
vital to the war effort overseas."

"Spy work?" Kat said, more as a thought out loud than an actual
question. "So I wasn't that far off when I said your name was on the
nose."

"No. But you are the first to note the connection."

She smiled, thinking of Gavin. Had he received the same furtive
instructions to be seated in the back of a dark vehicle? Or ordered off
the same bus? Or arrived at the very same camp-like span of fields,
and how many weeks before? No matter where he was now, Kat had
to believe he'd been trained well—well enough to survive and, one
day, write those letters he'd promised her.

Birch held out his hand, offering the wide span of a gravel road
that led to steps up to a wooden building.

"This way. We'll have them make you presentable. Give you something to eat. And check in with medical and administration before
we show you where you'll be bunking."

Kat nodded and started off walking with him.

The world of spies and saboteurs was certainly not as Kat had
expected.

She could have just as easily been brought to an office in DC as
to a rugged camp in a Maryland hillside. But to find that the veil
wasn't lifted, even when the recruits were fully admitted into whatever this OSS training ground was, was almost laughable. How was
Kat to work with them—for the United States government—if even
her superior's name and the simplest of answers were met with
impenetrable resistance?

"I'm not here for a new haircut. Not to run around an office fetch-
ing steno pads in a cute little skirt. And not even so Uncle Sam will
be satisfied with my sacrifice when this is all over. I couldn't care
less about that. I just want to know where my brother is."

"I know you do." Birch sighed, as if the last thing he'd be around her was surprised. "And so do we."

Kat froze, unsure whether she'd truly heard him say the words or only imagined them on her deaf side. "What did you say?"

He stopped on the path when she didn't continue, turning back to address her. "We didn't want to tell you like this, but your brother has gone missing after an airdrop in France. Under normal circumstances, we wouldn't be concerned had an operative not reported back by now. It takes time to reach a safe location. But there were . . . complications."

"What complications?"

"An entire unit of SOE agents was turned over to the Reich." He paused, as if having read something on her face. "SOE: Service Operations Executive. The Brits' answer to espionage needs in occupied Europe. They paved the way for us to join this war through sabotage and subversion, even if in the end they were betrayed by one of our own."

"You can't be serious. You have a double agent?"

He didn't deny it. "Baker Street is still trying to work out how twelve agents would report to the same safe house, only to be picked up and interrogated one after another when they arrived. So in order for our handful of OSS agents not to be caught themselves, they've all had to go underground. Your brother was a part of that team, I'm afraid."

"Fine. Then tell me where he went, and you drop me in the same spot."

"That's not possible." When she stepped up to countermand that, he fired back. "Look, I understand you have a certain personality—"

"This isn't a bathing beauty revue and I'm not up for Miss Congeniality. Personalities aside." She returned fire, the anger of such an insinuation roiling up from her middle. "You brought me here under false pretenses. How else should I react?"

"I didn't bring you. Your brother did, remember?"

"You delivered his letter."

"And that's why you're here. We tend to keep things in the family, recruiting siblings when we can. So when we first looked at Gavin, it didn't take us long to learn about you. Your years at Wellesley. That you're unmarried. Proficient with languages and mathematics. Possess a working knowledge of mechanics. You give attention to endurance and physical fitness. And especially your mistrust of anyone who crosses your path. You seem to use that to feed your instincts—all assets that can be useful to us. But there can be no more of that back there, at the bus. Do you understand? Not while you're on my team. We're doing everything we can to make contact with your brother. And in the meantime you don't get to make demands. You follow orders. This is the only time I'll say it."

"What orders would those be?"

Birch held out his hand then, palm to the sky. When she didn't move, he reiterated, "Do we understand one another?"

The instructions at the hotel had been clear: If you do this, you leave everything behind. You sever your name. Your connection to family. Every last detail that made you who you were before would be expunged. For Kat, that had been handing over the auto shop operations to her aunt and uncle. It was cutting her hair—chopping with abandon as she watched the clock in the hotel room. And as for what carried her forward, Birch was saying the hope of finding out what had happened to her brother would come in mismatched pieces, if at all.

If she wished to continue, those were the terms. Period.

"Fine. We'll do this your way. Kat Harris is dead." She sighed. Nodded. Then handed over the scissors. "But Gavin Harris had better not be."

"I hope not, same as you." Birch pocketed the scissors. He led them in a walk across gravel again. "And there's one more thing."

"More than all this?"

"Your ear . . . It won't pass medical." When she raised her chin in defiance, he tilted his head a tick, like he was changing his mind on something. "But I suppose we could keep that between us. If you answer me this: How did you know to use your alias back there?"

"You said it. I don't trust easily."

"No. I'd say you don't trust anyone at all. I'll bet you wouldn't risk needing another person if it's the last thing you do. And it just might save your life one day. But for now, you don't have a brother. Not anymore. Like the rest here whose real names are to remain unknown, you are Mrs. Betty Prior. That goes for when you address the Jeffreys of this camp, or me, or any leader up the rungs to OSS Major General Donovan himself. You are married. From Baltimore. You were educated in shorthand and English literature at Mount Saint Agnes College. And you are my secretary until I tell you different."

"And in exchange you'll give me information about my brother?"

"If it comes in, yes, I will." He looked down at the plain gold band she wore, shining in the sun. "That ought to help the gentlemen remember to keep their hands to themselves while you wait."

It was the most whiplash-inducing conversation she'd ever had. "And if I said I didn't come all this way to answer your telephone or to find a ring on my finger? I could have done that in Boston."

"Of course you could. But that's not enough for you, is it?"

She shifted her weight to the other hip. "Meaning?"

"My guess is you've been itching to get into this war any way you can. Whether you're ready to admit it to yourself, you have a fighter spirit that wants more than the upper echelons of Boston society can offer you. Or that you'll find frittering away your days in an auto garage. This war is bigger than Gavin or you or any one of us. But I think you already know that."

Birch shook his head, offering a subdued smile. As if it were a foregone conclusion that Kat wouldn't care about cutting her hair. Nor leaving behind the trickle of prospects left to her in the Boston marriage mart. Nor to show up on a bus without those scissors on her person, not if she was a recruit worth her salt. And it seemed they both knew her well enough to see the obvious.

He knew what Kat wanted before she'd known it herself.

"Yes, Mrs. Prior. I'd say you know exactly how this works. Because you already agreed to it the moment you got in the car."

⌒

1 January 1952
92 Avenue d'Iéna
Paris, France

Regret didn't follow rules. Nor did it consider all the good intentions in the world when their first kiss between man and wife had been a chaste peck in front of five hundred guests in a Boston cathedral.

Gérard might not have regretted everything in life, but he did regret that.

Not because he was caught out—that was no surprise. He knew Kat well enough by now to judge that once in battle, she could pivot faster than anyone he'd ever met. But regret accompanied seeing her panic-stricken face when she'd been presented with Xandre again. Kat had looked up, scanned the salon, and in that split second her gaze connected with his, a tiny something squeezed in Gérard's chest, telling him she'd been searching for an anchor. Someone to trust in this mad scheme.

Had she been looking . . . for *him*?

Pity that thought was dashed in a blip.

Kat must have realized he'd known who Mimi's husband was all along. A look of manufactured serenity had replaced surprise, and she resumed mingling as a conscientious hostess would with her sweet simpers and flawless French. Save for, now that the guests had gone, she'd used up her last smile. Their salon was empty. And with most of the furniture shoved up against the edges of the room, a chasm had opened up between husband and wife in its center.

"That's the last of them gone," Gérard said as he stepped through the salon doors. "Except for the staff. But they'll let themselves out when they've finished cleaning up."

Clean up indeed. He glanced around. Stray champagne flutes topped the mantel. Gold-rimmed dessert plates littered side tables. A few dotted the floor along the far wall. (Who left porcelain on the floor?) Discarded party hats and confetti covered the hardwoods, the gold and silver dots having exploded from holiday crackers of the long-gone revelers. And his wife sat in silence on a lone ivory chaise near the fireplace, entranced by the dying embers.

*Do something, you coward.*

*The biggest mess is your fault.*

Kat was American, so unlike the European girls, she wore her wedding ring on her left hand. The garish diamond he'd given her flashed in the firelight as she bent to unfasten gold straps at her ankles. It made Gérard look to his right hand, the band he'd wanted accusing him now of the truth that the first thing he'd done as her husband was break their vow . . . and lead her into a trap.

"Mind if I close these?" Gérard palmed the French door handles, thinking the service staff who were left didn't need a show from supposed happy newlyweds.

Kat said nothing, just tossed her heels aside.

He sighed, low, so she wouldn't hear, and clicked the doors closed anyway. "You are going to at least speak to me?"

"What should I say?" Pulling pins from the chignon at her nape, Kat dropped them on the side table with tiny *tinks* against the top, then ran her fingers through her dark hair so it spilled to her shoulders in a riot of waves.

Odd bedfellows crashed within him. Necessity, for what he'd done by not telling her the whole truth about the telegram, or Xandre, when he'd had the chance. Genuine remorse, for Kat had the right to give him a tongue-lashing and, thus far, hadn't. And curiosity as to why. It forced Gérard to turn away and land his gaze on the first distraction he could—the sideboard with a decanter and an impressive shelf of crystal tumblers lining the wall.

He went for it. And poured a drink he didn't even want.

"You could yell at me," he began, loud enough so she could hear with his back turned. But with an unaffected tone, too, even though his insides churned.

"And if I'm not the yelling type?"

"Then I would say we may already have found ourselves at an impasse in this marriage, my love. That is, if you let me win every argument."

"Please—don't call me that." Kat's entreaty was quiet, automatic, and . . . pained.

Gérard clamped his eyes shut.

*Fine. I deserved that.*

He straightened his shoulders, turned, and swept through the party chaos left behind. Walking slowly, with his dress shoes tapping the hardwoods, he stopped by the mantel so she could see his lips if she did care to talk. He leaned his elbow against the marble and swirled the amber liquid in his glass in absent-minded distraction, the ornate mirror on the wall doubling his movements.

Kat sat quietly, only pulling her legs up under her—she probably didn't realize how elegant that was, with toes pointed like a dancer. Then she simply stared into the glowing coals again. The icy indifference could mean only one thing—any second her anger would boil over. The boom would surely fall. And that fighter spirit Kat had possessed during the war would show itself to him again.

But when too many long seconds ticked by without a move, he had to seriously consider that one thing could be worse than regret where she was concerned: *silence.*

"What have we done, Gérard?"

"I'd say we just threw the most enviable wedding party Paris has ever seen, this side of the war at least."

It was the first time she'd looked at him, really looked since the masquerade of hooking her into some Parisian wives' cooking class and then nuzzling her neck on the dance floor so the gossips could get an eyeful. Those brilliant blue eyes pierced his with a gaze of true bewilderment now. And with a sense of shattered trust that felt like a bullet ripping through his chest.

"That's not what I meant."

"Non." He sighed and punished himself with a long, burning drink. "I suppose not."

"We are married."

"We are that."

"What I don't understand is, why?"

That was a stretch. "If you remember, you were the one who left me at the château. And then showed up in France again after eight years . . ." Gérard paused, creasing his brow yet still choosing his words with caution. "And asked me to marry you."

"I did," she snapped back. "But you didn't correct me when I assumed it was you who'd sent that telegram. You know that missive became the one hope that drew me here, even after you and I parted as we did all those years ago. And I wanted to believe there was something good in you."

No, he hadn't sent it. How he wished he had. Or knew who did. Because Gérard would have enjoyed putting a fist in their face for dredging up the past just to hurt her.

"Non. I didn't send it."

"But why would you let me think you did?" Kat searched his face with tears building in her eyes, then stared down at her lap to hide them from him. She probably didn't even realize it, but her left hand rose and toyed with the dress strap covering her right shoulder, fingertips grazing the gathered fabric that covered the scars she hid there.

"I'd moved on from all of this, Gérard. From France. From who we had to be in those terrible years during the war. And I promised myself when I had to go back to Boston I'd try to go on without my brother. Until that telegram arrived on my doorstep. And I thought someone—you—finally had answers. And now we don't even know who sent it, though I'd have to suspect Xandre, given he showed up in our salon tonight, and married my only friend in Paris. But then you knew that too, didn't you?"

A rough sigh huffed out. He still couldn't bear keeping the truth from her, even if it could hurt her again. "I did."

Kat's hand formed into a fist at her shoulder.

*Come on, give me something . . .*

His insides begged it. For the Kat he knew to finally show up. To be honest with herself—and him.

"This isn't just about you or me now. It's about others we're pulling into this. My family and Mimi are innocent. How dare you let that man back into our lives. How dare you give me hope, all the while knowing it wouldn't last!"

"What if I did want to give you hope?" Gérard slammed the tumbler against the mantel, the clip of glass to marble only amplifying the tension between them. "Because I learned you were hiding out at that auto garage. With no answers about your brother. Having nothing for yourself. No family, save for a mother and stepfather who would smother what spark of life you still have left by chaining you into a loveless marriage. I might not have sent that telegram, but you did come to France in search of answers. And you found me."

Before he even realized what he'd just revealed, the spark hit touch paper, and Kat rose with a fierceness that cut him to the core.

"Yes! Why do you think I proposed to you? Because a loveless marriage means nothing to me. You have money. And connections. And I'd exploit every bit if it means finding my brother!"

Hating himself for what he'd had to do, Gérard steeled himself from reaching for her, from offering a tender remembrance of how they'd first been thrown together in the war when her sleeve sagged and the angry scar peeked out from the shoulder. She stepped up to challenge him, nearly tripping over the heels discarded between them on her way to stop mere inches from the tips of his shoes.

"You *knew* Xandre was in Paris. Yet you said nothing to me."

"It's true I'd learned Xandre was in Paris. But once you did arrive and I'd realized what was happening between Mimi and him, I threatened him to steer clear."

"And still, you let me walk into our wedding party, unprepared, to find that depraved coward now married to my friend. Knowing he is more than likely the man responsible for my brother's disappearance. Why?"

Gérard clenched his jaw, only whispering, "You know why."

"I know you fed me some fairy tale about contacts in the French government. I might have been dealing with my questions for years, but you, Monsieur Fontaine—you made me believe it when you waltzed into my nightmare with all the right answers. *'Of course I'll marry you and help you find your dead brother . . .'* And now, months later, I'm still asking myself whether it was grief over Gavin's death, the lies you so easily make everyone believe, or my absolute insanity that I sought you out. What were you hoping to get out of this by saying yes? Is it just a ruse to save your own skin? Surely if a millionaire colonel's stepdaughter and former OSS operative married him, how could the man have consorted with the Reich on every single level during the war? And how could he be prosecuted as a traitor to France now? Admit it! It was all to save your neck. Let's enroll his wife in a cooking class to pump the rumor mill for information. Surely the tittle-tattle of Paris's female society can save him!"

"If you believe the rumors, then why did you marry me?"

"I hadn't decided whether to believe them. Yes, you wore the uniform at the château. And it was your orders the Vichy police followed—the very same orders that you took from the Reich. But I know the contradiction I saw in you. And I have yet to find my own eyes have failed me when it really matters. So, you are an enigma,

Gérard Fontaine. And it is more than Paris society who is attempting to unravel your past. Consider this fair warning that I intend to do the same, no matter what it costs me."

Gérard slipped his hands into his tuxedo pockets before he could think better of giving a visual show of defeat. "This is what you think of me? That I am a traitor?"

"I don't know what I think. Save for that you are an intelligent man. Too intelligent to lure me into a little wives' cooking class simply so I can learn how to serve roast duck on Sundays. I may have the misfortune to be married to you, but I am *not* your wife. And I won't stay in France one moment longer than it takes to find out what happened to Gavin."

Her words were a razor that liked to cut.

The pull to tell her more—to give Kat the truth she wasn't ready for—clawed at Gérard's insides. She hadn't a clue what it was to stare into the sea of those blue eyes when they searched his face. Or to gaze at her mouth, pursed and challenging, when she refused to let something drop. Nor to carry secrets of his own that no matter how Gérard had tried to conceal, this woman always managed to fling right out in the open. She was a masterful, terrifying mix of both seeing through him yet not seeing the real him at all.

And at the very same time.

"Why didn't you tell me about Xandre?" Kat accused in a breathy whisper, though the words weren't laced with anger. This was as forthright as she'd ever been with the question, adding a soft, "The truth. You owe me that much."

"Because I needed to see your face when you saw him again. And . . . I needed to see his when he saw you."

"Why would that matter?"

Regret or affection—was there a difference between them now? What good was trying to protect a woman who didn't need protecting? That ground was rocky. Untillable. And no kind of foundation to build something as lasting as a marriage should be.

Perhaps truth could blot some of the sins of his past. They each possessed something the other wanted and what the other needed, whether they cared to admit it or not. And standing here now with Kat staring back, asking for his honesty if not fidelity, with the firelight dancing over her cheekbones and hair and every curve of her in that dress . . . Gérard had to remind himself that this—a real marriage between adversaries—would never work.

"Xandre knows more than he's saying about what happened to your brother. I believe there's one reason he married Mimi Dover. You're right. I didn't send the telegram. But I did need to be certain that it could have been him who did. And I believe it's the same reason why he's in Paris now."

"Which is?"

Gérard sighed, wishing the world were not so cruel as to the answer he must give. And the chasm between them were not so great, even as his wife stood a mere breath away.

"You."

# CHAPTER 8

21 July 1943
Château du Broutel
Rue, France

Not knowing when the dinner menu could shift at the last possible moment, Manon had learned to hold a calligrapher on retainer. That way the man could pen menu cards up until just before the château guests were seated in the dining hall.

Too often his services were required.

A chef did what she must when potatoes had long since been replaced by topinambours, turnips, or swedes, and standard main course accompaniments were doctored kale or red cabbage. Oat, barley, and buckwheat became the mainstay of *pain de campagne*—the denser, seeded boules Manon would send upstairs to the breakfast buffet a poor substitute for the French country classic. And coffee and tea had disappeared almost entirely, leaving behind only chicory, which the Reich soldiers loathed for its bitter, woody taste and reported laxative effect.

Even with the tricks employed to work around shortages and stretch every meal as far as possible, rations often ran thin and forced Manon to improvise. They bred rabbits on the grounds for meat. Milked goats for cheese. Armed police protected valuable chickens and vegetables in the gardens for the times when the nearby farms' supplies ran thin. Manon herself foraged on the château grounds for blackberries, nettle, wild garlic, and cèpe mushrooms. And Valens had the footmen bleed the woods dry of every living thing that could be put on a plate: doves, pigeons, guinea hens, wild hare, and the occasional prize of venison. Even the sea was dredged clean by fishermen—as soon as the fish could grow scales, it seemed they were caught, shipped to the château, and poached à la nage with lemon and dill.

Guilt hit Manon as she stood in the larder now and ran inventory after the last night's dinner. Her staff were not exempt from the same rationed portions as everyone else—ten ounces of bread per day and only ten ounces of meat per week. But the Reich soldiers' waste that came back to the kitchen and the disgust at such opulence on the shelves made it difficult to overlook the suffering right outside their gates.

Checking the supply crates against the rail delivery list, she slammed a tin down on the shelf. "Caviar? What am I to do with more of this fluff when people are starving in the village?" Manon looked up from her clipboard just in time to see Valens sway on his feet and grip a wooden shelf or else tumble to the floor.

"Valens!"

"Do not trouble yourself," he mumbled, waving her off as he clamped his eyes shut. "I am well."

"Non, you are not."

Ignoring his meager protests, Manon hooked the pencil behind her ear, dropped her clipboard on a nearby shelf, and swooped in to brace Valens at the elbow. Then she led him over to a barley barrel.

"Sit. *Now.* That's an order from your chef de cuisine." She tried to be stern as she used her full title but smiled when he glanced up and rolled his eyes at her mothering tactics. "You will listen to me. Or I'll have you chopping shallots and polishing silver the rest of your days."

"Paradise . . ." he mumbled and fell onto the barrel to catch his breath.

They'd cleaned the mess Frédéric had made the day of the fish delivery from the broken wine case that sent a dozen bottles of Sancerre to crash upon the parquet floor. They'd watched as the priceless white wine swam in the cracks to all corners of the kitchen. What was left were soaked linens, shards of broken glass, and labels that were the only remaining witnesses that the wine had perished. And even then, Valens had scarcely been able to push a broom.

Manon's unease had only grown after he'd been unable to travel to the dunes. While the meeting with Dominique had gone favorably and they'd placed Henri's team in position to have regular association at the château, the matter of Valens' rapidly declining health was her primary concern. He could scarcely keep his head up through their breakfast preparations that morning. And he had been sleepwalking through the dinner preparations the night before.

"We ought to tell the mistress. You cannot keep working like this."

"Non. La Marquise has her hands full with this château stuffed to the gills with these Reich wasps. And the last thing I wish to do is give that overzealous police captain a reason to have me dismissed."

"It is good then that I do the sacking around here. Not Captain Fontaine."

"That may be. But your authority is an illusion—all of ours is. At least where they are concerned. You know the Reich does not approve of women who work. Nor of tired old men. If not for your skill as chef nor the pâtisserie I make for the officers, we would be of no use to them. So I must work. I must have value. To have no value to them is the greatest danger now."

He paused, as if pained more than in his physical person. Loss had a look, a deep indwelling sadness in the eyes that never fully dissipated. It was that depth of pain Manon saw as Valens shook his head and bit his bottom lip to cover a surge of emotion, physical pain, or both.

"I made a promise to my son." His hand trembled a shade as he braced it against his forehead. "If anything should happen to him, I'd look after his family."

"I know that. I do. And you've done a fine job."

"Then listen to me and let this go."

"But I could lessen your workload. If I knew what was wrong, I could protect you from doing too much. Won't you let me help?" When he waved her off, Manon stepped up to challenge him with as much care as he'd allow. She paused, trying one last time with, "Isn't that what Julian would want?"

"S'il te plaît?" He'd shut down any protestations with a firm "Please?" on the matter and then reached out for the clipboard. "Give me the list."

"Why?"

"I can write if I cannot stand."

Sighing for the love and yet absolute exasperation of this man, Manon did as he asked.

They'd slipped away after luncheon to catalog the larder, organizing foodstuffs for the upcoming dinner and what they ought to transfer to the much smaller icebox in the kitchen for ease of use that evening. And though Valens' skill as a pâtissier was unmatched—he could make notoriously difficult confections in his sleep—he was still near walking into walls these days.

It wouldn't be long before someone of note . . . noted it.

"We are striking the soufflé from tonight's menu. We can do a simple parfait with berry compote. The officers won't know the difference after they've had drink. We could give them jam and a spoon and they'd still think it high cuisine."

"We will do no such thing." Valens hugged his waist then, a seeming wave of pain hitting him ill-timed to win the argument. When Manon pivoted again and tried to press a careful hand to his shoulder, he shook his head with vehemence. "Lemon soufflé with raspberry mousse stays on the menu," he gritted out, his breathing slow and deep until the wave of discomfort passed. "And we will move the lemons to the icebox since the refrigerator is full."

"D'accord." She turned back to the shelves, reaching for the crock with bright yellow lemons stacked to the brim. "But I beg of you to listen on this one count."

Manon glanced to the doorway, checking that no shadow darkened it.

The door was cracked, just what propriety demanded of a man and a woman the rest of the staff didn't know had a family association. A sliver of daylight streamed through. Were prying ears listening outside the door?

"Here." Manon pulled the note Dominique had slipped them from inside her shoe, handed it to Valens, and allowed him to read as she carried the lemons to the icebox. When she returned, he was standing again. Counting boxes on a shelf and ticking marks off on the paper as if he were right as rain.

"Well?"

"Non. There is far too much risk."

"Maybe we can't do it now," Manon protested, trying any route that would make the man see reason. "But we must soon. There's nothing to fixing a breakfast on my own. And we can make the croissants the night before, so there's no worry."

"Forget this talk."

"Fine. If you won't go, then I will go to the village myself," she blasted back, snatching the paper with a firm whisper. "I can be there and back after breakfast one day. You can direct the kitchen to prepare the luncheon until I return."

"You will not. I will go when I am better."

"And if you do not get better?" She placed a hopeful palm to his shoulder and squeezed with a soft entreaty. "All I need is a list. Give me your symptoms, and I will pass them to this village doctor. And he will give us medicine to help you. The doctor must be safe or

Dominique would not have given us the name. I think he was trying to help. You must have worried him when he saw you."

Valens placed his hand over hers, giving a little return squeeze of thanks, even if to him it must have seemed futile.

"You don't know what you are saying, Manon. What you are offering. I beg of you to take that paper to the kitchen and feed it to the stove. And forget we ever had this conversation."

"But this is the name of a doctor who can help us. Why won't you let him?"

"Because, Chérie, I promised to protect you—even from yourself."

"What does that mean?"

A stark flash of reality washed over his face. "The day your husband and daughter were killed is the day I promised my son I wouldn't let anything happen to you. But if you do this—if you go to the village now—you might never come back."

"But why? Can't a chef go to the village doctor if someone on her staff is ill? Who would suspect that?"

"That's just it." His sigh was weighted, and the fear in him radiated when he gripped her hand. "The doctor isn't who you think he is. And there's no telling whether the authorities will use that information to suspect you too."

# CHAPTER 9

2 *August 1943*
Lothian Farm
Clinton, Maryland

R*aus! Raus!"*
Floodlights blasted Kat, blinding her as she was yanked out of bed. Disoriented, she was muscled from her bunkhouse with a potato sack pulled over her head and her toes making trails through the dirt when she was dragged outside.

Heart ramming in her chest, she battled to remain calm. And focused.

*Breathe in, Kat . . . and out.*

*One. Two. Three and four . . .*

Instinct told her not to fight—at least not yet.

Listening with her good ear, she could hear more shouts—all in German—and the sound of an auto engine rumbling, but little else. She could feel the cold steel of a rifle barrel bumping against her arm. And when the finality of a hatch slammed down over her head, she knew she'd been tossed in a trunk.

Trying to count time, she memorized turns. (Three.) And listened for any conversation she could hear over the rumble of the engine. (At least two men.) Though with her good ear pressed up against the trunk's floor and the roadway rough with gravel, it proved futile. She worked on shimmying the sack off her head, but with her hands tied high behind her back, there was little else she could do.

There'd been rumors around The Farm of a simulated Gestapo interrogation; it was an unannounced operative test that held either a pass or fail, but the rules weren't clear. While she couldn't begin to understand why they'd chosen to throw her to the wolves now, Kat was in this. Just like her decision in the hotel where she'd lifted shears to her reflection and cut those first locks of her hair.

There would be no turning back.

If this took her to Gavin, she would pass whatever test was laid out. Though, after weeks of training . . . why now?

Birch's summation of her role in the war had been exactly what he'd offered at the start. To the letter, in fact. Mrs. Betty Prior sat behind a typewriter. Accepted high-ranking military guests to Birch's inner office, and hung trench coats and trilbies in the foyer. And fetched piping-hot coffee until she was blue in the face. She ignored the catcalls and lurid shouts from recruits as she went from outbuilding to outbuilding, meeting to meeting. And tried not to find basic secretarial work a bore when all she wanted to do was spend her days digging through field reports for any scrap of intel about her brother. While Kat did not know Gavin's field name, she had learned he'd been sent to France as a pianist with the code name Magellan, and she scoured stacks of reports for any possible mention of it.

Coming up empty, Kat had nothing to do but wait.

In the few times she'd been admitted into meetings where German was the language spoken, she'd remained silent. But when the projector rolled newsreel footage smuggled from inside Berlin or Nazi-occupied Paris, she began reading lips over what she couldn't hear. And Birch, knowing this skill, began using her ability with linguistics to translate in all of his meetings.

One bright spot in her days was that Birch had given Kat increased

security clearance, and she began translating missives or review reports from OSS operatives stationed in the field, in places like Cairo,
Ceylon, Naples, and Normandy, and even once from Casablanca—
though the context was nearly always spotty. Too often she was
translating messages that turned out to be nonsense in code or read
endless agent field names that had no connection to one another.
And included no mention of a Magellan who might still be alive
somewhere in France.

As Kat's exposure to the inner workings of the OSS grew, to her
surprise, Birch arranged for her to be included in other recruits'
summary lessons in espionage, even assigning her the code name
Atalanta.

They were given tactics on how to lose a tail if being followed.
How to manufacture a new identity in the field. When to stay in a
safe house and when to go. How often a wireless operator should report back, and how long they might stay in a nest before their signal
could be seized upon by the enemy. (No more than five minutes at
a time or some twenty minutes in a day.) She relished instruction
in how to snap photos with a microfilm camera and hide it on her
person. The OSS had even sprung master con men from prison and
used their expertise to teach skills in making ink in a pinch or forging identification papers or how to pick locks or . . . any number of
whatnots an operative might need to stay alive in the field. But all of
this was variable on the location and specific circumstances of each
agent, which meant training would take a person only so far.

Survival was more about luck meeting gut instinct than true
preparation.

In the OSS operation Kat was afforded all of the information an
agent might require in the field via reports that came across her
desk, but she was given no luxury to actually try much of it out.
She hadn't fired one bullet, been allowed to repair a single engine, or learned how to defend herself beyond the basics. And
now, stuck in a trunk with only suffocating heat and little oxygen

as her companions, she was trying to recall what she ought to do, even as the brakes sang and the auto screeched to a halt.

Fresh air was a godsend . . . until it wasn't.

The trunk opened and Kat drank in coughing breaths, seeing only a starry sky and one face she recognized—Jeffrey, from the first day—before the sack was tugged back down over her head and she was hauled to her feet again.

*Okay . . . not a test interrogation.*

*Think, Kat. Think!*

*And listen. Find your chance to strike.*

*Then run.*

Revenge from a group of Jeffreys who hadn't forgotten her tumultuous entry into OSS training wasn't exactly on her radar. Neither was the shuddering walk over prickly crabgrass and rough soil in bare feet—was she being dragged across a field? Or worse, into the woods?

The silence around them was too loud, save for the footsteps of men and trilling crickets in the pines. And the shroud too dark. All Kat could think was that they were taking her to a remote spot on the outskirts of the camp. It was the why and to what end that gave her the greatest pause.

A door slammed open, sounding like it had been banged against a wall.

Kat was hauled up four wooden steps, her feet raw from scraping against them as she was dragged through a threshold. She was led down what seemed like a hallway. Until she was forced into a wooden chair, her ankles handcuffed to the legs. Strong arms shoved her forward, doubling her over the instant the shroud was pulled free.

There was a blast of light. And then nothing but water . . .

Over and over, with a fist yanking her hair, Kat was dunked in a bucket with an ice shock that stunned the breath out of her.

An unknown voice blasted, shouting curses and *"Sag mir deinen Namen!"*—Tell me your name!—and demanding information over and over. Her breathing was choppy. Coughing thundered from her chest. And the numbing intensity of fluorescent lights shone so bright in a sterile-walled room that it made her equilibrium nonexistent, so she couldn't tell which way was up or down. Nor when she'd be able to steal another breath in between bouts.

Drowning no longer seemed a distant fear but a sincere possibility.

After what seemed like hours—but surely could only have been a torturous minute or two at most—Kat's lungs rebounded in a fit of coughs. She lunged to free herself, or at least knock the chair over, but swallowed a wave of water instead. And hacked again so violently, she clenched her jaw, her teeth clamping down and ankles kicking against the cold metal cuffs with her body's flailing response.

Searing pain hit before blood filled her mouth in a warm, salty wave.

The metallic taste of it overwhelmed her and she continued to cough, this time spitting a mouth full of blood on the torturer nearest her.

"Sir!" a man yelped, jumping back as blood spray peppered the front of his shirt.

Kat felt the steel grip of one hand freed at her left shoulder, though she still couldn't move. Her body had begun shaking—the tremors sending locks of wet hair to stick over her face and mix with blood she could feel dripping off her chin.

"Is she sick?" one demanded. "She's bleeding!"

From the next voice: "What's wrong with her?"

"Let her up," another shouted, and hands freed her other shoulder as a fist pulled her hair back to lift her chin up. "You hit her!"

"I didn't."

"You must have, on the side of the bucket. You busted her mouth."

"No—they said no marks. No marks on her face!"

Shuddering, and her whole body shaking, the searing lights finally came into focus, and Kat could see the silhouettes of three men who stood over her. With blood dripping down the front of her nightgown and her body still racked with trembling but slowing into a rhythm of breathing again, Kat could finally see their faces as she looked around.

Jeffrey was front and center—no surprise.

Two other recruits she'd recognized from one of the newsreel meetings the previous week stood by, though they'd never spoken. At the very least, she'd managed to free her shoulders, endure the shock of the water bath, and, in the end, had told them nothing. No matter what they planned now, Kat was bolstered by what she hadn't known she could endure.

With what surely must have looked a sight with blood seeped into the spaces between her teeth, Kat smiled and lifted her chin, as if to say, *"Again."*

Clapping sounded from the corner of the room, beyond the brawn standing guard over her. The men parted, and one shadowy figure emerged.

Birch strolled over. Shrugged out of his suit jacket to place over her shoulders for decency's sake. He knelt in front of her, pointing to the flow of crimson dripping off her chin. "Which one of these men do I punish for doing that to you?"

Kat spit a stream of blood on the floor, hoping it ruined every last one of their shoes. And stared back in defiance. "Me."

"And how did you manage it?"

"I read about it."

"In a James Fenimore Cooper novel."

"No. In one of your reports." She pierced him with a steel glare behind ropes of wet hair that clung to her face. "A female operative from the Brits' SOE division was arrested in France in '41. Knowing what could be coming, she'd thought ahead and had a dentist file down her tooth before she was placed in the field. In the event of torture." Kat paused and coughed, for good measure. "She could clamp down. Pierce her cheek. Cough up blood. And convince any fool torturers she'd contracted TB. Everyone who reads a report knows the Nazis are terrified of sickness and will stumble back rather than be infected—never suspecting a woman might not fold with the first blow."

"What happened to her, this agent?"

"It saved her life. She escaped from hospital when they dumped her off in the quarantine unit. Met up at a safe house, was over the border to Switzerland the next day, and returned to the field within the month."

Birch nodded. As if knowing. "This is why you saw the dentist last week?"

"*Mm hmm.*"

Her superior did the one thing he'd never done, not in the weeks she'd worked in his office—he laughed. A good, hearty rumble that said any woman who would be willing to file her tooth down on the off chance she'd be interrogated was committed at a level few might have guessed.

"I thought the US government didn't perform torture for information. At least not in this way."

"We don't, as a rule." Birch confirmed matter-of-fact, though his retort had a layer of grimness about it. "But *they* do. The Geneva Convention protections extend to service personnel only, not OSS agents. And certainly not female ones. In fact, any methods they use on you will likely be more severe than on the men. Do you understand?"

"Yes, sir. I read that too."

Birch stared back at her, his eyes boring into Kat's. "You see, boys? I told you. I have the best secretary the US government could find. It's a pity I'll be forced to lose her."

"Lose her?" Kat perked up and wiped a trickle of blood off her chin with the back of her hand.

"Get those cuffs off. Now." Birch snapped at the men and pulled a handkerchief from his shirt pocket to offer to her. "We need Mrs. Betty Prior in France."

⌒

21 *January 1952*
29 Rue des Saints-Pères
Paris, France

It was rumored Michaud's kept a special table for Ernest Hemingway.
The upscale eatery on the left bank was where the celebrated
author had dined with F. Scott Fitzgerald. Its dining room had welcomed writers James Joyce and Sylvia Plath and owner of the famed
Shakespeare and Company bookshop, Sylvia Beach. And it was in
this ivory building on the corner of Rue Jacob and Rue des Saints-
Pères where Mimi and Kat had come for an exclusive luncheon
with L'Ecole des Trois Gourmandes, to meet their culinary instructors for the first time. More than that, it was the first solo outing Kat
had with Mimi since the wedding party—all hopes were pinned on
finding something useful out of the distraction of a mere cooking
class.

Kat swept through the bistro's brass-lined French doors with
Mimi trailing her, the latter who fidgeted with everything on her
person—from fumbling with long leather gloves to smoothing
her champagne mink to patting perfectly coiffed blonde curls
under her pillbox chapeau.

After informing the petite proprietress with flaming hair (called
simply *Madame*) that they'd arrived, Mimi slipped out of her mink.
Kat shrugged out of her luscious Schiaparelli shock-pink cape coat
too—both styles her friend had managed to procure for them from
a Paris runway. Only then did Kat notice the ashen tone to Mimi's
features when her friend began scanning the wood-paneled dining
room. Gone was the confident socialite from New Year's to be replaced by a jittery expat whose nervous energy kept a stiletto tapping
the art deco tile beneath their feet.

"Are you well?"

Mimi ignored the concern in favor of adjusting ivory ruffled cuffs at her wrists. "Of course."

"What's the matter, then? You've been looking forward to this for weeks."

"I know. But somehow it's different now that we're here." Mimi scanned the dining room while they waited to be seated, then cut in with a disappointed, "Voilà! Would you look at that?"

"Look at what?"

A Parisian *chat* lumbered down an aisle on lazy paws. Birds twittered from somewhere in the loft of the high ceiling. But Mimi nudged Kat away from those oddities (at least to an American) to look in the direction of a table where two Parisiennes nursed opera-length cigarette holders and a lion-cut poodle peeked out from under the tablecloth. Its lush apricot coat and diamond collar matched its owner's spring suit.

"It looks starving, poor thing," Kat joked, not seeing the allure of having an animal simply to match your wardrobe. At least not in the same way Mimi had. "I've a mind to order a roast chicken and roll it under the table between courses."

"That's it. I simply must have one."

"A new suit? Or the . . . dog?"

"The poodle of course." Mimi drifted for a breath, then offered a bright smile to cover her thoughts. "*Hmm.* But who wants the added work? A new frock won't soil the rug, will it? Poodle or not, you and I will receive invitations to the swankiest parties in this city *if* we play our cards right," Mimi chirped as they were led through the dining room. "Now smile. Remember, the devil is in the details on these things."

Details indeed.

Paris in the fifties bombarded the traveler with contradictory examples of them. Rations were slow to be lifted. Buildings lay in rubble piles on random city blocks next to new construction and fresh paint. Cosmetics and coffee were still priced at a pirate's ransom. Even the leftover wage strikes from the previous year's Confédération Générale du Travail meant travel times were murder to get just about any-where in the city. The electricity frequently went out. The metro was jammed. And doused streetlamps were not dissimilar from wartime blackouts. Les Parisiennes, while chic, still wore black even though brilliant colors longed to return to shop windows along the Champs-Élysées.

But then, rain glistened on the cobblestoned streets of Montmartre. Snow frosted the bridges of Paris so they looked like lace stretching across the Seine. Music lilted through the streets, from Latin Quarter cafés coming back to life. And soon Kat found herself falling for it—the sights and sounds, the tastes and culture that were the heartbeat of a wintery Paris, despite the upheaval of Xandre's presence and the briskness of her own marriage.

Gérard and Kat had discussed how to take full advantage of all that postwar Paris had to offer. While expats swarmed hidden corners of the city with their pocket-size copies of the *Paris par Arrondissement* guidebook, he'd escorted Kat to dine in the finest restaurants, walked with her arm in arm through museum exhibits, and insisted they visit the opera just to be seen. But each time they returned to the flat, they went their separate ways and hadn't spoken of their stalemate the night of the wedding party. That meant except for Kat's outings with Mimi, she was alone in a city still trying to breathe again from war.

This small luncheon might serve as a step back into the darkness of the past, yet still bring her closer to Gavin. And if so, Kat was keen to allow it. The job was to fly under the radar. Stick close to her friend. And wherever possible, keep the mood light as they were exchanging pleasantries of married life. And perhaps useful information about Xandre might seep through as well.

"A Paris poodle and matching suit does not determine our worth. Neither will party invitations." Kat's shot of truth seemed to ease the tension in Mimi's shoulders. "We have just as much right to be here as anyone. All we need is the spirit to learn, and we'll fit right in."

"*Absolument*," Mimi whispered back, butchering her French accent as they were led through the dining restaurant toward a reserved, glass-walled dining room at the back.

"And what does your husband think of the Paris life? Has he always lived here?"

"Well, since you asked . . ." Mimi pressed a delicate finger to her lips in a *shhh* gesture. "I'm not supposed to know, but I think Léo is planning a wedding gift on par with the one your husband gave you. One that will take us out of Paris though—north to where he used to live."

"Where is that?"

"The coast. Baie de Somme."

Kat's middle hitched on, she didn't know what exactly. Nerves, maybe.

"Is that so?"

"I've made inquiries with our man of business, mostly to sneak funds from Daddy into the bank books without my proud husband knowing. But I learned he's been searching property along the coast. For months now. It's a harbor with a funny little name I can't think of. But it must be beautiful if it's on the beach. Isn't that sweet?"

Kat swallowed hard. And this time took a chance to delve deeper into what could not have been mere coincidence. "It's not Le Crotoy?"

"Yes! That's it. How on earth did you know? Unless it's already popular with the expat crowd and I should have been aware of it? I wouldn't mind having a summer home there, if that's what the other Paris couples do." She paused, then shifted to a jittery tone again. "Is it what they do?"

Had Xandre been looking for Gérard?

Worse yet, was he searching for Gavin?

"I'm sure I wouldn't know. But did Léo live along the coast during the war? Or did you say he's visited Le Crotoy after it?"

"Oh, Léo travels for business so often that I can't pin him down. But he doesn't like to talk about the war years. He says we should focus on our future. And that's here." She dropped her voice to a whisper as they approached the party. "Look—they all know each other. We're new. And new money isn't the same as old money in Paris."

Disappointment reigned every time Kat attempted to turn the conversation to Xandre. And she feared, seeing the sparkle in Mimi's eyes, it would be a losing battle to divert her friend's attentions away from the finely dressed ladies they'd be poised to meet.

"Well, I for one am encouraged it's called L'Ecole des Trois Gourmandes—'The School of the Three Hearty Eaters.' I appreciate the freedom to be seen as women with healthy appetites." When Mimi gave a pert little eye roll, Kat offered a genuine smile and hooked her elbow through her friend's. "This cooking class is looking better by the minute. Let's go."

Madame led them around the corner of a glass wall with lush green planters, elegant brass lights hanging low from high coffered ceilings, and full booths, until their party came into view. Kat could feel Mimi relax at seeing women gathered near an oblong table who looked completely and utterly . . . normal. And with the exception of Évelyne Auclair's superior airs, the rest appeared both curious about the new students and warm to receive them.

"The blonde woman with glasses is Simone Beck, but everyone calls her Simca. She is French and also a graduate of Le Cordon Bleu. With Louisette Bertholle—the Frenchwoman with the kind smile on the left—she is working on a French cookbook for American housewives. I believe they are collaborating with the other instructor on the methods and recipes."

"And we're the test subjects?"

"It would seem so." Mimi tugged the sleeve of Kat's dove-gray peplum suit to direct her attention to the woman who'd just breezed by. "Oh, there she is, Kat."

"Who?"

"The tall one is the leader of this thing—that's Julia Child."

*Julia Child . . .*

The name rolled off Mimi's tongue a little whisper soft and dreamier than she'd probably intended. But to Kat, the woman seemed to warrant the admiration.

For every ounce of chic oozing from Paris, this American woman— a would-be French chef, as it were—exuded a larger-than-life presence that was anything but the cutting edge of trendy. Though clothed in a tailored navy suit, smart silk blouse, and matching pillbox hat that whispered she came from money, her tight-cropped chestnut curls and warm smile refused to be seen as pretentious. Her joy seemed to radiate from engaging a gathering of friends with the expectation of outstanding cuisine, fine wine, and brilliant conversation.

"Come. Let me introduce you." Mimi turned on her charm and waltzed them into the fold, reaching for the instructor to offer a Paris kiss to the woman's cheeks. "Bonjour! Simca? Louisette. And Julia. May I introduce Madame Kathryn Fontaine?"

"Ah—we've procured another American!" Julia exclaimed, with a distinctive, birdlike voice that seemed able to bring the room extraordinary light. "Can you debone a chicken?"

Kat couldn't contain the heart-smile had she wanted to. How her maman would have swooned at such an unorthodox introduction. Perhaps that's what she liked most about it.

"Ah yes . . . I can probably give a chicken a run for its money on the way to a Dutch oven."

A distinct twinkle sparkled in Julia's eye; a hidden delight of sorts either in Kat's answer or for the meal to come. The instructors took a seat at the head of the table, and Julia offered an exuberant smile when Madame presented them with the menu. One might think by the sheer delight in her face that this was the pinnacle of life, to chat with the proprietress of a favorite Paris restaurant and try out her delightfully lopsided French on the garçon. For the way she *oohed* and *aahed* over the menu offerings, one might think Mrs. Child had a pound of butter packed away in her satchel just in case the kitchen ran out before her order went in.

A flurry of names and smiles followed. And taking chairs around an oblong table as introductions were exchanged, and orders were placed.

Never had Kat sat in a group who might talk for hours of the best brand of French kitchen knives. Or how to haggle at market stalls like a local without insulting the seller. Or where to find the best olive oil in the city—which Julia passionately defended was purchasing a crock from the tucked-away L'Olivier on Rue de Rivoli. It was the epitome of contradictions—to dine on rocket salad, d'Anjou pear, and watercress, and to chat over pleasantries while her heart was reeling from the knowledge Mimi had unwittingly shared. Kat's mind raced through the baguettes with a smoky toasted brie and the French delicacy that followed: *moules marinières*—mussels in a white wine sauce.

To be seated with these women, listening to their zeal for similar pursuits was eye-opening. Most were married. But they were also professionals. Educated. Unashamed and passionate. They were masters of their own fate, who broke the mold of expectations where women were concerned. And, like Julia, they sought to do it all through what was a traditionally domestic pursuit, which ultimately proved unyielding for Kat to compartmentalize her life.

For the first time she was willing to consider that the glimmer of something new might be on the horizon.

Kat didn't miss the auto shop as much as she thought. Nor did she think of Boston before the war, the horrors of France during it, nor the tumult of the years that followed to leave it behind. But here, somehow, Kat was no longer adrift in the world. She might focus on finding the answers she and Gérard sought, but she wondered too, as she brought the wine glass up to her lips, where her husband might fit into this picture of a new life.

"What do you cook, Mrs. Fontaine?" Julia Child's high-pitched voice carried across the gathering.

The table quieted as the question hung on air.

"Pardon?" Kat set her wine glass back to the clothed table, whispering a "merci" as she leaned back so a passing garçon could set a petite plate of *tarte au fromage blanc* before her.

"What have you cooked? We're trying to decide on the menus for our first outings and going down the line to form an opinion. Madame Allmand next to you stated she has made omelets."

Mimi gave Kat a little nonverbal nudge, offering her friend the sweetest, most innocent smile to goad her into finding a suitable answer. And Kat had no wish to mislead, even if visions of her first horrible kitchen disasters at Château du Broutel flashed through her mind, next to the later triumphs . . . Manon had shown her how to sauté lemon sole. Make tarte tatin from apples of a nearby orchard. Valens had instructed her in whisking mousse for hazelnut crêpes. And the boules of pain de campagne Kat had learned to bake convinced her there was no more intoxicating scent in the world than bread fresh from the oven.

"Oh, I'd say this and that," she stumbled, looking for a safe place to land.

Best keep it French, and as basic as possible.

"It's not glamorous, but perhaps a bœuf bourguignon? Or a stout coq au vin? They are the French dishes that most come to mind."

"Why, bœuf bourguignon is the stew of stews! And coq au vin the quintessential dish for a savory meal on a rainy Paris day." If it were possible, Julia's face brightened. "We will add them to our list. And what else, since you have us rolling downhill?"

"I suppose the most important thing I was once told about French cooking is that a chef ought to choose a meal where she must be required to add copious amounts of butter. And no matter what you'd set out to make in the beginning, in the end it will turn out all right."

"Here, here!" Julia's laugh was open and automatic as she used her fork to pound a mock gavel to the table. "And if you run out of butter, use cream. That is the best thing about French cuisine. It doesn't have to be perfect to be exquisite. Merci to Mrs. Fontaine for reminding us of exactly why we are here."

They'd pooled their money, would shop for ingredients from the best markets in Paris, and made a plan for their first class to convene in two days' time at 81 Rue de l'Université—the Childs' Paris flat. And with that, Julia pushed back her chair and stood, their table head initiating an inaugural toast to their society.

The ladies joined, all standing and raising their glasses. Mimi beamed at Kat most of all, for the triumph of the moment that seemed to equal success for one meant swimming success for both.

"To Mrs. Fontaine, the return of butter, and to our class of hearty eaters." Julia raised her glass. "Bon appétit!"

Julia was quite tall. Inordinately interesting. In love with butter and Mr. Child—her husband, Paul, a photographer and artist who led the Visual Presentation Department for the United States Information Service (USIS) in Paris—whom she spoke of often and with great affection. And Julia owned an electric wit like no one Kat had ever met before. It was safe to say that among the gaiety and laughter, the savory world of French cuisine and unexpected expat smiles, she liked this enigmatic instructor immediately.

For Julia Child had managed a rare feat: to make Kat forget the nature of her troubles, even for a few rare moments, and allowed her to find her smile again in a city of truly exceptional things.

# CHAPTER 10

8 *August 1943*
Place Anatole Gosselin
Rue, France

How should a saboteur cross a public square swarming with enemy uniforms?

Manon's heels clicked upon rain-misted cobblestones that fanned out in crescent patterns on the street as she walked her bicycle through the medieval village's market square.

The lacy spires of Chapelle du Saint-Esprit were up on her right, the petite Flemish-style chapel looking morose in the rain, and its once exquisite exterior and fourteenth-century statues eroded from centuries of salty sea air. She passed a *librairie* on the way, the war having shuttered the poor little bookshop so that yellowed newspapers peeled away from the windows and tacked boards formed great X formations over the glass with splinternet tape. The *papeterie* was closed too—the lack of paper goods for stationery compounded by citizens keen to avoid writing letters that the Vichy police would only tear open and read when put to post. The *boulangerie* and *boucherie* shops boasted frightful queues out front, mostly women with little ones or old men and women who ignored posters that shouted slogans of the Nazi and Vichy régimes' ideal: *Travail, Famile, Patrie!*, or "Work, Family, Fatherland!"

The weekday market was set in the center square, with shoppers haggling for fish or unremarkable root vegetables under the watchful eye of the Franc-Garde—French paramilitary troops who since January had infected France with their brutality to root out Resistance factions across the countryside.

The brown shirts and midnight-blue military-style uniforms posted there noticed Manon. One even tipped his blue beret. But they didn't appear to realize it was the chef passing by—a good thing for her frayed nerves. Save for Captain Fontaine, the Nazi-loyal authorities rarely ventured into the château kitchen. And those who did come in contact were either focused on deliveries in the courtyard or scarcely noticed service staff at all. It wasn't likely they'd recognize her in the square now. Even if they did, it would not be out of the ordinary for the chef to be in search of foodstuffs for the château or to visit the doctor on behalf of one of her subordinates.

Though her hair was a memorable deep auburn, Manon had tucked it up under a navy cloche and kept her head down against the misty rain. Best to be forgettable. She tossed a few fleeting glances toward the fish market stall, hoping to see Dominique's familiar face working there. A tinge of disappointment followed as she found it empty and walked on.

The doctor's office building came into view just beyond the chapel. Its plain façade of weathered ivory boasted two stories, three simple windows on each level, and a cherry-red wood door too welcoming to belong in such a place. Manon parked her bicycle in a lean against the stoop, took her satchel and a tin from the basket, then climbed the few stairs to the door.

Dominique's instructions had been clear: enter the physician's office through the front and announce yourself as from the château. The doctor would know what this meant. It had taken Manon weeks of prodding when Valens' symptoms did not improve, and he'd finally agreed that a humble Frenchwoman might waltz through the front door for a medical appointment right under the noses of the Milice uniforms across the market without a second notice. And she was to bring a tin of sweets as payment—macarons Valens had provided.

Feeling the Miliciens' eyes upon her from across the square, she gauged they'd keep a Frenchwoman's bicycle from theft. And if by some chance they did not, losing the item would be worth it to find some answer to Valens' condition.

Manon shoved the door against a warped wood post and lintel from the constant moisture in the air. It stuck, then gave, rattling a brass bell as she fumbled into an entry with a garish lemon-and-white tile floor, sterile white paint, and a series of sky-blue brocade chairs pushed up against the front wall. Blessedly, the waiting area was empty; she could breathe a little easier. The only other occupant was at a reception desk wedged in the back—a secretary of some sixty years with a plain rust suit, bifocals on a gold chain, and waves of gray-brown pinned out of her eyes so she could clack away at a typewriter.

The woman glanced up over the rim of her spectacles when the bell clanged its last.

"Name?" She paused to pick up a pencil against a receiving ledger as Manon approached the desk.

"Madame Altier," Manon tried to sound confident when she added, "from Château du Broutel. Here to see Dr. Rousseau."

"Very good, madame."

The secretary said nothing further. Just rolled her chair back from the desk, marched across the room to a frosted glass door with **DOCTOR** stamped in a sharp block print, and gave a light rap before she ducked her head inside. After a second or two delay, she left the door cracked and stepped away again.

She returned to her swivel chair, and the wood creaked as the secretary sat. "The doctor will see you now."

The woman had gone back to typing by the time Manon could utter a "merci." Having been dismissed, she took the few furtive steps to the office, then entered.

"Close the door," he said.

She obeyed and clicked the door closed on an exam room with mint-hued metal cabinetry on a far wall, a central exam table, and natural light brightening the room from a large frosted-glass window facing the market.

Dr. Rousseau was as common a man as she'd have guessed would own a medical practice in the village but as unassuming as a Resistance fighter could be. A good tick beyond middle age, he wore a tweed suit under a lab coat that had seen far better days. A pair of spectacles accentuated a round face topped with a thinning gray crown. His manners offered an air of neutrality—not friendly but not aloof either.

"Madame Altier, is it?" He was direct and scribbled something on a clipboard from a desk opposite the door.

Valens had finally relented to let Manon go to the village for him but had coached her for this outing too. *"Keep your story simple,"* he'd said, *"and as close to the truth as you can make it."* Giving her real name would authenticate the visit as much as anything, even if she'd gone back to her maiden name while in Paris at the time of the occupation.

"Oui," she said, clutching the tin of sweets perhaps a little too tightly in her gloved hands. "I've come on account of a friend. He wishes you to have this. For payment." She cleared her throat, then offered the tin.

Dr. Rousseau stood, crossed the room, and, having received it, opened the lid to two dozen of the most perfect macarons Manon had ever seen. The luxurious scent of lavender and coconut perfumed the air as the man nosed around inside. Then, as if satisfied, he closed it up tight again.

He set the tin on a nearby counter, then offered Manon a spindle chair by the door. "Please," he said, taking a metal stool for himself and carrying it across the room to position in front of her.

Manon obeyed again, holding her satchel tight at her waist.

"Monsieur Moreau sent you."

Relieved a little to hear reference to Dominique, she nodded. "He did."

"I see. And how may I assist you?"

"As I said, I'm here for a friend who is ailing. Has been for several weeks now." Manon flipped the latch on her leather satchel, taking the list of ailments Valens had prepared for her, then handed it over. "These are his symptoms."

Dr. Rousseau read over the list, tipping his brow just over the top of his spectacles when he got to the end. "I see." He folded the paper and handed it back. "Tell me, what does your friend eat?"

"The same food as everyone in the kitchen."

"Which is?"

"Staff eat at the odd hours, around the schedule for the officers' meals. We breakfast with a tartine—a slice of pain de campagne of barley or oat flour served with jam. Apples, apricots, or plums. Whatever is in season. And tea if it is in supply. A hearty soup or stew at midday. Fish and veg sometimes, if left over from a dinner the night before. And the occasional pheasant or guinea hen, but that's a rarity. More for holidays and such. As supplies continue to run thin, we've taken to substituting staff meals with a hot malt porridge as needed."

"*Hmm*. And what does he drink? You said tea."

"Oui, though we don't often have it these days. Goat's milk, water and chicory, but he won't drink the latter. Occasional wine at meals, again if left over. But the gentleman prefers not to drink spirits, so he generally avoids even that."

"What does your friend do at the château?"

"He is pâtissier."

"Valens." The doctor looked to the tin on the counter. "He made these?"

"Oui."

"And what do his hands look like? Have you noticed patches of darkening skin perhaps? Or lesions? Just here." He ran a finger on the outsides of his hand.

"I don't believe so. I've tried to prod, but the gentleman is private. He wishes to keep this confidential—whatever it is." Manon cleared her throat as a tremor of anxiety winged its way through her middle at the thought of the rumored brutality of the Vichy police standing right outside the window. She lowered her voice, offering, "What do you think troubles him?"

Manon flitted her glance to the window, then back to the doctor.

"Madame." The doctor leaned forward too, to whisper, "I am sorry. I cannot be certain what ails your friend."

"But you must have an idea."

"I may. Is anyone else on your staff suffering the same symptoms?"

"Non. We are not."

He rolled the wheels of his stool over to the counter and took the tin into his lap. Opening the lid, he pressed fingertips through the mass of macarons, their robin's-egg-blue mound rising above the rim as he sorted through.

"The macarons will be useful with some of our female clientele." He pulled an empty metal basin from a nearby counter and dropped a handful of the macarons in. "They come here from a nearby gentlemen's establishment . . . frequented by the officers from the château."

*Oh.* Manon hadn't been aware of this association, though it did make a connection in her mind. Valens was frequently called upon to make pâtisserie creations for the Reich officers, though she'd thought this had merely been to feed a collective sweet tooth. But now it made sense—the officers were encouraged to socialize in their off hours, the idea being that it made them in better spirits to fight.

Seemed they brought gifts to their companions in the village.

As Manon was processing the association of what the officers called their *französische törtchen*—French tarts—a false bottom of the tin came away, and she jumped when he revealed a small stack of papers from it. They were wrinkled from having been wet and then air-dried, but there was no mistaking the wine bottle labels clearly marked with the Loire Valley *Sancerre* on the front. The very same that had been broken in the last château delivery.

Manon's mouth fell open, but she recovered and pursed her lips again.

"Monsieur Moreau said it was safer if you did not know." The doctor offered the tiniest ghost of a smile, as if the mercurial fisherman from the dunes had mentioned something of the chef who might arrive at his door. And certainly the extent of what she would or would not know.

"What is it?"

"Iron-gall ink does not bleed when wet." The doctor held out the labels, then flipped them to the other side. Scrawled notes were on virtually every speck of space—what looked like hand-drawn maps and tables of times and corresponding deliveries.

"Only the white wine works, mind. The merlot would stain the labels. And would be a crying shame to waste for no great purpose."

"I knew I was delivering something to you. I just never guessed . . ." Manon exhaled, disbelief washing over her. "But what of my pâtissier? He still looks unwell, and I believe he is genuinely suffering from something—"

"Non. That is a very real concern. Valens must be ill to have allowed you to come instead. But we will see to his problem. And, I trust, find the source. It must be either within the château walls— food supply only he would handle, for example—or from outside the grounds. Think of where he goes. Ask him to whom he speaks. And where the pâtisserie he makes changes hands. If he barters or trades or brings anything back to the château but does not share it with you or the rest of the staff, this would be the place to start."

Espionage was not for the faint of heart.

Manon's palms were trying to sweat through her gloves as she took in what the doctor had said. Her middle was twisting faster than a bicycle wheel speeding downhill. And even as the doctor stalked across the room to a cabinet and opened it, searching through bottles for some specific cure, she was trying not to think of what might have happened had the Franc-Garde stopped her.

All it would have taken was a single question. For the bike to hit a rut in the cobblestones and empty the tin's contents onto the market square. Or for her bicycle to have been stolen and the goods discovered along the way, and all of them in the château kitchen denounced to the Vichy police.

Short of stealing foodstuffs and repurposing them to the hungry in the village, Manon had been active only in small pursuits up until now. If she couldn't abscond with the Nazi goods for fear of being caught, she could aid in making the Reich officers' lives as difficult as possible. Pricking the cans of tinned fish. Spoiling carcasses of meat so the soldiers would have to make do with a thin soup instead of a true rib-sticking meal. Wetting dry goods so they'd be rendered unusable. The housekeeping staff was a part of their scheme by putting itching powder in the officers' sheets when they fetched spent breakfast trays back to the kitchen. Even setting aside sugar to pour in gas tanks or spitting in the highest-ranking officials' food were petty acts of subversion.

Traveling as a courier to the village, however, required a new brand of courage Manon wasn't certain she possessed.

Was she really ready for this?

"Give these to your friend." The doctor handed her two small glass bottles of pills. "Instructions are on the bottle. If he does not improve, come back in a week. And if anything changes, bring Valens to me at once."

Manon took the bottles, deposited them in her satchel, and stood to leave. "Merci, Dr. Rousseau."

"Madame Altier?" he asked, and she turned to find the doctor crossing the room with the tin again. He opened the lid, kept the false bottom, and returned it to her hands. "If you would, s'il vous plaît, take the rest of these and offer them to the Miliciens waiting outside."

"What? You wish me to speak to the Milice?"

"I do." He took his glasses off and slipped them into his lab coat pocket.

It was the first time she'd noticed the gentleman's weariness. It seemed subversion might not come naturally to him either, for they both appeared to be dangling on similar tenterhooks with dark shadows under their eyes.

"If they ask, tell them you were offering payment to the doctor and I accepted some of the macarons. But the rest are a gift. They will not question this."

"They don't know I'm from the château."

The doctor chuckled low, enjoying her innocence. "They know exactly who you are, madame. Or else they would have stopped you and questioned you on the spot. What I need you to do is offer these sweets to the officers, and make sure the square sees when you do it."

"But if I speak to the Franc-Garde troops . . . if I act as though I befriend those devils, the entire village will label me a *collaboratrice*."

He nodded, as if resigned to something she ought as well. "And this will ensure your safety."

Blind acquiescence was not a game Manon played.

It was one thing to be rumored a sympathizer of the Reich— there were still enough of Pétain's loyalists to turn in friends and neighbors who gave even the slightest hint of rebellion against Vichy rule. But to be branded a collaboratrice, to exchange pleasantries with their Nazi occupiers . . . This was a risky tightrope to walk.

Manon left the physician's office, making a play at the tin causing her distress to fit back in the small bicycle basket in the rain. And as a consequence of her frustration, she offered the tin to the Milicien who'd tipped his beret the first time she'd wheeled by. She nodded when he accepted the gift, subservient but without the least bit of guile, and moved quickly to be out of their reach.

To the desperate few villagers left queuing in the rain, clutching ration coupons for what remained in the shops, it might have been an exchange of little importance. Why wouldn't the chef of the grand château admire the officers whom she served? And if this was a little part Manon had to play to aid their cover in the kitchen, she'd take their stares of disgust. She'd weather the judgment and ire, clutching Valens' medicine in her satchel as a reminder of what mattered now. But just as she'd begun to wheel away, Manon caught a glimpse of a fisherman unloading a catch in his market stall.

And she could breathe again.

Across the square, through the rain and glances from citizens who judged the woman with the bicycle, familiar eyes said different. Dominique connected a gaze with hers to say he knew what she'd done. He'd seen the handoff and was as relieved the drop was over as she. And from under the brim of his flatcap, he seemed to wish those light blue eyes might convey something true: He was proud of her courage when Manon was certain she'd none.

# CHAPTER 11

17 August 1943
Baie de Somme
Le Crotoy, France

B*ail out!*" the pilot screamed over his shoulder as the C-47 Sky-train bay door flew open.

Kat fought her body's fear-racked reaction when explosions lit the night sky with brilliant orange bursts that blasted outside the windows.

Her head knew the truth: They'd been hit. Flak had torn apart their portside engine so it sputtered and coughed flames. And the only logical thing to do now was jump. But even then, as the pilot's shout hung on air and the open cargo bay rattled in the sky, shock stacked upon terror rendered her unable to move from her seat.

"Where are we?" Carter, their crew leader, shouted back, then unbuckled his lap belt to lean into the cockpit.

Seemed they'd decided to keep it quiet from the agents in the hull. But Kat could read enough of the men's lips to know the worst—they were only at Baie de Somme, and they were going down. The map of France Kat had memorized stateside reminded her now how much trouble they were in.

"We're at the Baie de Somme?" she demanded, leaving their leader astonished by her ability to have overheard—or read—what he'd been trying to keep quiet. When Carter didn't answer, she shouted again, "That's eighty kilometers from our drop zone, sir!"

"I know!" he bit back as the bay rattled again, flak hitting like starbursts around them.

Double-fisting her parachute harness in a death grip, Kat pressed her back harder against the metal wall, willing her training to take over as she stared back at the OSS agents across from her who'd make up their three-person team in France. Birch had assigned Jeffrey, who though brash and young, had turned out to be an efficient pianist. Carter was their seasoned crew leader, who'd spent eight months in France with an SOE team the year prior. And Kat was assigned the role of their communications specialist, with the code name Atalanta—the Greek goddess of running. How she wished she could run from this now.

It had been a whirlwind three weeks since Birch brought Kat into the fold as a full-fledged OSS agent. Her instruction held back nothing, from the basics of survival to weaponry, to the use of propaganda, and even learning the brutal torture tactics Vichy police and Gestapo were rumored to inflict upon their captives—especially women.

Along with that, the select few tools on her person were a pack of Benzedrine. (Should she need to stay awake in the field.) A "kill pill" all agents carried if torture became too unbearable. (The dreaded cyanide that if swallowed was coated to pass through the system, but if clamped down upon would bring death within seconds.) A ladies' leather satchel containing "pocket litter," such as receipts from local hotels and cafés, invisible ink matches, French brand cigarettes and cosmetics, and travel papers that would authenticate Kat's identity. And a pair of serviceable shoes with hollow heels concealing a boot knife in one and a tiny case with uncomfortable glass contacts in the other, to tint her ice-blue eyes a more common shade of brown.

Orders were to land with their team intact on the outskirts of Amiens.

From there they'd rendezvous with their contact on the ground at Lyon—a Brit SOE agent code-named Tempus, who'd been deep-seated for some time, working as a clockmaker in the old town. Once establishing her cover as Lucette Garnier, Tempus's niece, Kat would begin courier work carrying OSS and SOE messages, translating documents lifted from Nazi officials, mining for information, spreading propaganda, and wherever she could, assisting OSS agents and loyal locals to build Resistance networks through the heavily fortified Occupied Zone of Northern France.

That was her formal assignment.

But to Kat? Her presence in France began and ended with digging for information about Gavin. And though there was no expectation Kat would see hand-to-hand combat, she'd also been given a crash course in espionage, including self-defense, how to load and fire a weapon, and the best place to shove a knife—up under the ribs where it could do the most lethal damage.

The last rumor before takeoff was there had been a recent B-17 mission over Rouen-Sotteville that had gone spectacularly for the Allies, the heavy bomber raid leveling railroad marshaling yards and making a significant dent in the Nazi stronghold in the skies over Northern France. That meant with such an Allied success, the Luftwaffe was on high alert through the night of their take-off that brought fair weather, a bright moon, and favorable winds ticking just under twenty miles per hour. Their C-47 Skytrains had swept over the Channel for the planned drop of OSS agents and arms cargo over France but were doomed now that they'd been spotted.

"Get them out of here!" the pilot screamed.

"Nine hundred feet and falling—" The copilot shouted, then with desperation, turned back to the bay filled with cargo drops and the three ill-fated OSS agents whose lives hung in the balance. "We'll hold you up, long as we can. But if you're going to make it, you have to go! *Now!*"

Carter tried to catch his balance, bracing his knees at the increasingly tumultuous bobbing of the plane as he crossed sideways to Jeffrey.

In the split seconds it took to watch as Jeffrey unbuckled, Kat unbuckled too, and Carter helped hook the suitcase that doubled as the piano wire to Jeffrey's chute harness. And without the agent looking back, Carter slapped a hand to Jeffrey's shoulder to send him out of the plane.

Turning to Kat next, Carter yanked her with him to the open bay door.

Whether terror or insanity or something caught fire inside that said if this was it, Kat knew she had to go down fighting—*no one* was going to push her into France. If it was jump and die or go down in flames, she'd still be the one to choose it.

"You can do it, Prior!" Carter shouted, as the wind and flak and deadly ratcheting of explosions whooshed by. "*Go!* And roll when you hit ground."

Kat nodded, and not daring to think or reason or even look back . . . flung herself from the bay.

The night sky enveloped her, and the great span of France spread out hundreds of feet below. As her heart rammed in her chest, the wind punished and pushed and railed against her. Kat reached up, clawing until she found and executed her chute pull. She was yanked back, *hard*—the chute billowing above her head. And for a few agonizing seconds, she was able to stop the wild careening toward earth to catch her bearings.

Kat's body went rigid, tensing when a thundering explosion painted the sky. The horror of orange flames sent the C-47 in a nose-dive against the treetops, then split the hull into an inferno that sent a fiery mushroom cloud to rise.

Their pilots were most assuredly dead.

Whether Carter had made it out or what had become of Jeffrey . . .

Kat couldn't think as she sailed toward earth. All she could do was stare down, try to judge what was sea or air or trees, and head for it with the moon providing a backlit coast of France.

The terrible *crack* hit as her chute careened toward a grove of trees. Was it splintering trees? The Nazis' dreaded Wasserfall surface-to-air fire aiming for the chute that billowed above her head? Or, heaven help her, was it her own body breaking apart? Another *crack* sounded and Kat was split, first from shock and driving pain, and then as her world shifted from waking terror, she fell into darkness.

$$\sim$$

"Drink," a voice demanded. Followed by something that patted her cheek.

Kat stirred, starting awake with arms flailing for a fight.

"Don't move, Lucette," the voice ordered again, this time holding her down with a firm hand, applying pressure to her collarbone.

Kat obeyed, tears squeezing from the corners of her eyes as she awoke blindly, then adjusted her view. Stars sparkled like diamond pindots high above. Treetops waved in the moonlight around the silhouette of a man's head and shoulders bent over her. And before Kat could realize she was on the forest floor, a wave engulfed her.

Searing fire stabbed through her body and Kat cried out, the white-hot pain radiating from her shoulder down through each limb. She sputtered and choked on water he'd offered, then screamed again with a guttural cry that echoed through the trees.

He covered her mouth.

"*Quiet!* Or we're both dead!" he snapped in French. And then softer, maybe even with compassion, the man whispered, "You're going to be okay. Here—just drink."

This time water was a lifeline.

Coolness trickled in, softening the razors in Kat's throat as she swallowed. And finally, in the darkness, his face came into focus when he shot a glance over his shoulder and the moonlight illuminated his profile.

Remembering Jeffrey's field name, she muttered, "Clément?"

"*Bien*, Lucette." He smiled at the name. Even for hating her from that first day, it seemed she'd won something over in him. Enough that he didn't mind showing a tiny measure of pride now. "You remembered your name. That's good."

Pale gold light glowed through the trees, illuminating gangly limbs on small, knotty trunks spreading out in neat rows behind them. She remembered then, the plane . . . the pilots . . . the jump . . . and the explosion.

"The crew?"

He shook his head. "Dead."

"Non. We have to go back."

Kat refused to believe it. Surely Carter bailed. Maybe the pilots too. She'd read too many accounts in the OSS files that came across Birch's desk to underestimate any of their agents now. And unless she saw bodies with her own eyes, Kat couldn't give up on the rest of the crew.

There was always a chance they'd survived.

"They're dead. All of them."

"Non . . ."

Pulling against Jeffrey's clothes, Kat grasped for something to cling to that could help anchor her to rise but found only odd stones on the ground around them. She fisted one, felt a soft spot give under her thumb, and drew it up to the light.

"Apples." Jeffrey took the fruit from her and shoved the rest away from the ground so she wouldn't roll over one at her side. "We landed in an orchard."

Kat reached up to her right shoulder, desperate to alleviate the pain that coursed through, grasping at the source of her agony.

"I wouldn't do that."

"Why not?" she gritted out. When the expected feel of warmth on

her fingertips—blood—met the jagged shards of something rough
and immoveable, she closed her fist around the thin cylinder.

"That's why." He swatted her hand away. "Because you have a tree
limb sticking out of your shoulder.

Groaning, Kat clamped her eyes shut again on the pain that radiated with even the slightest movement.

"But forget that now, d'accord? You have to push the pain away."

Her mind battled, first from fear and panic, then to logic, thinking through the next steps to solve this.

*The closest city to Baie de Somme is . . . where?*

*If we were eighty kilometers off course, that would put us at . . .*

*How far from Lyon?*

Kat pushed up but her right arm was useless and fell like dead
weight at her side. Jeffrey helped her instead of holding her down,
this time bracing an arm around her waist to help her rise to sitting.

"Take this," he ordered, pressing a pill to her lips.

She clamped them closed and shook her head, bracing her palm
at his chest to shove him off.

*He's trying to give me cyanide . . .*

"Will you stop being a fool? I'm not trying to kill you! If I wanted
to, I'd have already done it." He tried again. "Take it. It's for the
pain."

Kat stared back into his eyes, only seconds to make a decision.

The agony already too much, she relented, allowing him to drop
it on her tongue. And swallowed when he again brought the canteen
to her lips and cool water barreled in.

"Your satchel and canteen are at your side, on the ground by your
left hand. I hid our chutes and harnesses. But I can't hide that plane.
Nor the bodies they'll find in it." He screwed the canteen cap and
wound the strap crosswise over his body, then shrugged a jacket
over his shoulders to conceal it. "You must have a story. There's a
ladder over there . . ."

"What?"

"Listen to me. There's a ladder. You are a local girl—from that village." He pointed to the moonlit line of rooftops and smoke rising from chimneys in a valley nearby. "You were reaching for the apples from the treetops that haven't been picked clean. And lost your footing. A limb went through your shoulder as you went down."

Mind muddling . . . from the pill he'd given her?

Not yet. Not possibly that soon. Still, Kat found herself swimming. Feeling herself falling into a tunnel. And her eyes were no longer able to focus on his face. She wanted to see the stars behind him but felt herself fall back, her gaze drifting off to nowhere in particular.

"Stay awake!" Jeffrey palmed Kat's face, shaking her to focus through fluttering eyelids. "Repeat it, Lucette. Tell me the story."

"The ladder . . . apples. And I fell . . . But why?"

"Because they're here."

"Who?"

Frantic, Kat looked right and left, finding only rows of apple trees as far as the eye could see. A rock fence lined the orchard to one side. And the dim light of the smoldering plane lit the sky in the distance on the other. There was no movement. No sound ahead from the sleepy village. No crashing waves to indicate they were at the coast. And certainly no boots on the ground or ratcheting machine guns to say it was all over. And thank heaven, no sound of tracker dogs barking in the distance.

All was haunting and still as the plane erupted in the distance.

"Who's here?" she repeated.

"Them," he whispered, gesturing over her shoulder to a far-off road she hadn't even known was there.

The terrifying outline of a box truck became a shadowed silhouette in the distance. Only Vichy police or Gestapo were likely to have access to petrol—it was the enemy if anyone.

"They must have seen the plane go down."

"Fine. *Allons-y*," she muttered, muscling herself up again from the apple-strewn orchard floor with her good arm, grabbing the satchel handle to go with him. "I'm a strong runner. I can run."

Thank heaven Kat's mind had clicked over to French even on autopilot, and she'd remembered she was not an American. She was Lucette. Her uncle was a clockmaker. And she was on her way to Lyon to find him . . .

Everything in French. She must think it. *Be* it now.

"Non. You can't." He pressed her down with a firm hand. Then began gathering his things on the ground around him: tucking a pistol in his waistband and a sheathed knife in his boot and filling his pockets with apples. "If I stay, we're both dead. And I can't give up the piano. Not now. But if they find you, they're less likely to hurt a woman."

"You know that's not true!"

The absurdity of it—the Boche weren't likely to kill her outright, not if everything the OSS had taught her was true. Graphic visions of agent torture blasted through her mind, warning of wires shot up fingernail beds, or rusty pliers twisted in her mouth for one gruesome tooth extraction after another. Or, heaven help her—Kat envisioned the unspeakable atrocities enacted against women, over and over, just to get them to talk.

She'd most certainly take her current state over the one they promised.

"If I go, we both have a chance. Do you understand?"

Disbelief racked her, possibly more than the pain. Kat grabbed at his elbow as he rose to a kneel, ready to run. Yanking him back, she demanded, "You can't leave me here!"

"I'll get word back that we both survived the crash." He shook her off and hauled the suitcase radio back into his hand. "Remember Tempus in Lyon? We'll meet there. Soon as we can. Say it back to me."

"Tempus . . . Lyon," Kat repeated, though furious and now

grasping at his ankle, even though she could not possibly hold it. "And then I'll kill you when I do find you, for leaving me alone."

"I wouldn't expect anything less. Just stay alive, Lucette," he whispered, then disappeared like a ghost into the night.

Kat listened to Jeffrey's retreat, the sound of breaking sticks and disturbed underbrush fading the farther he went. She tried to crawl after him, or at least drag herself out of sight as footfalls and distant shouts came closer from the other direction. And though the pain was muddling on the edges of her body now, it was still there. Pounding with every heartbeat. And the stick in her shoulder disallowed her to move far at all.

"Over here!" came a whisper-shout.

Bleeding through the agony, dragging herself through dirt and grass and rotting apples to get away, Kat finally decided it was futile. She gave in, collapsing so she could roll onto her back again. Gritting her teeth through the pain. Fighting to ignore the cyanide pill concealed in her boot. She'd vowed never to use it, but it might come in handy to use on an enemy, should they need a quick getaway. She just didn't expect that time to be in the first moments she'd landed in France.

"*I'm sorry, Gav,*" Kat mouthed, tears squeezing from her eyes as she stared up at the innocence of stars twinkling overhead. "*I tried.*"

One breath after another, the stars winked back. She stared up, wondering if he was looking at the same sky from somewhere in France . . . until a rifle barrel appeared, demanding her attention as it cut off her view between the eyes.

"Are you her?" a rough voice demanded.

When Kat said nothing, he paused, just enough to edge his face and a hat with a poppy emblem to the side of the barrel as he stared down. "I said are you her? Célène?"

Without thought of pocket litter that tied her to Lyon, or field names and a backstory she may bungle, or tinted contacts in her boot that should have presented her with brown eyes instead of a memorable blue, Kat's only option was a split-second decision to gamble for her life.

It was either yes or no. Life or death. Trust or risk.

"Oui. I am . . . Célène . . ." she breathed out, just as a wave of pain blotted out the sky.

Oblivion beckoned once again.

⌒

*25 January 1952*
2 Place de l'Opéra
Paris, France

Mimi had sent over a new opera gown that evening from an up-and-coming designer just making waves in Paris: Hubert de Givenchy. Kat arranged the skirt of the couture design in the auto's back seat now, ensuring contrasting layers of the nude-peach and deep ochre train kept to the invisible line on her half of the bench as Gérard slipped in beside her.

It was a rain-soaked, bitter night when he'd taken her to the Palais Garnier to see the Théâtre National de l'Opéra's popular ballet *Le Palais de Cristal*—another in their whirlwind string of public appearances to woo Paris society from the inside out.

Though stunning to start, it was when the ballerinas' performance morphed into intimate movements by demi-soloist pairs that it proved too much for Kat to endure another performance of her own. They'd sat in the opera box with cool indifference. Until Gérard reached for her hand and rubbed his thumb against the inside of her palm—but only while others were watching.

With the buildup from weeks of silence between them before that, Kat had endured enough. She whispered she was unwell and fled the box the instant the call lights blinked for intermission. And before Gérard could protest, she slipped out to their auto to wait in the cold.

The silence between them extended now to the drive back to their flat.

Kat stared out, attempting to subdue the riot of frustrations coursing through her as raindrops cried down the window and smudged the Paris streets into a watercolor world beyond the glass. It seemed to be what Gérard favored too, the watching instead of talking. Always contrived and calculating instead of genuine. He'd braced his elbow to the window frame with fist anchored to chin, as if intent to hold his ground.

Each backed into their respective corners. And both wary of the other all the way home.

"I ran into Monsieur and Madame Allmand in the lobby," Gérard pronounced from behind his hand.

"Can we not call them Xandre and Mimi, even when we are alone?" Kat glanced in her side vision, finding his profile unaffected through the shadows. Even if his jaw did seem a bit tense.

The flashes of memories came, of him in a Police Nationale uniform instead of the smart tuxedo he wore now. But this Gérard was older, more mature as the postwar years had passed. With a clean-shaven jaw and the distinguished note of silver at his temples, even with the lack of the streetlamps. The few lines at the corners of his eyes were not unpleasant, on the rare occasion they softened with a smile while at a party or social event. And those golden eyes that rarely looked her way now seemed distant, as if in possession of some private pain he often visited but never shared. It had become the contradiction Kat couldn't untangle between the memory of the captain and the singular man who now sat next to her.

"My apologies," he muttered, after a long silence. "I was simply trying to update you on our progress."

"And what is that?"

"Probably not what you're thinking. I meant only that Mimi is too dear for her husband. And it is going to take more concerted effort to ease Xandre into giving us anything useful."

"I thought it was useful to learn he'd been visiting the coast at the Baie de Somme. Inquiring about real estate so close to where you live cannot be mere coincidence."

"I don't believe it is either. And he'll trip up, even if he doesn't realize it. Because Xandre thinks himself clever enough to fool everyone. And it will give us an advantage if we're willing to wait for it."

"I see." A pause, and her thoughts shifted tracks. "And what of you?"

Gérard's shoulders stiffened against the seat, as if she'd taken him by surprise. Perhaps he thought she was asking if he, too, was hiding something?

"What about me?"

"Surely you've learned something about the rumors against you, after a month of parties with government officials packing the guest list. I'd wager you don't particularly enjoy attending a ballet or the opera. It doesn't seem the type of evening you'd favor unless you were certain there would be a return on your investment."

He nodded, as if she knew him well enough to judge, and a tick of ease returned as he leaned back against the seat.

"I managed to survive the *épuration légale* trials in '49 based on the testimony of La Marquise, but her word can only last so long. With *indignité nationale* the main offense in being a former Vichy police captain, my solicitor believes the Courts of Justice are building a case. And if what I've learned is true—that Xandre is planning to testify against me—then it's strong. Unless I can provide proof against what appears ironclad accusations of collaboration." He paused. Let out a lengthy sigh. And added, almost as an afterthought, "It's finished. So I ought to take in all the opera I can while I'm still free."

Kat sighed too, over the same set of questions always on the tip of her tongue. She'd wanted to ask about Gavin. Perhaps whether Xandre had said something about him at the opera. Or that terrible night at the château when they'd hidden the weapons. But she'd only just realized how high the stakes might be for Gérard.

"After Gavin's disappearance, I pored over articles about liberated France, reading anything I could get my hands on about what was happening here. It didn't sit right that those we know helped us might be unjustly pulled into the mire of it all." Kat paused, not mentioning of course that she had also searched for Gérard's name and somehow felt relief that she'd never seen it in print. "You do want me to testify? I mean, that is why you married me?"

"We will see if it's necessary. Though I think Xandre suspects something is amiss between us, even if his wife does not. She's convinced we're in love."

"What did you say to them?"

"The truth. That you were unwell and we'll call it an early night." He shook his head then. And a chuckle escaped his lips.

"What is so funny? Certainly not your pending prosecution."

"Non—it's that you are playing your part well." He turned to look at her. "So well, in fact, that Mimi is positive you must be with child."

"Oh . . ."

Thank heaven it was dark and there was an inch-thick separator between their back seat conversation and the driver, or else the whole city could have seen the blush burning like fire on her cheeks.

*That* was not a topic they'd discussed.

Never even come close to discussing it since saying "I do." And certainly it was nothing to consider when all between them had been a business transaction. From the little caresses on the small of her back when he led her to a dance floor, offering his hand to help her from a car, or the tiny kisses Gérard would press to her wrist—their intimate interactions were only ever when others were watching. And even those owned a measure of detachment Kat could discern meant neither of them desired a real marriage behind closed doors.

Kat cleared her throat over the mortification. Calmed nervous hands from fidgeting in her lap. And with as much an unaffected tone as she could muster, she looked straight ahead when she responded, "And why would she think that? Besides that I was ill tonight, of course."

"Because she said she's never seen you happier."

"Happier?"

"Between the luncheon at Michaud's, your outings across the city, and your first class at Mrs. Child's flat, she says you are in heaven. Or seem like it. You have taken to cooking as if you've been doing it all your life. And in her words, have managed to charm the entire class with your passionate nature and intuition in the kitchen. But you are not just happy, are you? You've found something to distract you. Perhaps something to make you smile again. Naturally, Mimi's understanding of a bride's new life is that the groom must be the catalyst of all her smiles. As opposed to what is actually supplying them."

"Certainly you don't suspect anyone is . . . supplying any such thing."

The auto might as well career off the side of a cliff to follow where this conversation was going. Kat didn't dare try to reason with him. To try to confess her fidelity in an arrangement that, to his own words, was a means to an end for them both.

"I'm not trying to embarrass you, Kat." He paused, his words laced with humor. "I was talking about cooking."

"Cooking?"

He turned. Those eyes gazed on her, twinkling a shade too much. "Oui. Cooking. What did you think I was referring to?"

Heaven help her when he allowed a rakish smile to meet her from across the bench, something Kat had not been entirely sure he was capable of, at least not unless they were on a stage. They might have been a couple on an awkward first date someone else had set, not a man and woman who'd once placed their lives in the other's hands and, by some miracle, had survived.

How could they pivot from the memory of all that to . . . small talk and smiles?

"I was merely trying to talk to you. Even though we've known each other a long time, if this is going to work, we must have some measure of trust between us. I know I broke it at the party, and I am sorry for that. But I'd like to earn it back if I may. However that might be possible."

"We knew each other once, a long time ago," she qualified, instinct pulling her mink stole up to cover her right shoulder after it had slipped down. "There is a difference. And questions that linger even today."

"You're right. Of course." He nodded. And braced his arm against the door when the car slowed to a stop in front of their apartment building.

Neither moved. Not to go inside, and not even when the driver came back and opened Gérard's door to let them out. He simply asked the driver to wait and yanked the door closed again. Then turned back to her.

Kat glanced at their poor driver, holding his umbrella against the rain. And tried not to note the little hitch of breathlessness that seemed to come from nowhere and announce its presence in her middle. "What are we doing?"

"Do the other wives know how well you can cook? Or that you were trained by a Paris chef during the war?"

"Non. The OSS was another life for me. As far as Mimi and the rest are concerned, I simply went away to work like many women did during those years. I could have been a Rosie with my rivets for all they know. Some in Paris seem able to recount war stories, but I don't talk about those years now."

"But if it would help, would you talk about it? Do you want to?"

Hiding for one's good and outright deception were two entirely different beasts. Though in this—the secrets she'd not yet been ready to trust him with—they felt very much the same.

"What's to say? I don't know what, if anything, Xandre has told Mimi about his past association with us. But if you want me to remain in her confidence, I'd prefer to keep war talk at bay unless she brings it up. At least for now. I'm not one to give up the cards in my hand to anyone on the first deal. Probably not on the hundredth either. Distrust has saved me too many times to abandon the armor now." Kat swallowed hard, not wanting to say what she knew she must. "I don't trust anyone. Not anymore."

"That's what I thought." Gérard opened the door again but this time stepped out to address the driver. She could not see all of their conversation, just that he'd given the driver an address: "To Rue des Saints-Pères, s'il vous plaît."

The driver nodded, and she could read his lips offering a "Very good, sir."

And Gérard slipped into the back seat beside her.

"You thought what?" she demanded when the engine revved to life again, and the auto turned around to head back toward the Seine. "What's going on?"

"There's something we need to see."

They crossed over the Seine again at the Pont de l'Alma and slipped through the streets back to Saint-Germain, where the auto stopped in front of a café not far from Michaud's, with a glowing marquee: *Le Comptoir des Saints-Pères*. It was a charming 6th Arrondissement eatery known for its French classics of *soupe à l'oignon gratinée*—onion soup—and perfect pairings of French charcuterie, pâtisserie, and the sweetest dessert wines France could offer. It was rumored to be an unforgettable haunt that some of the cooking-class attendees had lauded. But how he knew Kat had wanted to stop by, had even thought maybe she'd take an afternoon and go there on her own, she couldn't guess.

Incredulous, Kat stared up at the marquee, the rain pelting through the glow of streetlamps, and the warmth of a cozy dining room beckoning from behind the drizzle on street-facing café windows.

"What could you possibly want to see here?"

"You," he said, whisper soft. "And I should like for you to see me, with no one else watching us. Or judging our every move."

Gérard didn't wait for the driver. Instead, he flung the door open on his own.

Stepping out on the curb, he opened an umbrella and, with one nimble hand, buttoned his tuxedo jacket. Then extended his palm and waited, as if he'd just requested Kat to join him on a dance floor. Save for there were no high-society couples to convince this time. No Mimi and Xandre watching to see if she would accept. Everyone else was still sitting under dimmed lights at the opera house; there was no one in the world to care what they did in that moment except them.

"I'm not asking for anything but a conversation, Kat. You won't trust me if you don't know me. The man who brought you to Paris is not the one you think you knew all those years ago at the château."

"And if I believe I already know him?"

"You might be surprised. There must be a hundred cafés in Paris." Gérard shimmied his hand in front of her, as raindrops pinged his palm. "Come on. If it takes that many dinners to reveal our hands to someone, then we might as well start now."

# CHAPTER 12

18 August 1943
Château du Broutel
Rue, France

"We found Célène."

It was the very last thing Manon had expected Dominique to say.

He'd left a note in their fish delivery that morning, asking for an urgent meeting that afternoon at a new place closer to the château grounds. But rather than journey to the dunes this time, Manon had set out with a seagrass basket and a cover story to go foraging. She came across their meeting point at an abandoned groundskeeper's gîte buried in a wild, unruly part of the woods.

Thank Providence the posted warnings of electrocution were far worse than their actual bite. Dominique's instructions noted that the electric current had long since been cut and Manon could slip through a barbed-wire fence at the back of the grounds. She'd find a gate left unlocked, which would allow her to pass through. And were Manon to be stopped by any patrol along the way, it would be easy enough for the chef to explain herself with a foraging basket in hand.

They stood behind an abandoned groundskeeper's gîte now, tucked in a shadowed alcove between the structure's crumbled side and the bramble that had grown thick around a rock wall. Birdsong twittered overhead. Rays of sunlight pierced the trees. And a breeze toyed with webs of ivy that covered an opening in the rock wall, where Dominique kept a watchful eye on the bend in the road that led to the village down below.

Manon had left her uniform behind and instead had worn a forest green frock and a thick plait that drifted over her shoulder, the braid woven with the scarf she'd worn to the dunes. She shifted the basket hooked over her arm so she could brush a stray lock of hair the wind had lifted to her cheek, finding it took her a few seconds of absorbing shock just to register what he'd said.

"Célène is here? How is that possible? And after all this time?"

"She's not *that* one. This is a new agent who was found yesterday, in the orchard rows near Le Crotoy. We've not been able to speak, but I have seen her. Henri said he came upon her just in time and was able to glean enough information to make the switch with her identification papers. So she is safe from Gestapo inquiry, at least for now."

"Is she British?"

He shook his head. "American. Though we know she has similar skill to the last one, with languages and intelligence. And if the state we found her in is any indication, a similar grit to other operatives in the field."

He must have heard from the Americans then, to know who the agent was and what her skills were. Regardless, this was good news, even if it added a layer of risk to their present activities. The benefits of having an agent in the kitchen would certainly outweigh any mounting caution. To have an OSS operative who could listen in and translate German conversations and a capable souschef who could share in Manon's duties of the kitchen too . . . It would free them up to make more message drops in the village. And give Manon the trusted confidant she'd been looking for alongside Valens.

Her mind flew through the dinner preparations. There was much she could use help with, starting with Valens' pâtisserie. This news might be the godsend they'd needed.

"I'm relieved to hear we have found our replacement. Should we expect her soon? We have a dinner tonight, with many officers coming in. I can't tell you what this will mean to us to have her help."

After seeing Dominique's features darken, unease flooded in. He diverted his gaze, enough that Manon knew he could not possibly be that fascinated by the ground at his feet.

"What is it?"

"It's going to take some time to get Célène here. She was injured in a parachute drop." He sighed, braced hands at his hips, and stared down at his shoes as if pained. "And is badly hurt."

"I'm so sorry. Has she seen a doctor?"

"She has. But the last I've been told, she still has not regained consciousness. And it will be at least another week after she wakes before we could consider moving her. Perhaps longer, with a serious wound to her right shoulder. We can't risk transferring her and having Reich officers come across her in the kitchen only to question how she received such an injury."

"But you said she is safe."

"She is, to a point. We had to leave her at Captain Fontaine's cottage."

Unease turned to terror in a blink. "What? But you cannot leave her there, at the Vichy police captain's home!"

"It is the only way."

"What on earth was Henri thinking? The captain will surely ask questions. He will arrest her. And then whatever happened to the first Célène will become this second one's fate. And ours as well."

"I won't let that happen. And Henri didn't have a choice. Captain Fontaine was in the delivery truck on a ride to his home along the coast. An OSS plane crashed in front of them, not far from the orchard where Célène was found. Henri scarcely had time to come up with a plausible explanation before they had to get her to a doctor. Under the circumstances, she couldn't be moved. It would have been far too suspicious."

Manon braced finger and thumb to the bridge of her nose, thinking through possible ramifications. What it was to be under the captain's watchful eye Manon understood. But to be under his roof? Where he kept umpteen weapons and could have Vichy police or—because of the high-ranking names at the château—even the Gestapo parading in and out any time of day? It was horrifying to think of the girl's pain and suffering from injury, let alone the flood of panic the homeowner's title would bring on top of it all.

"That poor girl . . . to be in the same house with a monster."

"Whatever the captain is, he was the one who saved her life. That ought to count for something."

"I don't know what when he's one of *them*."

"Even then I assure you, this one is not a poor girl." A slight glimmer of hope took over his face. "Only myself, Henri, and Xandre know who she really is. Though you may inform Valens she can be trusted. The Yanks have delivered; she's exactly what you've been asking for. Except maybe for one small thing."

"What is that?"

"She can't cook."

"You cannot be serious."

He nodded, with something of pity in his eyes. "Not even to save her life."

The dread that had swept through Manon moments before returned now, to an impossible degree. She nearly dropped her basket when the realization landed, and she had to set it on the ground at her feet or risk losing the meager harvest of cèpe mushrooms she'd found. "I can guess what you are thinking. But it is impossible. You cannot learn to bake, to butcher, or to prepare pâtisserie overnight. I am a chef, not a magician."

"But you can teach her the basics of what she needs to know. Just to make her believable in the post."

"There's far more to French cuisine than that. The Vichy police will know she doesn't belong. Or, at the very least, my staff will. They are always watching and they will see. This could be infinitely worse than having no operative at all."

"An OSS agent is selected because they are skilled, intelligent, and resourceful. I'd stake my life on this: she will prove sure in your kitchen just as she will anywhere else." He paused, then the ghost of a smile pressed back to his lips, like that day they'd met at the dunes. "And I've no doubt if you're the one teaching her, Célène will learn fast. And with great skill."

"You know me so well to say such a thing?"

"I do, if tinned fish in the larder is any indication. In any case I've brought a peace offering. No fish this time. But it's a gift I hope you will accept."

Dominique retrieved a muslin pouch he'd concealed under his coat and transferred the sturdy bundle to her waiting hands. Manon untwisted the fabric to find a rich and nutty aroma inside— the buttery seeds a prize long forgotten in their world.

"Pine nuts?" She brightened, offering an unconscious smile for such a rare treat. "We haven't had these for ages. Where did you find them?"

"At the dunes. The pines are full of them if you know where to look."

"But it must have taken you hours. Just like the fish. You spoil us."

It had been mere weeks since the deliveries began. But already in that time, Manon had found a quiet comfort in Dominique's presence. There was a measure of safety when he was near, as if a watchful eye held her from harm even from a humble fish market stall in the village, or with a simple glance from across the château courtyard. And of all the days that had managed to meld together in a string of miseries since the war began, there was one Manon held back as dear—both in secret and in the hidden corners of the heart she'd thought long would not beat again.

She'd not shared with anyone how that visit to the dunes had lifted her spirits. Maybe not even with herself until this very moment. And she certainly couldn't make heads nor tails of why a muslin bag of pine nuts warranted such a burst of joy, but she didn't want to stop smiling.

"I don't know how to thank you—"

"Manon . . ." He cut her off, his whisper pained as he removed his flatcap and turned it over in his hands. "Things have changed. I won't be able to make deliveries at the château for a while."

The first thought to bridge her happiness was anxiety, that perhaps they'd been found out. But then Dominique wouldn't have been standing here, his crown and beard tipped by the sunlight streaming through the trees as he could offer nothing else to say on it.

Disappointment ravaged her. What was once a secret place of solace now made the dunes feel as though they were slipping away.

"Why? Captain Fontaine does not suspect anything, does he?"

"It is not because of the captain. And I wish I could say more." Dominique looked back to the road for a breath, less like he was keeping an eye out for an auto but instead was avoiding telling her the truth.

"I know. It's better if you do not."

"Oui. I don't want to put you in any more danger than we already have with courier visits to the village. I admit, I'm more relieved than I can say each time you step back out the doctor's door and hand the tin off to those devils in uniform. I've, uh . . . worried about you." He cleared his throat and corrected in a snap. "I mean, all of you. Here. At the château."

"Of course you have."

Though her old life seemed a million tears away from where she stood now, Manon's heart pricked with the notion that something felt alive again. And to see Dominique was disappointed by this turn of events too . . . It meant something. His features were resolute, his eyes calm as he stared at her for long seconds. But a weariness weighted them that she could see clearly this time.

"Henri will get a message to you once we know when Célène can join you here."

"Merci. I appreciate that."

An engine approached, humming beyond the rock wall. Dominique stepped in front of her, shielding her with his back while he checked through the ivy. "That's my ride."

When he slapped the hat back on his head as if to leave, without thinking, Manon reached for his arm. "Wait!"

Not even knowing why she'd done it, before leaving the château Manon had woven the paisley scarf into her plait. Now the fabric seemed to burn against her neck, for wanting to put it in the hand that on softly spoken words had once returned it to her.

"Wait," she said again and, on impulse, unwound the plait and threaded her fingers through her hair so it spilled over her shoulders. Manon pulled the kerchief free and held it out, letting him see her hand tremble against the edges of satin, and the tips of her hair dance on the breeze.

"What if I need to send you a message?"

Dominique stood before her, lips parted but struck with silence. It seemed an eternity while she waited for his answer, with wind toying with the trees, the breaths between them and the hum of the engine the only sounds louder than her heartbeat.

"The village. At the fish market stall," he whispered, and bent to pick up her basket. "We can still accept your messages there."

Ever so gently, he brushed leaves off its bottom with his palm. Then he reached for her hand, the warmth of his fingertips lingering like electricity on her bare skin as he took the token she'd offered. In exchange he slipped the basket to hook over her hand, slide it up her wrist, and secure it in the crook of her elbow, drawing himself close enough with the action to brush back the locks of hair that tried to blow over her cheek.

"And if I wanted to see you?" Manon swallowed hard. This was a step she'd neither expected or sought, but it was happening nonetheless. She couldn't bear letting that cord of connection break between them. "What should I do then?"

His hand chose to rest at her cheek, waiting and wanting too, as he looked back in her eyes.

"If you want to speak with me, you don't need to ask. Just come to the dunes. I'll always wait for you there."

# CHAPTER 13

20 August 1943
1 Rue du Château
Le Crotoy, France

The world was not at war.

Not where the sea air was sharp to the senses and gulls danced on the wind. Not where the sun blazed like fire over the horizon and the sky was so calm one could hardly believe planes existed in the world at all, let alone could fly over such an otherworldly place.

Kat awoke not marooned in an old orchard but to the sight of a wood-beam ceiling, a cozy cottage room, and a thin stone-lined window left open to welcome sea air.

She lay in an oversize wooden bed next to a simple chest of drawers and a stone fireplace, with a faded quilt in a soft cerulean-and-white block print pulled up to her chest. Provençal toile curtains danced in the salt breeze, and the sun painted the sky over the water as far as the eye could see, with the rhythm of waves and gulls mixing with the barking of a dog somewhere in the background. It was sunny. Warm. And wonderful.

Her first thought: *You are dead. A place like this cannot exist.*

And the second, when Kat moved and her shoulder protested with searing pain: *No, you're not dead. You're being tortured.*

She reached up to the throbbing spot.

Her fingertips found gauze wrapped against her bare skin, under a sling braced tightly over her collarbone, and the strap of a knit camisole. The strange surroundings started to become clearer, and she scanned the room: the ceiling, the opposite wall with a generous armoire, the hardwood floor peeking from under the rug at the foot of the bed. A trunk sat there, with her shoes sitting atop. But no clothes. No satchel stuffed with French pocket litter. And no idea where she was as her thoughts turned frantic.

*I need my shoes . . . my clothes . . . a paper knife. Screwdriver. Fountain pen—anything to use as a weapon if I have to run for it.*

*What about my contacts? Can I still hide my eye color?*

A hinge creaked and Kat turned her head on the feather pillow, senses now sharp to the danger she was in.

A Dutch door opened in a mudroom alcove just beyond her room, where a man in a white-collared shirt rolled at the forearms and dark weave trousers paused to set a metal bucket down on the flagstone. He tapped sand from loden gumboots and then had to fight for his balance as a German shepherd nudged its way past and shook seawater from its coat to splatter the walls. He must have scolded the animal because it responded, stilling in the center of the kitchen, then nosed lovingly under the man's palm and sat to wait for the next command.

The man took a tea towel from a wooden butcher block and stooped to dry the animal first, shuffling the linen about its neck and pointy ears and whispering like the naughty animal had still won the prize of his endearments.

He moved methodically about the cottage kitchen, with no action wasted. He draped the tea towel on the back of a chair to air-dry. Set the bucket in a sink and pumped water over it. Lifted an armful of kindling and bent to light the stove in an alcove outlined by an impressive stone wall. And when it seemed he'd realized she was awake and watching, he turned, and golden-hued eyes locked on hers.

It was easier to see him in the light of day.

The man was clean-shaven with a strong jaw. His ebony hair was short and neatly trimmed. He had a brow that, once she got a good look, said he might be trusted. He seemed to own a genuine openness about him as he looked at her—a rare quality in this time and place of the world, to be sure.

Kat scolded herself as remembrance struck. Jeffrey had left her. And someone thrust a rifle in her face.

That was all she'd recalled until now.

As the waves of memories came crashing over her, Kat realized she'd kicked at being subdued in the orchard. Fought when strong arms picked her up and carried her from its orderly rows. Scratched at hands that probed her shoulder when she'd been laid in a bed. She'd even thought, in the sheer madness of fits that had taken over, that Gavin had been there. Watching over her somehow. Telling her, *"Hush, sis! Let them help you."* But Kat slipped out of consciousness again and could only remember one comfort when she'd woken in a state of drug-induced heaviness—those eyes.

Between the rigid cold kicking off the sea and the warmth of the Bordeaux pressed to her lips, Kat's senses had been dulled. And with a fire glowing amber on the bedchamber hearth, she'd slipped in and out of the sleep of the dead. Where no Gestapo chased her. No police dragged her off to be tortured. And no pain dared touch her.

Somehow she knew this stranger had posted vigil next to the bed. And each time she awoke, those eyes were there. Watchful. Afraid? Reassuring. Bringing water to her lips or reading for long hours as he sat alone in the glow of firelight.

The same eyes looked on her with curiosity now that she was fully awake.

"Bonjour." He offered her a slight nod to punctuate the greeting.

"Bonjour," she replied, soft and far too jittery. Then broached the big question: "Where am I?"

"You don't know?"

She shook her head.

It was believable. A woman who'd had an accident in the orchard oughtn't know where she was, especially if she'd been traveling. The admission meant nothing.

"I am Gérard, and you're at my home. In Le Crotoy harbor." His voice was deep but not smooth. And matter-of-fact with a sharpness that said he was used to asking the questions. "And you are Célène?"

"Oui. Célène."

So that memory was true.

Kat had remembered something of a man with a rifle who'd peppered her with questions and repeated a name that was not her own. But perhaps it was hers now, at least for the interim.

The man turned and unwrapped waxed paper that concealed a meager portion of a treasure: bacon rashers. He leveled an iron skillet on the stovetop and snapped a command to the dog dancing around him, who instantly settled again. The man said something else over his shoulder, but Kat didn't know what because he'd turned away. And without being able to read his lips from that distance, she could offer nothing in return.

When she didn't respond, he turned again. "I asked, are you hungry?"

*Hungry?*

After a week of naught but military rations on one side of the Channel and upon landing on French soil, who knew how long had passed since the disaster in the orchard? Hungry didn't begin to describe the intolerable pang that seemed to claw at her core. It was all Kat could do not to tackle the man, shove him out of the way, and fight the dog over who'd devour the rashers raw.

Kat swallowed, her mouth like cotton. "Oui. I am."

"You must be, to have stolen apples that belong to the Vichy government."

"I did?"

"You did. Most people wouldn't have been brave enough to risk pilfering the orchard in the dead of night. Even if it is only a hefty fine if you're caught, to land on the radar of the authorities is no subtle wish." Before Kat could inquire over the fine she faced, or possible punishment, he shook his head. "Don't worry. They won't arrest you. The authorities have decided you went through enough punishment with a tree going through your shoulder."

"Last night . . . I don't remember much. But if I hurt anyone, I'm sorry."

"You think you hurt someone?" He seemed to find amusement in that, his profile softening a shade.

"Oui. In fact, I know I did. I seem to remember biting an arm or—"

"It was my hand." He cleared his throat and flexed fingers a little before he tossed a rasher to sizzle in the pan. "Still works though. And that was nearly three days ago. But apology accepted."

"Three days ago?"

"You've been out for that long."

She reached a hand up to the sling. "What is this?"

"The doctor's been here twice. You were fortunate—no broken collarbone, no punctured lung. But your shoulder will be sore for a while. And he said the morphine will sour your stomach if you go too long with it empty."

Gérard turned to a butcher block. Removed cheesecloth from a boule of crusty bread and held it up. And placed a palm on a wooden bowl of fruit with soft green and ruby skin.

*Pain de campagne and Anjou pears.* Her stomach cheered.

"There's tea." The man turned to her, set a kettle on the stove, and pointed to a leaded-glass window. "It is a fair day, so the doctor should be able to visit again. No doubt he'll be relieved to see you're finally awake."

Kat didn't know much at the moment, but she did know this: They'd missed their drop zone by more than fifty miles. They'd lost their rendezvous with the only contact they had in France. And then she'd lost Jeffrey. Without knowing, Kat had placed herself in the untenable position of making herself dependent on a stranger—one who for reasons unknown appeared to be in no hurry to push her out of his home.

Wincing with the effort, Kat rose to sitting. And found that, mercifully, she was covered enough to be decent.

As if reading her thoughts, he offered, "There was a woman from the village. She looks after my home when I'm away. It was she and the doctor who . . . helped you."

"Merci." Kat nodded, then looked to the door that was calling her to freedom. "I ought to go."

He shifted his gaze to the sling that immobilized her right arm. It was rendered useless. And, in turn, made her statement laughable.

"You're late for something? Or didn't you realize you've been knocking on death's door these last days?"

"Je suis désolée," Kat apologized but still pulled the covers back to swing her legs to the floor. She paused when her bare feet hit hardwood, feeling woozy enough to brace a hand to her brow. "I've a, uh, job. I've promised to begin work and I'm already tardy—"

"Don't worry about that. Chef Altier has given you grace to heal before you report to the château. There is no hurry."

Had Kat muddled the backstory in her sleep? She reran it in her mind: *Your uncle, Jacque Garnier, is a clockmaker in Lyon. You're to rendezvous with him there. And work in his shop.*

"The château?"

"Château du Broutel. Did the employment agency not tell you where you would be working when they placed you?"

"Oui, of course. I'd forgotten the name."

He cut thick slices of the boule with a bread knife. "The chef has been looking for a skilled worker for some time, since the last one left. You bake, too, I understand?"

The key was to stick as close to the truth with every lie. Answer, but do so in a way that revealed nothing of consequence. Avoid small talk and personal details. Go along with any preconceived notions, even if they were false. And, for heaven's sake, do not make him laugh because that he'd surely remember.

"Evidently, enough to have secured the position."

The man tossed a knob of crust to the dog, who caught it in her mouth and swallowed it whole. "You are already weeks overdue your appointment. What is a few more days? The doctor said you should not move yet or you could tear your sutures. And you need to regain your strength or infection could set in."

"Forgive me, but what appointment?"

"Your position as chef de tournant." He paused now, as if curious—with no more cutting—but to her inner caution kept the knife tight in his hand. "Isn't that why you're here? I saw your travel papers, for Célène Montrose. You've been through a full Gestapo check, oui?"

*Think fast, Kat.*

"Oh, oui. Of course. And my travel papers are . . . ?"

"In your satchel. Over there." He pointed the chopping knife to the armoire opposite the bed. "With clean clothes my housekeeper brought. And your uniform. They've been holding it for you until you arrived."

This was not all bad. If Kat could gloss over the inconsistencies, get the clothes and shoes, and her travel papers, it wouldn't be anything to jump out the open window and run for her life. All she had to do was close the door on the man and his knife.

"Merci, Monsieur . . . ?"

Blast—she'd forgotten his name already. Or did he not give his full name yet? Kat would have to refuse any more morphine from now on or remain foggy-headed when what she needed was to think sharp.

"Gérard Fontaine." He ran a hand over the shepherd's head,

stopping to scratch behind its ears. "And this is Bella. But don't worry. She looks mean as a gale but wouldn't hurt a fly, this one."

Indeed. Even though the animal had stretched out on the kitchen floor, blocking the only path to the Dutch door. Kat wasn't sure she was ready to challenge that even if she did need to get out of here.

"Well then, if you don't mind, I should like to . . ." She padded from the bed, hoping to appear as frail as she could as she stopped behind the shield of the door. Though her shoulder did burn like wildfire, he should think her far weaker than she was. He should never dream Kat would run, especially if that was exactly what she intended to do.

"I should probably change."

"Of course. But the doctor said it might pain you to move too much. He should be here shortly to check your bandages if you'd like to wait." When she gave no reply, Gérard tilted his head toward the other side of the kitchen, where there must have been a door she couldn't see. "I'll put your breakfast on a tray. And the bath is just there, first door around the corner."

"Merci." She offered her most innocent smile and closed the door between them.

Kat pressed her good ear to it for a moment, half sure she might hear him cock a pistol on the other side. Struggling, all she heard was the sound of rashers sizzling on the stove and Bella's nails once again clicking on the hardwood floor as she danced about the intoxicating smell of breakfast cooking.

Gérard Fontaine had said it looked to be a fair day.

Perhaps it did to some. But all of that crashed down the instant Kat opened the armoire to fetch her clothes and satchel. If anything, she'd walked into the storm of her life, for hanging next to her clothes in the armoire was the horror of a freshly pressed Vichy police uniform, which meant there was nowhere left to run.

12 *February 1952*
92 Avenue d'Iéna
Paris, France

The hardwood creaked in the hall. Gérard looked up from the pile of papers on his desk to find Kat lingering in the doorway to the study.

"You're still up."

"What time is it?" He glanced at the mantel clock, shocked to find it had ticked over to half past three in the morning.

From the moment they'd returned to the flat from dinner, through dense fog and drizzled streets, Gérard had fallen headlong into research mode. By the time he'd loosened his necktie, unbuttoned his collar, and rolled up shirtsleeves on his forearms, the desk seemed to fan out with endless files and Gérard had forgotten all else.

"I lost track of the hour." He started tidying up the mass of papers. "My apologies if the light kept you up."

"I was awake."

Kat hadn't asked to come in.

In truth, Gérard liked that. She'd assumed the study door was open to her. It was, of course, but she'd still eased through on her own.

Drifting in with a porcelain dessert plate in her hands, she surveyed the space as if discovering it for the first time. And maybe she was. Gérard didn't know what rooms she favored when he was not at the flat. Whether she'd seen it before, Kat surely took it in now—the high coffered ceilings and Baroque-style fireplace, the gilded portrait hanging over the mantel, a horseshoe of furniture framing the focal point of the room. Ivory built-ins lined the walls with books, and an oversize mahogany desk had been tucked by the windows. It was where he sat and where her gaze finally rested after circling the corners of the room.

She walked over, set the plate and golden fork on the edge of the desk, and slipped into an ivory wingback opposite him.

"What's this?" He gazed at the cut-triangle dessert hemmed in by a gold-embossed rim.

"Banana tarte tatin we made in class. Mrs. Child sent it home with me. It's never as good on the second day."

"You're offering?"

"It was mine, but if you're hungry . . . go ahead. There's more in the kitchen." She leaned her cheek against the side of the wingback as if comfortable and, as she preferred to do often, turned to watch the embers burn down on the hearth.

Gérard tried not to linger on—or at least not admire—the vision of the woman sitting before him. And certainly not feel his breath quicken as she ticked a glance to his bookshelves, as if she wished nothing more than to thumb through the spines and discern his tastes.

For some reason, he wanted her to.

While many Parisiennes still wore black, American expats had swooped into the city with bright, nipped-waist frocks, and chic chapeaux. Yet Kat sat in the gentle glow of firelight without poise or pretension, as though she'd just stumbled out of bed. Her glossy brown hair was knotted at her nape. She had bare feet. And dared to sport the more risqué Parisian trousers and a simple red shawl around her shoulders to ward off winter's chill.

No more was she the young Célène who'd been dropped into the orchard and had flirted a little too close with death. And in the days that followed, of her healing in the bedchamber he'd given up, and of Bella abandoning her place by the sofa to instead sleep at the foot of Célène's bed . . . They'd spoken very little. Kat had not been dispirited or panicked as he'd have thought one might be in her position. In fact, quite the opposite. She'd improved quickly, kept an unyielding gaze with those ice-blue eyes, and was keen to learn once transferred to the château kitchen. And Kat appeared in control of her emotions regardless of the state of affairs she found herself in.

The woman before him now owned that characteristic steel resolve yet was much changed at the same time.

Kat now went by her real name, which suited her. She still favored reading but had also taken to fine food and the Paris friendships she was forging, even in a short time. And she likely hadn't a clue of the beauty she'd matured into these last years since the war. Nor that the glow of firelight against her cheekbones made her more alluring than a Parisienne in a couture gown could ever be. It was in the quiet moments though—on a dance floor, at a dinner party, or when Gérard might find her sitting by the fire in their flat—that Kat was given to heavy sighs or gazes that said she was lost in some secluded place. Even for the conversation between them and the private dinners they'd frequented as of late, she was battling some sadness he didn't know how to allay.

She didn't trust him enough to share it. And he hadn't the faintest idea how to breach that wall she'd built around herself.

"So you went to class? Anything new from Mimi?"

With a firm-lipped grimace, she shook her head. "And you?"

"Just what we discussed at dinner," he offered truthfully, and ran a weary palm through his hair. "Timelines and bits of information about Xandre's movements since the war. From the château that night of the Christmas party, he goes on- and off-grid until the end of the war. There were stays in Marseilles. Lyon. Rouen. Portugal and Spain. And I can't find anything on him from 1948 until he showed up in Paris a year ago. And even then there's little information until Mimi splashed onto the scene. It's as if he's afraid to be tied to one place for too long."

"He does not strike me as a man who fears much. But I do believe he fears that. What do they say—when a man shows you his character, believe him? Xandre would have to keep moving, if only to avoid being discovered for who and what he truly is."

"Or for the trail of sins buried in his past."

Kat's glance snapped back to his and he knew he'd hit a nerve. Though what it was, she wasn't revealing.

"Especially in this case. Xandre had covered his tracks well by the time Mimi and her family's money came into his life. I thought I could get through more of this tonight . . . maybe connect the dots. Find what it is I'm missing." He gathered up stacks to drop them back into the bottom drawer but pulled the telegram out and left it on the desktop. "I keep going back to this."

"What about it?"

"It doesn't make sense. If Xandre sent you that telegram, why? Just to goad you back to France? He could search for answers without your involvement."

"Maybe. What if he's looking for Gavin too? And knows that no one would fight harder for answers than his sister?"

"But why would he care if Gavin is alive?"

"Maybe that's the question."

"Right." Gérard sighed into it, letting the questions linger. "In any case, I suppose it'll keep until tomorrow."

"Will it?" she whispered, then turning back, looked at him for long seconds.

Gérard stopped cold. With half the papers buried in the drawer and the others still in open folders before him, he braced elbows on the desk and laced his fingers together over them. "Is there something you want to ask me, Kat?"

Those ice blues froze him with their coolness as she considered.

One question could take them in too many dangerous directions. Why had Gérard worked at the château? Why had he continued to don the Vichy police captain's uniform, even when he could not bear to do the enemy's bidding? Why hadn't he fled France after the war like so many others had, preferring instead to return and prove his innocence against claims of collaboration? Or why, after all this time, could Gérard not forget the face looking at him with such intensity now?

"Let me guess. All this time, you've thought me a torturer? You think I ordered men to their deaths? Or suspect I raised a pistol and did the deed myself?"

"War is war; it brings out the worst or the bravest of men. And we all do things we regret."

"I know. I regret many things, most of which was not being able to stop the executions in the village square that day. But I assure you, I did not do the worst of everyone's imaginings."

"I know that."

"Do you?" He palmed the remaining stacks of papers on the desk. "Because all of this—letters, timelines, telegrams, and train tickets—it means nothing if you believe the rumors about me."

"I said I would give a testimony, and I will. At any time."

"My solicitor says we are not quite ready for that. At least you won't have to lie under oath though, if you have doubts. Seems you're off the hook for now."

Seeing her face soften puzzled him. Those eyes broke contact with his. And her lips parted as if to say something when she tore her gaze away, only to be pursed again when she changed her mind.

"Go on," Gérard invited, expecting the worst. "Whatever you want to ask, I can take it."

"You misjudge me. I saw your face that day at the executions. Even then I could see what happened cut just as deeply for you. You are not an executioner. And it was confirmed the night of the Christmas party. You did what you had to in order to help our team. I didn't understand then . . . but I do now. You could have turned me in at any time. Still, you didn't. And I haven't forgotten that fact."

"Is that what you're asking then, why I didn't turn you in?"

Kat shook her head, then flitted her gaze to the open drawer.

"Non. I want to know why you haven't shared this with me. You said you wanted trust between us. But what you've offered is to fund our lives in Paris in what amounts to a handful of dinners and mere pieces of a story. I don't ask for more than we're willing to share; we both know where we stand in this arrangement. But as for the search into Xandre's past, to finally find out what happened to Gavin, and to form a defense for you . . . I am not wired to play second team."

"You want more."

"I do," she said, firm. "If we're going to find Gavin, I want it to be because I've fought just as hard as you have. I'm capable enough to dig for answers. So let me."

"Fine. What do you want to know?"

"For starters, tell me who you are."

Gérard looked to the fireplace, to the mantel and the portrait hanging over it. A raven-haired beauty in a pale yellow gown stared into the room with a soft gaze that spoke of happiness from summers spent by the sea and contentment when she'd sat for the portrait. She was serene. Forever young. And lived only in his memory now, the place he did not allow others to freely go.

"You asked me once about my family."

"Oui. And I believe over a café au lait and plate of pastries you confirmed that you now have a Paris wife, a brother-in-law last seen somewhere in France, and a kind father-in-law married to a troublesome mother-in-law, the latter who is invited to remain in Boston just as long as she wishes."

He tried not to smile. "I did say that."

"Because it is true." Kat rewarded him with a genuine smile in return.

"Before the war, my, uh, family was my mother." He tipped his chin toward the portrait. "I have no siblings. And my father was a distant man, so when I was young, she and I spent much time together away from him—at the cottage, in Le Crotoy. After my mother's death, my father sent me to school near her ancestral home in Britain. He died not long after leaving me sizable estates there and here in France, that if I'm honest, I haven't the foggiest idea what to do with them. That's pretty much the whole of it."

Kat lingered on the painting, but her gaze drifted back to him for a breath. "I'm so sorry. A child should never have to lose a parent."

"It was a long time ago. But La Marquise de Longvilliers had become friends with my mother here in France. When she feared the Nazis would invade, La Marquise thought we could help each other. It was she who secured my post at her Château du Broutel very early in the war so I'd be in place with the Vichy police who ran security on the grounds. And she has proven a staunch advocate for me in the years after. If not for her, I believe I'd have been arrested in those first few months after liberation. And who knows what would have happened?"

"But you weren't. And you won't be now. Not if we can do anything to stop it."

Kat's gaze lingered on the portrait for long moments, all through his declaration and in the silence that followed. She'd raised her fingertips to her shoulder, in that little absent-minded move that said she might be thinking on her own scars as she listened to his.

"What was her name?"

"Madeleine. And I think she knew somehow that her time was coming, when she gave me a gift not long after she got sick—a shepherd. We spent endless hours on the beach after she died. It seemed the only place in the world that made sense somehow."

"Bella," Kat breathed out with a soft smile of remembrance and turned back to him. "I wish she were here now."

"In this flat? That dog would tear down the walls to be stuck inside instead of chasing gulls on her beloved beach. She was a faithful friend for years. But then, you could have guessed that."

"And you?" Kat asked, a frankness in her gaze as she looked back in the firelight. "What do you want to know about me?"

He ticked his head to one side. "When did you lose hearing in your left ear?"

"I might ask you how you knew. Or when. But . . . from birth. I've never known my life but as I've lived it. Like this. It seems everyone else sees it as a sort of deficiency, when to me, it's all I've ever known. I hardly think about it until someone brings it up."

This was risky, drawing Kat in. Trading smiles. Sharing memories. About his mother. And Bella, the beloved shepherd who'd been gone for years now. About secrets and the lives they'd lived. And if at the end of this thing they'd go their separate ways, telling her more than he'd shared with any soul before could prove a fatal mistake. Who could believe the Vichy captain who was so by the book at the château, and detached from the world since, actually had a very real heart beating in his chest?

That is, if she chose to believe it.

"Well, if we're to be partners in crime, Madame Fontaine, then we have a serious problem."

"Which is?"

Gérard looked to the dessert on the desk and the lone fork shining gold in the firelight. "There's only one fork. And I don't give up dessert that easily."

"Non," Kat countered, and revealed the second fork he hadn't realized she'd held. She placed it with a golden *clink* next to his on the plate. "There has always been two. You just didn't know it until now."

Few things in this life surprised Gérard. Even fewer people. But with Kat, all bets were off. He'd known it that first night when she'd fought the paratrooper injury that almost claimed her life. She couldn't remember what he did when she'd opened those searching blue eyes and stared up at him for the first time. In her terror and her pain, Kat had grasped out for a lifeline, found his hand, and held on as she'd asked him to stay. So he did. For two nights he'd sat by the bed, held her hand in his. And now, years after that first touch, Gérard still hadn't been able to walk away. Not really.

"I'll trade what's in this file for half of that dessert."

She used an index finger to push the plate across the desk. "Then I have real questions. Starting with why you think Xandre's telegram is not just some lure to draw us into a trap. The US government declared Gavin missing and then legally dead in 1947. I want to know why you think he could still be alive."

"You wouldn't believe me if I told you."

"Try me."

He picked up a fork and cut a bite off his side of the tart. "Because, Kat, you haven't given up on Gavin yet. And if you haven't . . . then I can't either. If you have one shred of hope left, it can be my hope too."

The early morning hours faded between them as they talked about everything and nothing and polished off the rest of the tarte from the kitchen, until the sun began its slow rise over the mansard roofs of Paris and the fire had smoldered to ash.

While Kat went to bed to catch a few hours of sleep before her cooking class that morning, Gérard had taken their dessert plates back to the kitchen, washed and dried the dishes, and had to open nearly all the cabinets to find the proper place to tuck them away. He flicked off the remaining lights as he strode down the hall. And for all the beauty of connecting to another in a simple night spent together and a bitter-cold Paris sunrise peeking through the drapes as he passed her door, Gérard hated himself all the more.

His wife couldn't know that the answers she so desperately sought—the same secrets he would die to keep hidden from her—were only one wall away . . . behind the heavy bolts of his locked chamber door.

# CHAPTER 14

4 September 1943
Château du Broutel
Rue, France

There were few more chill-inducing sounds than the unannounced rumble of jackboots coming down the stairs in the middle of a high-ranking Nazi dinner party happening upstairs.

*It's just a drill.*

*It must be a security drill . . .*

The captain must be overseeing security measures for the party. Oui, Manon had to calm her thoughts. And still remind herself that it was not uncommon for the kitchen staff to endure extra checks, especially with the frequency of packed guest lists.

The château had short notice on this night, however, that it would entertain a host of some of the Reich's most revered names. The lack of notification had been a security precaution to take it down to the wire, and for the last hour, a steady line of sleek automobiles sporting swastika flags had rolled through the front gates. Though the Gestapo would not arrive in occupied France as a commonality, fresh waves of their uniforms had arrived with high-ranking officer after officer, including the man rumored to have been at the helm for the slaughter of thousands across Europe—the chill-inducing SS chief himself, Heinrich Himmler.

Manon couldn't keep a pit from forming in her stomach when

she'd been handed the demand of producing an upscale dinner with inadequate time in which to prepare it. Since then, it had been all they could do to take in specialty items shipped directly from the rail lines to their kitchen, culminating in a seven-course autumn menu of stuffed squid; duck pâté en croûte; *soupe de courge musquée*—a hearty garlic-infused butternut squash soup; the Baie de Somme's specialty of lemon sole; roast pheasant with zucchini relish; a fruit, cheese, and nut board; and fig tartlets with cinnamon frangipane and crème fraîche.

But no sooner had Manon sent Frédéric and the other footmen off to the dining room with sterling aperitif trays than the footfalls descended, and the Franc-Garde accompanied by the afeared Gestapo swarmed her kitchen with Walther pistols drawn.

*Alle halt! Halt!*

*Aufhören!*

Activity ground to a halt.

The few who spoke German understood and froze in place. For the ones who didn't, it took little to discern from the shouts what was meant. Steam rose from abandoned saucepans. A kitchen timer pinged in the background. And knives were dropped to the counters with a chorus of *clang clangs* as the kitchen brigade raised hands on air and nervously peeked out from their stations.

Manon's chest rose and fell in time with her wild heartbeat as she held firm in front of her staff. Captain Fontaine had arrived at the château but was engaged with security at the gate. It left her as the lone leader to face the Gestapo, the only support in a glance she shot to Valens at his pâtisserie station in the corner. He gave a tiny shake of the head, begging her not to move. Telling her without words to stand firm. To wait and see who they'd come for.

Pity that was not how Manon was wired.

Nor was it the reason that while the rest of Paris fled south away from the Reich's advance in 1940, she and Valens had moved north and applied for the post at the château. It wasn't to stand back but to step up. In any way they might fight the overlords who'd taken their whole world from them in Paris and had layered miseries upon the world in the years since. It seemed that this war would end not because of the big battles the Boche celebrated upstairs, but because of any one person's willingness to battle them in secret downstairs.

"What is the meaning of this?" she demanded, her head held high.

"*Zurücktreten!*" a man in a Gestapo uniform snapped.

"But we must be allowed to—"

"He's telling you to step back, Chef," a voice interrupted, in French. "They are the authority here. I would do as he bids."

Manon looked to the service door leading to the starry-skied courtyard.

Captain Fontaine filled the doorway with a slender woman about Manon's age, positioned in the half shadow at his side. She wore a chef's coat and plain chignon, held a toque blanche in one hand, and presented an air of calm sustained by striking blue eyes that searched the room. She stood in stony silence as if merely curious instead of terror stricken like the rest. Regardless of what had just exploded in the middle of their dinner preparations, it seemed neither the captain nor the stranger was caught by surprise as the kitchen staff was.

"Thank you, Captain. But I would ask that you tell them we have a dinner to prepare. And unless they wish for SS Chief Himmler's meal to arrive cold . . . on . . . his . . . plate"—she slowed, nearly spitting the words for emphasizing the last syllables to the nasty horde of Gestapo staring back—"we must be allowed to proceed unobstructed."

Captain Fontaine entered the kitchen and rattled something off in German to a Gestapo official out front with the most litzen on his collar. They engaged back and forth for brief moments. Manon looked to Valens as her breath hitched in her middle, he looked back with equal apprehension, and she wished now she knew enough German to follow what they were saying.

It wasn't until the captain nodded and pointed out Valens' corner that her breath caught, almost choking the air right out of her lungs. And to her horror, the captain stepped back to allow the uniforms to have their way.

A butcher knife shone on the counter nearby, mere inches from Manon's grasp. She felt her fingertips curl around the hilt and drag the blade against the counter in one expert swoop as the Franc-Garde soldiers pounced. But she slipped it down, hiding it at her side just as fast, when she realized they did not seek Valens but . . .

*Franz? Our sous-chef?*

"What is the meaning of this?" Manon demanded, shouting in French.

All to deaf ears.

The sous-chef had only made it midway from the larder back to his station when the kitchen had been swarmed. He'd frozen in place, and the Franc-Garde surrounded the poor man now, tearing the crate from his arms so it tumbled into a crash of ice and fish to the parquet tile. His glasses went flying as he sputtered cries in French, asking—What had he done? Who'd reported him? How could they, as he'd committed no crime!—and encircled his wrists with steel manacles before dragging him away.

Captain Fontaine extended an arm before the woman in the chef's coat, to ease her back and let the authorities pass. The rest of the staff stood by, glancing back and forth between the door and Manon, stunned and barely breathing as their sous-chef disappeared into the night.

Only after the last pair of jackboots left through the courtyard door did the kitchen seem to break from its stupor. Poor Frédéric bounded down the stairs and stared, wide-eyed, in the aftermath. A neglected pot boiled over and sizzled on the stove. And Manon glanced at Valens for a breath, her thoughts pinging so fast she wasn't certain she could find her voice.

"Back to work, everyone," Manon squeaked, then turned to Frédéric. He would unleash a mountain of questions unless she gave him direct orders to focus on their tasks. "Take up the fish course now, s'il te plaît. It has already been plated."

To his credit the lad seemed to understand.

He nodded, sidestepped the captain, and swept over to Franz's empty station to silently instruct the footmen to carry on with him.

Never had retaliation emboldened Manon so as she stood there gripping the knife hidden at her side. There seemed no surprise the Reich would not author, no evil that should not be expected of them. And even without explanation now—as was their method of brutality—she had to wonder . . . who was next.

"Chef?"

The captain's voice broke Manon's composure, and she spun, ensuring the knife was concealed behind the fold of her chef's jacket. "What is it, Captain?"

"This is your new chef de tournant, Célène Montrose. We have already seen her through a full Gestapo check. I just assured the commander of this, and he will not trouble you further." He gestured with his hand to present the uniformed woman behind him. "This is Chef Altier, head of the kitchen here. She will see you into the fray."

"But my sous-chef . . . Why have they taken him?"

"We will see about finding you a replacement" was all he replied.

The captain stared back, the coldness she knew him to possess belied only by the clenching of his jaw. He did not go on. Rather, he turned back to the courtyard and stalked off, disappearing with the Gestapo into the inky night. And left the untested addition to their staff standing there awaiting Manon's expert instruction, when all she could do was try to endure the wave of relief that crashed once he'd gone.

The woman did not wait to be invited.

"It is good to meet you, Chef. I'll just take this and get started," she said, matter-of-factly, and reached over, deft in exchanging the chef's hat she'd held for the knife clutched in Manon's hand.

Looking over a crate of produce nearby, she inquired of Manon, "Shall I prep for you, Chef?"

"We have this in hand. The dinner is all but ready to go up. So if you should like to settle into your room instead . . ." Manon cleared her throat. She turned to face the wall and clamped her eyes shut, trying to calm her racing heart. And defied tears from daring to squeeze from her eyes.

They'd come so close this time.

Too close.

A mere breath from disaster, as she'd been sure Valens was the one who would have been taken. And Manon hadn't fully understood until that moment what it could mean to lose the one person on earth left who was tied to the loves she'd lost.

Tears glazed her eyes as she continued. "It's up the service stairs, um . . . on the top floor. The ladies' quarters are to the right. Our room is the last door."

The woman seemed to unpack the moment. She squeezed in next to Manon, nodding here and there for the benefit of any eyes that watched them, making it look as though the chef was instructing her in the ways of their brigade de cuisine instead of shaking in her shoes from the adrenaline that had emboldened her just moments before.

"I should like to start work now. If that is agreeable?" And inclining her head closer to Manon's, the woman lowered her voice to a deliberate whisper. "Have you noticed any wine is missing?"

Had they? She tried to think back.

"Some, I suspect. Oui. But that was weeks ago. I'm ashamed to admit we've been under a cloud of activity, and I haven't inventoried stock in some time. I thought it was my error in accounting and meant to go back over the numbers."

"Wine is missing. That's what the Gestapo commander told the captain. The sous-chef has been identified as a proprietor of goods on the marché noir. Apparently he's been pilfering the Reich's wine from the château and has been attempting to sell it on the outskirts of the village. The Franc-Garde had been brought in to arrest him for it, now that a witness has come forward to say that he is operating an illegal black-market business."

"Our wine . . ." Manon's heart thumped harder, like a rock rising and falling in her chest.

They'd been so careful, so intentional to keep track of the labels so they shouldn't fall into the wrong hands. But what if Franz had seen something? What if the sous-chef had unknowingly passed Resistance messages from the château to the wrong eyes in the village? Or worse, what if he'd learned of the messages and would report them all to the Gestapo for Resistance activities? Severe questioning was surely to follow now that the man had been arrested. And heaven help them, but what would he say?

Though Célène's explanation of what occurred did little to assuage her fears, Manon nodded, especially when Valens had gone back to plating fig tartlets with a complexion whiter than a ghost's.

For the first time she considered the possibility that Franz could have something to do with Valens' illness. But what? Now that he was gone, perhaps Célène could slip into the fold and all of those fears would cease. Dominique's request came to mind then, when he'd advised that OSS agents were selected for their skill, intelligence, and resourcefulness. Manon dared hope if she should be called upon to give this woman cooking lessons, it just might become the answer to all of their prayers.

This new Célène had proved she could handle herself, even in the few moments she'd been there.

"Are you certain of this?"

Célène nodded. "Quite."

At the next thought to terrify Manon, she said aloud, "Who is the witness?"

"They did not say. Just that one has come forward in the village. The sous-chef has been denounced as a thief against the Reich. I cannot think that good news for him."

"But how do you know all this?" Manon asked, noting Célène's position had been adjacent to the door—much too far away to have overheard. "The captain was not speaking loud enough for anyone to hear."

"Let's just say I've been hired to help in this kitchen in any way I can." Célène gave her a pointed look as she placed the knife on the counter between them. "And I intend to use every weapon we have in order to do it."

# CHAPTER 15

28 September 1943
Château du Broutel
Rue, France

From the first nail-biting moments in the château kitchen, Kat had been thrown to the wolves.

Coupled with pretending to possess a skill at which she was not yet at novice level and the chef's ardent advice to keep a wide berth from the officers in their midst, the first days Kat had been at the château proved an education. Weeks into her position, she was running on pure luck and gut instinct to know how best to blend in.

Being thrust into the foundations of cooking began with identifying tools. Learning how to chop veg without losing a finger. How to deglaze a pan, debone a chicken, and fillet a fish. She could discern the difference between a full-puff and rough-puff pastry. And it seemed now they were muddling through the vast mire of French sauces . . . at a snail's pace.

Manon projected efficiency with a cool head and sure hands. That came as no surprise; Kat could have believed the woman could chop down an apple tree and have it prepared in bite-size pieces by teatime. What she did not expect was that Manon possessed a tender heart for those under her direction, even if not entirely sure of their allegiances.

Her orders were calm but firm. And always followed. Her words were kind. And her attitude no-nonsense. She expected excellence from herself just as much as anyone working alongside her. And so believed Kat could retain the encyclopedic knowledge she tossed out at the speed of light—no small feat when one was tested on the nuances of a bavarois, a *crémeux*, a *crème diplomat, crème chiboust,* and something or other called *crème mousseline* . . . All were varieties of French custard that to Kat looked, smelled, and seemed to curdle in just the same manner.

"Non—not yet. Keep whisking," Manon cut into Kat's thoughts with a tap to the wrist when she'd made the fatal error of slowing her whisk over a warmed copper pot.

She sped it up again. "Like this?"

"Not faster, but . . . even. It is the same as the mirepoix we made yesterday. No matter the ingredients, you cannot rush excellence. You need slow, even heat to release the flavors. And you must give the pan consistent attention. If you do not respect your roux, it will burn on you."

"I thought I was, you know, doing all of that."

They were fortunate that the scent of buttery croissants in the air provided a believable excuse for the early morning cooking lessons. They could stand over a stove while the pastries baked—Manon teaching and Kat failing almost everything—but if caught, they could fall back on the convincing excuse that it was simply early prep for the officers' breakfast.

The lights were dimmed and the kitchen still asleep, as they'd risen hours before any of the other staff. Blackout curtains were drawn. Deliveries were still half a morning away. And they had the added security of Valens providing watch while sipping tea and pretending to read a newspaper in the servants' hall just around the corner.

Should anyone come downstairs and discover them, they'd have warning and a credible cover story. Now it was just for Kat to wrangle this roux before it got away from her.

"Let's go through it again. The five 'mother sauces' are?"

"Right. The roux—equal parts fat and flour. Whisk until your arm falls off or it will go lumpy." Kat winced inside at the ache in her shoulder. Who knew chefs needed biceps of a Greek god to endure preparation of a French staple? "There is the velouté, espagnole, *tomate*, and . . . béchamel. And you would add hollandaise to the list. Though, if I'm honest, that one still slightly terrifies me."

When Manon didn't respond, Kat looked up from the roux to find the chef's gaze fixed on some point beyond the wall.

"Was that right?"

"Oui. It was." Manon exhaled on a breathy sigh. But shook her head just the same. "And I am sorry."

"Sorry for what?"

"Dominique warned me what a task this would be."

"Did he? And how could the gentleman judge my culinary abilities without knowing me?"

"I suppose your organization gave fair warning of your skills. Nevertheless, you are doing quite well. Just as he predicted. But I only saw this through my eyes—how difficult it would be to teach an understudy from the ground up. I did not consider what all this might be like for you." She lowered her voice. "So far from home. And in such a dark place as France has become."

Clear-eyed and open, she glanced to Kat's shoulder, that still had a slight lump from the bandages Manon helped her change in their servants' quarter room each day. "I'm sorry for it now."

"Don't be. I chose this. Same as you."

Kat tried not to think of the ten years she'd aged in the nail-biting weeks she'd been in France. Nothing could have prepared her for what she'd experienced already. And if it meant learning a few basic cookery skills, it seemed a small task in the larger sea of what might be helpful to them should she succeed.

One tiny, unexpected thing in the midst of it? Kat liked cooking. And the way Manon instructed her in it.

"You mentioned Dominique. I have not met him yet, but I have the others who make deliveries: Henri and Xandre. I understand they are with the local Maquis." Kat tossed a furtive glance over her shoulder, double-checking they were alone. Then continued with her real question. "They've told me not to trust the captain who oversees the delivery schedules. But . . . are you certain of his loyalties?"

"I wish I was not. While he's not shown himself to be as brutal as they are, he does collaborate with the Franc-Garde and Vichy authorities and, by extension, the Reich officers within these walls. You saw that on your first night here. He stands back and allows them to pass by, to do as they may. He takes their orders and carries them out. That is as bad as pulling a trigger himself."

"What orders are these?"

"Whatever they demand of him, I'd wager."

The times Manon and she were alone in their service staff bedchamber at night was the perfect time to share information. Kat had been schooled in the rail shipments and regular deliveries, the wine labels, their arrangements for passing correspondence to the Maquis in the area. Who could be trusted. Where to go for help in a pinch. About the safe house at the dunes. And they'd even discussed the orchard and Captain Fontaine's cottage. And how they'd play their parts for subversion while at the château.

It was exactly what Kat had imagined of France when reading reports behind a typewriter in Birch's office. This was where she could be most useful. And she knew in her heart of hearts it was the best chance to glean information on Gavin. Last reports were he was somewhere in Northern France. If that was true, Kat would take every advantage—including learning the art of French sauces—if it aided her mission to find him.

The conflicting hints of the captain's loyalties, however, she must set to one side.

"Henri and Xandre will arrive with deliveries today?"

Manon flitted a glance to the shadow of the stairs, dark and mysterious now with only the clock ticking in the background. Even though they were talking in code, Kat had to appreciate the ongoing caution. It gave her confidence in Manon's abilities as their leader and in their safety overall.

"They will. We have a delivery of fish coming. And provisions arriving by rail. Though those are nearly always inconsistent."

"And Xandre is still the liaison for these rail deliveries?"

"Oui. You've probably already learned that the captain keeps a tight ship on the delivery schedules and the goods coming by rail. And save for the occasional . . . hiccup, like you witnessed the night you arrived, our duties run like clockwork. We much prefer it that way." Manon eased the copper saucepan off the heat. "I think this is done. It is a blond roux, so it can go longer—up to ten minutes to give it the desired nutty flavor. But a basic roux should not take more than five. Just enough for the raw flour to cook down."

"I wish I could say I can see all that." Kat stared at the creamy mess and just couldn't understand how it could be the anchor of France's gastronomic prowess. "It's just not as impressive as the croissants."

"Maybe they prove that in any meal one should add copious amounts of butter. No matter what it was in the beginning, it will turn out all right." Manon glanced up at the clock. "We should have about five more minutes on the croissants before we—"

A loud clatter echoed from the hall, followed by the shattering of a teacup and a harrowing *thump* a split second after. Their glances shot up, one to the other, a scant second before Manon dropped the whisk and bolted toward the door. Kat swiped up a knife from the counter along the way and trailed behind.

Manon reached the servants' hall first. "Valens!" She ran, throwing herself on the floor next to the man. Kat followed, shoving the overturned spindle chair out of the way as they knelt on either side of his body writhing at the foot of a long center table.

"Valens? What is it?"

"Je suis désolé . . . ," he apologized, whispering, "Julian . . . ," as he groaned and wretched, vomiting on the newspaper that was fanned out on the hardwood floor.

"Who is Julian?"

"His son. He's dead." Manon tried to undo Valens' chef's jacket at the collar, but he protested, clamping his eyes shut as he hugged his stomach.

Kat hid the knife on the underside of the table lip, just in case. Then gave a gentle pull to open the man's eyelids, finding them glassy and the pupils unfocused. He crinkled his forehead in pain and pressed the side of his face to the floor as he wretched again.

"I'm not a doctor, Manon. I don't know what to do."

"Neither do I," she cried, and if it were possible, her eyes begged to be wrong more than her words. "Can you go for a doctor?"

"There is a doctor in the village?"

"Oui. By name of Rousseau."

"I know him." Kat breathed a sigh of relief. "Can he be trusted with this?"

"Oui. The doctor is safe—" Manon dropped her voice to a cryptic whisper. "His office is in an ivory building with a red front door. It is next to the chapel. Adjacent from the square. If you go there and tell him what has happened, I know he will come."

Kat saw the desperation in the chef's eyes as she patted Valens' cheek.

War was not for the faint of heart. Nor was it for the reluctant. Decisions must be made. Even if instinct was followed, survival was not assured after. And while this was not the first time Kat had been thrown into the fire at breakneck speed, the original strategy to climb out the captain's seaside cottage window and run for her life had been abandoned.

This could be another of those flashpoint moments that could have a ripple effect on either side.

"S'il te plaît?" Manon begged again, tears trailing from her eyes. "He means everything to me."

"Of course I will go," Kat whispered, and stood to leave.

Though when she'd braced a hand to the hardwood, her palm landed in a puddle near the stove. And she'd almost tripped over a hefty ceramic jug overturned on its hidden side facing the wall. Kat turned to find its contents had spilled in a wide, dark amber half-moon on the hardwood and sopped up two corners of the newspaper.

"What is this?" Kat sniffed the jug. The woodsy scents of apple and walnut and deep fermentation met her nose with a fierce slap, and she drew it away. "Could this be alcohol poisoning?"

"Non. He doesn't usually take spirits, but . . ."

"He must have taken it up. If he is struggling with his son's death, perhaps? He wouldn't be the first to find solace there."

"It's not that. I have seen this jug before." Manon swiped it out of Kat's hand and, as if on a mission, knelt to crawl on all fours and search the tile near the stove.

"And?"

"And it won't help to explain now. But I believe we may have found the culprit for his illness."

"Chef? You don't think . . . actual poisoning?"

"I wish I could be certain." Manon knelt for a moment until she found a cork shimmed under one of the stove's cast-iron legs and stood again.

She corked the jug and, with panic building in her eyes, cast a glance around the deserted hall. To the shadows clinging to the stairs. And to the windows that faced a courtyard behind blackout curtains. As if all had eyes and watched them, even then.

"Just go, Célène. Tell the doctor what has happened. And bring him here?"

"I don't know if I should leave you."

It was admirable of the chef to care about her staff so. But as she'd taken the jug in hand and did her best to help Valens rise to his feet, Kat jumped in on the other side, anchoring under his shoulder. Walking him to the foot of the stairs, she watched as the depth of feeling in Manon's features grew, saying she was pained far more than simply for a leader and employee. This man, whoever he was, meant a great deal. It hastened Kat to be quick on her feet.

"I can get him upstairs. But take my bicycle; it will be faster. It is locked in the larder. The key is on the back wall, slipped under a barley barrel."

Kat nodded. And stripped out of her chef's jacket to the simple stone-blue frock she wore underneath.

"I remember passing the village on the way here. It can't be more than 3 kilometers. I could be there and back in a half hour. Twenty minutes if I hurry."

"Here." Manon plucked her navy cloche and rain trench off the peg in the hall. "Take this. The Franc-Garde may already be in the square. But we look similar enough that they won't think anything if they see you and believe it is me, even in the dark. Just keep your head down. Go with confidence, straight through the square to the doctor's door. They will not stop you."

"I'll be back as quick as I can."

"And Célène?" She caught Kat at the elbow, drawing her back. Manon's chin quivered when she squeezed her fist around the jug handle and added a tearful, heart-wrenching gaze. "I told you not to trust the captain. I hate to say it now, but if you should meet Dominique at the fish market stall, whatever you do . . . do not trust him. Don't trust anyone else until we know for sure who is on our side."

⌒

12 *March* 1952
81 Rue de l'Université
Paris, France

"The meat must be dry before you sauté," Julia noted to the gaggle of ladies who'd gathered in the Childs' third-floor kitchen for their

Wednesday morning class. "If you don't pat it dry, the meat will steam instead of sear, and you lose that wonderful flavor. Remember: This must be classic technique."

The class had been invited into the Childs' multistory Paris flat, known affectionately by its shortened address, "Roo de Loo."

Kat stood among the ladies who were enamored by how their instructors—and for her, particularly Julia—allowed their culinary passion to be on full, winning display. Julia wore her usual uniform of a polished yet functional skirt, a button-down blouse in flint gray under a kelly-green cardigan with mushrooms embroidered on the lapel, a navy apron tied taut round her waist, and their cooking school badge proudly pinned on the front.

As Kat and Mimi were the only ladies under forty-five years old, it was no surprise the latter's pink cocktail apron and cool wasp-waist frock stood out. With that exception, the rest had followed the route of serviceable but respectful attire; there was room for only one ruffled apron and strand of pearls amongst the lot.

It was comforting—and a surprise—to find how similarly Julia's hands worked as Manon's once had. Swift yet safe. With skill and purpose. She patted the brisket dry, made quick work of slicing it into hefty portions, and talked the wives through as she dropped the flanks to sizzle and sear in a pan of hot olive oil.

The aroma of fine flavors sealed the air. The Childs' cat, Minette, had drifted upstairs from the second-story salon and circled the ladies' feet now as the happy chaos of cooking and conversation reigned.

"Here. Let me help." Kat squeezed in shoulder to shoulder with Mimi at their wooden chopping board. Angling the blade's side against her knuckles, she used her hand as a guide to chop carrots while still curling her fingers out of the way. "See? This way, you don't worry about slicing your fingers."

"I shall never understand why there must be a methodology for every tiny movement in the kitchen."

"You get used to it. Then before you know it, it's second nature."

Kat gave even, slow chops before speeding up. "And you get faster over time."

*Chop. Chop. Chop.*

Kat ran her knife through the carrot and onion on the butcher block. Set them in neat piles in a flash. And moved on to give a rough chop to the remaining elements for their bœuf bourguignon.

"C'est bon. You keep going on with that and I'll just organize this . . ." Mimi crossed her eyes a bit, staring down at the list of ingredients. "Where are we again?"

"We have bacon, onion, and carrot. A half dozen garlic cloves," Kat noted, and moved on to peel and mince those next while they cataloged. "Then pearl onions. Fresh white mushrooms. Our spice is here . . . three pounds brisket over there . . . We've also beef stock, tomato paste, bullion, butter, and bay. And the olive oil is in the crock by the stove."

The stove boasted an enormous space in the Childs' third-floor kitchen, opposite a wall of windows in a multistory flat that was homey but extravagant in size and flamboyant in style.

The master kitchen was on the third floor and chock-full, with a Magnagrip magnetic cutlery strip, cookware lining the walls, a soapstone sink that ran only cold water (and they'd learned, did not work at all when pipes froze in winter), a shelf holding an impressive number of stewpots and stockpots, and a pirates' horde of gadgets, including Julia's beloved Daisy can opener and copper pots and pans that gave the space they were cooking in now a Byzantine glow.

"That's it." Mimi tossed their list, allowing it to flutter across the counter as she flounced in a high-back chair. "There are so many ingredients it might as well be a new volume of *Moby Dick*. I am exhausted. Where's the wine?"

"It's not as bad as all that." Kat chuckled under her breath, holding judgment as her friend peered around for witnesses, then took a generous swill from their bottle of Merlot without getting caught.

"Easy for you to say, teacher's pet."

"Why do you say that?"

Mimi dropped her voice to a playful whisper, eyeing their enigmatic host as she used tongs to turn browned meat in the sauté pan. "You can do no wrong in Julia's eyes. I'd go as far as to say she is smitten by your passion for putting produce under the knife. Seems rather murderous if you ask me."

Kat smiled to herself, thinking of how the much younger Célène wouldn't have believed that in a million years, nor that her hands could work as fast and efficiently as they were. And certainly not that her heart could swell to be back in a kitchen.

What would Manon think of it now, this little society under the tutelage of Julia Child? Manon should be here instead of Kat. Yet this place was the home and classroom the ladies had been invited into, and every moment she spent in it felt golden. It wasn't until she looked up from her mince and realized Mimi had been watching that the magic moment fizzled and Kat came back to the now.

"What are you thinking?" Mimi asked, then walked her fingertips over to the edge of the cutting board. She tapped an index finger to the wood. "I know. It's that handsome monsieur of yours. Oui?"

Kat shifted her stance and tried to refocus them. "Can't a woman enjoy herself without a man being behind it?"

"Of course. There is wine. And galette for dessert. But it is more fun if there's a monsieur behind your smile, non?" Mimi kept tracing her finger on the edge of the cutting board, teetering a mushroom back and forth with a perfectly manicured index nail in cherry red. Her attention faded, and she stared down as if transfixed.

"Mimi?"

"Have you ever wondered . . . ?" She stopped. Sighed. Swiped her hand back and stood, pressing imaginary creases out of the front of her ruffled apron. "Well, do you ever think of . . . ?"

"Do I ever think of what?"

"Someone else? I don't mean to make you feel uncomfortable. It's just—" Mimi stopped and looked up, her eyes meeting Kat's. And her whole visage softened. "I look at you. And you remind me of him sometimes."

"Who?"

"Your eyes—they're so similar. The same shade of blue. I've not forgotten."

The string of words clicked into place in Kat's mind, and she set the knife down on the board. "You mean Gavin?"

Mimi nodded, and bless her but those pretty eyes were tearing under their winged liner, and her pink lips were quivering a shade.

This was not chatter. It was an opening—but to something far different from subversion. Kat could not weasel her way into Mimi's affections as she'd promised Gérard before she left their flat. Not when Mimi's gaze was so wholesome and her face registered a deep hurt that was rebounding from somewhere Kat couldn't nail down.

It had been the goal of course: Find out what Mimi knew that could be helpful. Where did she meet Xandre? When? What were his plans while in Paris? Did they exchange letters? (Documentation.) Did they have old photographs? (Connections to associates.) Did Xandre have his own money, or was he spending hers? (Dry finances led to the best clues.)

All manner of things could be gleaned. And useful.

But this? Tears? Emotion? And having them both rocked by the one name that Kat could not subdue in her own heart? If she wasn't careful, she'd find herself crying into their stew and downing swills of wine alongside her friend.

"Gavin taught me to swim. Did you know?"

"No. I never knew that. But it sounds like him."

"We were at a beach party and I wouldn't get in the water. Gavin couldn't stand seeing me sit by the bonfire all alone. So he took me out. And spent the entire afternoon helping me until I'd learned how. He was like that."

"Fearless?"

"Yes." Mimi let a little laugh escape her lips at the thought. "But also unfailingly kind. Too kind for this world. I was deeply saddened when I'd learned about his death. I am so sorry, Kat. The war took so much from us. From all of us. But I still cannot believe it took him."

It was enough raw sentiment to claw at Kat from the inside out.

She felt her middle retract, winding tight. And her eyes mist. She breathed in deeply. And gave attention to the recipe, the ingredients, the sight of the other ladies prepping their meat for the pan at Julia's stove—anything to turn the conversation around to something she could possibly endure.

Mimi stared off in the distance for a breath, to the windows where streams of sunlight illuminated flecks of dust dancing on air. And the cat stretched itself on the sill now, pawing at and nosing the glass while looking to the street down below.

"I loved him, you know."

"What?" Kat did turn at that.

Mimi gave a little flutter of her hand, as if waving it off. "It was nothing—a schoolgirl crush. We've all had at least one of those in life. And Gavin never did anything improper. I think the only time he ever touched me was to save me from drowning under a rogue wave. How romantic. But that's both the tragedy and beauty of love, isn't it? By the time you learn what love isn't, it's only then you real-ize what it might have been. Maybe what it should have been."

"Mimi . . . what's wrong?"

"When I saw Gavin at a party one night in the summer of '43, it turned out to be the day before he left. I came to every one of your maman's parties after that, hoping I'd see him. And I never did."

A flood of memories came rushing back. Of Gavin standing in the garage the night before he'd left for the OSS. Asking for the compass. Chiding Kat for her bare feet and sleep-induced blowtorch attack when he'd come from a party with a rumpled tux and the weight of the world on those broad shoulders.

"I've gone back over it in my mind, Kat. For years. Wondering. What would have happened if I'd asked him to stay that night? What if I'd just been brave and told him how I felt?" Her voice stalled, hitching on emotion. "I may not be standing here now."

"None of us can say that for certain. But rekindling yesterday's choices is a luxury we don't have. I still wish I could tell you what happened to him. I wish I knew myself."

"Bless you," Mimi cooed. "Of course you do, Chérie. All of us wish that."

A vise squeezed inside Kat's chest.

There was truth in what she'd said, far more than her friend could know. Between unconfessed feelings and reality lurked a little something like torture. The questions of what might have been would inevitably stack up against the disappointments of yesterday. Decisions could not be undone. Regrets became untenable. And for the one whose love remained evasive or whose pain was left unchecked, this was a prison from which one could not escape.

Kat knew it. Felt it burning within her. And, for the briefest of moments, could not untangle why, when thinking of a complicated or unspoken love, her mind produced an image . . . of Gérard.

"How could you fall in love with someone you hardly know?" Mimi shook her head then, tossing sculpted blonde waves as she sniffed and pushed back misty tears with an energetic smile. "C'est la vie, right?"

"What's brought all this on? It's not Xandre, is it? Or the summer home on the coast? Is he treating you well?" For the life of her, Kat could not clamp her mouth fast enough.

Mimi's brow creased. "Who is Xandre?"

"Mrs. Fontaine?" Julia chirped with her pleasant air, calling their attention to the stove. "Can you bring your bœuf? We are almost ready for you."

"Of course." Kat painted a quick smile on her lips. "I'm sorry, Mimi. I must have remembered his name wrong and—"

"That man." Mimi waved off Kat's misstep and took up the knife to aimlessly chop. "He has lived a hundred lives before Paris. I'm sure he has a few names back there to match. He told me about that kerfuffle during the war and the authorities' questions after it. I'm just relieved they finally saw truth and will leave us alone to go after the real culprit."

"What kerfuff—?"

Mimi let out a pert but potent, "*Ow!* I told you," Mimi muttered, though more knowing than actually upset as she gripped her finger, now dripping bright red. "I am *une disaster* in the kitchen."

"Don't worry. We've all had accidents." Yanked out of the moment, Kat sailed into action, helping Mimi over to the sink to stem the flow of blood under cold water. "Here—let's see to this."

Kat reached out, quick in unbuttoning the petite pearl cuff at her friend's wrist, in hopes of saving the ivory satin from bloodstains. She stretched Mimi's sleeve up before her friend could protest. And for every hope and dream and definition of love that had passed between them, her heart sank to see the unmistakable outline of fingertip bruises marring Mimi's porcelain skin.

# CHAPTER 16

28 *September 1943*
Château du Broutel
Rue, France

Manon was convinced a woman was never as strong as in the moments she could single-handedly muscle a loved one up three flights of stairs.

Fear was the constant companion now, as Valens did not give the usual fight for her wanting to help. Instead, he'd slung an arm over her shoulders and mumbled incoherent words in reply to her questions about the jug. And as she battled to keep them both upright, he dragged up each step so she had to readjust the weight to keep going, taking far longer than she'd anticipated.

Time was bleeding thin.

It wouldn't be long before the officers' breakfast must be on the table. To have a chef absent at this time could be disastrous. Blessedly, Manon had the presence of mind to stow the jug where no one else would find it and had swept up the shards of porcelain from the broken teacup. The remaining hope now was that Célène would return soon. The doctor would indeed be able to help Valens. And by some miracle, it wouldn't be known in the kitchen—nor under the scrutinizing gaze of the captain—that anything was amiss.

"What's this?"

"Oh! Frédéric." Manon's shoulders sagged in relief when the footman bounded around the corner on his way downstairs, nearly crashing into them. "Can you help me?"

The boy took an immediate cue and slipped in to shoulder one side of Valens' body before he crumbled down to the floor of the attic landing. With wild eyes Frédéric shifted his glance from their leader to the obviously ailing pâtissier, questioning without words even as he helped muscle the poor man along at a faster pace.

"He is unwell."

"That's obvious. Here." Frédéric led them down the hall the direction of the men's quarters. "We can put him in my room—first door. It's closer. And private."

He turned the knob and kicked the door wide. They carried Valens to the cot in the dark chamber and eased him down in a heap upon the mattress.

Manon stood breathless for a moment, shock rebounding as she caught her breath. Frédéric rushed over to close the door behind them, then flicked the light switch by the door, washing the plain room in a glow of light.

Valens lay still, his color woefully pallid.

"Is he breathing?" The footman approached the bed.

Manon knelt at Valens' side to check him over. Thank Providence his chest rose and fell. But he rolled to one side on instinct and cradled the pain in his middle as he seemed to slip out of consciousness. This could not be good at all.

"Oui." She nodded, as Frédéric filed in at her side. "Barely breathing. But he is."

The footman leaned over Valens, too, angling to check the man's head and body, then pulled back arms from his torso as if looking for a bullet hole or wound somewhere on his person. He found nothing—just a pâtissier who looked strangely at peace, even while fighting for his life.

"What happened?"

"Just what I told you. He is ill."

"Is he?" He rose from kneeling to move toward the door. "Someone should report this."

"I've already sent Célène for the doctor."

Frédéric stopped cold, giving Manon a double take that said he'd not expected that. "Célène? She was awake this early?"

"We were up working in the kitchen. And she had been baking with Valens."

"With Valens . . ."

"Oui. And when he fell ill, I sent her to the village straightaway. She's to come back with the doctor as soon as possible."

This was the part Manon had to judge rightly. How much information would be wise to share, and with a young man who had no idea of their ongoing activity with the Maquis?

He eyed Manon, staring back with a frankness—and perhaps acute interest—she'd not seen in him before. "Tell me again. What happened exactly?"

"We were preparing breakfast and he collapsed. That is all I know."

Frédéric tipped his brow, as if confused. "But where was he then? Not with you in the kitchen?"

"Non. He was in the servants' hall."

"Is that so?" He crossed arms over his chest, staring at the poor figure in his bed, then peered back at her. And waited. For long seconds—*too long.*

The young man was bright; Manon knew this well enough. But beyond "bonjour" and *"bonne nuit,"* and "Take this service tray upstairs," they'd rarely spoken. And she could discern little of his manners. It became clear in that instant that Manon did not know the people working with her well enough. Nor had she stopped to consider how the young footman might have been helpful, and long before now.

"We must tell the captain."

"What?" Manon shot to her feet, then crossed the room to stand in front of the young man. She lowered her voice to a steady whisper, trying to exude authority while keeping their conversation hushed from any who might pass by in the hall. "There is no reason to do that. I am certain Valens will be all right if we can get the doctor to him soon. The captain would only suppose we're telling him because we suspect it's something other than illness."

"And is it?"

Rebounding, she asked, "What do you suggest it would be?"

Frédéric glanced over his shoulder to the door and the silent hall on the other side.

It was as if he also expected someone to be listening, maybe even coming for the ailing pâtissier even in that moment. He, too, must be aware of the precarious position they were in, with officers taking up every bit of breathing space in the château. And with the guest list chock-full of illustrious names of the Reich that turned over with regularity, he could not ignore the ominous undertones of their situation.

"Chef," he said, voice lowered to a cryptic whisper. "You couldn't know this, and I take my life in my hands by telling you, but some have begun to suspect staff here at the château."

"What?" Manon stared back, hoping the mock surprise she tried to paint over her face would read as genuine. Save for mention of the captain's suspicions—which was new information—the rest had been bang on.

"Prepare yourself for a shock. There may be the Maquis working among us."

"Surely not. Captain Fontaine would not believe that we have been infiltrated by the Resistance. Not without notifying me."

"But what if there is something more happening here? Healthy men do not just fall flat. Not without reason. Valens may have witnessed something. Or he may be a part of something himself . . ."

"What are you saying?"

"We ought to go over the captain's head and notify the Franc-Garde. Immediately. And allow them to sort this out, like they did with the sous-chef."

Manon swallowed hard.

All of a sudden, she realized this young man had been far more in tune to château activities than she'd given him credit for. She didn't fear for herself—his eyes were not threatening as they looked from her to Valens. But Manon did wonder what he and the captain had discussed before. Or how a certain jug had somehow made it from a high shelf in a Resistance safe house at the dunes to spilling over the servants' hall floor at their Reich-occupied château.

"Chef, how well do you know Célène?"

*Oh no.*

Her heart sank.

Through his innocence, this boy had landed on the truth—even if by accident.

Célène was not who she'd claimed on the surface. But then, neither were Manon and Valens. And all she could think to do now was to divert this boy's attention by bolstering the one asset they had: The captain trusted Célène. And if Manon could ensure that fact remained, surely everyone else would too.

"I know her well enough," she rebuffed with a flat tone, though inside, her middle had gone to mush. "She has been a model worker since her arrival. I have no reason to question her, especially when she has passed a Gestapo check. And she was brought to us by the captain himself. Surely you do not accuse him of anything."

"Not at all. But that's just it." The boy took a cautious step forward. "The captain does not let our chef de tournant out of his sight."

"What do you mean?"

"He watches her—keenly. When he thinks no one else is looking. And he remains close. Always appearing around corners when she is nearby. Lingering during deliveries she accepts. And even once staying in the kitchen the entire time you were gone on an errand to the village. He remained back out of our way but always kept her in his sight. I know. I've had my suspicions and was there to witness it."

"Did he?"

"Oui. And what's more, Franz's arrest was not coincidence. I think the witness who came forward against him might have been connected to Célène in some way. That maybe his position was conveniently vacated so she could come here, to work amongst us. And for who knows what dark purpose."

"Those are very serious accusations."

"I know. It is why I've remained quiet. And I wouldn't bring them up now, if not for this. I believe the captain may suspect she is not who she claims." He looked to Valens with pursed lips, resolve washing over his features. "We cannot take a chance this château has a saboteur right here in your kitchen. We must report this to the Franc-Garde."

Reporting suspected activities to the Vichy police captain was one thing. But to inform the Franc-Garde was to poke a sleeping dragon. There was little to do now but agree. At least that would buy them some time, and once Célène returned, together they could figure out what to do without the Boche cocking pistols against their heads.

If Manon must be put to the test with the captain, so be it.

"I believe you are right." Manon gave a firm nod. "For Valens' sake, we must follow protocol and notify the captain first. Go and fetch him at once, please. And then he will decide what action to take with the Franc-Garde."

Assuaged for the moment it seemed, Frédéric straightened his livery at the waist, turned to the door, then slipped out into the darkened corridor with a determined chin held high.

Manon stood in the center of the room for long seconds, trying to calm her racing heart as she considered what in the world she might have just done. She dragged a spindle chair from the corner over to the bed and sat. Then reached out for Valens' hand. Held it. And dared to hope beyond hope she was both wrong about Dominique and right about the captain.

In a world of spies and saboteurs, you never knew whose actions you could trust . . . unless it was a man who was falling in love with a woman when he thought no one else was looking.

# CHAPTER 17

28 September 1943
Place Anatole Gosselin
Rue, France

Rain cried from the sky as the bicycle tires spun along the village road.

Thunder snarled overhead and leaves blustered around Kat as she pressed her head into the wind, the punishment warning that autumn had arrived. Village lights had long since been doused against the threat of planes in the sky, and without the benefit of daylight yet, she had to do her level best not to fly off into a ditch. The tires splattered mud puddles, spraying her one uniform skirt, socks, and shoes as she pedaled. But as long as she could get to the doctor in time, it would be worth it.

The one thing that puzzled Kat was that the château security had not stopped her at the gate. Even for kitchen staff running out to the village at an ungodly hour, the uniforms under Captain Fontaine's authority did not appear interested and allowed her to pass through the gate with little more than a wave. Though uncharacteristic, she took it as a triumph that saw her down the village road. And no matter how it arrived, she was grateful for the good fortune if it led to saving poor Valens' life.

The country road soon faded to cobblestones that bumped beneath the tires, and Kat slowed up as the outskirts of the village came into view. Medieval streets appeared, twisting and turning in a dark maze, with tight pathways of row houses and closed shops on each side. Windows were shuttered here, too, as if the village were locked in sleep or safety. The few autos she saw were parked—one, a Franc-Garde paramilitary truck that gave her shivers, and the other, an old model Renault that was half tarped with a canvas shroud and little sprigs of weeds growing up around the tires.

A stray cat tipped a discarded sardine tin and darted across her path, its half-starved calico body rattling Kat as it fled down the street. She gripped her hands to steady the handlebars, regaining her balance.

Thinking it would be wise to dismount and walk from here, Kat moved on, wheeling the bicycle to a clearing at the far end of the street. The view soon opened up to a square with a central fountain and wide expanse of cobblestones, and a market that was just waking up for morning. Precious few shopkeepers tooled about their stalls, setting up stores of apples and root vegetables, fish and pitifully thin game birds, and foraged herbs that were not on the long list of rationed goods, all under the hush of a fast-fading darkness.

*There it is.*

The little ivory building just beyond the chapel doors sat like a ghost beyond it, the rain and fog hanging low so only the red door shone stark through the haze. Kat wheeled past the chapel, stowed the bicycle in the metal rack, and trotted up to the door, taking the stairs two at a time.

She pounded a fist to the red wood with a call through the door of, "Bonjour? *Le docteur est là?*"—asking if the doctor was in—and listened for stirring to respond behind the portal.

*Nothing.*

Trying again, Kat knocked. She kept her voice low and watched blackout fabric at the windows to see if it moved at all. And this time she took the liberty to jiggle the doorknob, finding it locked and the door bolted firmly in place.

Flitting a glance over her shoulder, Kat could see more activity in the market, but those who noticed a woman shouting for the doctor were wise to stay out of any potential for trouble. And Kat could just make out the reason why: A pair of Miliciens had wandered into the square and now lingered with the fire-orange glow of lit cigs pointing in her direction, warning that the Franc-Garde were keen to her presence.

She peeked around the corner to the shadows of an alley. Daybreak was just crowning through the fog, and Kat could discern a mountain of weathered crates stacked in a jumble to one side, with rubbish that had been scavenged for anything of use. A woodpile on the opposite wall had been picked for firewood like meat off a bone and was barely recognizable as an old wagonette with a broken wheel. And save for rain trilling on the roof, water gurgling through the downspout, and the hushed murmurs of shopkeepers in the market, all was still.

Movement from the alley caught her eye, snapping Kat's attention back.

Though her hope was dashed to see the red front door open, it was a side door that creaked in the alley. And to her astonishment, a figure trotted down a short series of steps.

The man bore no warning that she could see—no flash of brass buttons or litzen on a uniform. He was thin but sturdy. And nimble as he wasted no time avoiding the obstacles to head toward the back of the alley.

OSS operatives would say they survived in the field by a strict adherence to protocol, iron wits, and often a hefty measure of luck. But for every report that had come across Birch's desk, Kat had found one commonality amongst them: The agent who survived did not surrender his or her instinct. And though Kat knew she should not approach those stairs, instinct said to seize upon the opportunity anyway.

A split-second decision had Kat wheel the bicycle out of sight for inquisitive Miliciens, and disappear through the fog into the alley. She threaded her way around crate piles and the busted wagonette, and avoided the scurry of little feet as rats darted into holes burrowed in nearby rubbish piles.

Kat braced her bicycle against the stair rail, reaching for the metal spindles to swing around and run up the stairs before the door closed. It wasn't until a hand clamped her wrist in a viselike grip that she realized what was happening.

An attacker thrust her against the alley wall, slamming her cheek against wet brick in a jolt to her senses.

Seeing stars, Kat shook her head and tried to wrangle free but instead found her injured right arm twisted behind her back with ease. A firm arm crushed the base of her neck, holding her immovable even as her instinct—which was to fight like mad—could not best the man's strength and speed.

"Non! Stop, you fool!" A voice protested, almost in a whisper-shout, as hands sailed in and wrestled her free from the attacker's grip. "Can't you see? It is the chef!"

The instant Kat was free, she whirled around and drove a knee into the first attacker's groin, then used his imbalanced weight to send him straight into the brick wall—face-first. The man melted to the ground and lay still, giving her the split-second chance to get away.

*Leave the bicycle behind . . .*

*You don't know whether the Miliciens heard that . . .*

*Just run.*

Kat's mind raced with calculations as she fled in the opposite direction.

She exploded through the fog, as if hitting the open trails of Boston Common, at an all-out run. Where there were no questions, no arrest, and no more hostile attempts made to subdue her. And the memory alone of what her legs could do carried her from threat to freedom.

"Manon?" She thought a voice called out from behind.

The alley bled round a corner and then twisted to another. Until Kat sucked in a despairing breath—*a dead end.*

She stopped on a dime before a wall of brick, the fog still hanging low as she faced the barrier. The footsteps slowed behind her, the pursuer's in-and-out breathing harsh as a gentler hand reached out to grip the shoulder of her coat.

Kat allowed herself to be turned to face the assailant. But with a knife he hadn't known she kept in her boot now raised in defiance at her waist, she waited for the exact right second to slash and skirt the man or, if she must, give everything she had to shove the blade up under the assailant's ribs.

The man whispered words she couldn't fully hear but sounded again to be murmuring a cautious, "Manon? It's me."

Daylight was just breaking across the sky in between the buildings, the shadows pierced by the slight glimmer of dawn streaking the sky. The figure froze in seeing the knife, with a silhouette that had stepped into the growing slivers of light. And every ounce of grit in Kat's body that had been ready to strike only seconds before did an about-face when disbelief washed in to take its place.

There was nothing familiar of the beard, the wispy overgrown hair, or the broad shoulders under a threadbare coat. That man ought to have been a stranger, save for staring back was the familiar sight of her own eyes—the trademark Harris blues—that she had seen in the last many months only in her own reflection.

The knife-grip released almost on its own and fell from her hand, clattering to the cobblestones. He looked down at it with wide eyes, then back to her as she pulled the cloche free to give him an unobstructed view of her face.

"Gavin . . . ?" Kat breathed out, and threw herself in her brother's arms as doubt, shock, and unencumbered joy crashed within her. "You're alive."

12 *March* 1952
92 Avenue d'Iéna
Paris, France

Not even Paris in the springtime could release Kat from the cloud
that hung over her heart.

It had been a quick pivot at the cooking class, from absorbing the
innocence of Mimi's declarations to Kat's slipup over Xandre, and
the unintended revelation of what her friend might be enduring at
the hands of a monster. Kat had fallen into the solace of the study
since returning to the flat and tooled around with their project, but
not really doing much beyond staring out the window at the clouds
hanging low over the mansard roofs.

The flat door opened and closed.

Keys gave a high-pitched *clink* when they hit the porcelain dish
on the sideboard by the door. She thought she heard the flick of a
light switch—back and forth—echoing in the hall, followed by the
cadence of heavy footsteps in her direction.

Gérard passed by the door. Stopped in the shadows, then came
back.

"You're here," he stated rather than asked and stepped in. He
pointed to the doused chandelier hanging overhead. "But the electric
is not."

Blackouts had continued to grip the city, and many neighborhoods
were still enduring several hours each week without power—much
to the dismay of Parisians trying to go about repurposing their lives
postwar. The Childs seemed to have some diplomatic dispensation
and did not suffer blackouts at Roo de Loo. Mimi's injury had cut
short Kat's opportunity to probe for more information, and they'd
both left soon after.

A lack of electricity was the least of her worries.

Gérard slipped his hands into his trouser pockets. "Does that
bother you, the electric going out?"

"Why? Would you do something about it if it did?"

He seemed to read her apprehension and looked to the mantel clock, having realized she was home early instead of lingering over conversation and savoring the meal the class had cooked. "How was class?"

"A disaster."

"Mimi finally burned down the Childs' flat, did she?"

"She cut her finger and we left early."

He seemed to expect she'd match the teasing energy. Maybe even laugh. But when she didn't, Gérard's manner shifted, and he grew serious again, staying within direct eyeshot so she could read his lips if needed.

"Do you want to talk about it?"

"Not really. But I suppose I must." Kat paused, feeling the need to fight rear up within her again.

Like that day in the alley, there seemed an innate instinct within Kat that needed to exchange blows whenever something threatened one of the few beloveds in her life. It had been Pops first. Her brother after that. And for reasons even she didn't understand, it had become her maman and even Lou as a father figure—especially in the years after the war, when they were so hollowed-out by grief.

And now it was Mimi.

Xandre had been Kat's enemy since the war. His callousness extended to sending nameless telegrams, marrying for money, and showing up at a wedding party fully prepared to exploit every bit of the bride and groom's past. But to know he could be capable of what she suspected now made a fire combust within, a fury Kat would never be able to hide from Gérard.

"I made a mistake today. I said the name Xandre to Mimi."

"That's not so bad," he admitted, his deep voice somehow edging closer to soft—almost understanding. "She'd have found out sooner or later. It may even help things along if she begins to question her husband over some things. Might as well start with the many names from his checkered past."

"That's just it. I don't know that she's in a position to challenge him. Or whether it would be right to goad her to do so."

Gérard ticked his head to one side. "Why is that? You don't think her clever enough?"

"Of course she is. I meant I'd mentioned his name without thinking, in the open way I speak to you instead of being guarded about what I should say. And it's not like me. I protect . . . everything. I don't trust anyone and I don't let things slip. But this was different. I can't see Mimi as a means to an end any longer. She opened up to me, Gérard. And I don't want to rebuff that confidence. I can't toss away someone's trust like it's nothing. Especially not when it could mean her life."

"I know that. And I'd never ask you to."

"He's beating her," she blurted out. "That monster put his hands on her."

The words felt foreign and pained to have to say them aloud. Heaven help her, but Kat was so furious her hand formed a fist and pounded the desk. And she had to bite her bottom lip not to cry in front of him when she'd said it. "I can only imagine what he's doing behind closed doors, and in places we can't see."

"How do you know?"

"Bruises. On Mimi's arm. And . . . I wanted to kill him for it. I still do."

Gérard gave a rough sigh and raked an agitated hand through his hair. "And you thought you'd changed from all of that, what we had to do during the war. The people we had to be then."

Kat felt the sting of tears glazing her eyes as she nodded.

However wrong it was to trust this man, and for how long it lasted before everything crumbled between them, there was something in Gérard's eyes that felt familiar. She didn't have to look away. Didn't want to look away as she bared the raw and real and ugliest parts of herself. If she must share it with someone, Kat hated the vulnerability it cost to realize she wished it to be him.

And something inside didn't want to let that go.

Rolling her eyes a little, Kat made fun out of the fact she could cry before him. Then swiped at errant tears from under her eyes and waited.

Gérard glanced out the windows, considering something. And after nodding again, he offered, "Right. We can figure this out. How about a walk?"

"A walk? Now?"

"I know the sky looks like rain, but it's still a warm day." He flipped his wrist, checking his watch. "Le Grand Rex is playing *An American in Paris*. We could just about make it if we leave soon."

"You want to go to the cinema . . . with all that's going on?"

"Oui. Don't you think as an American, you ought to see the film? At this point it would be almost embarrassing not to. And you said you need to talk. It'll take us a bit to get there. So, two birds."

"I've just taken a Pithiviers out of the oven."

"*Hmm.*" He seemed to think about it for a breath before adding with a hint of a grin, "And if a man had no idea what that is but was too self-important to admit it?"

Kat could smile then. And did, through the fading uprise of emotion. "It's a fancy way of saying a *jambon*-and-*fromage* pie."

"Then far be it from me to refuse anything made by the hands of my fair French chef wife. What do you say we light a few candles through this blackout, eat here, then grab an umbrella and take our chances in the streets? I have yet to be disappointed by Paris in the spring, even if it does rain."

"Fine." Kat stood, however uneasy, and started tidying up the desk.

"Leave the mess—we'll get it later. I just need to drop something off." He headed toward the door. "Two minutes. Meet me in the kitchen?"

She nodded, thinking as he left, was this what married couples did?

They talked and teased and lived through the normal little things that, before long, added up to something much bigger. It seemed their little things were to endure blackouts together. Eat at home in their historic Paris flat. Stroll down the Champs-Élysées for a late showing in a theater the Nazis had commandeered for German soldiers during the occupation. And instead of bearing the truth that stared them in the face, Kat was about to steal away hours with this man and pretend everything in their world wasn't falling apart.

The undefined truth was, in secret . . . she wanted to.

Kat stepped into the hall toward the kitchen, slowing up as Gérard's chamber door closed and the sound of a bolt's sharp *click* cut the silence in two. She looked to the shadows, staring at his door with that same gut instinct dashing her hopes again by setting off warning bells that this time she could not ignore.

That, and the electric never clicked off in their flat again.

# CHAPTER 18

28 September 1943
Château du Broutel
Rue, France

All was still until the doorknob turned.

With a mere breath's worth of warning, the footman's chamber door was thrown open, banging against the wall, and Captain Fontaine's brooding figure swallowed up the doorway.

Manon jumped and gave a quick swipe of fingertips to her bottom lashes as she rose to her feet. "Sir." She nodded in deference as he marched in.

"What goes on here?" Captain Fontaine demanded, his glare piercing.

Frédéric hovered behind, regulated—the captain's authority rendering him as if a soldier called to attention from the hall.

"Is it true, what this footman has said?"

"Oui." Manon watched as the captain's glare shifted to the bed, where Valens was stone-still in sleep. "Our pâtissier has fallen ill."

"We *believe* he has fallen ill." Frédéric had the gall to correct her, even if he stepped in from the hall behind the captain. "But there are still questions that linger, sir. And I think we ought to—"

"Leave us," the captain snapped, silencing Frédéric. He ticked his head to the door, ushering the footman out. "Back to work. The officers' breakfast must not be interrupted."

The young man seemed genuinely taken aback.

Manon watched as he slipped out of a soldier's stance and stood there gaping, arms hanging at his sides as if not knowing what to do with himself if he were not to be involved in what came next.

"You heard the captain," Manon echoed, though softer. "I appreciate your care for our pâtissier. But I ask you to go please, Frédéric. I entrust you and the butler to serve until I can return to our duties in the kitchen."

With a sharp nod to them both, the door clicked closed on Frédéric's back, and she was left alone with the captain and Valens in the haunting silence that remained.

Captain Fontaine stared at Valens with his customary stony glare, like a pillar with hands anchored at his hips. Silent and calculating. And without giving off the slightest hint of what could possibly be going through his mind.

"Tell me what happened."

"Sir . . . ?" Manon sputtered, praying her unease was not noticeable to him. "I don't understand your meaning. I've told Frédéric everything I know. And if he was able to relay that, then you know why we brought this to you. As a matter of château security."

"Non, Chef." He breathed out the denial on a deep exhale, as if he were letting something free from him. But his glare seemed to ease so that it did not appear police-like at all. Instead, his features softened. And he asked, "I need to know what's really happened, or I won't be able to help him. Do you understand?"

With her heart pounding in her throat, and as the seconds ticked by and the captain waited, somewhere in the mire of the moment Manon's thoughts turned to Julian. And to Collette. And to how her every prayer for deliverance from evil had once gone unanswered.

Manon wished she had strength enough to know what to do now. Even so, for Valens, she was willing to risk it, and the truth tumbled from her mouth.

"I believe he has been poisoned."

"How do you know?"

"He has been ill for some time and under the village doctor's care. Though it has been in secret. Only the pâtissier and I knew of his illness. Something's happened today to make it worse. Though I'm not certain what that is."

Captain Fontaine nodded—not in shock. And not at all as she'd thought he'd respond, but it seemed in a sad sort of resignation. "You sent for the doctor?"

"Oui, Captain. Célène went out to fetch Dr. Rousseau straight-away."

She watched the captain with ardent attention, waiting to see his response when he'd heard that Célène had gone into Rue and had done so alone, where any manner of circumstance might befall a woman traveling through occupied France.

If this concerned him, he covered it well.

"Célène was willing to do this?"

"Of course, sir. She is not afraid. Not of much that I can see."

"Non. She is not," he whispered. He pulled the service pistol from his belt holster and took a seat in Manon's chair. "You may go. I will stay with him until she returns."

"Non." Manon stared at the pistol, shining like cold death in the lamplight, and shook her head. "I cannot leave him."

"It would be noted if the chef were not in her kitchen or if the officers' breakfast is late. That would be suspicious to the Reich officers." He paused, then drew in a deep breath as he held the pistol braced against his thigh, as if ready to point it toward the door. "I promise you that no harm will come to him. Nor to Célène. I will look after your pâtissier with my life until they return. I've held vigil by a bedside before."

What that meant, Manon didn't know. Only that Frédéric had been right; if anything in her memory of having loved once could be trusted now, it appeared the captain had taken special notice of

Célène. And if that was the case, perhaps it could be used to their advantage.

With one last look to Valens, she nodded agreement and turned toward the door.

"Wait." The captain's order caught her just as she'd opened it to step out.

Manon froze, her fingertips just tipping off the edge of the doorknob. "What is it, Captain?"

Captain Fontaine clamped his eyes shut for a breath, then turned and looked beyond her to the empty hall where Frédéric had disappeared. And with an openness she did not expect, he gestured in silence for her to close the door again.

"*Reste s'il te plaît*, Chef?" he whispered, changing his mind by now asking her to please stay a moment more. "Close the door. And I will tell you how we can save his life."

# CHAPTER 19

28 September 1943
Place Anatole Gosselin
Rue, France

W hat on earth are you doing here, Gav?"
Kat squeezed his neck, then pulled back, only just realizing the full shock of seeing the brother who'd chased her down in an alley.

No longer was he the posh and polished law student from the Beacon Hill mantel pictures, but a man who'd been much altered by war. A wiry beard stood out, with longer hair that curled around his ears and a build that, while thin, looked as though he'd been plowing all summer in the sun. Kat barely recognized him— wouldn't have if not for the familiar eyes staring back and the compassionate care in the way he stayed in the fraction of light where he knew she could read his lips.

"Hey, sis," Gavin murmured, then pointed an index finger to the throbbing spot on her cheek. "Did that happen just now?"

Kat reached up and pressed fingertips to the scratch, finding blood smeared on her skin when she drew them away.

"I'm fine." She gave a hasty swipe against her uniform skirt. "Where have you been all this time? You didn't write."

"That's what you want to say to me? You of all people know why I couldn't."

Of course she did, but she whacked his shoulder for good measure anyway.

"That's not the point."

"I've been everywhere up and down the Normandy coast. And then on my own here with the Brits in the Baie de Somme for a while now. At least until you showed up."

Kat glanced beyond him to the twisting street and the fog still hanging on air, checking for any ears that might be listening or eyes watching.

She lowered her voice even further. "Wait—there is SOE here?"

"The rest of the team that was here before me were arrested months ago. Turned over to the Franc-Garde by someone on the inside. I've been working with the Brits and the local Maquis on my own since. Fishing in the harbor and attending a fish market stall in the village at Rue. And trying to get my hands on a wire to contact the Yanks back home."

"But you said until 'I showed up.' You knew I was close by?" When he shifted his weight, and uncomfortably so, she had her answer. And couldn't fathom it one bit. "How long have you known?"

"A while now," he confirmed, but halted her from a bitter retort with an earnestness about his features. "But hear me out, please? There's more to it than that."

"I'll say. You left that letter with Birch. And when you went missing in France, you knew well what he would do with it. He'd recruit me, and the first thing I'd do is come looking for you."

"Of course I knew, stubborn woman that you are. You always have been."

"Oh yes, let's slight the sister who nearly died trying to find you."

"I didn't mean that." Gavin sighed and glanced over his shoulder, noting the sounds of the market awakening through the mist behind them. "Look, with a whole crop of agents lost to someone from the inside, both governments want answers—and someone's head on a platter. I have orders from the highest office in the OSS to find out how far up the ladder this goes. Under the circumstances, I couldn't come back for you. When Henri found you that first night, you were out cold and bleeding all over. He'd brought you to the only place we could think of that would be safe."

*So it wasn't a dream . . .*

The blur of the accident had been in the recesses of her mind, but Kat knew now there was some truth to it. The fighting off the hands that had pulled at and pained her after the parachute drop and crash in the orchard . . . and in the madness of that night to have thought she'd seen Gavin's face staring down at her . . . was real. And she wondered now if her mind could be trusted at all, for flashes of memories were bobbing their way to the surface at lightning speed.

What else was she missing of that lost time?

"You were there that night. Weren't you?"

He placed a hand gingerly on her shoulder, the one throbbing now from her arm having been twisted behind her back. The same one he had to have seen was injured.

"You think I would have left if I wasn't sure you'd be looked after?"

"But you did! I woke in a Vichy police captain's home. Alone. Am I to believe you were part of that too? That you agreed to leave me there?"

"Kat, it was my idea." He sighed and gave her that boyish look she knew so well, the one that said he was caught and knew it. "But only because I knew the captain wouldn't hurt you. You were safe."

"You said that. What if he would have turned me over to the Franc-Garde? Or the Vichy authorities? There were enough unanswered questions about my story. And there are no assurances in France unless it is to trust no one but yourself." She narrowed her eyes, fury taking over. "I've lost my team too. But instead of being able to go on to Lyon and find the last one of them, I've been commandeered to some château full of Nazis on the outskirts of the village and . . ."

*Oh no.*

Her breath caught as remembrance of why she was there came back. Kat grabbed his lapel, tugging him in the direction of the doctor's building back down the alley. "We have to go back. Right now. I was sent to find a doctor for a life or death emergency—"

Gavin stopped cold, the color draining from his face when he grabbed her shoulders and demanded, "It's not Manon, is it?"

"Non. The chef is fine." Kat slapped his hands away, shrugging out of his grip. "What in the world is the matter with you?"

"I'm sorry. I . . ." He started and stopped, though the pained expression said enough.

Kat looked down at the rain-speckled trench, her cloche hat, and thought of the bicycle standing alone by the square.

And it clicked in her mind.

For the playboy he'd been in Boston, and the literal stranger he was standing before her now, Kat couldn't ignore the relief that hit him when she confirmed the chef was indeed well. Gavin's breathing hitched. He closed his eyes. Nodded. And for all the love in the world, he looked positively weak in the knees until he drew in a fresh breath and let it out again.

"Wait. That's why you chased after me. You thought I was Manon? You know her?"

"Yeah. I do."

"What on earth is going on? And the sixty-second version as we turn around if you please, because Valens needs the doctor. And also the man who I laid out in the alley back there, who I suspect may be a friend of yours."

"Or yours," he muttered, offering no explanation as they hurried back. "I should have warned him about your right hook. And your killer disposition."

"I'll have a go at anyone who shoves my face into a brick wall, thank you very much. Though I'd love to pummel you too for leaving me to fend for myself, twice now."

"So no blowtorch this time?" Gavin ticked his head to one side, giving her another hint of that boyish grin. "I know it won't make sense, but from now on at least, I'm Dominique—"

"Wait. You are?"

"Why do you ask?"

"Just something Manon said as I was leaving."

He gave a perplexed look she could discern, even through the shadows. "And as far as anyone knows, we've never set eyes on each other before the night of the plane crash. I can't explain, but you have to trust me. Can you do that for once—listen to someone without putting up a fight?"

She nodded, though she couldn't let it go without giving a characteristic answer. "I'll consider it."

"Even those working with us don't know the extent of all that's happening here. Manon is risking her life on blind trust because she doesn't know who I am. She doesn't know the truth of who you are either, for that matter. Not all of it anyway," Gavin whispered, as they approached the alley door and the heap of man who'd been knocked out cold. "Even if someone else does."

Kat swept her hair back over her shoulder as they stooped, and a breath escaped her lungs when daylight dawned on the man's face.

*Jeffrey?*

"I do know him. Clément?" She remembered to use Jeffrey's field name and patted his cheek to rouse him. The OSS operative groaned and sputtered blood. Then snapped back out of her hold like she'd better not dare try to help him up.

"He's been looking for you—Lucette. For a while now."

"And I thought he was in Lyon all this time."

"Lucky for us, he came back. With his piano, I might add. It's the only way we've been able to make contact back home."

"He's right here, you know. And can hear both of you talking about him." Jeffrey groaned again.

Gavin grimaced at Jeffrey's eyes, already turning an impressive purple either side of a bloodied nose. "*Ouch.* Good thing we're at a doctor's office. Looks like you may have broken his nose, Lucette."

He hoisted Jeffrey's arm over his shoulders, helping him back toward the stairs as he mumbled something about "I should have known she'd get me back" and "at least it wasn't a pair of scissors this time."

Kat ignored the quips, sorry but satisfied at least that she'd made contact with Jeffrey again. And that they might find answers to the questions that had built up from finding Gavin. She swept up the couple of things that had been in the alley—her knife, which she took from her pocket and hid back in her heel. The bicycle, which had been turned over somehow in the struggle. And Jeffrey's hat that had flown off into a corner with windblown bits of paper and a collection of wet leaves.

"The doctor is inside. We can get him and you can leave straightaway."

She caught up to Gavin on the stairs and tugged his sleeve. "Wait—what was in the jug?"

"What jug?"

"Manon found a porcelain crock in the kitchen. It's possible Valens had been unknowingly poisoned by whatever was in it. And she seemed to allude you might know something about it."

Shades of indecision covered Gavin's face, and his lips parted for a breath, as if he wanted to say something but couldn't. Or wouldn't.

"What's wrong?"

"She thinks it was me." Gavin cursed in frustration and readjusted Jeffrey's lax weight over his shoulders. "Manon thinks I poisoned Valens."

"Well of course you didn't. I know that now."

"I don't blame her for thinking it." He slipped a key into the doctor's office door and held it open with his shoe. "But I'll have to fix that later. We have a bigger problem staring us in the face."

"Which is?"

"There's a mole at the château. And I'd say that mole and the jug go hand in hand. We have to decide what we're going to do about it."

Digging into the inside pocket of his jacket, Gavin pulled a folded cardstock item out and handed it to her before angling Jeffrey into the back of the doctor's office.

"Second row, dead center."

Kat unfolded a faded nine-by-twelve-centimeter photo with crinkled edges and a crease down the middle. But even for the quality, it was still enough to see a chill-inducing group shot of a Hitler Youth rally and a banner that read: *Hitlerjugend, 1938*.

In the middle of the bright, shining faces was one cadet in the lot . . . with the same face as their French footman who'd been in and out of the Château du Broutel kitchen a hundred times before.

∼

7 *April 1952*
La Rue Cler
Paris, France

The spring markets were just starting to come alive again after the war and now seemed to regain an open-air magic all their own.

The city was just shedding the cold of winter and had not yet welcomed the swell of summer crowds, making spring the prized time to enjoy Paris—the locals came out of doors, flocking to the open-air markets under blossoming cherry trees, as wisteria and magnolia blooms scented the air with a sweet, citrusy perfume.

The Childs hadn't a telephone, so when Kat received Julia's handwritten note the day before, asking if she'd like to visit the market to shop for next week's class, she was hard-pressed to be on time.

She'd stepped onto La Rue Cler a half hour early in a smart spring frock of sky blue and with a seagrass basket hooked over her arm, and from that instant she was enveloped by the bustle and color of Parisian life all crammed into one remarkable pedestrian thoroughfare.

Kat passed fresh produce piled high: in-season asparagus, artichokes, and earthy garlic bulbs ready to flavor Easter tables. Florist wagonettes boasted a rainbow of spring peonies. Boucherie stalls offered leg of lamb, veal, rabbit, and pork cuts for the traditional Easter pâté. Not far off, fresh fish, the dark blue-black of mussel shells, and iced octopus glistened in the sun, with the scent of the sea still clinging to their sheen. The sweet French delight *fraises des bois*—wild strawberries—were just ripening, and patrons tucked them away in picnic baskets with smoky fromage, baguettes, and sweet dessert wines for a leisurely lunch along the Seine.

Julia's unmistakable laughter cut the air, and Kat turned to the familiar sound, finding her mentor's tall form tucked under the striped awning of a *fromager*'s tent. It appeared she'd been spirited away too and was happily engaged in conversation with the proprietor of the golden bricks and wax-covered rounds of cheese piled like mountains in the stall.

"Madame Child!" Kat called, uncaring that it was very American to shout across a market. Knowing Julia as she did, there was every reason to believe her compatriot would do the same.

"Bonjour, Madame Fontaine!" Julia spotted Kat and waved her over with the booming greeting. And without pageantry or pretense, Julia inducted Kat into the world of French grocer relations.

"You see?" Julia instructed, as they strolled away to their next haunt. "The French grocer will not offer up his cordiality straightaway—especially to an American. You must show genuine interest. Fan the flame of their passion and they will warm up. And incidentally, save the best their stall has to offer for *you*."

They walked on, both baskets bearing selections for the aperitif the class would make next: baked brie with fig jam and walnuts. Finding the choicest cuts of lamb for their Easter-inspired meal came next. And produce last, where Julia now leaned in and hunted through the prized white asparagus to pick the freshest bundles.

"If you don't mind the question, what did you do during the war, Mrs. Fontaine?"

"Please—call me Kat. And like so many, I was proud to serve."

"You must call me Julia. Ah! This is what you want—firm to the touch." She jumped from one thought to the next and pressed a bundle of asparagus stalks with her thumb. "And the bundles ought to be able to stand on their own. So, you served. Where?"

"Same as you as I understand it. In the OSS."

"Really? But not in Ceylon. I'd have remembered if our paths had crossed there."

The little kindness brought sunshine to Kat and she smiled.

The instant fear of being backed into a corner to talk of the war faded with Julia's pragmatism. She wasn't fishing for gossip. Rather, it seemed she'd found a similar spirit in Kat's growing affection for cooking and was simply making conversation as one did in Paris, talking of life and the war, and living beyond the past . . . with a friend.

"I was here—in France, actually. A field operative who ended up at Baie de Somme before the Normandy invasion. But our team was broken up during an operation, and I was sent to Lyon until the liberation. After the war, I served on a communications team in London for two years. And then"—Kat raised her shoulders in a light shrug, as if that was that—"I went home."

"Where was home?"

"Boston."

Julia did stop at that and looked over at Kat. "But you don't talk about the war now. Not with the other ladies. And not even with your friend Mrs. Allmand?"

"Non. This is the first time I've spoken of it outside of with my husband. I suppose I haven't been ready to. For a number of reasons."

"*Nous en voudrions trois, s'il vous plaît,*" Julia said to the seller, buying three bundles and tucking the asparagus in her basket. As they walked on, she added, "This is not surprising. Some are free to talk. To move on. We have a circle of acquaintance of former OSS here in Paris, and they are the most interesting lot. We have dinners and talk about the old days. But I worked in communications, reporting to Wild Bill Donovan. So the information we saw was varied, to say the least."

"I know of the director. My superior was also a direct report of Donovan's. He and my stepfather, Colonel Sullivan, are quite close acquaintances to this day."

"I believe I have heard of the colonel. Our outfit coordinated field reports that came in from the front, and I believe we saw his orders come through more than once."

Kat couldn't remember Lou having been behind enemy lines. He'd always told Maman when he'd gone to Washington, but never overseas.

"You saw my stepfather's name on reports from the front?"

"Oh yes. It was the raw and gritty portrait of war in those wires. So I can understand why for some who served in the field, the weight of all has not lifted enough to share those experiences. You would be someone who understands that, I think."

"It's something like that, I suppose."

"We are not so unlike these grocers. Given time and genuine attention, you win their trust. And earn their favor. You have enough of it in the kitchen." She turned with a smile lit by the sun. "But then, this is not your first time preparing French cuisine, is it?"

Kat shook her head. "Non. It's not. But I suspect you've known that for a while."

"Why do you hide your skill? Our class could benefit from your contributions."

"I don't know exactly. But having been trained by a French chef during the war, it still feels private, given the way it ended."

"I see. And it is evident you hold those memories dear. Your technique is classic—too much so to have been taught by anyone other than a proficient." Julia paused at baskets overflowing with rich purple aubergine and turned to Kat before sorting through them. "Does Mr. Fontaine know this side of you?"

"He does."

"And what does your husband say about your culinary pursuits?"

What did Gérard say? Many things.

He knew the weight of the guilt Kat carried. Over Valens. Over the atrocities that happened in the village square in Rue one terrible day. And, heaven help her, for Gavin's disappearance not long after.

They'd won the war, but she'd lost everything else.

Kat had placed her trust in Xandre the night of the Christmas party, and all had crumbled from that one disastrous error. Their team had broken up and scattered. Their covert position at the château was lost. And her family was shattered. It was a whirlwind of pain and questions and seeking but never truly finding answers to stem the bleeding from the deepest cuts to her soul.

She'd still not been able to tell Gérard all of what happened the night of the château Christmas party. But even then, in the quiet moments they shared, the pain of those memories had somehow become easier to bear. They existed as if nothing was hidden between them. Maybe it wasn't. And if Kat was honest with herself, that scared her more than anything else.

Gérard didn't seem to be afraid of needing someone.

Not like Kat always had been.

In that instant, under the romance of cherry blossoms and a sweet Parisian sun warming the market stalls, what had begun as a ruse of a marriage clicked over in Kat's mind . . . to the naked truth staring her in the face.

She gaped in the silence as reality sank in.

"Are you quite well, Kat?"

"Oui. I think I . . ."

*I think I may be falling in love with my husband,* was her first terrifying thought. But knowing she couldn't say that aloud—even to herself—Kat pivoted instead to the safer notion in that instant.

"I've just realized something has changed for me in France. It no longer feels like a country I'm visiting. Or simply staying in. Boston is where I grew up. But somehow I wonder if this could feel like home one day."

"I see." Julia nodded, thoughtfully but not as one taken aback. And turned her attention back to picking through the aubergine harvest before them. "And this is a problem?"

"For me it is."

"But this is Paris. And the war is over. Look around you; anything is possible here."

Julia paid the grocer and led on with a little sparkle in her eyes as they passed market stalls, shoppers, patrons, and tourists, and the gentle sway of cherry blossoms lining the street.

"Do you see this beautiful city? The color and flavor at our very fingertips? It is awakened now from years of death," she said, leading them past the rainbow of a French flower cart. "And you are here, alive in it. Why wouldn't you want to embrace that, even share it with someone?"

"I suppose I'm still mucking through the mire of yesterday—not allowing myself to really look back at all that's happened, but also not moving forward. Until the class. I never thought I'd enjoy cooking like this, but I do. The kitchen has become a place where I can breathe again. Does that make sense?"

"Ah—yes. You know, the first meal Mr. Child and I had in France . . ." Julia closed her eyes for a breath, as if revisiting the splendor of a cherished moment. "We stopped in Rouen, at a little eatery called La Couronne. That was more than two years ago now, but I can still remember that moment like it was yesterday. We had *Portugaises*—I'd never had Portuguese oysters like that! Sole meunière, *salade verte*, fromage blanc, and *café filtre* . . . I hadn't a clue then, but that one meal has changed the course of my life. And I find myself here, just like you, looking at the world with new eyes. Perhaps you see your life in a similar way?"

"I hadn't thought of it that way before." Kat soaked in the color and life bustling around them. "Being here in Paris? It makes me not want to forget the past. Because it's how people live on. To look back is not to lament all we've lost, but to see how past experiences have shaped us into who we are. Neither of us would be standing here if not for having lived every one of those moments."

How in the world had they landed here?

Kat would never have made such an admission to herself, let alone to a mentor who'd never broached the subject of the heart in the months they'd worked together. It had been student and teacher, never friend to friend. And she'd certainly not entertained what might be happening—maybe what her heart wished would happen?—between her and Gérard.

"Someone close to me used to say, 'Don't look back.' It started as a silly thing we said, between children. But without realizing, I've embraced that advice these last many years. And I'm afraid it's kept me from living. Almost as if I, too, died in the war."

"Who said that?"

"My brother, Gavin. He served in the OSS too. I only signed up because of him."

Julia turned to face her now, forgetting the pirates' horde of riches piled in the stalls, and instead seemed taken by Kat's silly anecdote of brotherly affection.

"What happened to him, may I ask?"

"He's . . . gone. He actually went missing here in France in 1943. And was declared legally dead in '47. I'm afraid some of my time here in France has to do with him, that I'm just not ready to let go."

Kat's world was not ready for the tipping, not in the beauty of such surroundings. But as she looked up at her mentor, that world was eclipsed by the genuine care in Julia's brow and the hint of emotion glazing her eyes.

"I am terribly sorry for your loss." Julia steadied the basket between them, offering a careful hand to Kat's wrist. "But your brother is still with you every time you say his name. And in every moment you're brave enough to look back despite everything you've been through. The power of that is choosing to *live*, and Paris is the one place you will not regret doing it."

# CHAPTER 20

30 September 1943
Fort-Mahon-Plage
Baie de Somme, France

*Just get there . . .*

It was all Manon could do to pedal faster.

Through her ragged breathing and tears, calf muscles that burned with each turn, and the painful stitch in her side, she told herself that Captain Fontaine must be wrong. That the Franc-Garde couldn't have learned of the association she and Valens had with the cottage at the dunes. That they hadn't arrested Dominique with the others—they couldn't have gotten to him that fast. And please, Providence, the enemy hadn't snatched Manon's whole world away from her again.

Not a devastating second time.

The sun was bleeding behind the trees after an hour's ride from the château, leaving twilight to descend with sharp light that pierced through the pines. She glanced over her shoulder as she cycled, checking every now and again for the terror of a phantom engine's hum that warned she'd been tracked that far. Mercifully, she found none. Just readjusted sticky palms, sweat mixing with the blood dried between her fingers and smeared across the handlebars.

The old shed with the sea-weathered walls where she'd hidden the bicycle before came into view. She slowed, coasting as the dunes took shape along the sea. And finally exhaled when the jagged cut-out of the cottage eaves appeared against the sky over the rise.

Manon skidded her bicycle to a stop, then dropped it in a hollow alongside the shed so she could run the rest of the way. The wind whipped her hair about her shoulders and pressed her bloodstained chef's jacket tight against her form as she ran up the stone steps two at a time, not pausing until she reached the top.

Stumbling off the lip of the last stone, she hunched over, holding her hair back at her nape as she battled to catch her breath.

"Dominique?" Manon called against the wind, turning circles to search the yard and the path down to the dunes. Then she looked to the trailheads that cut secret paths into the woods surrounding the fisherman's cottage. *"Dominique!"*

Desperate, she shoved her shoulder into the front door, thinking the bolt would block her. But the door was unlocked and gave way without a fight. She ducked in, her body surging with adrenaline as she searched in the dim light.

"Dominique?"

Finding no signs of a struggle—not even a fire on the hearth—meant at least neither the Vichy police nor the feared Franc-Garde had stormed in. She ran to the back and flung open the quilt partition to find a single room with a rolltop desk, chest of drawers, and bed over a soft blue area rug covering the floor. Then she came out and called his name again as she hastened to the last trailhead that led down to the dunes.

A dingy was marooned onshore, overturned in the distance and piled against a mound of windswept sand and beach grass where the tide couldn't stretch. As if he'd used it and simply left it there until the next time.

*He's not here . . .*

*They've taken him.*

Staring out to sea, Manon drank in deep breaths as her heart bled. Battling her quivering chin and a surge of emotion that came with realization that the dunes were deserted, she cupped a hand over her mouth to bury a sob.

A stirring on the roof caught her eye—a tiny blip in her peripheral vision, and she looked over. Dominique popped up from the highest eave then, like he'd been disturbed patching the roof, and wielded a hammer like a weapon.

His face softened the instant he saw her.

"Manon?" he called, and dropped the hammer in a wood caddy nearby. "Stay there!" He motioned with his palm, shouting, "I'll come down."

Dominique disappeared from view as he climbed down at the back of the cottage, then came around the side toward her, his face brightening as he jogged her way—that beautiful smile behind the beard and the strong visage of the man she could see now in her dreams. But his features darkened when he registered the state Manon was in, with crimson stains splashed over her clothes, hair wild as it whipped over her shoulders, and hands blood red . . .

The look of shock on his face lasted a split-second before he took to a run at full speed. She tried to run too, but wobbly legs refused to cooperate after the exhausting ride. Dominique met her, not stopping until his body thundered against hers and she was cradled in his arms.

"What's happened? Are you hurt?" He pulled them both down to the ground, knees in the sand together.

His hands were everywhere—palming her cheeks, grasping her shoulders, running down her arms, and parting the sides of her coat to find an abdominal wound that could have caused the massive crimson stains to mar her front.

"Non! It's not me," she sobbed, shaking her head. Grasping for his hands to stop their search. "It's not me."

Dominique brushed her hair back from her tearstained face,

holding it against the wind so he could stare, steel-boned and un-restricted, back into her eyes.

"What happened?"

"I'm all right." Manon shook her head again, though every nerve ending in her body was raw with grief over what had happened. But she was also filled with sheer joy for finding Dominique alive and unharmed, and in her arms.

He cupped his hands on either side of her face. "What happened to you?"

"The Vichy police have arrested Valens," she cried, collapsing against his chest. Crying into the hollow of his neck. "And I thought they were coming for you too. I thought you were gone . . ."

"I'm not," he reassured over the wind, cradling the back of her head with a steady palm. His arms tightened their hold around her. "Feel that? I'm alive. I'm here with you."

"I would have been here sooner, but all I had was the bicycle."

"You mean you rode all the way here?"

Dominique didn't wait for an answer to her exhaustion. He lifted her into his arms, pressing a hard kiss to her hairline as he hurried from the trailhead back to the cottage. He kicked the door open, bolted it back with one hand, swept her over to the cot by the hearth, and set her down upon it.

He knelt in front of her, taking her bloodied hands in his atop her lap. "What's all this now?"

Manon didn't answer right away. How could she?

The brutality of what she'd seen . . . the sight of the body thudding to the ground at her feet. And the river of crimson flowing from the hole in the side of his head filling the cracks in the courtyard's cobblestones under her shoes. Manon had risen up from that shock only when the captain had dragged her to her feet and told her to hurry—to go.

So she did, pedaling all the way to the dunes.

To *him*.

"I should not have trusted the captain . . ."

"What do you mean?" Dominique brushed a soft thumb over her palms.

"The day Valens fell ill, the captain and I had a secret plan. He said we could get Valens out of the château just as soon as it was safe. When he was well enough to walk." Tears squeezed from her eyes and she shook, her entire body trembling with the trauma of what she'd seen. "But he must have reported Valens to the Franc-Garde instead. The château's Vichy police stormed the kitchen this morning. They went straight up to the servants' quarters and dragged Valens away. I could not stop them."

When Manon paused, he brushed careful hands over her palms. And almost seemed to hold his breath as he asked, "And what about this? Whose blood? Not Célène?"

"Non. It was Frédéric. Our footman."

"He's dead."

"God help him, he is," Manon cried, rubbing her hands together, hating the sight of the crimson stains smeared up to her wrists. "When the captain's Vichy police were attempting to arrest Valens, the Franc-Garde soldiers arrived and Frédéric intervened. He chased the soldiers out to the courtyard, shouting about there being 'more of them' and 'why had they not arrested Célène with the others in the village?' I didn't know what to do. I knew Célène had found you in the village two days ago, because she came back here telling me not to worry. That all was well and we could trust your team. But the captain made me vow not to reveal anything to the staff; he said it would be safer. I tried to get the footman to quiet down. Told him to be sensible. But Frédéric followed after the captain where they were loading Valens in a truck and threatened to sound the alarm with the Franc-Garde soldiers at the château . . ."

"And he was killed."

"I think one of the Vichy police shot him. Right there in the courtyard," she breathed out. And closed her eyes, trying to think it through. "I'm not sure what happened exactly. Just that there was a *pop* and he fell to the ground, dead at my feet. And when I knelt and tried to help . . . That's when . . ."

Manon held out shaking palms before him.

"Stay here," Dominique whispered and rose, leaving her for a moment.

The sound of a match struck and a flicker of light cast a glow as he touched flame to a candle in the center of the table.

The cottage was washed in a faint warmth, illuminating the same place that, for a brief respite, had become their makeshift hideaway from the world. She'd visited Dominique here many times now, where the scents of pine and the salty sea air filled her lungs . . . where she had a friend and did not feel so alone in the world . . . where that wretched calvados jug used to sit on the high shelf above the stove.

All of that was gone now; the illusion of peace in this place had shattered.

She watched as Dominique found a basin and pitcher on the sideboard and poured water, then returned to kneel in front of her.

Gently, fingertips brushed against her skin.

They coaxed, pulling her hands free from her lap. Manon hadn't realized how she trembled until she gave up her hands and the touch of his skin warmed hers. He dipped a tea towel in the water and brushed cool linen across her skin, turning her hands over in his, washing away the stubborn bloodstains between her fingers and dried to her knuckles.

"The captain did this?"

Thinking back, it was too dark to make a determination.

She shook her head. "I do not know. But at the very least, it could have been one of his officers."

"Listen to me, Manon. No matter who pulled the trigger, this had to be done."

"Killing Frédéric? Non. The captain said he had a plan to get Valens out of the château and then he would—"

"Arresting Valens *was* getting him out. And the only reason that footman is dead is because he would have given all of us up to the Franc-Garde—You. Me. Valens, Xandre, and Célène. And the captain for not reporting this. It was by pure naivety on the footman's part that he hadn't turned us over already."

"I don't understand."

"Frédéric was German."

"Non . . . But he worked with us. Almost since the start of the war. I know—I hired him."

"We learned before that he'd once been a rising star in the Hitler Youth. And now we know he's been working with the GFP as a plainclothes agent—a junior one, but with no less zeal to root out anyone disloyal to the Reich. We believe he was the one who reported Franz to the Franc-Garde over the matter of the stolen wine. Somehow he must have become aware of the coded messages on the labels and fingered Valens for it."

"How do you know this?"

"Dr. Rousseau sends Resistance messages out, but he also takes them in. There are some women in the village, the ones the Nazi officers go to see. They put their lives on the line to photograph documents or steal information from the officers when they are asleep, then feed those back to the Resistance through the doctor. Among the effects on one officer was documentation of Hitler Youth rallies. It was only then that we recognized a face in one archive photograph as working amongst us at the château. And it all came together, albeit too late."

"But the Vichy police work hand in hand with the Franc-Garde and the Reich. It is rumored the Miliciens can even be more brutal than the Nazi authorities, some practicing one-upmanship to prove loyalty to their overlords. Captain Fontaine is at the helm of that loyalty. Why would he not turn us in?"

"Manon . . ." Dominique's gaze bore into her now as he searched her face. He waited before continuing, like he was thinking something through. "For the captain to allow Frédéric's death would only be for a very good reason. It would have been kill or be killed. The captain wouldn't risk Valens' life—not any of us if it came down to it."

"But he set you up for deliveries at the château. And he was there that night Célène was injured yet kept her hidden at his home until she was transferred here. Why would he allow all of that?"

"What matters now is Valens will be safe. As will you. And we know who's been working against us. That's all I can say. But tell me, why did you think the Vichy police would come for me too?"

"It is rumored there have been more arrests. In reprisal for what happened to Frédéric."

"At the château?"

"Non. In the village. Frédéric believed the captain would have reported Célène and Valens, so he did not alert the officers at the château. And while he did not know about me, Frédéric did report those in the village he suspected of working with them. The Franc-Garde were going there to make arrests soon after."

"Dr. Rousseau. And Clément?"

She nodded. "Henri and Xandre are in danger too, at least we fear so. Célène left to go to the village. It was under the guise of re-supplying the larder, but she hopes to make contact there. To warn them if she can. Even Célène does not know anything of the captain trying to help us get Valens out, though I believe she has growing suspicions about him."

"To protect everyone concerned, we must keep that information secret." He caressed the side of her face, brushing her hair back off her brow. "You should know, what Valens endured may have saved many lives. And we won't let that sacrificial act be taken from him. No matter what happens now, I will get you out of here. As far from the château as we can. I will find a place where you will be safe."

"Non, Dominique. You won't."

Manon's heart lurched, so she leaned forward, unhooking the chain from her neck and pulling the wedding band from under her collar to drop into his palm.

"Three years ago the Nazi régime killed my husband, Julian— Valens' son. Along with our daughter, Collette. She was not four years old. With dark brown hair like her father and the sweetest green eyes. They both died the day the first bombs fell on the out- skirts of Paris. They were in our flat while Valens and I were working in the Hôtel Ritz kitchen. I thought they would be safe when Paris had been declared an 'open city.' Bombs were not supposed to fall. The art and architecture would be spared. And that horrible mistake of judgment—that human life would be valued by the Reich as they did the art—is why we're here now. To fight. To use our skills in any way we can to overthrow this evil. And if necessary, to give our lives to do it. It felt like I had already died once, but I am willing to again if that's what it takes."

Dominique rocked back on his heels, his breathing suddenly ticked up a notch as he stared back, blinking, holding still with the gold chain and ring in his open palm, and searching her face for explanation of what she'd just said.

"I am so sorry for your loss. That must have been unbearable."

"It was." Her bottom lip quivered a shade. "It is. And I will never lose someone I care about again. Not in that way."

Tears glazed his eyes as he tipped his brow in question.

"You came here to die?"

She shook her head, thinking now of what Valens had said so long ago. "Non. I came here to live. And I never thought I would again . . . until I met you."

Manon stared into the deep blue pools of his eyes, and he gazed back, the connection that somehow had existed from the first time she'd ever stepped foot in the cottage entwining them now.

"Is it wrong of me to say that? That I want to live, even while it seems the rest of the world is dying anyway?"

"It's never wrong to want to live."

"And if I thought I could"—Manon swallowed hard, not knowing up until that very second whether she could say the words aloud—"or wanted to . . . love again one day?"

"I'd say that's a very, very good thing," he whispered, and set the linen and basin of crimson-tinged water to one side.

Dominique scooted in so his waist pressed into her knees and placed the chain and band on the coverlet. He then pulled up his shirt cuff, unbuttoning it so it revealed a paisley scarf he'd kept knotted at his wrist. Her lips parted to see it, surprise catching her off guard as he unwound the satin from his skin and folded the scarf over the ring and chain.

"We have something to live for, don't we?"

Breathless, she repeated, "Do we?"

"If you want to stay at the château and fight, then I'll stay. I'll fight alongside you." He opened his hands before her, palms up, on either side of her on the cot. "But I can't pretend I don't care. Nor that I haven't for some time. No matter what this crazy world is and does, I know that much. I won't let anything happen to you."

War was not for lovers, nor courage for fools.

Manon stared back at the man now who would be hers, understanding that courage was not for the faint of heart but reserved for those who would willingly risk no less than everything they held dear. And amid the brokenness of bombs and blood and gut-wrenching loss, the tiniest shred of beauty whispered that if a heart was but willing, love could grow there again.

"And I won't let anything happen to you." She accepted his hands, leaning close so he could wind his arms around her and stopping her lips a breath from his. "We stay, we fight. And maybe one day, you could change my mind."

"Keep coming back here, and I will."

# CHAPTER 21

30 September 1943
Place Anatole Gosselin
Rue, France

The Franc-Garde swarmed the village like a cloud of locusts.

Kat watched as midnight-blue berets bled into all corners of the square in stark contrast to the morning market's usual calm. In response to increased subversion by the Resistance, or perhaps—as Gavin had noted the last time they'd spoken—the Germans saw the tides shifting and knew they were in grave danger of losing another war.

Brutality was their answer.

Milice troops had been issued the primary task to root out the Resistance and make it pay. Rumors ran rife through the underground to beware of the blue berets, as well as the plainclothes Geheime Feldpolizei—the German secret military police would swarm into any space where subversion was suspected. And like their cousins, the Gestapo, they were rumored to be brutal in their submission tactics. Only this enemy was not just hungry for informants. Nor for rooting out the Maquis or unveiling foreign operatives or even digging for the information their torture might bring.

Their goal was singular: make France bleed.

To all in the village square, Kat should seem interested only in the fresh catch at the fish market stall. Whiles sunrays streaked through the building tops to shine against dew on the cobblestone streets, she passed by the clusters of Milicien uniforms as if she hadn't a second thought for the authoritarian presence. And gave no notice to anything save for picking over baskets at the fish stall: fresh mussels and clams, sea bass and lemon sole, and mounds of fresh squid glistening in the morning light.

She had far more than a regular message drop to Dr. Rousseau's that day.

The château had awoken to Valens' arrest by the Vichy police and the shock of Frédéric's death. And now Kat had gone to the village under the pretense that they needed supplies for the kitchen, when it had ballooned into a full-scale operation to warn those at the doctor's office that arrests could be impending.

She noticed Gavin was not in the square. It could be a good thing—he might be at the dunes. Or a bad thing, if arrests had already been made. She did see Henri in his usual beret, stooping to scratch chalk on a slate board with prices for the day's fresh catch.

Henri set the chalk back on the slate ledge, then stood, dusting hands on his waxed-canvas smock, and stopped cold when he saw Kat on the other side of the stall.

"I've come for lemon sole," she whispered, picking over the catch iced in the wagon. "Where is the other fisherman who sells with you?"

"He's stayed in harbor, mademoiselle."

Relief washed over her to hear him confirm Gavin was not tied up in all of this. But Henri's manner was still deadly serious, and he kept his attention on topping off a basket of mussels with more ice.

"What do you recommend of the catch today?" Kat kept her eye on the uniforms across the square as she opened her satchel and began searching through, as if retrieving payment.

"You ought not speak to me. They are watching," he whispered, turning to lift a basket of cod from the wagon to the stall. And, with grave caution in his eyes, he inclined his head to the horde of Gestapo flowing into the square.

The details of the situation began to take shape.

To her horror, Kat swept her gaze over the square to find a string of frightening realities. Dr. Rousseau's windows were shuttered, an oddity for midmorning, given how many patients he'd see on any given day. Wooden boards had been nailed up over the red front door. Low-ranking Vichy foot soldiers stood guard on either side of it. The nearby chapel doors had been closed too, turning worshipers away. Drapes were drawn on all the windows facing the square. And lines at the shops were nil, with not a single child among the few citizens who did move about.

Kat's breath caught in her lungs.

"Go. Now," Henri snapped, his fists white-knuckled on the handles of the basket between them. He held out a newspaper-wrapped parcel—fish she hadn't asked for. (A Resistance message.)

Taking the parcel, she placed the fish on top of the tin in her basket. And turned to hurry off but was startled to crash into a Milice soldier who'd managed to sneak up behind her.

"Show me your basket, mademoiselle."

Knowing confidence was key, Kat raised her chin a fraction. She offered a respectful, "Pardon me, sir. I must return home."

The officer eyed her, the coolness of suspicion marked upon his face. He leaned in, nosing the tip of his pistol over the top edge of her basket's rim.

"No one leaves the square. We have extra security checks during the Gestapo's Schutzhaft. And we are to search all parcels before the event begins."

Any second she expected the tension to combust.

The knife in her boot screamed to be let out, to be made useful in its purpose. She had to believe that somewhere, buried under squid and ice and waterlogged wood, Henri, too, must have a weapon hidden. And if the worst happened, he would step in to aid her so they could flee.

Kat swallowed hard. "Please, sir. Allow me to pass. I am late."

"I will see to this."

A familiar voice was the only thing that penetrated Kat's will in that instant, the surprise flooding relief to her insides. She looked up, the streams of morning sun cut by the captain's shoulders, creating a shadow against the officer in front of him.

"Move on, soldier," Captain Fontaine demanded, his voice calm, cool, and unaffected in the least. "Stop bothering this lady."

The soldier eyed Gérard's Police Nationale uniform with its many decorations. Still, he stood firm. "You have no authority here, Captain."

"I do when this is one of the château staff. Or would you prefer to explain to your superiors why you've spent your time pestering the under-chef for the Reich's regional headquarters instead of going about your real duties—to protect France?"

The soldier seemed to bite at the notion and moved on.

Henri flitted his glare to the captain and tipped his head toward the side street, as if encouraging him to see Kat out of harm's way. It could have been nothing—just a little tick of restraint between men who'd frequented the same château courtyard for deliveries. But even as Henri ignored them to go back to work and the captain led her away, it was that look and the hand he'd braced at her elbow that dared her to relinquish a bit of the fear she was supposed to have for this man.

Leading her to the corner of the chapel, the captain eased her toward the back of a crowd of citizens who'd been herded into an audience before the open square. "What are you doing here?"

Kat raised her chin. "Shopping. What else?"

"Did you find what you needed?"

"Non. But what is happening?" she breathed out, as he handed her a pamphlet with the title *Combats* splashed across the front.

"It's a copy of the Franc-Garde's newspaper. They've printed names of the accused for today's demonstration."

*A demonstration?*

*What in the world could they wish to show now?*

Surveying the square, Kat felt the hairs on her arms prickle as she watched a tunnel form, with two rows of uniforms lining up so an open space—like a parade route—unfurled between them.

"We should go. Now," he whispered back, his breath warm against her good ear. "Stay with me. I'll try to lead us out."

The captain reached for her basket and shoved the pamphlet inside.

When Kat couldn't give reason why she wouldn't give it up— knowing Henri's message was surely in the parcel of fish— she allowed him to free it from her hand. But in her internal deliberations, she did not expect he'd replace it with his palm in hers. The captain tugged her behind him then, pressing them along the back edge of the crowd, trying to cut into a side street. It was then that the world opened up for the horror it had become, and Kat halted them in their retreat.

A half-life swallowed the square, like a dream turned to a nightmare that sucked them all in together. Time was suspended as blue berets marched prisoners out before the throngs of terrified citizens, their captives with faces bloodied and bruised and forced to kneel before the crowd.

One woman was marched out in the lot of men. Kat's middle hitched when she recognized Clarice—Dr. Rousseau's secretary, the woman Kat had learned had lost her fiancé during the Great War. She'd never married. And had risked her life to work with the doctor in any way she could in the years since the occupation began.

Kat watched as the Franc-Garde shoved the poor woman along, her hair coming undone from the chignon at her nape to toss salty waves about her shoulders in the tiny breath of wind that swept the square. Heaven help them, but Dr. Rousseau followed behind, the lapel of the poor tweed suit Kat had seen so many times now dripped with blood from his busted lip. He stared straight ahead as the procession continued, and prisoners were marched out to be lined up before the central fountain with the Gestapo looking on from the perch at all corners of the square.

And in a moment of shock, a young pianist she knew was marched out too—the OSS operative with intense eyes still marred by purple bruises from a broken nose and a gait she hated to recognize from their days at The Farm.

*Jeffrey . . .*

His gaze was fixed somewhere far off, cast wide over the crowd, as if he could see through the buildings and behold the coast.

Kat's breathing racked in and out now, causing her to fight with her body's response to tremble. Her hands shook with such violence, it must have been evident to the captain with his shoulder pressed up against hers. And with the last bit of determination she'd possessed to remain quiet and still and unobserved by any uniform in the square, Kat drew in a steadying breath as a pair of eyes scanned the crowd . . . and landed upon her.

Jeffrey's gaze locked with hers from across the square.

His eyes held a steel resolve she'd never before witnessed in another person. Shame punished, as her eyes must have been terror stricken in return. In anger. In fledgling support as she gave a tiny tick of a nod. And with anguish that was so real, Kat had never tasted such an all-consuming bitterness in her life.

The Franc-Garde's first shot rang out to a collective yelp amongst the crowd.

With each blast that followed, executions down the line, the crowd's reaction reverberated as Kat kept her eyes locked on Jeffrey's. His jaw was set, but his hands shook in their rope shackles as the blue berets' pistols claimed the back of each skull. Coming closer. As some wailed in fear and others kept silent. And filling the cracks in the cobblestones with blood that soaked the knees of his trousers.

Clarice was next.

Tightening her hand in a fist at her side, Kat watched the poor woman's fate enacted. The doctor followed, the shot to his head echoing as seabirds stirred in the sky overhead and his body thumped to the ground in a heap.

Kat steeled herself not to question. (War was a bloody slog. It wouldn't help the poor souls now.) Not to cry out or fight. And not to close her eyes to the horror of each life that was snuffed out in such bloody brutality. Holding firm, she clenched her jaw and lifted it in resolve, giving the only measure of solidarity she could.

Jeffrey locked his eyes on hers, Kat reading the silent recitation of the Twenty-Third Psalm upon his lips in the horrible connection they'd now have as silent comrades in his last moment on earth.

The pistol braced the back of his head.

A shot fired. Life drained from Jeffrey's eyes, and blood poured from his skull as his body thumped to the cobblestones face-first.

Her heart quickened. And Kat felt her feet try to bolt, only to be tugged back.

"S'il te plaît, Célène," the captain pleaded and reached for her hand. Pulling her up against him and holding tight as if he'd read the murderous thoughts racing through her mind. "You cannot help him now."

The horror was over in mere minutes.

The crowd dispersed with a German warning shouted in French that this was what awaited saboteurs—the blood-soaked square having made its demonic impression upon them all as Franc-Garde soldiers dragged the bodies away and tossed them onto a waiting wagonette.

The captain led Kat out of the chaos, gripping her basket in one hand and her palm iced in the other as they fled the square. They did not speak. Did not let go once they'd made it to the road. Just walked along at an uncomfortably swift pace to where the lane curved and a soft breeze rustled trees in a grove at the back edge of the estate.

He glanced over his shoulder to see that the road was clear.

In her stupor, Kat allowed him to pull her through a hidden rock wall to hide amongst the trees. There was an old outbuilding— a worn little gîte that mirrored the grand château on the rise. Barbed wire and a gate with warning signs of electrified fencing were posted in the distance. And there a rock-wall fence and crumbling stones hemmed them in, with birds singing innocent lullabies from the protection of the trees.

In that place of hushed beauty, their resolve shattered.

The basket dropped to their feet—the *Combats* pamphlet fluttering out with it—and they reached for one another. Breathless. Broken. And both numb it seemed, as the captain swept his arms around her in a protective hold.

Kat invited him in, hooking her arms under his shoulders as she pounded a soft fist against his back and the tender weight of his chin met the top of her head. Burying her face in the front of his Vichy police uniform, Kat's caged tears finally released as she broke apart.

Uncaring now, she allowed the will that said never to trust this man—certainly never to care—to die, and chose instead to cling to the momentary haven of his arms.

$$\sim$$

28 April 1952
92 Avenue d'Iéna
Paris, France

It took zero spy effort to dig up the trail of secrets Gérard Fontaine would not divulge.

Kat's husband made no point to cover his tracks as he strolled through the Paris streets that day. No doubling back on his way to Le Grand Véfour café near the Palais Royal park. Nor choosing a table tucked away in a corner of the ornate, gilted dining room.

Instead, she watched as he met with Madame Auclair for all to see, greeting the woman who'd been the icy guest at their wedding party on New Year's Eve. And then ordering cocktails and engaging in laughter and smiles in full view of the café's street-facing windows. It was as if he wanted to be caught. Or seen. Or found out in whatever her husband did in these clandestine meetings that took him from their flat so many days of the week and at all hours.

As soon as the pair were served their meal, she'd seen enough. And hurried home to the flat, knowing if there was anything of consequence to be unearthed, there was no more perfect time to discover it.

The door lock was easy to pick; Kat let herself in Gérard's room within a moment or two of trying.

He was neat. (As expected.) The French Baroque-style bed was made, the deep slate duvet smoothed and pillows lined along the headboard even when the housekeeping staff would not arrive to tidy up until the next day. (Ordered.) And didn't appear to need much: Only aftershave, razor, and a comb were lined up by the gold sink fixture in the oversize en suite. (And unpretentious.) His suits and shirts were starched, organized, and neatly hung in the armoire. A pile of books lingered on the bedside table, though it, too, was arranged to a tight four-corner stack. And naught but a brass lamp and telephone sat atop a scrolled-leg desk by the chamber's floor-to-ceiling windows.

She went there first, rifling through the desk drawers.

They were unlocked yet bore nothing incriminating. Kat skipped over the hiding places of bureau drawers or closet shelves. (Too obvious.) Gérard was smart enough not to hide anything in the first place a novice would. Instead, she inspected the unseen areas, seeking truth in the places she'd have hidden something herself.

Kat unscrewed the iron-scroll ventilation plate from the wall and checked inside the ductwork. She ran her fingers around the inside of the overhead light fixture that hung low over the bed. Tapped the tile in the bathroom, looking for any that served as a false front. Peered under the sink, felt behind the claw-foot tub faucets, and checked for loose stones lining the windowsill. She even paced the floor, listening for any hollow sound to tell her something had been tucked under the hardwoods.

All nothing.

A clock measured time from the mantel, its hollow *tick-tock* echoing off the high coffered ceilings—a little mocking that said she'd spent too long in his bedroom already, and if she hadn't found something by now, she wasn't likely to.

Kat moved back toward the door, remembering to flick the light switch before leaving. But as natural light pinged off the gilted fireplace grate, it struck: Gérard favored the glow of firelight and kept a fire lit as often as possible in any room in which he frequented. Always in the study. In the formal salon when they'd give parties. Even in his bedchamber at the seaside cottage at Le Crotoy harbor.

The hearth in this chamber, however, was pristine.

She rushed over, muscling the ornate fireplace grate aside.

*There's dust on the hearth . . .*

Kat reached underneath the lip of the mantel, racing her fingertips along cool marble until—a lump. She gasped as her palm wrapped around the unmistakable butt of a pistol and retrieved a black Walther PP that fell into her hand. After a breath of absorbing the shock, she set the pistol on the mantel, then moved along until her fingertips hit another.

*Leather?*

She pulled out a journal—its long leather strap wound tight around worn covers, with a thick binding and beveled edge. With trembling fingertips Kat unwound the strap and turned over the first few pages to find the book's hollowed-out center.

Melting to sit at the foot of the bed, Kat pulled out the bundle of her husband's secrets one by one: a passport bearing a British seal, a recent photograph, and the name *Jonathan Ashford*. A US passport with a similar photograph but with the name *Eric Doyle*. A French passport with *Maurice Lavigne*. And five more with aliases of nationals from Spain, Greece, Poland, the Soviet Union, and—her middle hitched to see it, given their wartime lives—even Germany.

A parcel of cash was tucked in the bottom, in too many foreign currencies. And her heart bled to find at the bottom of the secrets, with worn edges and a familiar face smiling back, an OSS photograph . . . of her.

A fire glowed in his bedroom hearth when Gérard slipped a key into the lock and stepped through the door. His gaze landed where Kat waited for him, sitting shadowed behind his desk with long legs crossed under her black wasp-waist skirt, and her ballet flats extended out the front.

"Bonjour, husband."

"How did you get in here?" When Kat tipped her brow, as if asking how ignorant he thought she was, he corrected. "Oh—bravo. Your skills are still sharp, I see. But you could have just asked our housekeeper for the extra key. Save you some time."

"It didn't take me a minute to pick the lock. I actually saved time by doing it myself. But since you favor using our time together so well"—she pushed the journal and pistol across the desk to the edge nearest him—"perhaps we should talk about this over dinner tonight? Shall I cook something, or have you already eaten?"

Gérard clicked the door closed, looking a little too dangerous in his crisp white shirt, cobalt tie, and powder-gray vest, and waltzed in with a matching suit jacket draped over his shoulder.

"Care to tell me what we ordered?" he asked, his tone flat as he tossed the suit jacket on the bed.

Fluorescent light flooded the room when he flicked the light switch in the en suite, spreading in a path from the bathroom sconces to the desk. Kat watched as he rolled shirtsleeves, removed his watch, and washed his hands before he tossed a hand towel on the sink and doused the light again.

Finally acknowledging her, he loosened his tie, unbuttoned his collar, and slipped hands in his trouser pockets as he paused for a casual lean against the doorjamb. "I've been wondering when we'd have this conversation."

"It wasn't as if you were trying to hide it. It's almost like you wanted to get caught. Why would that be?" She tapped the pistol with her index finger. No way they were going to gloss over it. "And don't try to tell me this is left over from the war. I checked; it's loaded. Just sitting in that fireplace over there, waiting to be used."

Gérard shook his head, caging. "What is it you really want to know?"

"Fine." She lifted her chin in defiance, breathing out a disbelieving, "Who are you?"

"I thought I was your husband."

Kat shot to her feet and slammed her palm to the desk.

"No more games! No more clever tit-for-tat deception or late-night desserts or strolls in the rain. And no more fairy tales about telegrams and my brother still being alive. Either you tell me everything—right now—or I will walk out that door and never look back."

When he dragged his hands from his pockets and took an ardent step forward, Kat raised her palm on air to halt him.

"I will not be made a fool again, Gérard. Not by you. Not by anyone."

He gave a weighted sigh from the center of the room. "I am Gérard Fontaine. I was born in France. And after my mother died, I was sent to my family's estate in the Midlands. All that I told you is true."

She gestured to the pile of aliases on the desktop. "And where did all this come from?"

"I attended school in Britain, at my father's insistence. By the time tensions with Hitler grew in France, my father had long since passed. I was of age. And I thought my family name and father's wealth might be of some use. The fledgling SOE found me and through La Marquise de Longvilliers, we contrived a way to place me at her château, to help mount a fight from within if the Nazis were to take over. They did. And you know the rest."

Moments and memories flashed through her mind.

From their first meeting at the seaside cottage. To the château. Valens' arrest. That harrowing day of executions in the square. The moment of solace they'd found in each other's arms after it. And the Christmas party at the château when everything changed . . . It all clicked into place.

"You were SOE? All that time?"

"Oui. Henri knew at the start. He was too and had been sent over to prepare the way for the first agent we'd place: Célène. Then your brother dropped into the picture around the same time Xandre came in with the Maquis. We'd have a proper team to focus our efforts. But then the real Célène disappeared. And that's when you came to us."

"Why didn't you tell me who you were? I was OSS. And had a right to know."

"That was Gavin's decision, in order to protect you. I vowed to honor it."

"But that wasn't his choice to make! Or yours." Kat shook her head on a furious denial, the rush of emotions hitting like a wave. "How could you take that away from me?"

"I'll give you one guess."

"But I am not a child! And didn't need protecting from either of you."

That brother of hers, always doing the same as she—blasting through the door to shield her, even when it wasn't needed. Making decisions she'd never asked for. And treating her as the fairer sex when there was no such thing.

If anything, Kat's mock interrogation at The Farm had taught her something about herself, and it wasn't that she was weak. After everything they'd been through in France, Gérard ought to have known it too.

"You still work for the British government?"

He nodded. Just once, but slow, to punctuate the truth laid bare between them.

"When you showed up, I had to question why someone would send you a telegram about Gavin—what would they gain? Why would anyone want you back in France? And it led me to one conclusion."

"Which is?"

"Maybe the G in the telegram wasn't about Gavin; it was about me."

That couldn't be . . . could it?

Kat shook her head, unwilling to believe the lure had been to bring her back to France not for Gavin, but to root out Gérard instead. Why that would be she didn't want to consider—couldn't consider. Because if Gavin wasn't a part of the equation, then all of this they'd done would be for nothing.

"Why would someone send the telegram to tell me you were alive?"

"They wanted you to know where I was. To lure you back to France. I still don't know the full reasons why. But I put a tail on Xandre as soon as I learned he'd come back to Paris. That's how I knew he'd pursued and married Mimi. And how he'd show up at our wedding party with her on his arm." Gérard inched forward, with a renewed sense of openness now alive in his eyes. "I never wanted to hurt you. But it's long past time to tell you all of this."

"Saying you don't wish to hurt me is a far cry from promising to love, honor, and obey until death do us part. I should never have come to France. Or listened to your fairy tales about Gavin, though dangling that carrot of the telegram was a clever ploy to keep me from getting on a boat straight back to Boston. The thing I don't understand is why you would even care. The war is over. I left France. And I made a life for myself again. You could have gone on with yours, as you said that first day in your kitchen, and left me out of it."

"This is what I do, Kat. It is a job. A compulsive act maybe, but it's not who I am."

"How could I ever believe that?"

He took several steps forward this time, long strides that ended with only the desk as an obstacle between them. "You know, because you know *me*. I've never lied to you."

"Non? You just conveniently omitted an encyclopedia's worth of backstory about who you really are! Is our marriage even legal? You know what, don't answer that." She shook her head and skirted the side of the desk, intending to leave. "We haven't . . . Well, it's not a real marriage anyway, so it can be undone."

"And if it's real to me?" He caught her, cutting off her path to the door with a gentle hand to her elbow.

Kat stopped. Turned. And faced him, but with a protective shield of crossing her arms over her chest.

"What if it has been real to me this whole time?"

"How can that be? After months, the first time I've seen the inside of my husband's bedroom I stumble upon a pistol and enough money to put a down payment on an estate in the south of France. Any woman who doesn't find a problem with that hasn't considered the glaring reality of her husband's double life. Or am I just your Paris wife? Perhaps you have a flat and a female in every city of the world. Is that why you play this game? So you're not that recluse returned to his seaside cottage?"

"There are no games here, Kat. The life I lead is the one I want. There is only you and me in this room." He paused, considering before he asked, "You saw everything in that journal?"

"I did."

"And . . . ?"

She swallowed hard. "And you couldn't share any of this unless it was with your wife. I understand that part."

"That's not why I married you."

Standing firm, she whispered, "Where did you get that photo?"

"Wouldn't you rather know why I have it?"

Gérard stepped up then, not asking if he could touch her with words, but if it was possible, with everything else. His gaze intensified with unmasked longing and rested on her pursed lips that remained silent before him. Then to her eyes, suspended with his. And the hands anchored in fists at his side said he was doing everything he could to hold back from acting on the impulse to reach for her.

"Because if you asked me why, I'd tell you that the photo is worn at the edges because it belongs to a man who's carried it with him every day, from the end of the war until you came back into my life. Or that every look to you from across a room . . . every kiss pressed to your hand . . . every dance . . . every single dinner and walk and moment shared with you here in our city has been genuine. It's because I wanted to do those things. No one made me fall in love with you, Kat, but *you*."

He paused, waiting. Breaths heady in the noticeable rise and fall of his chest.

"I'd have given you the money. All you had to do was ask."

"And I . . ." Kat paused then too. And tried to start again, her lips parting with the revelation. "I'd have given my testimony at any time. Even without the ring."

Defenses within Gérard must have shredded in the same way they did for her, because they gave, breaths crashing in and out as each rushed forward and swallowed up the space between them. He swept arms tight around her waist and they fell back together so fast the underside of Kat's legs bumped the desk.

A tiny gasp escaped her mouth just as his lips closed over it. They stood entangled. Allayed. Rescued, even. And all of a sudden realizing each hadn't been so far away as the other had thought. And making up for lost time was a longing they shared.

"I have more to tell you if you'll let me. More I couldn't say before now," he murmured, trying to catch his breath against her mouth.

"I don't want to talk."

Kat felt him smile against her lips. "Then, please. Stay?"

"I asked you that once before. At the cottage in Le Crotoy that first night. And you never left. For three days I woke and you were still there."

Gérard nodded, his forehead bumping hers in a soft brush. "I'm the one asking now. And I swear you'll never wake up alone again. Not if you don't want to."

Twilight skies bled to ink, and night took the room.

Only the glow of dying embers on the hearth and a stout spring rain kissing the windows remained. They welcomed the quiet hours, with the unearthed secrets on the desk long forgotten in exchange for the hope that come morning, the sun would return and they'd no longer have to greet it alone.

# CHAPTER 22

26 November 1943
Le Crotoy, France

Manon tapped an index finger to the windowsill, waiting and watching the road from the shadows of the old thatched-roof barn.

Crows flitted about rain-soaked orchard rows, cawing and picking at rotting apples left over from the last harvest. And clouds lingered over the fields, the gray plumes hanging low in the sky as they drifted inland from the sea. She checked her watch. Again, for the tenth time in the last five minutes, as raindrops dripped from the eaves and ticked away the minutes at an excruciatingly slow pace.

*A quarter after ten o'clock . . .*

If Dominique didn't arrive soon, she'd have no choice but to start back to the château without having met him at all. And in the midst of darker days now with Célène as her only ally in the kitchen, Manon longed for nothing more than to feel the assurance of his presence. At the least that could bolster her to go on.

The message Henri had given Célène in the village the day of the executions was not positive news. Nor was the aftermath in the square with its lasting impression.

On top of the enormous loss of life to their team, Henri had sent a warning that meetings would become scattered, with few safe places left in which to organize Resistance activities. Their village connections had been all but severed with Dr. Rousseau's execution. And with the mishap with the dead footman, the châteu grounds had been on virtual lockdown since. This clandestine meeting only came about from a message Manon slipped to Henri during the latest fish delivery. She had something to report—a spark of hope they'd stumbled upon in preparations for the Reich's upcoming holiday fêtes.

Hinges creaked and Manon turned, her breath quickening as she peered into the darkened interior of the barn.

"Manon?" Dominique whispered through the maze of hay bales, fermentation barrels, and cider bottling tables. And what remained of the orchard's apple harvest that hadn't been sold, stolen, or commandeered by the authorities.

"I'm here." She edged out, then seeing those beautiful eyes brighten when they landed upon her, charged forward and threw herself into his arms.

Dominique enveloped her back, lifting her from the ground as he whispered, "You found it" and "You're safe," and pressed kisses to the tender spot at the junction where her jaw met her neck.

"I thought you weren't coming," Manon whispered, leaning back to look him over. "I didn't know how much longer I could have done this without at least seeing you—without knowing you're safe. Tell me you're well."

He edged back a shade, a little play in his eyes as he settled the wisps of hair that had fallen, windblown around her face.

"You mean you were worried about me?"

"I was, if you must know," she admitted, letting him enjoy toying with her. "And do try not to be so smug about it."

"I'll do my best. Forgive me if I fail?" Pressing another quick kiss to her lips, he peered through the window and grew more serious. "We don't have much time before the others will be here. I need you to listen to me."

"What is it?"

"I don't want you to go anywhere alone. Not you or Célène. Not unless I come for you. Promise me you won't take any unnecessary risks."

Ticking her head toward the road and orchard teeming with beady-eyed blackbirds, she wasn't certain how realistic that was.

"Of course I won't, if you ask me not to. But I did come here alone."

"I know that." He brushed another lock of her hair back, but with his finger tracing a slower line against her brow. "And when we leave, I'll follow you out. At a distance but all the way back to the château. After that, you and Célène stay together as often as possible. No visits to the village. Nor the dunes. And don't mention this to anyone else. I'll sleep better at night for knowing, at least until some things are settled. I couldn't bear it if anything—"

"D'accord. I promise. We will be safe."

With his usual way, Dominique had lifted her spirits, even when delivering less-than-desirable news. But the way he was watching her now, looking on her in quiet and as if they had all the time in the world just to breathe in each other's presence—it felt like the whisper Valens had once spoken of, that a day would come when she'd want to love again.

"And what is it now?"

"Nothing. It's just . . ." With an almost boyish grin behind his beard, he paused as if discovering something anew. "I've missed you. You can't know how much. I don't even think I did until this moment. I'd despise everything about this terrible war, except that it brought me you. I don't know whether to be soul-angry or grateful down to my bones. Maybe I'm both."

It was always the hint of something beautiful next to brokenness with him.

Dominique was as serious as they might come. And it was no jest that people everywhere were desperate. It seemed the worst time in the world to love. And yet, something warmed in her, and Manon leaned up, pressing a softer, slower kiss to his lips.

"I've missed you too." And remembering the other part of her heart then, she dared ask, "How is Valens?"

"He is well. And sends his love. He made certain I relayed that or he said something about having my hide for tea. Oh, and that I'd better not hurt his daughter or he'd find a convenient way to make me disappear. As if the war needed any help with that."

"That sounds like him. Though I'm sure he said it in a much more musical way."

"As he does. I promised when it is safe, you'll be reunited soon." He exhaled low, relief quick to wash over his face. "Now, what do you have for us?"

The door creaked again, and Dominique stepped in front of her in a protective half step, until they saw Xandre and Henri come through, shaking rain from their coats.

"Dom. Chef." Xandre tipped his flatcap to them both.

Henri's greeting was much more absolute. With a curt nod he got down to brass tacks without missing a beat. "We'd best hurry, Dom. The road will not be empty long."

"Right." Dominique welcomed them. "Chef has news."

"I do." Manon pulled a folded parcel of paper from the inside lining of her trench and handed it over to Dominique. "We have an opportunity. The lists for rail deliveries have arrived, with the usual foodstuffs for planning the officers' dinners."

"So?" Xandre leaned in, peeking over Dominique's shoulder as he unfolded the papers. "I've been helping the Maquis disrupt the rail lines for months. We've stolen supplies before. We can do it again."

"Oui, but this is different. See? Here." She pointed out columns on the page—the ledger written in stark lines from top to bottom. "Célène translated it for us. We couldn't pass up the chance that the Maquis might find it useful."

"It's in German?"

"It is." Dominique nodded to Xandre's question, just as his face melted into a relieved smile. He looked up at Henri, then Manon. "And it's brilliant. How did you get this?"

"We have Célène to thank. She came across it at the château. This is proof that the Germans are concerned about an Allied offensive somewhere along the Normandy coast as early as this spring."

Dominique shook his head, as if the news was too fortunate to be true. And maybe it was. "An Allied invasion? What that could mean for France. And for the world."

"The Germans see it as a credible risk. So much so, they're fortifying around the Baie de Somme right now. These rail schedules confirm it—more Nazi soldiers, more tanks and concrete and building supplies for the construction of additional lookouts on the cliff tops."

"They're expecting this soon, aren't they?" Xandre questioned, his voice sounding a fraction worried.

"Oui. But most important for us," Manon continued, "is that a bevy of arms and military supplies will be sent to the château, likely within the month. That means with the preparations for events, I'll know when the shipments of arms have arrived based on what shows up in the kitchen."

Henri smiled too, the usually reticent man showing himself to come alive at any instance to aid in the Reich's eventual downfall. "And if we could relieve the Boche of those arms . . ."

"We'd be ready to fight when the time comes," Xandre finished.

"Célène translated it all. She made copies in French for the Maquis, there on the back pages. And we'll do our best to keep you informed of what shipments arrive. There's still a chance the arms could be diverted. Or not arrive at all. Though you can see, it is a steady stream expected through the end of December. This is the best chance we've had."

"And you'll know when to alert us." Dominique took the German ledger, folded it, and shoved it down in his boot. Then handed a

French version each to Xandre and Henri. "Is that enough to get you started to arm the Maquis?"

Xandre scanned the list and nodded with a glow of triumph on his face. "I'd say that's enough to hope Christmas will come early—at least this year." He, too, shoved the ledger in his boot, then nodded to Henri. "Allons-y. And Chef?" He turned to Manon. "Merci. The Maquis will be on alert for when you say it's time."

"We'll send word when the shipments arrive."

Henri nodded to Dominique and then to Manon, adding a "madame" as they fled back out to the rainy November landscape.

When she moved to follow, Dominique pressed a finger to his lips.

"Wait—" He whispered and held her elbow, keeping her behind him as he watched at the window. And when the men hurried by through the drizzle, only then did he continue. "How did she know?"

"You mean how did Célène know to leave off the additional columns on the French translations? She is more intelligent than you give her credit for."

"You can't mean she has reason to suspect two men who've been loyal up to this point?"

"Non. But Célène does not trust anyone it seems, except for you. Though she would not say why. She knows Xandre does not speak German, as he cannot follow what the officers say during the courtyard deliveries. And I think she'd wager Henri might not either. She guessed getting a message to you in German would be the safest way not to tip them off. Célène has no proof to the contrary, but she put the safeguard in place just as a precaution."

"So an extra shipment of arms is coming by Christmas. But this one is assured whereas the others are only a guess?"

Manon nodded. "Oui. And now you can decide what to do with this information. Célène and I have put it to you to ensure those arms do not fall into the wrong hands. And until we learn whose those are, no one else should know about it."

A look of sheer relief washed over his face. Or was it . . . pride? "There is something I need you to do for me."

"Anything."

"I know there is a fête planned at the château for Christmas Eve, with the Nazi elite in attendance. I need Célène to attend that party with the captain."

"She'd never agree to it. Not without explanation."

"You'll think of something. I just need her to be there for the toast at midnight. She has to see the faces of everyone in that ballroom."

Manon shook her head, the puzzles only building upon one another. "Why?"

"We've known there is a mole in our network for some time. We believe he has been operating at a singular level, collecting and disseminating information from the château. I'd have guessed it was Frédéric after what happened. But we believe there's someone else. Someone higher. Someone the Yanks and the Brits together can point to as the one who set a trap for the SOE agents when I'd first arrived in France. I can't get in the château to that party to see his face, if he shows. But she can."

"How do you know this man will even be there?"

"I can't say how, as it would endanger someone else."

"But you need me to do this."

"I do. Convince Célène? If the man is indeed OSS, she might pick him out from a sea of Nazi uniforms. Give her this." He retrieved a tube of lipstick from his pocket. "It's a microfilm camera. She's to photograph the gathering. Take as many pictures as she can. And smuggle the film downstairs and hide it in the kitchen after. I'll come by to retrieve it in the next fish delivery."

"And if the weapons arrive?"

"We've a rough plan. I'll take the lead at the rails to ensure the weapons are lifted. I'll make the transfer to Henri at the old grounds-keeper's gîte. While he uses Xandre's contacts with the Maquis to fan the weapons out along the coast, I'll return to the dunes and send a wire back to the Allies that it's done. It would help if you and Célène could distract the kitchen staff and the Vichy police both when the shipment arrives. However you can."

"This is a lot to ask."

Dominique exhaled heavily; the ticking clock always the overlord in the background making men sigh. "I know. But she's capable. And so are you."

"I understand." Manon smiled, leaning in close so she could palm his chest. "Should I say Merry Christmas now?"

"Non, Chérie," he whispered back, his lips brushing hers. "I will find a way to see you before then. A man knows when he's defeated. And sometimes that's the best feeling in the world."

In war every goodbye was torture.

Manon stepped out into the orchard, stirring the crows from their feast as she walked her bicycle through the fields. And knowing those brilliant blue eyes watched her from some safe place behind, she stepped up to the road and, with all the hope in the world, blew a kiss on the wind.

# CHAPTER 23

18 December 1943
Château du Broutel
Rue, France

How about now?" Kat plunked down the porcelain plate in front of the chef with a wedge of her latest creation and a fork ready for tasting.

It must have been the tenth Pithiviers she'd made that week, but this time with a savory mushroom, leek, and potato crème filling and an intricate fluted pastry edge she'd hoped to serve for the kitchen staff meal at midday. But not if this one, too, belonged in the bin. Call it a small victory, but Kat was determined not to fail at this feat of cookery for the umpteenth time in a row.

Manon cut a bite from the tip of the triangle, loading the fork with a creamy bite to taste, while Kat chewed the corner of her thumbnail and watched.

"Well?" Without waiting, Kat threw her hands up. "I knew it. It's the pastry, isn't it? Soggy bottom again."

Putting the fork back, Manon turned away to the mosaic of copper saucepans she'd been watching on the stove. She picked up a knife from a chopping board nearby and began mowing through a colander of garlic bulbs.

"What then? Surely the pastry needs salt or I've overworked it or the butter leaked out?"

"Did you see flash-fried butter in the bottom of your pan?"

"Non. But it must be something." Kat took the plate back and peeled off a corner of the fluted edge to taste test the pastry herself. "Look—you could barely eat it."

"Célène, please do get back to work. We haven't time for theatrics when we have a staff meal to serve." Though she was firm in her kitchen, Manon did let the softest hint of a smile press into her profile as she moved to a pan of heated olive oil and tossed in the minced garlic.

"You mean it's right?"

"*Bien joué*," Manon echoed with a genuine smile this time. "You no longer need my instruction. Not to know when you've made something that should be celebrated. Judge yourself fairly next time."

It was as much a moment of praise as Kat had ever been offered.

In the weeks Manon and she had rebounded from Valens' absence and the gutting display of the public executions, they'd worked side by side and developed a mutual rapport. Kat's job was to keep her eyes and ears open, to continue filtering the deliveries for potential messages, and to aid in the subversive efforts around the château. But the in-between moments had filled her with a genuine desire to learn in the kitchen. And after the hiccups of split crème au beurre, burnt pastry, boiled jam, and one batch of undercooked pheasant pies that nearly poisoned the entire kitchen staff . . . Kat was determined to get something right.

The Pithiviers was it—her moment of triumph in the days that bled together with waiting for word on what came next for their pared-down team.

Before she could rush off, Manon placed a gentle hand to her wrist. "Wait, Célène," she entreated with a serious whisper.

Kat set the plate back down and flitted a glance around the kitchen. There was activity across the way—shiny pots and pans being put in place for their dinner preparations, and the new German-placed pâtissier piping méringue to his lemon tarts in the far corner. But thankfully, no one was close enough to hear.

She turned back so she could read Manon's lips as they spoke. "You have news?"

Manon nodded. "The captain has informed me that our shipment for the kitchen will arrive on the twenty-second, so we might prepare and have our menu approved by the Reich officials in advance of the Christmas holiday. But the remainder of the rail deliveries we are hoping for are to arrive two days later . . . on the same day the Reich's minister of propaganda is set to join the other officers here."

Leaning in to whisper, Kat couldn't help but state the obvious. "But that's the night of the Christmas party! We can't be expected to serve a seven-course meal and coordinate this at the same time. It's not possible. Especially not with the heightened security should Joseph Goebbels himself actually decide to attend."

"I think it's worse than that. I've seen paperwork for the Gestapo checks of a bevy of food testers who will be paraded through to sample from our kitchen. That can only mean one thing."

"Oh, my word," she breathed out, hand clutching invisible pearls at her collar. "Their führer himself is coming?"

Manon gave a quick nod, then turned back to her saucepans. "I'm afraid it appears that way. I've never seen such security. The Gestapo will be in the kitchen that night, scrutinizing everything we do."

Kat pinched finger and thumb to the bridge of her nose.

How she wished Gavin were there at the moment.

At least that way they'd have some intelligence from outside the château to offer information on the view looking in. They'd been virtual prisoners in their own kitchen these many weeks. Not to mention the Franc-Garde were known to pop in and out with more fervent regularity. And Captain Fontaine's former ironclad security detail was under the watchful eye of many more now, not just the officers upstairs.

The very air they breathed was fragile.

"You think we should abandon the scheme and try another time?"

Manon shook her head. "And allow those devils to put more bullets into Allied soldiers who might storm a beach to take France back? *Never.* We'll simply have to find a way around it."

"What could be worse than that?"

She looked back at Kat, this time with a heavy sigh and empathy in her eyes. "I've been informed that you'll be in the ballroom too. I'm afraid it's been requested by Captain Fontaine that you attend the party at his side."

$\backsim$

29 April 1952
92 Avenue d'Iéna
Paris, France

Paris was not known for subtle mornings.

Pedestrian traffic woke early. Sparrows and greenfinches twittered about at sunup, nesting in the trees that lined the avenue. And automobiles clogged the thoroughfare on the way to l'Arc de Triomphe, with the hum of engines and random horn honks that broke the stolen silence of their room.

The sun warmed Kat's bare back in a last temptation to lull her from sleep. She let out a soft sigh, blinked awake with her cheek buried in the pillow, and at once remembered where she was—where *they* were.

The view of white sheets, gauze drapes filtering the sun, the masculine desk and mound of troubles still sitting atop it, and the husband next to her all combined in a flash of unease. And without having been schooled in wedded bliss thus far, Kat hadn't the faintest clue what came next.

"Bonjour." Gérard greeted her when he'd stirred and pressed a sleepy kiss to the scar on her shoulder that just peeked out from the sheet.

"Morning," she whispered, and turned to face him, her hair falling over her eyes at the exact wrong time. He brushed it back over her shoulder, out of the way. But left his fingertips next to her on the bed, the warm touch just grazing her arm.

Gérard's ebony hair was mussed over his forehead. He seriously needed a shave. And Kat would have hated to admit it, but the sun on his face almost stole her breath more in that instant than he could have with the confessions he'd murmured against her lips the night before.

"Um . . . what time is it?"

He stretched over to his bedside table and swiped up a pair of glasses from the drawer to read the mantel clock. "Half past nine."

"You wear glasses? I never remembered that. You must have had contact lenses all that time during the war."

"I wasn't this old during the war. And in my defense, that clock is pretty far away." He dropped the glasses again, the soft smile he rewarded her with tinged with the casual comfort of familiarity. "You going to tell my superiors? Get me fired for nearsightedness now that you know what I do?"

"I'll think about it after I hear the full story. Then I'll decide."

He let out a little laugh that ended with a yawn and ran a sleepy hand through his hair. "Coffee?"

Kat sat up a little, her delight unmasked.

War rations were still in place as Paris recovered. Little luxuries like chocolate or cosmetics were priced at a very pretty penny, when you could find them. And coffee? That was very much a dream that she wasn't about to pass up, even now.

"You found coffee?"

"Had to pay through the nose. But oui. Though it is French roast, I thought my American wife might like it. Maybe help her feel more at home here in Paris."

*Wife . . .*

*And home?*

Those words were going to take every bit of getting used to hearing now, even though they'd been floating between them for months. But with umpteen complications sitting in the very same room, the thoughts goading Kat now were that the argument that had turned into a monumental leap forward the night before seemed far more reckless in the light of day—the offer of coffee or not.

An awkward silence dropped between them again, accentuated by the muffled sounds of the Paris streets below. Kat stared at the ceiling and seriously considered bounding from the bed under the guise of making the brew, just so she could dress and escape through the flat's front door.

"The Christmas party."

"What?"

"You asked when I knew about your ear. It was the château Christmas party."

She sat up, pulling the sheet up to her neck, and looked down at him. "You never said."

"I'd suspected it before, at the cottage. I was talking to you from the kitchen, but you only answered when I was looking directly at you. I put it together when I could see what you were doing the night of the party, reading the lips of the Nazi elite from across the ballroom. You asked me to get you a drink. And I watched as you sat in a chair against the wall, tilting your head to keep the visual connection as waiters walked through your line of sight. Taking in everything those Reich commanders said."

"Is that why you needed me to go to the party? We didn't know who it was—still don't. But I was the eyes to find a mole if they were from the OSS. And you were the eyes to find one from the SOE."

"It was supposed to work that way. But then you got up and crossed the ballroom. And left. Just like that. Without a word."

"How did you know I hadn't gone to powder my nose?"

Gérard leaned up on his elbow, soft and slow, and grazed lips to the spot where her neck touched her ear. "Because you left your clutch behind, love. Remember? I placed it on the table so we could dance? I tried to call out to you for it, but you didn't hear me." Gérard tapped her earlobe with his finger. "That pretty ear again."

"You're right. I didn't hear a thing."

"And it all made sense when you missed the toast and I found you in the woods afterward, trying to untangle a bigger set of problems."

"Yes. You did."

"Nothing's changed from that night, Kat."

That deep voice of his wasted little time in reminding how well he knew what was racing through her mind.

"Everything's changed."

"I meant nothing's changed for me. I'm not afraid to admit I love you."

Kat stiffened and drew in a steadying breath. Before she could think of how to respond, he reached for her hand and brushed a thumb against her palm.

"And before you think you have to say something back, know I've wanted this every day we've been in Paris. For years, before you showed up in my kitchen with that telegram. Even from that last moment we were together during the war and I had to break your heart. It killed me to do it. So the way I see it is, whether I sent that telegram or not, I thank Providence every day because it became my second chance to make some things right."

She looked around at the state of where they'd found themselves now, in his bed with a heap of proverbial baggage filling the rest of the room.

"Quite the second chance to end up here."

"I didn't plan this part. Oh, I wanted it—believe me. But I realize this . . . took us both by surprise. I'm not asking for anything except that you let me show you I meant what I said last night. There's more I need to tell you. More to say. I just don't know how to do it without—"

A booming knock pounded the flat's front door, cutting him off.

Kat jumped.

"No need to worry. Probably the staff forgot the key again." He squeezed her hand and brought it to his lips, brushing a kiss across her knuckles. "I'll get it."

"You sure?"

Gérard winked at her. "If you're lucky, I'll make the coffee too." He pulled on trousers and an unbuttoned collared shirt, then stepped out as the second round of pounding began. A few seconds later, it was followed by men's muffled voices that carried down the hall.

Alarmed, Kat rose.

She shrugged into Gérard's robe she found hanging on a hook in the en suite and gathered up the items on the desk. Never mind they'd been too swept up in each other and left them out all night— she'd have to slip them back in the fireplace now. She stepped into the hall after, only intending to listen. But because she couldn't hear and needed to see in order to do so, Kat padded down the hall and slowed to tiptoe in the shadows where the entry led to the kitchen.

Her legs almost dropped out from under her when she witnessed a horde of Vichy police standing by the open flat door and handcuffs being drawn around Gérard's wrists.

"What do you think you're doing?" she blasted and rushed into the light.

"Don't worry, Kat." Gérard raised shackled hands to hold her at bay. "I'll be all right. I promise."

"How dare you! Take your hands off my husband this instant."

An officer stepped up, offering a folded piece of paper to Kat. "This man is under arrest, madame."

"Is that so?" She swiped the paper out of his hand. "On whose authority?"

"The Courts of Justice. There will be a hearing within thirty days' time, in which the gentleman may present a case against the charges and the witness testimony."

"What witness testimony? I've yet to give mine."

"Witnesses are confidential, madame."

The uniform droned on: "And after a set amount of time, he may then appeal any conviction to the—"

"Non," Kat snapped, bristling at the notion that the man standing before her could in any way be a candidate for prosecution under a supposed testimony as weak as Xandre's. "You will release Mr. Fontaine this instant, or you will find every solicitor in France on your doorstep within the hour. And I'd wager you will be out of a job by the end of the day."

"That is your right, madame. But you will stand aside, as we have orders to take the captain with or without necessary force," the police pushed back, ordering Kat to stand down.

A uniform gripped her arm to shove her out of the way, prompting Gérard to wrestle free and drive a shoulder into the officer's chest. They crashed the sideboard in a furious *thump*, shattering a lamp on the tile floor.

"Telephone my solicitor. Mr. James—his number is in the file," Gérard called as they hauled him up to standing.

"I will," she vowed, crying out over the scuffle. "I promise."

"And telephone Betty Prior."

Kat froze—that name was so foreign now she could have just received a slap to the face. She shook her head in disbelief, not understanding how he could possibly know it, nor for what purpose he used it now.

"What?"

"Mrs. Betty Prior. Telephone her. Tell her the man I've been looking for is somewhere at the château. I just need to know where he is, and all of this will end." Gérard rushed the words out, terrifying her all the more that he'd allowed his eyes to glaze in an entreaty when he'd said it. "Can you do that for me, love?"

"You want me to telephone Betty Prior?"

He nodded, and mouthed back, "*Kat . . . I am so, so sorry.*"

With eyes that begged her to believe him, Gérard pleaded for only a split second before he was shoved through the entrance and the flat door slammed behind them.

Kat was left trembling, covering her mouth with one shaking palm and the other holding an arrest warrant that had gone limp in her hand. Her breaths racked in and out. *Remain calm. Think. Focus on what Gérard said because there must be a very good reason why he said it.*

*The telephone . . .*

She snapped her view up to the hall, then ran back to Gérard's room.

Standing in the doorway, she saw it—the black rotary Peohud sitting in innocence on the desk. Rushing forward, Kat dropped the warrant on the desktop and grabbed the telephone. It had a wire running at the back, down the desk leg. But that's where it appeared to stop, plugging into no outlet and making it a device of no use. She flipped it over, the handset falling to the desktop in a clamored ring against the rotary dial base.

Prying the face off the bottom and with a host of questions pinging wildly through her mind, Kat's world shattered when the bottom came away and revealed what had been hidden inside.

An old brass Testrite compass fell cold into her palm.

Kat shook her head in horror.

Tears blurred her vision. And all of a sudden, the pain-racked emotion in Gérard's eyes made sense. This must have been the heartbreaking piece to the puzzle he'd not been able to tell her yet but had hoped to share had they been given the chance that morning.

Kat melted down to the floor on her knees, closing her fist around the compass as sobs racked her. There was only one way Gérard could have found the compass. Either Gavin was alive and her husband had been keeping it from her all this time, or her brother was dead and Gérard had found the treasure on Gavin's body.

Heaven help her . . . Who had she helped Xandre bury at the château?

# CHAPTER 24

20 *December 1943*
Château du Broutel
Rue, France

The ballet-pink dress box had a layer of dust an inch thick when Manon pulled it down from the top of the armoire. She stepped down off the chair, the top of the box clouding the air like flour when her feet hit the floor.

A petite cough later, she presented the box on the bed, its top christened with *Bruyère* in gold-leaf lettering.

"It's been up there a while. But here it is."

"Are you sure this is really necessary?" Célène asked, the lamp-light of their service quarter room glowing dimly in the space between them. "I can just wear one of my dresses."

"My dear, it doesn't matter for what occasion a woman should wear a pretty dress; she always makes it shine in the end. And for this party, we need all the luster we can get. Besides, you don't want to stand out for lack of attention to detail. We must do everything to make them think you are one of them."

Slipping her fingers under the lip of the box, Manon opened the lid and swept back the layers of tissue to reveal the one last treasure she owned from her old life.

It was a masterpiece.

Still.

After all the time that had passed.

Emerald satin caught the light with a luxurious sheen as she raised it from its slumber in the box. Gathered fabric formed a strapless sweetheart neckline, a cinched waist, and decadent haute couture waves that rolled to a sleek hem, creating a fluted skirt and train worthy of a fashion feature in *Vogue* magazine.

"Where did you get this?" Célène asked, sounding as breathless as Manon felt to see it again.

She held the gown up against Célène, noting the similarities in their figures.

"It should fit nicely. You're a shade taller than I am, so we'll have to put you in flats to ensure the train goes down to the ankle. But other than that, it's a fine last-minute save if I do say so myself."

"I'm sure we can find a pair of flats somewhere."

Accepting the gown with gentle hands, Célène held it up before the floor-length mirror in their chamber. A wave of understanding seemed to dawn, perhaps in how Manon had stood behind in Célène's reflection, taking in the view of the gown Julian had always wanted her to wear. It couldn't have been more heart-tugging if it were a never-worn wedding gown, though at least she'd worn one once upon a time.

"But this is custom made. I couldn't possibly wear it. It looks like a gift." After a pause, Célène added, softer, and much more endearing, "Oh my. Was it? A gift?"

Tears always muddled the best of things and broke hearts in the worst. It was the memory of that Christmas in 1939 that provoked the glaze in Manon's eyes now.

Julian had been secretive that year, never letting on he'd met a guest by the name of Marie-Louise Bruyère once after a shift while working at the Ritz. He'd spoken so fondly of his wife that the woman—apparently a renowned Paris fashion designer— offered to design a custom gown for her. Julian had borrowed one of Manon's dresses to give the haute couture house of Bruyère the proper measurements and had siphoned extra francs out of their household ledger to pay for it, which she'd found out later was a jaw-dropping sum. She'd even learned Valens had given up more than one of his own pay vouchers from the Ritz, all so her husband could give her this one surprise.

When the worst had come and Nazis stormed into Paris, Manon and Valens had left everything behind . . . except for this.

The blush box had come all the way from Paris, cradled lovingly in her arms. Had ridden on her lap in automobiles as they trekked north for a job placement in a château kitchen. Was carried with pride past the Reich officers when she'd first climbed the service stairs. And with too many tears shed later in that very room, Manon had left it to sleep atop the armoire until it could be useful—a precious gown that had still never been worn.

"My husband, Julian, said one day he'd take me dancing at the Ritz, instead of me having to work their parties from the kitchen. How he would have had a time twirling me with that train. And our daughter—" Manon's chin quivered, and she stopped over a hitch of emotion. "Collette, said she wanted one when she grew up one day, just like her maman. And she'd have had it too. My husband would never let his girls down."

Célène offered a compassionate nod. "He sounds like a very fine man."

"Oui. He was. Too fine, as I recall. Too good for this war. They both were."

Despite the stripping down of personalities to become a member of service staff, Manon could not help but notice now that they were far more like two sisters in a dress shop than cooks planning a grand scheme to arm the local Resistance. They might have been Paris wives—perhaps of new acquaintance but growing close enough to share deeply guarded corners of their hearts and have them understood by the other.

It was a surprise, to talk of her loves like this. And to find a friend in it.

"Have you ever thought it might find you again?"

Manon glanced up, meeting Célène's gaze in the mirror. "What might find me?"

"You know. *L'amour*. Or does it only happen once in a lifetime, if we're lucky?"

"Love? Here? In this madness? I hadn't until . . . Well, it is remarkable isn't it, how war cannot blot even that from the world? It's how we know we're still alive, when love hasn't gone completely from our hearts. But none of it matters now," she said, running a finger along the bottom rows of her lashes, swiping away the moisture that had gathered there. "All I know is he'd want you to wear it, and he'd be proud knowing what we plan to do. It's almost like he's here. Fighting with us."

To her credit, Manon's understudy in the kitchen seemed a woman practiced in the art of subtlety. She didn't argue or press. She chose not to intrude. Instead, she slipped out of her frock and pulled the gown up in its place, allowing Manon to fasten her up the back.

"You've done this before," Manon qualified, seeing the way Célène knew how to move with elegance.

"A time or two."

Célène looked more like a princess in a palace than kitchen staff who was to be elevated for the night. She could hold her shoulders square, projected an air of effortless grace when she moved, and knew the most flattering way the train would sweep out behind her as she walked the length of the room and back, trying it out.

"My mother wished me to attend society parties when I was younger, hoping I'd make a good match. But I always resisted that life. I'm afraid a party for me is a good book and a fire on the hearth." Célène pressed a palm to her middle and turned to the side, checking the gown's nips and tucks at all of its best angles. "You know, this is the first time I've actually looked forward to attending one. Or am anxious about it at the same time."

"No one will know that. You are exceptional at keeping your features calm, no matter what's stirring up on the inside."

"I am still attending with a Vichy police captain. Let us hope I can play it off next to him."

"But after that day in the village . . . do you trust him at all? You have to admit, it is a contradiction that he didn't turn you over to the authorities."

Kat sighed and met Manon's gaze in the mirror's reflection.

"I don't know what to think. Should I trust my head, which only sees his uniform? Or do I trust the something else in me that wants to believe there's good in this man?"

The chef tipped her head to one side, considering. "Why does it have to be one or the other?"

"Maybe it doesn't. All I know is, the Franc-Garde will be watching. Too close. That's what keeps me up nights now. Wondering how I'm going to work this out, as if I don't know what Dominique will be doing at the rail lines. What if the night patrols do continue as normal?"

Manon shook her head, a firm denial to that. "I've been assured they will not. Out in the woods, where the barbed-wire fence and rock wall meet, that area is supposed to be electrified. At least that is what the soldiers will think. They won't want to waste their time patroling an area thought secure, not when they can enjoy a Christmas tipple and a night off. I'd wager they'd much rather be toasting their spirits over a burning barrel than out enduring the elements for no good reason."

"And by then, the weapons will be in Henri's hands."

"And they will be none the wiser. You just keep the captain occupied as long as possible. Get the photos during the officials' toast. And there will be no more patrols on the grounds until the party is over. By then Henri will be gone with the weapons and you can slip back down to the kitchen. It's the best chance we have now."

"What will you do, having to serve an entire dinner on your own?"

"I won't be on my own. We'll choose the menu carefully and work together until you have to go up. Besides, this is what I've trained for. It's the moment I've lived for these past years, to use my skill for retribution. And incidentally, to have the honor of spitting in the food of their führer himself. I'm only sad Valens shall have to miss out on this moment." Manon reached out, fluffing the wrinkles out of one layer of the train. "You just walk in that ballroom with your wits sharp and your head held high."

"I will, even if there are no pockets in this beauty." Célène swiped up the lipstick tube with the camera inside and tucked it into her clutch with a gold compact, a sewing kit, invisible-ink matches, and her forged French identification, just in case. Then she turned again in the mirror, twirling the train with a dangerous smile on her lips.

"Now . . . if I can just figure out where to fit my knife."

Manon felt genuine laughter roll up from within her, for they should have been terrified for the undertaking that faced them all. Instead, she felt proud.

"Well, that's the very last thing I'd expect a French glamour girl to say. But in this case, I couldn't be more pleased. You will stun every one of them in that ballroom."

"Let's hope so." Kat smiled back, her reflection piercing with blue eyes full of expectation. "Because if our plan works, the officers at that party will be stunned in more ways than one."

# CHAPTER 25

24 *December 1943*
Château du Broutel
Rue, France

*S* howtime . . .

Kat started down the circular staircase, slow and steady as she eyed the party below.

Nothing could be done about having missed the lavish sit-down dinner; Manon needed help to ensure everything went off without a hitch from the kitchen. But the instant the last course had been plated, Kat slipped into the couture gown, twisted her hair into a chignon at her nape, and was off to meet the captain at the Christmas party, her ivory opera gloves and ever-important clutch in tow.

German conversation and laughter lilted on air. A string quintet set the formal tone, the violins and cello crying the familiar notes of "Stille Nacht" in the background. Guests nursed cocktails as they stood against the palette of spruce-green walls and gold trim in the hallways, and moved between open dining room doors and the after-party that extended to the ballroom.

Scanning the crowd, Kat searched for tuxedos. (All the possible OSS mole.) Noted the swarm of Reich military uniforms. (Keeping the enemy close.) And passed over ladies in diamonds and opera gowns in search of a midnight-blue Police Nationale coat—all things she'd need to orient herself to the task ahead.

"Célène?"

She whirled around at the sound of her name.

"Oh. Good evening, Captain."

"It is you." He almost smiled—a shock to her system to see—then seemed to think better of it and tempered his features again. "I almost thought I'd been stood up."

"My apologies. Were you not expecting a working member of the kitchen staff to accompany you tonight?"

"Of course. I just wasn't expecting her to show up . . . in a dress like that." He shifted to a more serious tone before Kat could process the surprise of a compliment, and added, "But it seems everyone's come out for the big show tonight. Let's hope we'll be lost somewhere in the crowd."

He pointed out the Franc-Garde positioned along the wall, not far from the horde of Gestapo watching the revelry like hungry hawks guarding a nest.

"Shall we go then, mademoiselle?"

The captain offered his arm. She took it, with a measure of relief to find the gloved hand she laced through his elbow did not feel like pageantry, but more like solidarity. His hold was firm but his touch light. And Kat had to actively look away from the front of his uniform so she wouldn't be reminded it had once held her and mopped her tears.

Why did she no longer feel so alone when he was near?

"A pity the führer was unable to attend."

"Indeed." Kat answered his statement with cloaked sarcasm, feeling her back stiffen the deeper they were enveloped into the Reich's fold.

They'd learned that in the kitchen hours ago, bless them, that the führer had been called away from Northern France at the last minute. And Kat couldn't pretend she wasn't encouraged by it, even if the night had turned into a twofold celebration now: to inaugurate the new National Socialist Leadership Officers task force that had been formed just days before. With the minister of propaganda on hand, this was to bolster Nazi soldiers' morale. And, in turn, it was believed the venture would boost the régime's efforts.

This party was to launch a new era that, in the Reich's view, would surely win them the war.

Fir trees were positioned at each corner of the ballroom, flecked with twinkling white lights, cinnamon stick bundles, clove-flocked oranges hanging from crimson ribbons, and blown-glass baubles in a mosaic of colors. Tuxedo-clad waiters wove around the room, offering ginger-lemon cocktails and mulled glühwein, alongside raspberry and dark chocolate petit fours. And Kat had to stomach the sight of it when mere kilometers away villagers were starving in Rue.

"Seems they've pulled out all the stops," the captain noted as they stood just inside the main doors, scanning the ballroom. "No doubt they'll be satisfied to have the minister of propaganda on hand to make their toast."

Why did he do that—supply an answer that sounded good should one of the Reich officers hear but still manage to sound noncommittal at the same time? Kat hadn't noticed it at first. (Who would?) But now, what one would believe is the captain's ironclad loyalty could be viewed in the opposite way the closer she listened and the harder she looked.

An ornate cuckoo clock chimed high on the wall, noting the time: ten o'clock.

Somewhere near the rail lines, Gavin was about to face the bitter cold with the Maquis, avoiding planted mines and the possibility of patrols in the woods as they commandeered the crates of small arms. On the château grounds Henri would sneak the fish market truck to the meeting point beyond the rock wall. And there, in the glimmer of a gilt ballroom, Kat would play the role of a French glamour girl on the arm of the Vichy police captain, all while trying to ignore the knots in her stomach, the covert camera in her clutch, and the presence of a knife sheath strapped to her calf.

The captain led her in and introduced her to officers who'd lately arrived at the château. She pretended to nibble on Manon's confections without any real appetite. (They'd spit in the cake batter too.) Kept watch on the time, the same as she did the Franc-Garde posted at all entrances and exits. (The devils were so thorough.) And eyed the Gestapo moving about the party like worker bees in a hive.

"Care to dance?" the captain asked, interrupting her surveyance.

Of course she didn't. But Kat accepted, as she must. And tried not to react when the captain lifted the clutch from her hand and set it on a nearby table before leading her to the dance floor for the Christmas waltz.

Heaven help her—if Kat had no lipstick, that meant no camera. She'd just have to play along, keep an eagle's eye on it from the dance floor, and pick up the clutch after.

The ballroom whirled around them, with the glow of the chandelier and flickering candles blurring by. Kat read the lips of men in litzen, trying to discern any conversation and memorize faces. She allowed the captain to hold her close, even palm the small of her back as they moved. His stature was a bit too tall to dance cheek to cheek, but she could still ease in and gaze over the top of his shoulder. And that offered a perfect circular view of the ballroom.

"You dance well," he offered.

"Merci."

The side of his mouth tipped up in a ghost of a smile when he added, softer, "For a girl in gumboots."

That did draw her back to look up at him. "How did you know?"

"Don't worry. I won't tell. Besides, they rather suit you."

Of course the rest of the room wouldn't be able to see the only flats Manon could procure at the last minute were a pair of black garden boots that she assured Kat would stay safely beneath the flare of her train. But he was telling her he could *feel*. Or guess. Or that he knew. And somehow, knowing the secret between them gave him pleasure it oughtn't have.

The dance would have left her breathless for a host of reasons. But from the corner of her eye, Kat thought she noticed a familiar face—a waiter in state livery drifting near the edge of the dance floor, balancing a tray of cocktails.

"Excuse me," she muttered to the captain, stumbling their steps. And feigned an almost-swoon with one gloved hand splayed to her middle and the other fanning her face. "I apologize. It's just hot in here."

"Come." He glanced over his shoulder until he found a chair by the terrace windows, then led her over to and sat her in it.

"I wonder if I might I have a drink?"

"Of course."

The captain spotted the bar and bowl of Christmas punch at the end of the ballroom and nodded before leaving her side. Kat waited until he'd gone, then moved from the perch through the crowd toward her clutch on the table. She felt her stomach twist in knots as she looked again for the waiter. And listened with her eyes to the callous conversations all around that turned her insides sour.

She searched the maze of people as they passed, keeping her eyes trained.

"A cocktail, mademoiselle?"

"Merci." Kat looked up to find Xandre had drifted from the edge of the dance floor to her side—the waiter in the state livery—with alarm on his face. She turned to take a flute from the tray. Then lowered her voice. "What is it?"

"Dominique sent me. There's trouble. At the rails." He tipped his brow, as if to say, *"The weapons shipment . . . ?"*

Her throat nearly closed up.

They'd decided Gavin would steal the weapons. Henri would take the transfer at the drop point in the woods. And while they'd use Xandre's Maquis contacts to fan the weapons out to the bands of fighters rooted along the coast, Gavin had never expressly noted that Xandre was to be part of this operation. But then, he always had before.

What would change now, especially if Gavin was in trouble?

"How did you know?"

"Henri pulled me in. Let me know what the plan was. Now we need your help," he whispered, head down. "Take the service stairs to the courtyard. It's not passable, but they'll let staff through." He darted his glance—eyes only—to the Gestapo circling the end of the ballroom. "You know where the old groundskeeper's gîte is, in the woods?"

Of course she did. It was the place the captain had held her that day. Kat pushed the intensity of that memory back, then nodded and took a sip of champagne to avert suspicion that anything had affected her.

"Meet me there. As soon as you can."

"But what can I do . . ."

"You can save Dominique's life, if you want to."

The world could have spun off its axis as he walked away, and Kat could hardly have noticed. A member of their team that could be down was bad enough. But that it was Gavin . . . God help her. And without knowing whether he was in peril or what that might mean for the rest of them, it left her one option.

Kat glanced at the clock as Christmas lights twinkled in the reflection of the château's leaded glass doors. With a last sip for courage, she made the decision of her life to leave the champagne bubbling on the sideboard, slip through the doors, and vanish into the snowy night.

2 May 1952
81 Rue de l'Université
Paris, France

The Childs' usually inviting Roo de Loo felt different on this day.

Their second-story salon was still warm, with its charming contradiction of a rumpled Palace of Versailles look. Paper peeled off the walls, the ceilings were lofty, and the span of windows impressive—storied touches characteristic of historic buildings in the 7th Arrondissement. Plants sunbathed in the windows. Stacks of books belonging to Julia's husband, Paul, lay on armrests, like old friends left until his return. And a writing desk basked in the warmth of the front windows, where Julia would correspond with her friends and family.

They sat there now, with Minette sunning on the rug while Gérard's London solicitor, Mr. James, reviewed the information Kat had managed to gather up to that point. Circumstances being what they were, there wasn't much more that could improve upon the present situation, even if the room did try to be inviting.

Once the Vichy police had carted Gérard away, Kat had fallen into a bevy of telephone calls and files and calling in favors, all to get to the bottom of his last message to her. One of those in-person calls had been to meet Julia for their weekly shop at the market. It was there in their special place that her tears had overflowed. The truth tumbled out. And Julia marched them back to her flat, flew over to her desk, and sent a message to Mr. Child straightaway.

Paul's contacts at the US embassy were in no way instrumental to finding a solution, but they were generous for the effort. And it meant the world to Kat that they'd try to help.

The worst was not knowing the extent of what Mr. James knew—about Gérard's work, his past, and the war. She made the decision to answer questions where she could and ask more than she'd answer.

It was the only balance she could think of to help and not harm any further.

"Well." Mr. James took off his glasses and settled back in the Childs' salon chair, folding the spectacles in his hands over the middle of his tailored suit vest. "First I'm to tell you that everything I'm about to say has been relayed to your husband's Paris representation, a Monsieur Tremblay. I'm to report that the Courts of Justice have a sworn statement from a Léo Allmand, denouncing your husband for collaboration with the Nazi régime. His claims are quite detailed, I'm afraid. And corroborated by others."

"But I'll give a witness statement. And I assure you I can refute any such claims, having served in the OSS with both Mr. Fontaine and Mr. Allmand at the same time."

"I'm sorry, but the courts will not permit the statement of an accused's wife."

The words hit like a slap in the face, and Kat leaned forward, resting elbows on her knees to gain her bearings.

"That can't be," Kat started, and then stopped. Thinking it through. "You see, this was our plan all along. It's in part why I even came to France. I'd always been prepared to testify. My husband knew this. We'd agreed. And he spoke with you about it on more than one occasion."

"Mr. Fontaine must have been mistaken. We informed him some time ago that were he to marry, the courts would never accept his wife's testimony. I'm surprised he'd even think it a possibility now. Any sworn statement from a wife would certainly be rejected for bias."

"Of course I'm biased! This is my husband's life we're talking about."

"Do you know why your husband engaged my services the last several years? Alongside preparing a defense, he has also been searching for information about the death of an operative who went

missing from a château near the Normandy coast in December
1943."

"I'm aware of that too." Kat flitted a glance to Julia to bolster her
strength before she had to say the next words out loud. "Gavin Harris."

"Peter Radcliffe," the solicitor contradicted in the same breath.

"I'm sorry?" Her memory pinged, finding no recollection. "I've
never heard that name."

Mr. James leaned forward again, sifted through his briefcase, and
retrieved a folder. Opening it, he handed it off to Kat, pointing out
a sepia-toned photograph of a man paper-clipped to the inside cover
and notes scrawled on paper bearing background information on
the name tucked inside.

The man in the photo was not wearing his customary poppy-
emblazed hat Kat had come to recognize during the time they'd
operated in France, but the face was true. The same strong jaw. Salt-
and-pepper hair. And identical eyes that had once peered back at her
from behind a rifle while she lay on the floor of an orchard row.

*Henri . . .*

"I did know this man. He was here in France, working with our
field team."

"For the past several years your husband has been attempting to
bring closure to the family of one Peter Radcliffe—a wartime SOE
agent who also went missing in 1943. He was a part of the group that
included an operative by the code name of Célène. She was named
one Penny Samson, from Fulham."

He turned around a photo of the poor woman whose life Kat led
in France but never met. She was pretty—brunette. With a bright
smile and a youthful blush on the apples of her cheeks. And no idea
when she'd sat for that portrait how it would all end.

"What happened to her?"

"I'm sorry to say, we've since learned she was denounced to the
Vichy authorities, subsequently arrested, and shot within days of
landing in Lyon."

"What an unimaginable loss for her family. I'm so sorry." Kat handed the photo back and shook her head, the revelations of the woman whose identity she'd assumed the last expected. "But I did know this man. He went by the name Henri. And when I was injured upon landing in France, he was one of the men who saved my life."

The sharpness of the memories paused her—the pain, the bitterness at Jeffrey having left her alone, and the sight of Henri appearing out of the darkness . . . It was beyond anything to know the real man who, in great part, she now owed her life.

"I didn't know he was SOE. I'd just assumed when our cover was blown and our team fled the château in December 1943, he'd gone on to arm the Resistance and fight somewhere along the Normandy coast. He was very convincing as a Frenchman. The invasion came months later, and it rendered communication virtually nonexistent until the liberation. And by then I was in London and we'd all lost contact. Though I did attempt to locate another OSS agent who'd gone missing around the same time."

"Yes. Mr. Gavin Harris—your brother, I understand?"

"I have yet to find him, sir. Or to learn what happened to him. So I can understand the importance of learning Mr. Radcliffe's fate, for his family. I just hadn't considered that fate to have been entwined in this, especially after all these years."

"I'm afraid it is, ma'am. Your husband has been attempting to find information on both men these last many years."

"What?" Waves of confusion landed, too late to do anything but further unsettle. "But I only came to find Gérard in France last summer."

"That may be. But he'd been searching for Mr. Harris for some time before that. And suffice it to say, he's engaged my help in financial matters in England to benefit the Radcliffe family. And yours. Pending the outcome of these matters."

"Mine?"

"He owns an estate—" Mr. James stopped. "My apologies. You and your husband own an estate passed down from Mr. Fontaine's maternal family that he has been attempting to liquidate . . . a Claxton Hall in Herefordshire."

"Do we?" Kat shook her head. "I've never heard of it."

"That's just as well. Mr. Fontaine has expressed he was never happy there. And should his suspicions prove true about Mr. Radcliffe, he's asked me to proceed with you to authorize the close of the estate sale so the funds might go to the Radcliffe and Sullivan families. And I'm to tell you this decision was made years ago, in the same year your brother was declared legally deceased by the United States government."

*1947?*

*Gérard* . . . Her heart reeled. *That was years before I'd come to find you.*

Ill-prepared for the heart-swell that followed, Kat had to take in wave after wave of revelation, but this time the biggest washed over her with a surge of tenderness for Gérard. He'd told her of his family—of the brokenness he'd seemed to run from yet held so close to him. That wasn't different from her own story. But to be willing to part with his mother's family estate for the benefit of others was more than she'd dreamed. He was willing to sacrifice the pain of his past for the benefit of her future.

The cataclysm forced Kat to look away from the faces around her and direct her tearstained eyes toward the view out the second-story window instead.

Mr. James cut into the quiet. "You'll find the bill of sale outlined in the paperwork at the back of the folder. Just there in your hands. You can sign at any time and we will set the rest in motion."

"I don't want the money."

"No. I should think not. But nevertheless, Mr. Fontaine has made a sizable provision for you too. Should things proceed with the current charges and the outcome go poorly for him in any way."

Giving a hasty brush to the moisture at her eyes, she asked, "And what of the cottage at Le Crotoy harbor?"

"No, ma'am. There are no French properties included."

"Very well. If it's what my husband wishes." Kat flipped forward to the bill, and Mr. James anticipated her agreement by offering her a pen. She signed and with an indrawn breath, asked, "But what suspicions?"

"Ma'am?"

"You said if my husband's suspicions about Mr. Radcliffe proved true. What might those be?"

Mr. James accepted the signed paperwork and slipped it into a folder.

"He believes Mr. Radcliffe was killed somewhere near the Château du Broutel on Christmas Eve 1943. It has been our belief as well. If we were to find a body, then it might put an end to the whole messy business. And his widow could receive the death benefits due her as a war widow. But we've not been able to thus far."

*If we were to find a body . . .*

Kat's middle knotted with the possibility she'd been wrong. All this time she'd wondered. She'd not even been able to broach the subject within her own heart, let alone with a room of people who knew facts of the case but none of the emotion behind it. And now she had to consider who she'd buried that night.

Was it not Gavin after all?

"I would be willing to give a statement. As long as it is overseen by our legal representation, and Mr. and Mrs. Child serve as witnesses."

"And it would be most welcome, ma'am. But as I said before, the statement from the accused's wife would not be admissible in—"

Raising her hand to halt the man, Kat shook her head.

"I do not wish to be rude, Mr. James. But it is not that kind of statement. I should like to inform the authorities on where there is a body buried at Château du Broutel, as well as the circumstances surrounding the gentleman's death."

"Circumstances?"

"Yes. I believe I know who killed Peter Radcliffe . . . because I helped bury the body."

The usually vibrant Paris outside the windows seemed to hit a standstill in that instant. Only the clock ticked and the cat purred on the rug, followed by the solicitor clearing his throat through the silence and shifting in his chair.

"Very well," Mr. James eased out, the discomfort in the room just held at bay by his commitment to due process taking over. He retrieved a leather portfolio and notepad from his briefcase, then readied his pen. "We can take a written statement now. And you may come to your Paris solicitor's office at your earliest convenience to give a recorded statement for the courts. And with all gentility, I must inform you that this may not absolve your involvement in this matter either. Even if it was an action committed in your wartime service, I shall have to report this to the American embassy as well."

"Fine."

"And as long as you are aware, ma'am, this may not be enough to release charges against your husband. We would need another corroborating witness statement. Perhaps from someone else who served at the same location at the same time?"

"I have none."

Kat shook her head through the throngs of hopelessness that threatened to overwhelm her with such candor. It was time to confront what had occurred in the woods at the château that night, if only for the Radcliffe or Harris family to be assuaged by the long-drawn pain of never knowing what had really happened to their loved one. Whether Peter or Gavin lay there, she could not go on without knowing. But now, to have the truth out yet no assurance any of it would be enough to set Gérard free . . . The hollowing-out pain of it surprised even her.

"Pardon, sir. But I believe it is time for a break." Julia, bless her, cut into the gentleman's proceedings by standing up. "Madame Fontaine? Come. I'll make some tea."

It was only when Julia had led her upstairs to the sanctuary of the

Roo de Loo kitchen that Kat could break apart. She did, her resolve crumbling as she fell into one of the dinette chairs, buried her face in her hands, and wept.

Julia moved around the kitchen without a word. Kat could hear the muffled sounds of water running. A kettle *clank* against the gas stove. The sound of a tea tin on the counter, and cups and saucers being laid out after.

"The water is set." Julia slipped into the chair opposite her with a creak of aged wood. "Kat?" A handkerchief was presented across the table, Julia offering a fold of white gauze with rickrack trim in grass green and the initials *JC* embroidered in the corner.

Kat took it gratefully and tapped under her eyes.

"What's this about a body?"

"From my time in the OSS. It's not as bad as you imagine, I promise."

"I believe you. And I should tell you that I spoke with your husband some time ago." Kat's head shot up, connecting with Julia's frankness staring back from across the table. "When he began to suspect this might happen. Well, not all of this, mind. But enough that I'm wondering if this isn't as dire as it may seem."

"You spoke with Gérard? About what?"

"I didn't want to alarm you—certainly not to give false hope. But Mr. Fontaine wanted to ensure someone was able to help you should he be arrested. He asked me to be that person. And it seems with all the revelations we heard downstairs, it's time I share one of my own."

"Go on."

"The first trip you and I took to the markets, you mentioned a brother who'd gone missing during the war. There was a tiny detail—something trivial, yes—but big enough that I remembered it. We processed reports from an OSS field operative from Lyon late in the war. He went by the code name Magellan. But I remembered this agent because the sign-off on his reports were so unique."

"But that's my brother. Gavin went by that name. How did you know?"

"I remembered Magellan sending word back about a château near the Normandy coast and the executions of Resistance contacts in the village, an OSS agent among them. He filed a report with evidence of treason on microfilm, outlining information about a suspected double agent in the field. I know this because all such reports were marked *Top Secret*—only those with the highest security clearance could access them. I always read these first if they were routed to us from the field, made notes and notifications to other teams as necessary, and then filed them with my leadership."

"To Director Donovan? You said once you reported to him."

"I did. And the reports did go straight through to his office. Though occasionally we were to file reports from certain agents to another intelligence branch."

"And you don't remember if Magellan was one of those agents?"

"I'm sorry. I do not. All I know is that when his field reports stopped, Magellan's last wire ended with '*Don't look back.*' I remembered it because it seemed so odd at the time—almost a hidden message. The operative filed no further reports that I am aware of after 1944. I asked Mr. Child to call in a few favors with his contacts at the embassy to inquire with the CIA and see if my memory has served me well. If there was no connection and we'd found nothing, you'd never have known of my suspicions. But if we did . . ."

She slid a note card across the tabletop, easing it under Kat's trembling fingertips.

"We found something odd—an agent whose final report is believed to have been altered. Of note, the microfilm evidence he filed with it is missing. And save for one mention of an associate in Lyon, that's where all contact was severed. It's from that altered report that your husband has been searching these last weeks and pressing on any officials he could, hoping to find a lead. And finally, he did."

"I don't understand. An address at the village of Estaing?"

The natural light shining in from the windows illuminated steam when the kettle started to sing. Julia rose and crossed the kitchen for it.

"You'll give your statement, dear. And then you will need to make a road trip, where I believe you'll find answers you've been looking for. Your husband wanted this for you. I assume he wanted to share this with you as well. But now I wonder instead if this will be the way for you to help him."

"Answers seem impossible to hope for now. I'm not even sure I'd know what to do with them."

Julia set a teacup in front of Kat, then slid into the chair again, the teapot momentarily forgotten on the counter.

"Have you considered this? That man married you, all the while knowing you'd never be able to testify for him. Now why on earth would he do that?"

"You don't think . . . unless he married for love," Kat finished.

"Do you remember when I told you of that first meal Paul and I had here in France? I've often wanted to go back to La Couronne just to see how I'd feel to order it all again and experience the blissful moment that changed our lives. But I realized that even when we do go back, it won't compare. You see, I am the one who is changed. Not because of where I went or what we did, but because of who I journey through life alongside. You see? That is the great adventure of it all—l'amour."

"I suppose that's the point. We cannot stay safe forever. And we can't run from trusting someone or loving again, or else we miss everything that matters." Looking up, Kat allowed her friend to see the vulnerability she knew must be painted over her face. With no masks. No secrets of the past. And no way on but forward. "But I don't know what to do. I don't know how to untangle all of this."

Julia rose and tended to their tea again. "You will know when you get to the address. Let the solicitors here earn their paycheck for once. In the meantime you can borrow 'The Blue Flash' and go save your husband's future."

"What in the world is a Blue Flash?"

"You'll find out." Julia's face brightened as she poured water in the cups and set the kettle on a trivet, then returned to the table. "But only if you promise to tell me every detail about the meal you order at the café."

# CHAPTER 26

24 *December 1943*
Château du Broutel
Rue, France

The muffled sounds of celebration erupted through the ceiling, the revelry in the ballroom echoing down into the larder where Manon sat on a barrel in the faint glow of light under the kitchen door.

They'd managed to make it through the dinner intact. From the traditional French menu with the opening drinks and small bites during the *apéro*, through the seven-course meal, to the finale of Christmas biscuits enlivened with German touches and coffee with liqueurs. The slowdown of activity in the kitchen emerged from the last of the dishes being sorted. Few wanted to celebrate another year under authoritarian rule, and much of the staff had retired for a subdued Christmas holiday in the privacy of their own chambers.

With all the bustle, it had become the first blessed moment of the day Manon could find a breath of time to herself. And as the seconds ticked closer to midnight and the cheers rebounded from what she guessed must be the minister's toast in the upstairs ballroom, the only thing to do beyond endure the gut-wrenching worry was to cling to a last shred of hope that there would be word soon.

Surely Xandre would return to the château with Célène and bring good news.

Any moment they'd come back to the kitchen to assure Manon that all was well with Dominique. Henri would have taken receipt of the stolen weapons. And neither the captain—nor the Franc-Garde who had taken authority over him—would be wise to their scheme until the Reich soldiers woke with thick heads in the morning. And that would be long after the Maquis had farmed the weapons out along the coast through the night.

The door creaked and Manon lifted her gaze.

"Chef?" Their dishwasher, the usually reticent Madame Larue, poked her head in.

Manon stood as the woman opened the door wider, and though there was no hiding the obvious, she cleared her throat in composure and stepped forward as if all was well.

Best perform as though nothing was amiss.

"Oui. What is it?"

"You have a visitor, madame."

Stalking across the larder, amongst wheels of the valuable horde of aged meats and rounds of cheese on the shelf and crates of wine that had been shipped in for the next day's dinner, Manon could think of nothing to celebrate. Not unless the holidays would usher in the new year, and with it, that these would be the last cheers of celebration their overlords would be free to make.

Madame Larue stepped aside, and Manon's breath hitched in her middle when the silhouette of a Vichy police officer was cut out by the light streaming in.

A clean-shaven man with dark hair and sharp uniform stepped in off the kitchen's black-and-white parquet floor. Her insides nearly turned to mush in the split second her mind registered that perhaps they'd come to arrest her.

But it was familiar blue eyes that met hers from under the brim of his uniform hat that whispered this was not his purpose in coming to the château. And if not for the strength of his arms to catch her when she charged forward, Manon might have knocked both Dominique and herself clean into the shelves without care.

She threw herself into his arms as the door clicked closed, not caring about pretense now—only the unabashed feel of being back in Dominique's arms.

He held her, brief seconds only, and pressed a kiss to her temple.

"What is this?" she cried, cupping his face in her hands. The feel of his smooth jaw against her palms and the warmth of his skin under her fingertips said this hoped-for moment was in fact real.

"Vichy police do not allow beards," he whispered, then took one of her palms and pressed a kiss to it. "It makes the uniform believable. It was the only way to get in without being stopped."

"All I care is that you're here . . . I was so worried when Xandre told me what happened at the rail lines. I sent him straight up to the ballroom to fetch Célène. And I've been going mad down here since."

"So Xandre was here. I was afraid of that." He exhaled a shaky breath, and with a crestfallen expression that said though he stood before her, all was not well. And only then did it register what he was wearing, and perhaps why. "We're going to need your help. And if you can, love, please don't cry out."

Dominique leaned back and rapped on the inside of the door.

With shuddering breaths, Manon watched as the imposing figure of Captain Fontaine stepped into view. Madame Larue allowed him to pass the threshold and closed the door behind again, it seemed holding a post as watchman outside.

"Where is Célène?" he demanded, the usual calm and cool captain looking as though he'd just seen his first real château ghost. When she hesitated, his face softened with what seemed genuine concern. "Please. I need to know where she is."

Manon darted her gaze between the men, unknowing what this could be about.

"What do you mean? Didn't she come back to the party?"

The captain shook his head with a resolute calm about him, but it was the wild look in his eyes that could not belie the truth. This was the shared fear that appeared on Dominique's features now as he drew in a breath, then continued, his voice low against the booming celebration muffled by the ceiling above.

"Célène left the party," the captain said, and set her evening clutch on the shelf. "And we need to know where she's gone, s'il te plaît. Before it's too late."

When she darted her glance to Dominique, he nodded, as if reading her thoughts. "It's all right. You can speak freely in front of the captain. He's a part of this with us."

"Oh my word . . . She went with Xandre."

"Why would she do that?"

"He came here and I helped him into a state livery. He said he was going up to the party, to fetch her to help you—" She turned to Dominique. "Out to the gîte in the woods. She was to help hide the crates of arms because neither you nor Henri showed as you were supposed to. He said you were arrested at the rail lines, and I . . ."

Manon's voice caught, the emotion of nearly losing him and then not. And compounded now by the possibility they'd lost Célène, and all because one little lie by an untrustworthy source had complicated everything they'd tried to do.

"I wasn't even close to that," Dominique confirmed, which helped allay her fears for him. "Our Maquis contacts provided a diversion outside the rail lines so Henri and I could get in and steal the crates. We did. And Henri was to bring the truck to the gîte. But Xandre intercepted us on the road, telling us that you were in trouble here at the château. I left Henri with him and the weapons and rushed here to you."

"How would he know you were on the road? I thought Xandre wasn't included in the plan tonight?" she questioned, distinctly remembering those supply logs Célène had transferred that left Henri and Xandre out of the more detailed information.

"He wasn't," Captain Fontaine gritted out.

Dominique stepped in to explain beyond what it seemed the captain could. "Remember that day at the orchard, when I asked you not to go anywhere without me? We've been watching him for some time. The only way he could have known about an arms shipment coming in tonight would be if he was tipped off—by them."

"So he's been playing both sides . . . and now Célène is somewhere out there with him?"

Captain Fontaine took the news with a clenched jaw and delivered a fierce look to Dominique. With a nod, he released the captain into some plan they must have discussed ahead of time, and the captain fled from the larder without looking back.

Dominique turned her attention back to him.

"Manon, do you have anything you need to take with you?"

The door was still cracked. She looked to it, worried that the old dishwasher would listen in. And report. Or heaven help them, reach for the nearest cutlery and hold them at bay long enough for the streams of Reich officials to flood down the service stairs and drag them away.

Manon tugged on his lapel and lowered her voice to a cryptic whisper. "We cannot talk about this. Not here."

"Madame Larue will not report us. And she won't stop us either. La Marquise has asked her to aid Captain Fontaine." Dominique cupped her cheeks in his palms, bidding her to focus. "That means we must leave tonight. You and I."

"We cannot. Not until we find Henri and Célène."

"The captain is headed to the road behind the drop point to track the fish market truck. And when he finds her, he will bring Célène to meet us."

"Then we must first go to Henri and see that the weapons are passed off before the Reich finds they've been stolen. I will help you." When he looked ready to slap that down in protest, she quieted his protests with a firm shake of the head. "Non. Remember what we said at the dunes? This is my time to fight. I have a weapon—a sidearm I've kept hidden under the radiator in my room. And I have at least some authority at the gate. They will not stop us. And together we will see this through to the end."

It wouldn't have been out of character for Dominique to fight her on this. But, instead, his jaw tensed; she could see it even in the dim light. He struggled, it seemed, to find his words.

"What is it?"

"Célène . . ." He shook his head, then reached in his pocket and handed over a tube of lipstick.

"What? She got the photos!"

"Non. The captain saw across the ballroom that the Franc-Garde were doing bag checks on the ladies. He convinced Célène to dance but lifted the lipstick from her purse before he laid it down on a table. They would never check the pockets of a Vichy police captain. That way she would be safe if her bag was checked," he said, pained. "But she never returned in time for the toast. He snapped the photos. And he has given the film to us to see it safely out of France."

She held the tube tight in her fist, nodding, proud, wishing like anything she could see Célène walk through the door in that couture gown that had been hers and tell her what her bravery had done.

"But she left the party without it and followed that devil out to the woods, all out of love for *me*." Before Manon could even understand what he was saying, Dominique uttered a pained, "She is my sister."

"How can that be?"

"I'll tell you everything, but not now. It only matters that the captain finds her. We've doubted Xandre for some time. But now with the film, we'll have proof both of his treachery and of the operative he's working with. And we've learned through the captain that Xandre plans to alert the Franc-Garde to arrest both Henri and me when we try to truck the weapons out. They could be waiting on the road to Rue now."

"And that's why you're dressed as a Vichy officer?"

He nodded. "It was our only option to get to you here, in the event something like this happened. The captain has a Vichy police truck. He will retrieve the weapons and, with all hope, meet up with Henri and Célène before the authorities do."

"But if he's stolen one of the Vichy police trucks . . . the captain can never come back. The Franc-Garde will know he had a hand in this. He will be arrested!"

"We know. And he is willing to give up everything, except her."

"What about Célène?"

A pained look flashed over his face, emotion glassing over his eyes. "The captain fears that Xandre lured her out of the ballroom because he believed that by being at that party, she would have seen the mole's face. And as soon as he gets the information he wants, Xandre won't need her any longer."

"He'll have her arrested?"

"Even with their brutality to prisoners, that would be a mercy compared to the alternative. Célène knows too much. And Xandre cannot risk letting her go free."

Manon swallowed hard, her lip quivering for the fear of Célène in that beautiful haute couture gown, unknowing, isolated out in the woods with a monster. And heaven help her, but Manon was the one who'd delivered the poor girl into his hand.

"I'll tell you more—I'll tell you everything. But we have to leave. Now. Before it's too late. We can meet up with Valens, then go south to Lyon where the OSS has contacts in the Free Zone. I'll make contact with the Allies from there. Then they'll know the truth. But not until we develop that film first."

That seemed a funny thing to say. Wouldn't it have been customary just to turn it over to the OSS and keep going?

"Why would we do that?"

"Because I want to see his face. I need to know who it is we're dealing with."

"And from there, what?"

"I don't know." He brushed a hand to the side of her face. "We'll have to take that as it comes. Can we trust each other in that?"

The sounds of the party did not foster as much care now, as Dominique led her out of the kitchen. She looked back over her shoulder, to the rows of copper pots and pans shining in the light, the great stove sleeping in the alcove at the back, and the expanse of parquet floor that checkered the length of the mammoth space to the larder door. She'd spent years of her life in the château—joyless many days, but with purpose. Perhaps that was what had allowed her to heal more than anything. And now, with Dominique leading her through the courtyard, she said goodbye to the door left ajar.

Their false paperwork checked out with the Gestapo, who were stopping all on the premises. And as the Vichy police at the front gate had been instructed some months back, the order from the captain of château security held fast, so the uniform who drove Chef Altier would not be stopped as the vehicle disappeared from Château du Broutel.

"What about our dunes?" she whispered, lovingly, staring out the window as stands of gangly winter trees whisked by on either side of the road.

"We can't go back."

"Somehow I thought we would one day. And live our lives. You fishing. Me cooking—maybe at an inn or a little café on the coast, when this nightmare is over and some part of the world makes sense again. It was my dream for a time; it kept me going some days. Now I can't bear the thought of leaving it behind."

"I wish we could," he murmured, sorrow lacing his tone, and reached for her hand. "But wherever we go from here, it will be together. I promise you that."

When Manon offered hers in return, he opened her palm against the bench seat. He slipped his hand into his uniform pocket with the other on the wheel and retrieved a treasure. Her chin quivered in realization as he curled her fingertips around the chain and wedding band he'd remembered to bring from the cottage.

Manon peered into the side mirror, the château gates blending into the night behind. She came back to him then, as heavy snow peppered the road beyond swishing wiper blades, and tucked her head in against his shoulder.

"That's right. Don't look back, love." He hugged her deeper into his side as he laid lead to the gas. "We go forward from here."

# CHAPTER 27

24 December 1943
Château du Broutel
Rue, France

Snow tumbled down in the woods now, blanketing the shovelfuls of dirt in the makeshift grave.

Kat froze at the click of the pistol trigger and turned slowly to find what she'd dreaded—Xandre, with a Luger raised to her head.

Though breaths rattled in and out of her lungs at breakneck speed, she covered the horror of seeing a Nazi service pistol pointed in her direction by going into immediate fight mode. For Kat, that was to remain calm as she dropped the shovel to clang on the frozen ground at her feet and raised both hands on air, arrested before him.

"Let me guess—you used a low-pressure cartridge?" she bit out, battling to keep her voice controlled no matter the terror stirring inside.

"You know your weapons, don't you?"

"I know if you wanted me dead, you'd realize the breech block won't clear the top without a high-pressure cartridge." Kat tipped her head to the dirt-covered jackboots in the hole. "You used the first shot on him before it jammed?"

Xandre nodded, giving her credit for knowing. "Even if you were foolish enough to have followed me out here, seems you're lucky enough that this Luger gave you another minute to breathe."

"Then that was your aim all this time? To kill me?"

"Non. To prevent you from seeing things at that party that you oughtn't, and to ensure this situation doesn't grow worse for me. I'd have turned you over to the Vichy police—earned points with them. But you weren't supposed to see the jackboots in this hole. And I can't let you leave these woods with that information."

"Célène?"

Kat turned at the shout that echoed from the other side of the rock wall, just as a shepherd bounded through the opening. Followed by the captain, his own raised service pistol glinting in the moonlight as he stopped to make a three-point triangle with their positions anchored in the snow.

"Captain," Xandre started, trying to clear his throat over the shock. "I can explain . . . "

"No need."

The captain flitted his glance from one to the other. From crates to the shovel on the ground. And eased one palm on air by his hip to hold the simmering Bella and her bared teeth at bay.

Moonlight cast a soft glow over his features, beset with furious alarm—not because of Kat it seemed but, rather, for her. It was contradictions like these that cast doubt on all they were doing. From steadfast glances and his support at a Nazi party, to now finding her a whisker close to death as he gripped a raised service pistol trained on her would-be assassin.

Together they forced Kat's instincts to turn more muddled than ever, and to see him standing there not as merely the captain, but as Gérard—the man who'd once shared his cottage kitchen. His home. Even his time by the bed of an injured stranger. And those golden-hued eyes that stared back now were more familiar than ever, and genuine with their pained expression.

Kat swallowed hard. Kept her hands raised. And didn't move a muscle while the two men calculated which side of loyalty they were on.

"You are to be commended, Xandre. You've done well by stopping her before these weapons left the grounds," the captain levied the accusation and, to Kat's horror, trained his pistol on her. "I'll take her in. I've a police truck just through the opening."

"You what? H-how did you know we . . . ?" Xandre's brow flinched, and he lowered his Luger to waist level. "Or, they . . . ?"

"You may go. Alert the Franc-Garde that we've found her and the stolen weapons. They've set up a roadblock at the crossroads to the village." Turning his attention to Kat, the captain ordered with a stinging command, "You. Viens ici—*now!*"

With hands still arrested, Kat obeyed, taking slow steps toward the only man she dared trust out of the options.

*One step. Two. Three . . .*

*Almost there.*

Without warning Xandre lunged as she attempted to cross over to the captain. And with an arm catching her collar from behind, he slammed Kat down in the snow at his feet.

Coughing through the mass of dirt and pine needles and face-stinging snow, Kat clawed at the forest floor beneath her cheek. Trying to rise in the unyielding gown. Battling with her footing in slippery gumboots. And failing through the flurry of stars before her eyes to see which way was up.

The shovel was too far away to reach. And the metallic taste of blood Kat could feel from having clamped down on her tooth now flooded the inside of her mouth and darkened the snow crimson beneath her chin. She was able to look up through her daze and register a growling Bella positioned out front, Gérard with his sidearm raised again behind the dog, and Xandre anchored over where Kat was laid out on the ground.

Xandre dragged her to her feet, with an arm creating a vise around her neck and the other pressing the Luger barrel against her temple.

"You almost had me there for a moment, Captain."

"Let her go," Gérard demanded this time, his steps iron as he inched forward.

"*Arrêtez!*" Xandre bellowed back, halting the advance. "And call that beast off, or my trigger finger may not stay where it is."

Gérard raised a palm, again giving the silent order. Bella eased, her stance still alert but held at bay between the men. And with a brow battling to remain strong against seeing Kat with a pistol raised to her, he held firm.

"I never said these were weapons, did I, Captain?"

"You didn't need to. I'm privy to our rail deliveries."

"Of course you are. And I see it's time to make an exit because of it." Xandre pointed to the rock wall with the Lugar barrel and the police truck on the road behind. "The keys. Throw them—easy."

The captain retrieved them, then tossed them in the snow at Kat's feet.

"Pick them up." Xandre squeezed her neck and let go, keeping his gaze fixed on the police captain in front of them as Kat stooped in the snow. Fumbling for the keys, Kat found them with a bloodied, shaking hand and dropped them into his outstretched palm. "Lower your weapon, Captain. *Now.* I won't ask again."

Gérard's eyes narrowed as he stared back at Kat, saying without words that he couldn't give up the one chance they had. If he put his weapon down now, there was little hope of this working out in any way that saw them both leave here alive.

But what were the consequences if he didn't?

"You are one of *them*," Xandre scoffed in the way a beaten man registered surprise. Or even respect, for an adversary one had every intention of killing. "I'll admit—even I was convinced, and that's some feat to accomplish. You've played your part well."

"There is no part to play. I'm here to arrest her. And you're going to let me do it. The Vichy police are waiting on the village road."

"Why not let us take her to the Franc-Garde together," Xandre fired back, his hold growing ever more desperate as he clamped down again on her throat. "Or are you afraid of what those beasts will do to your girl here? I've heard their interrogations are the most brutal on the fairer sex. Imagine how they would enjoy doing more than making her bleed from a cut lip, *hmm?* Maybe you'd prefer to interrogate her yourself. If you are worthy of that uniform, they'll ensure you prove it."

"I've nothing to prove," Gérard gritted as though in pain, though his jaw was clenched and his eyes registered barely contained fury. "It's not hard to work out what happened tonight. When she did not return to the party and we received word of missing arms down at the rail lines at the same time. I wouldn't call that coincidence. Would you?"

The captain gambled—lowering the pistol enough to show he was backing down. And in her horror, Kat realized he was securing the sidearm back to the holster on his belt, in exchange for handcuffs.

"Go down to the road. There is a Franc-Garde checkpoint at the crossroads. Tell them they'll find Dominique right this minute, traveling the road to the dunes. With a wire unit in his trunk he intends to use to contact the Allies."

Tears squeezed out from the corners of Kat's eyes.

How could she know what to believe? What to feel? And, heaven help her, with a vise cutting off her air and Gérard cutting out her heart by turning her brother over to the devils in uniform, what should she fear now? Even if it was meant to save them, his fidelity lasted only as long as it took to turn her brother over to the Reich, which would all but ensure Gavin's death. And if those shackles landed around her wrists, it would seal hers as well.

"You lie," Xandre bit back.

"See for yourself." Gérard motioned to the rock wall. "There is a Vichy police truck ready to take her in. And to return those weapons to the Reich officials who, no doubt, will find their Christmas far less merry when they have to explain the loss of a cache of arms come morning. That is, unless you were to hand them back, along with the OSS agent who right about now should be nearing the coast as we speak."

She could feel the deep rise and fall of Xandre's chest at her back, shock evident in the intake of breath.

*He didn't know Gavin is OSS.*

If ever her heart told her what to do, as the snow blew wild and her life hung in the balance, Kat looked in those golden-hued eyes and begged Gérard to tell her it wasn't true. When he couldn't— didn't, for having just revealed her brother's true identity—she made a decision then and there.

If she wanted to live, Kat had to bet on herself.

"*Bella,*" she mouthed, then flitted her glance to the dog standing guard in front.

The captain ticked his brow in misunderstanding, ever so slight.

She repeated it, barely a whisper but firm: "*Bella!*"

The seconds split then, Kat hoping beyond hope the long hours they'd spent in devoted companionship at the seaside cottage meant the animal would take an order from Kat. To her relief, Bella obeyed. And lunged, as a shot pierced the trees, and Xandre's Luger discharged against the jaw that sank teeth into his forearm.

With the precious opening she needed and the knife he hadn't known she'd pulled from the sheath under her gown when she'd knelt for the keys, Kat drove the blade into Xandre's side. And prayed if her hand-to-hand training wasn't sure in that instant, at least it would give her precious seconds to get away.

Xandre sank to his knees in the snow, coiling around his middle with a groan. And lay motionless thereafter.

Looking back, with the bitter air burning in her lungs and blood dripping down her chin, Kat saw Gérard was already lifting Bella from the snow, cradling the animal in his arms. Kat swiped up the keys and Xandre's weapon and darted for the truck. She threw open the passenger door, arms ready to receive and help level the wounded animal in.

Gérard ripped off his uniform coat, pressing it over Bella's flank.

"I'll take her. Just go," Kat coaxed, taking over as Gérard bounded to the truck's driver's side door. "We have to go now or she'll never make it!"

"Non," he gritted out, looking down at the bleeding animal with distressed eyes. Then he set his jaw and shook his head. "We can't. Not yet. We still have a job to do."

"What?" she breathed out, the ping-pong of whether Kat could trust him giving her near whiplash.

Gérard marched away, disappearing back through the opening in the rock wall. Was he was going back to finish off Xandre? Or to see whether Kat had done it herself? She peered through the darkness as heavy snow layered on the windshield and the engine chugged in time with swishing wiper blades.

Within a few terrible seconds he reappeared and, to her shock, was muscling a crate in his arms.

"Open it!" Gérard shouted over his shoulder as he charged to the back of the truck.

Kat jumped out. And through the madness met him at the tailgate. She flung the doors open. Climbed up. And in a silent partnership, accepted and stacked every single crate he transferred to her waiting arms.

When they'd finished, they said nothing. Just climbed back in the cab. And as the snow fell in sheets and the moon disappeared behind the clouds, they left the world of Château du Broutel behind. Thank heaven Kat had thought to conceal her identification papers in the bodice of her gown, just in case. Wherever this road might take her from here, she'd need them now.

"Where do we go?" She glanced from poor Bella's limp body

in her lap to the windy road and black night trying to swallow them up.

"Let me think." His eyes flitted between the whimpering shepherd bleeding on her gown and the never-ending landscape of snow and trees. He, too, realized at any second the authorities could blast headlamps through the windshield.

"Will we meet Dominique and Henri? They are safe, oui? You must have arranged for us to meet them somewhere else or you wouldn't have said that back there, that my brother is on the road to the dunes. Why did you tell Xandre that? Now he knows." When he didn't answer, she looked up and pulled a bloody hand up to clear locks of wet hair from her eyes. "Tell me they're alive."

"I don't know!"

"What do you mean you don't know? Where is my brother?"

If the truth was a revelation, he'd covered well.

Gérard kept his jaw clenched and fists white-knuckling the steering wheel, managing to keep them on the road through the deterioration of the elements in every second that ticked by.

Not daring to believe he'd truly turned Gavin over to the brutality of the Franc-Garde, she levied a glare at the man sitting beside her on the bench. "Surely you know where Dominique is. You told Xandre a lie to draw him off course. Right?"

In this seemingly never-ending landscape of threat, they couldn't see a thing, not even a speck of light to guide them through the dark, even as the truck coughed . . .

Lurched . . .

And died.

"Tell me it was a lie," Kat demanded, her voice deadly soft.

"We just need to drive right now. To think. We can't go back; I've stolen this truck and . . . they'll know. The mole will know one or both of us have seen him. Or that Dominique has too. We have to go our own ways for now—all of us."

When she sat in stoney silence, he waited. Gripped the steering wheel like it was his lifeline. And poor Bella whimpered low and pawed against her thigh.

"Tell me it was a lie," she repeated, staring straight ahead.

"Do you understand, Célène? We have to keep going down this road—just us. There's no going back after this."

Gérard slammed his palm to the wheel and cursed, then turned the key. Twice. With no luck. And no further explanation. Though his silence now was enough to give Kat the answer she needed. Maybe Xandre was right? The captain had been toying with her—showing a little interest. Perhaps even offering affection for the girl who'd once cried on the front of his uniform, who could dance in gumboots, and who, like a fool, had dared open her shut-up heart.

Even that fraction felt like a betrayal now.

"I trusted you, God help me." Kat clamped her eyes shut. "Put it in Park."

The engine coughed again, shuddering as Gérard ignored her and turned the key.

With gentle hands, Kat kissed Bella's nose, then eased the shepherd down onto the floorboards. And, steeling herself to remain calm, fixed her fist on the handle of her door. "I said, put it in Park."

He obeyed but dared to look her in the eyes when he asked, "Why?"

"Because if nothing else, at least I can fix this." Kat threw the door open to a burst of bitter air that slammed her cheek. And uncaring, hopped down, boots in the snow.

Tools didn't matter much; she'd use what she had and manipulate what she'd learned at Pop's garage to get the captain's truck in working order again. And just as Gérard had used her love for someone to his advantage, she'd do the same now.

He'd never leave Bella alone. And Kat knew it. If she fixed the truck, he'd save his shepherd rather than come after her.

"Try it now!" she called.

It might have been months overdue, but as the engine chugged to life Kat vowed she'd do whatever it took to make it to the dunes, and Gavin, before it was too late.

Without a thought or direction or even a warning to herself, Kat bolted—the muscle memory of her legs able to find their stride again through an open field of snow and bramble.

"Don't look back," Kat breathed out Gavin's line as she ran, leaving behind the stunned Vichy police captain, a truck with enough weapons to arm the Resistance for the impending fight to come, and one dear, courageous shepherd who, on that night, she hoped was too stubborn to die.

⌒

17 May 1952
2 Quai du Lot, 12190
Estaing, France

Kat stepped out of "The Blue Flash"—the mammoth Buick station wagon she'd borrowed from the Childs for the drive to Averyon and turned in a semicircle to absorb the spectacular view.

A square opened at the mouth of the Pont d'Estaing bridge, under the watchful eye of the Romanesque Church of Saint Fleuret and the Aubrac Mountains that overlooked the medieval village sleeping in the valley down below. Twisty and cobblestoned streets fed the square in typical French style, and the river babbled as patrons sat in cafés lining the avenue, sipped local rosé, and dined on fresh seafood trucked in from the coast.

A gentle wind kissed the hem of Kat's wasp-waist frock, tousling the mint skirt as she stood before the address Julia had penciled on the note card in Paris.

So this was it. The café.

*The hiding place.*

And the moment that all the years had been pointing to.

A black-and-white-striped awning stretched over outdoor tables, under a white marquee with Provençal-blue block letters on a three-story stone rooming house, which bore the name she sought: *Café du Château.*

Kat patted the chestnut curls sculpted at her nape, adjusted the black satchel she'd hooked in her elbow, and stepped through the establishment's front door.

A brass bell above the door gave a happy chime as her eyes adjusted to the light. She could have moved deeper into the dining room, toward the bustle of diners and waiters, but she stepped into what looked like a pâtisserie at the front, with cheery azure walls and a parade of confections overflowing in the display case.

She pinged the bell by the register and summoned a gentleman from the back. He dusted his hands on his apron with a bright smile. It faded when he spotted Kat. He was older, with time having tracked deep laugh lines in tanned skin around his eyes and mouth. And a trim beard of white. But the air was the same—his manner spoke of kindness and a welcome, despite the revelation of Kat standing in the middle of his shop.

"Bonjour, Kat," Valens said as he stepped up to the counter. "You look well, mademoiselle." He nodded then, his brow tipping in surprise when he cast a glance to her hand and saw the sparkler weighing down her finger. "Or madame, should I say?"

"Um—it is . . . Madame Fontaine, actually."

"Fontaine?" He paused, as if that name, too, sounded foreign. "You mean . . . ?"

"Oui. The captain."

"*Grand-père!* Les croissants," cried a boy who bounded out from the back, with flour dusted on his nose and panic alive on his little face. "They will burn! I need your help. You know I'm not to touch the ovens. Come, come."

Aged no more than six or seven, with dark hair and a button nose

Kat had seen before, and eyes as blue-green as the sea, he looked back at the patron in the shop, having no idea who she was. Then tugged at Valens' sleeve to get him moving. And while Kat's mind would need the confirmation, if Julia was right about the address, her heart fluttered with the truth it already seemed to know.

"Hush, Luc. Can you not see we have a guest?"

"Pardon, madame." The little boy tossed a bow in Kat's direction.

"Have patience; they will not burn. We wish only to allow them to find their perfect color, non?" Valens smiled down at the boy, squeezing a hand to his little shoulder as Luc nodded but grasped his aged hand to lead him to the back. "I must go. But I will send the owner out to speak with you." He nodded then, turning away.

"Valens?"

A knowing care in his eyes met Kat when he'd glanced back.

"It is good to see you," she added, hoping it was not out of place to feel emotion grip her and show him eyes that must have glistened from the sunlight streaming from the windows.

"And you, Célène. It is very, very good to see you."

Stomach turning flip-flops and having to hold herself from running back out the door more than once, Kat waited. And held her breath. Until a woman with auburn hair in a plait over her shoulder, a soft flowered-print dress in buttercup yellow, and a noticeable rise in her middle swept out from the back at a near run.

Manon skirted the display case and enveloped Kat in her arms.

"I told him you would come," she whispered at Kat's good ear, holding tight. Then backed up to get a look at her with a beaming smile. And then wrapped her in a tight hold again. "Kat—I told him so many times. How we've waited for this day."

"You told Valens?"

"She told me," a deeper voice echoed from behind.

Kat looked past Manon to the man hovering in the doorway.

The youth of Gavin's grin from the Boston mantel photos was mere memory now, to have been replaced by a man's smile. He'd kept the beard from the war years. The fuller shoulders too. Lines had matured at the corners of his eyes—only enough to highlight a pair of Harris blues not afraid to openly tear.

"I should have listened to my wife." He choked a little. Sniffed. And fused hands at his waist, as if he needed an anchor for the power of the moment. "She told me one day you'd walk through our door. And that I should be prepared for that."

"Gavin . . . ," Kat breathed out, the sight of him carrying her forward.

Her mind demanded answers. Why stay away? And where had he been? But all Kat could do was respond to the heart that carried her forward through the weight of questions, to embrace the brother she'd loved. Then lost. And searched for as if he were only a memory that would not let her go these past years. And now, to see him healthy and apparently even happy was the most confounding truth of it all.

"But why . . . ?" She tried to ask. Then stopped. Took a step back and had to start again. "Where have you been? I don't even know where to begin."

"Gérard found us. Weeks back, with the help of one of your friends—a woman named Julia? And before you blame your husband for not telling you, I was the one who asked him to wait. None of this is his fault."

"I don't understand. You've been here all this time? How could you just leave us like that, thinking you were dead? You *are* dead! As far as the US government is concerned. And the people at home who buried you."

"Come? S'il te plaît," he coaxed, with a hand outstretched for her to step through to the back of the café with them. "I'll tell you everything. Just please, come. Sit with us?"

Kat followed, moving as a ghost when he led her to their residence behind the shop.

This was just and simply a home.

Weathered stone tiles stretched through what must have been Manon's French kitchen. A behemoth gas stove dominated the back wall, bordered by an abundance of French vanilla–hued cabinets with furniture-like carved details, and wall hooks that organized a bevy of copper pots and pans. Industrial ovens had produced two batch-bake trays of croissants that now cooled on a wide counter beside—with the look and intoxicating scent she remembered now from the château kitchen all those years before. A butcher-block island overflowed with crusty, fresh-baked boules, wooden chargers of pears and apples, and a marble rolling pin that lay next to a round of pastry dusted with flour.

Gavin led them through a set of open French doors to the terrace, with flower boxes and a tiny iron dinette that overlooked the river below.

"Here." He offered Kat a chair. Then asked Manon when he pulled out another chair for her, "Won't you stay, love?"

"Of course. But I think I'll make some tea first."

Gavin sat but grasped his wife's hand as she swept by, giving her palm a squeeze. Manon returned the gesture with the warmth of a knowing smile and disappeared back into her kitchen. It was a little look to be sure, but Kat could see every ounce of affection between the two. And despite the questions and the hurt, she had to admit it was beautiful to see her brother in love.

"I'm sorry, Kat. I don't ask you to understand, but—"

"You're right. Because I don't."

"That is why. She is." Gavin pointed to the open doors and the auburn-haired chef moving about her kitchen. "My world is standing just through there. And I have to keep it safe."

"Please don't tell me this is about that childhood notion of not looking back. I don't think I could take it, not when this is about people's lives being destroyed."

"That's exactly what I'm saying. Think of your family, Kat, with your husband. What would you do to keep someone you love from harm?"

She did. Just then. And realized it was as messy an arrangement as any a novelist could dream up. A wedding night followed by an arrest and waves of revelations wasn't exactly in the same category as what he was comparing.

"I am not completely void of feeling, Gavin. I have lived the last eight years without knowing whether you were dead or alive. That warrants some understanding."

"Manon lost everything at the start of the war. So you know why I am not willing to risk our home, nor the peace we've found after it. I vowed to my wife that as long as the courts still had to punish the collaborators in France, we would remain hidden . . . and safe."

"This isn't like you."

"What does that mean?" With arms crossed over his chest, he leaned back in his chair. "Is that your way of telling me I've grown old?"

"No. But the Gavin I know wouldn't run from a challenge. He'd stand up and fight. He always did. He signed up to go to war, for heaven's sake! And risked everything at that château."

"I am fighting. Just in a different way. I can't expect you to understand."

"We buried you, Gav!" she blasted back, emotion nearly bleeding her dry for the joy at seeing him alive backed right up to anger at him having stayed away for so long.

"What?"

"Or at least we had an empty grave. Maman picked out a head-stone where we lay flowers every Memorial Day. For years after the war, she cried. Lou petitioned the CIA, or anyone who would listen. And even went to Birch himself—who happens to be an adviser to our president these days. Our stepfather spent a fortune and called in every favor he had, for years. He vowed never to give up until he found you. And became a shell of a man in the process. All for the love and loss of you."

Gavin's pain was obvious as he clamped his eyes shut and braced his elbows to the table, his fingertips holding a hung head.

"You were dead. And we had to go on."

He lifted his head. "Who said I was dead?"

"The government. They—"

Gavin shook his head, cutting her off.

And then, it dawned. "You mean you never knew you were declared dead? After the night at the château, I went to the dunes to look for you. I understand you fled to Lyon. You made contact with the OSS. And you filed your last report from there before you disappeared."

"That's right."

"The woman you spoke of—Julia? She worked in the OSS too, processing reports from field operatives overseas. It's she who remembered you."

"We did go to Lyon, long enough to get word back that I was alive. That message must not have gotten through before we left to go into hiding. But I never knew the worst of it. I wouldn't have done that to you."

"What did you think would happen when you didn't come home?" Kat closed her eyes for a breath, unable to believe it.

For the years of searching . . . the grief and loss and burden of never knowing . . . All of it might have been allayed had they simply arrived in Lyon at the same time. And her heart bled now to know they might even have passed each other on the same road.

"I swear I'll do everything I can to make this right."

"I'm not asking for penance."

"And you have no idea how deeply I thank you for that. But what I am asking for now is time. I have to protect my family from a man who knows the only ones who could send him to the executioner are the very same who worked at the Château du Broutel."

"What does that mean?"

He exhaled, as if resigned to something. "I saw him, Kat. The man who did this was in the photos. I know because I turned over the negatives—after I developed the film."

"But I've been in the very same room with Xandre in Paris, and I can tell you, he doesn't scare me. I am not afraid to face him again."

"Nor me. But it's not Xandre I speak of."

"Then who?"

Gavin shook his head again, then pointed to the shadow of the kitchen doors, his jaw clenched with it. "They are everything to me. And I beg you to forgive me for hurting you because of it. You are my sister and I will always love you. But please, don't ask for more than I can give."

Kat was not without a heart for his pain. Nor could she withstand watching her brother wrestle in a battle that tugged in opposite directions. They'd been through too much to cast aside a man's plea for those he loved without at least considering how it would impact all of them.

"What if I told you there might be a way out of this?"

"What way?" he asked.

"To see that Xandre and whoever protected him will answer for what they've done. And at the same time, we could ensure your family's protection here."

"I'd ask how that is possible when we both know this doesn't end with one man."

"Let's wait then, for your wife to bring out the tea. We'll sit and talk it through, all three of us. Then you two can decide together if this is what you want to do. And I'll honor your wishes, whatever they prove to be."

Gavin's face changed, the heady emotion giving way to a touch of amusement and faint sparkle in his eyes. He leaned back in his chair, shaking his head on a soft laugh.

"So pragmatic these days. Gérard told me you would be. I didn't believe him. Especially when I recalled how you used to blast into every conversation ready to fight—even with a blowtorch, as I recall. But he defended you. And had the gall to argue that I don't know the real you. At least not like he does. I had to stop myself from planting a fist in his face to talk about my sister like that."

"Is that so? And what else did my husband say?"

In authenticity it seemed, Gavin offered, "He said he understood my position. And didn't blame me, because if it was for you, he'd have done the same in my shoes."

"Oh . . ."

"That's why he couldn't let you go once that telegram brought you back to France. And by the time he'd figured that out, he was afraid it would be too late. That you would never forgive him. Gérard did give real information about where I was that night, thinking it would be enough to sway Xandre. But Manon and I had already gone from the dunes. We were safe and Gérard knew that. He'd have done anything to assure it, for you if not for me. I have to assume this is his way of sharing now what he couldn't then."

*The telegram . . .*

With all that had happened with Gérard's arrest and the legal wrangling that followed, Kat hadn't thought of it for some time. And yet the mention of it clicked something new in her mind: Xandre wouldn't have found Gavin his biggest threat. He wasn't even in the woods that night. Kat was. And Gérard.

So why would he have goaded her back to France at all?

"There's something we're missing. The telegram may have gotten me on that boat, but it's not why I stayed. Not all of it, anyway. I had to consider who else in France might be looking for you. Or for Gérard, and why. Without anything sure, I couldn't drop it. You know me well enough to gauge that as truth."

"I thought I did. In fact, I gave Gérard the compass and said to use it if he needed to. That it was the only way you'd trust him. But I see now that I was wrong. You'd have taken your husband at his word."

"I would have. I do." She nodded, emotion trying to make her a fool when she thought of the last thing Gérard had said to her before he was hauled away. "That's why none of this makes sense."

Kat's heart squeezed, thinking of the morning they'd awoken in Paris, how Gérard had wanted to tell her everything. How he'd said those beautiful words that he loved her and wasn't afraid to admit it. She wasn't either—not then, heaven help her, when she should have echoed every bit of her beating heart back before the police dragged him away.

"Gérard caught me reading lips of the Reich officers that night at the château, from across the ballroom. It's how he knew I have hearing loss in one ear. I slipped out of the party, leaving my clutch behind when I saw the Gestapo checking ladies' bags. I knew I wouldn't be able to take the photos—your life was more important, so I was willing to forgo that part of the plan."

"You've lost me now."

Kat leaned forward, elbows on the table. "Gérard took the photos. And he gave them to you to get to the OSS once you landed safely in Lyon."

"Which I did. I submitted a field report with everything from that night."

"I never actually saw the faces of the all party guests. If the OSS operative was at the château that night, he'd have done anything to hide his face. Especially if he knew you and I were there."

She shook her head, the weight of the implications heavier, broader, and far more high stakes than she'd realized. "There's only one person who would have altered your report—the one Julia read and remembered. And it's the same person who would be looking for you now, after all these years. It's why he's trying to send Gérard to prison for life. Gérard saw the man's face that night. But he didn't work in the OSS, so he'd never known the man's name."

"And he won't stop searching for us, will he? He won't leave us be until he's certain neither Gérard nor I can come forward with what we know."

Manon set the tea tray on the table with wide eyes and sat, searching her husband's face on the tail end of their conversation. Gavin reached out, took her hand in his, and laced their fingers together.

"Gavin, I am the one who's been wrong. My husband is my world too. And I'd give anything for one more chance to tell him so. But I can't do that alone. Nor can I fix this without you."

"We're listening." He squeezed his wife's hand. "What is it you want?"

"I need your help . . . in Paris."

# CHAPTER 28

20 May 1952
21 Rue de Vaugirard
Paris, France

Kat was shown into the formal salon in the eighteenth-century *hôtel particulier* that served as the Allmands' Paris home.

She waited in a typical Mimi Dover–decorated space with primrose-pink striped settees, Baroque wall insets exploding with freshly cut flowers, and an ornate gold mantel mirror that reflected views of wide windows and Jardin du Luxembourg across the avenue.

French doors were left open to the Allmands' private garden on the opposite side, with sun streaming through the gangly limbs of cypress trees, ropes of climbing ivy and manicured boxwoods, and peony bushes that still overflowed with blooms despite those cut for the indoor bouquets.

Kat supposed she was meant to be fazed by the luxury. Or by the sheer volume of space she would have to be in alone with Xandre. Even so, she tapped her heel against the marble floor as long minutes ticked by without the host's appearance. And only when the loud clip of footsteps echoed in the salon did her breath hitch at all.

Despite the relative safety of an exclusive mansion teeming with service staff, to be in the same space alone with him did cause her stomach to tighten. Xandre appeared unaffected, casual in linen trousers and white shirt cuffs already rolled against the pending summer heat, and with a haughty air as if he'd expected to see her walk through his door at some point.

"Tell me, Kat," Xandre's voice echoed against the high ceilings as he stepped in from the garden, a folded newspaper in his hand. "Did the shepherd live?"

*Down to brass tacks it is.*

"She did. Despite your best efforts to the contrary, it seems something survived after it crossed paths with you that night."

"I could say the same to you." Xandre patted a hand to where she'd driven a knife into his flank as he passed by to the sideboard. A host of decanters and amber liquids reflected in the sun. He held up a tumbler. "Care for one?"

"Non. I've no stomach for your calvados these days."

He chuckled as he set the newspaper on the sideboard and poured a tumblerful, topping it off before continuing. "And what finds you in this part of our city this morning? I thought you ladies frequented that little cooking venture midweek."

"We do, usually. But your wife did not arrive today. And I was worried."

"My wife should be reminded that we have staff for cooking." He dropped ice cubes in, swirled them, and turned with a lean against the sideboard.

"That is not why I'm here. I merely wished to inform you—as a courtesy—that your lies are at an end. And that right this moment, the Courts of Justice are processing my husband's release."

The exact look she'd expected to see washed over his face. Not panic; that would have been telling. This was doubt mixed with arrogance, and a tiny flit of his gaze to the garden said he thought she was bluffing.

"That is quite a statement, given where your husband finds himself at the moment. Tell me, do they wear stripes in a French prison?"

"I don't know. I suppose you'll find out when you get there."

Patience for the cat-and-mouse games appeared to wane, as he deadpanned with all humor having drained from his face. "What do you want, Kat? I've other business to attend to, and that doesn't include trading barbs with a pretentious skirt in my own home."

Kat stepped forward, showing confidence in her simple black peplum suit and heels, and lifted her chin in defiance.

"Perhaps I'll offer another statement then. You shot Frédéric the night Valens was arrested by the Vichy police. And Henri the night of the weapons drop at the château. The bodies the authorities have found on the château grounds do not lie."

"Is that so? And why would I do that—shoot a footman and a fishmonger?"

"For starters, Frédéric knew too much. You were our contact with the Maquis, and it was the Maquis who supplied the calvados to the locals—including our footman. You arranged for him to slowly poison Valens when you could have shot him on sight. Or turned him in. But I think you wanted to root out who he was working with to save your own skin. Arsenic is used in pesticides, is it not? You suggested the orchard as a meeting place the day you were given the Reich's rail schedule, and it had fermentation equipment. It was only a matter of time before he'd found out about you and you needed him replaced."

His chuckle was detached, a humorless peal that said he was more annoyed than alarmed. "We have gone back in time, *hmm*?"

"This is very much a tale of today, for how it ends. While you gave the jug to Frédéric and he used it to sicken Valens, only you could have known the names in the village to turn over to the Franc-Garde the day of the executions. You were playing both sides when Henri learned what you'd done. The last hope you had was to return a stolen lot of weapons from your overlords' rail lines on Christmas Eve. Dominique didn't trust you to share that information, and the only way you could have known was if the Nazi authorities had told you.

But they wouldn't have, would they? Not to an underling like you. So you took the German version of the shipment ledger he'd later given to Henri. That is, after you killed him. And before we buried him in the woods."

Xandre slammed the tumbler against the sideboard, sloshing liquid and ice to spill on the floor.

"Tell me," Kat bit out, boldness overtaking her words. "Was I digging my own grave that night too?"

"You've no proof," he gritted out from a clenched jaw. Exactly what she needed—to goad him to admission. "And no one to corroborate these tales, except that you are the wife of a man all know to be guilty of collaboration with the Nazi régime."

"You're right. I didn't have. Until now."

The sight of Dominique waltzing in from the Allmands' private garden with a black suit, freshly shaved face and combed hair, and a firm set to his jaw appeared to the man as the ghost of another life walking into his home.

"Xandre." Gavin stopped next to Kat, hands at his sides. "The chef has given her sworn statement. As have I—Gavin Harris. And Kat, my sister. As well as the pâtissier, who still lives and who should like nothing more than to read of your arrest in tomorrow's newspaper. And to see the release of Captain Fontaine alongside it."

"*Hmm.*" Xandre nodded, his index finger tapping the newspaper while he calculated.

"What I don't understand is why." Kat took a step, her heel echoing through the silence. "Why send me the telegram? It was you, wasn't it?"

"Of course it was."

"But I had no evidence to pose a threat to you. Why would you tip me off at all that Gérard was alive? Or were you really searching for Gavin? Because you knew he saw the photos. And that it was Birch who was at the château that night."

Gavin stepped up, fury evident in his profile. "It was Birch who turned over the SOE agents to the Boche before I'd even landed in France. And you helped him."

"If you'd have left well enough alone and never sent me that tele-gram," Kat blasted, shaking her head, "it would have all gone away."

"Because, Kathryn, the telegram wasn't meant for you."

The soft-spoken answer belonged to the man who, when she and Gavin had turned together, stood in the salon's open door.

"Lou . . ." Kat's voice trailed on reams of shock.

"You're not supposed to be here, Kathryn." Lou Sullivan looked to the son who'd been dead and buried, and offered an emotion-laden, "You neither, son."

"I don't understand," she pleaded, her gaze darting from Xandre's ire to Lou's unrepentant frown as he clicked the salon doors closed and crossed the room.

If anyone, it had always been Birch who should have walked through the doors. Not the man who'd loved the brother at her side. Or who'd wept with her maman and held her umbrella in the rain as they stood vigil over an empty grave. Or the man who'd given her away at her own wedding to Gérard, only to play a part in trying to now lock him away for life.

"All this time, it was Birch. Gavin knew it. Gérard had seen his face that night and would have figured it out sooner or later. But you?" Kat demanded, her voice cracking on its own. "How could you?"

"A telegram did come to our home that day. But it was meant for the eyes of the military colonel who'd have done anything to bring his son home. I paid off a director of intelligence in the OSS—Birch's cooperation was easy enough to buy, for the right price."

"You paid for what?" Gavin demanded.

"To keep your name off draft lists. To have your volunteer application lost. To keep you from harm once you did go—whatever I had to in order to save your mother's tears. And when I'd learned of Birch's activities in France, after you'd gone behind our backs and signed up . . . I merely pressed on it a little."

"You mean you blackmailed him."

"That man had too many sympathetic leanings for the Reich after the Great War. Everything he did in France the second time around was his choice. Turning over the SOE team. Even declaring you dead. It saved your mother grief in the end by it being over. And then I could keep looking for you on my own. I merely did what I had to in order to bring you home, son. I'd have done that and more."

Gavin clenched his jaw. Shook his head. And formed fists at his sides. "No. You let a war turn you into a criminal. And given the chance, you'd have been a murderer—two more times over."

"If we'd only appeased the Germans at the start, this war never would have happened. And the harsh reparations of the one before it would have been overturned. All of this could have been avoided. And you'd never have gone and broken your mother's heart."

"You know that's not true," Kat countered. "How many secrets did you have? How many more locked drawers are in your home office?"

"Let it go, Kat. He's destroyed whatever explanation he may have had." Gavin looked from Lou to Xandre, then gestured to the garden beyond the glass. "If either of you choose to leave, we'll let you. But you'll find French police waiting just outside. And you can sort out your own legal troubles with them."

Kat stared back at them—first to Lou, who'd stolen so much from them all in his years of deception. And to Xandre, thinking it poetic now that he couldn't even muster enough pride to stand and face the truth.

His head hung low, and his shoulders hunched over the sideboard.

"Gavin's right." Kat let the waves of emotion in to find the man she'd allowed to become a father over the years was nothing less than a coward who'd warped love in his mind. And made decisions that destroyed so many lives. "You have the option you gave no one else. It is your choice how you leave now. But you will hold our families captive not a single day longer."

Xandre reached for the newspaper, tearing at it the instant a hollow *click* echoed off the ceiling from behind.

"Arrêtez!" Mimi's voice wavered but still echoed off the ceiling in a clear shout for her husband to stop, as she slinked through the open salon door.

With shaking hands and the stark contrast of purple bruises that shone out against the porcelain skin under her eye, the Grace Kelly vision in pastel pink and soft blonde waves had not attended cooking class that day. Instead, she raised a Walther pistol and took calculated steps into the room.

"Mimi . . ." Gavin stepped in front of Kat and reached out, palming the air. "We mean you no harm. Think about what you're doing."

"I am." Her chin quivered as she advanced and trained the weapon on Xandre. "But he does mean harm—to everyone and everything he touches. My husband keeps a pistol on him. I'd wager it's in that newspaper, just in case a day like this came when his past would catch up with him. Or perhaps his present would as well."

"You don't know what you're saying, Chérie," Xandre pleaded. "There is a history with these people that you know nothing of and—"

"I said *stop*," she shouted again, this time with a steely resolve that echoed off the ceiling. "Thank goodness Mrs. Fontaine loaned me her husband's service weapon, or you may have continued your lies. But all I needed was to listen at the door, to the guest who'd arranged to introduce us on my first visit to Paris with his daughter. To the man who made his children's lives a misery. And to the military colonel who deserves every bit of damnation our country can heap upon his name. And I swear if you move one more inch toward that newspaper . . . I will use this. And then the Courts of Justice will no longer need my sworn statement along with theirs because you will be the one in a grave."

Kat flitted her glance from Mimi to Gavin, to the frozen Lou, and to the furious Xandre grinding his fists into the front lip of the sideboard. None seemed certain whether the wounded Mimi would fire, until she exhaled low and lifted her chin in solidarity.

"You will never hurt another person again. And as your wife and the lady of this house, it is my job to ensure you don't." Facing Xandre, she called over her shoulder a cool, *"Entrez!"*

French police swarming a historic mansion was a sight Kat could not understand how one could become used to. But as the uniforms flooded in from the gardens, it brought back the remembrance of the same sound of jackboots flooding down the service stairs at the Château du Broutel. Save for that this time, the powers that governed were in pursuit of truth and had found it with the strength of a petite Boston socialite whom all had underestimated.

Mimi collapsed in a fit of tears in Gavin's arms. Kat took the unloaded weapon back from her friend's historic bluff and, still with little sense of victory, watched this time as handcuffs were affixed to Xandre's and Lou's wrists.

Loss was not measured in years—not in those calendar days that had passed since the war, nor for those to come for shackled men led out of a lavish salon for the last time. Kat watched with sorrow as Mimi broke apart, while Gavin melted to a settee at her side, and hoped that if anything Julia had told her was true, that something could be rebuilt from the broken days of the past.

And that this, too, would make them stronger in the end.

# CHAPTER 29

25 *August 1952*
92 Avenue d'Iéna
Paris, France

The bells of Paris chimed across the city that day, echoing in the streets a siren song of commemoration.

Even as the summer months saw the locals flee the tourist crowds and stifling city heat for their annual *vacances*, Parisians did not wish to forget the liberation of Paris on that day in 1944. And for those who'd stayed on, neither did they wish to forgo an ardent remembrance of all they'd lost in war nor all they'd gained after it.

Kat glanced up from her place on the study floor as the bells chimed, her attention lifted from the wooden packing crates sitting in a maze of ordered chaos on the hardwoods. Drawn by the bells' invitation, she stood and carried the short stack of books she'd been sorting—volumes of Alfred de Musset poems she couldn't bear to leave behind—and padded to the windows in bare feet.

Parting the drapes, she leaned into the window seat, her cigarette pants–clad knee on the cushion so she could look out at the bold visage of l'Arc de Triomphe draped in the French flag. She tucked a stray wisp that had come loose from the kerchief holding back her hair and gazed out at the steel-blue sea of mansard roofs that fanned out for miles around the Seine and the ironwork Eiffel Tower at its center. Sparrows took to the sky with the bells' song, darting and diving as the melody rang out.

"I thought I'd find you either in the kitchen . . . or here."

Kat looked up at the sound of Gérard's voice, her breath hitching a little on instinct now whenever he walked into the room—though she'd never have admitted it, if only to save her husband gloating from then on. But she could appreciate the figure he cut, standing in the study doorway in a summer suit and tie loosed at his neck, with wind-teased hair and a contented smile on his lips.

"I guessed right."

"There's an endive salad with Anjou pears and blue cheese in the kitchen if you're hungry."

Shaking his head, he countered. "Try again."

"Or coq au vin just out of the oven? It's cooling on the butcher block."

"My girl." Strolling in, Gérard grinned and dropped his trilby and jacket on the settee as he went by. And met her at the window, with arms slipped around her waist from behind to offer a soft, "Hi" against her good ear.

"Bonjour, yourself."

He spied the stack of books on the cushion in front of her and tapped them with his index finger.

"What's this? I thought we agreed you'd only supervise the staff in the packing."

"*You* agreed. And I am supervising," she argued, half turning to lean up and press a peck to his stubbled chin. "I'm supervising everything into the proper crates. I can't have your books—"

Gérard squeezed her waist in a little shimmy. "Our books."

"D'accord. Our books, lost on the way to the cottage. If you think we can live contented by the sea without all of these things, I'd disagree. Everything that is important goes to Le Crotoy harbor with us. And I will put up a fight about it if necessary."

"I wouldn't hope for anything less. The more we fight, the more we get to make up. And that's what I can't live without."

They stood quiet for a breath then, holding fast to the rush of remembrance the bells brought. Gérard kept his arms in a tight circle around her with his chin pressed in a light graze against the top of her head.

Having fallen into the rhythm of reading each other's moods, Kat noted the silence as a tip that his thoughts were trying to carry him away somewhere. Maybe to look back? Maybe to the château and those years of war, when they hadn't a clue how far they'd have to journey to be standing where they were at that very moment?

"Are you thinking about Henri?"

He sighed, the weight of his arms adjusting her shoulders with it. "Are you thinking about Jeffrey?"

"I do, some days. And Pops, how he'd have been so proud that we put up such a fight to win the war. And of the years lost with Gavin and Manon. Or how I'll miss Julia and Paul when they move to Marseilles. Or of everyone who gave of themselves to get the world—and France—to this day. Even Lou, who will spend the rest of his days with a tarnished name, even if he doesn't end up sitting in a military prison alongside Birch. Looking back, I'm ashamed I didn't connect the father I knew to the man he truly was."

"You've nothing to be ashamed of. How could you know?"

"You're right; we couldn't. That's why I've decided . . . I'd much rather look forward now." She turned away from the windows then, hooking her arms behind Gérard's neck so she could gaze up at him. "How did the meeting go?"

"You'll be pleased to learn that Mr. James and our Paris solicitors have deemed your husband to be in the clear. With a full pardon from the French government, I might add, for Xandre's lies, Colonel Sullivan's deception, and with Mimi's corroboration. And a commendation from the British SIS, though no one else can know about that part of the deal but you."

"And . . . ?"

"And Xandre, or as the world knows him, Léo Allmand, will also spend the next decades in a French prison to pay for his crimes during the war. While that shouldn't cheer me considerably, it does. At least to know I won't have to be looking over my shoulder to ensure no one is coming after you. I don't know how your brother endured it as long as he did."

"Us, you mean. No one is coming after us."

He dropped a hand, palming the rise in her middle under the soft pointelle weave of her blouse, and gave a hint of a smile. "Oui. Us. Our family. And that's why I don't want you lifting any more books. And especially not the crates, d'accord? Call me and I'll do it. That's what husbands are for."

"But—"

He cut her off with a kiss, then shook his head. "I know you can do anything you set your mind to, Kat. I'm not debating that. But can you listen to me, just this once? And at least consider slowing down?"

"I still have several months to work yet. My editor may have something to say about it if I disappear to the coast this early—baby on the way or not."

"*Time* magazine will continue to have the most brilliant food editor that France has to offer, but only after she's taken a well-earned leave of absence. You can fix our autos when they break down and cook all the culinary delights you want. And write for whomever you choose for the rest of our lives, with Julia to use her pull to back you up. But I'll do everything else. Deal?"

"Never. I'm not wired to play second team, remember? But we can fight about that later." Kat looked to the windows again, gazing out at the romance of a perfect cerulean sky. "For now, just promise me we'll come back here one day. I don't think I could live without Paris. Nor you in it."

"Good thing you don't have to on either count. The flat will still be here, anytime you want to come back. It's not goodbye forever. Only for now."

Gérard paused, showing why he was so skilled at reading the people in any room in which they entered. Pity she was the only one under his scrutinizing gaze at the moment. He looked to the crates of books she'd been sorting through on the floor and saw the open letter atop one.

"I received a letter from Boston."

"*Mm-hmm.* I saw. Your mother?"

"I'm not worried about Maman—she's a survivor. And she'll survive this." Kat shook her head and sighed into the name. "It's Mimi."

"Don't worry about your friend," he coaxed, knowing her so well that her thoughts were hopscotching between the sorrow in her friend's life and the fulfillment in her own. "She'll heal. Just give her time. And your mother, too, come to think of it. She will find forgiveness faster. I have to imagine having her son back—and his family—will prove a balm to her wounds."

The bells faded then, their song ending with the ghost of an echo for several seconds after. And then the streets were still.

They paused. Looked at each other in the quiet, the haze of yesterday fading with the bells' final toll. And somehow, as France rebuilt and the people constructed new lives out of the ashes, they recognized their hope of tomorrow was soon to be in a cottage by the sea.

"*Je vous aime,*" Kat breathed out, saying "I love you" to the two beloveds at that window with her.

"That's all I needed to hear. Allons-y, family," Gérard said before pressing a kiss to her mouth. "Let's go home."

# EPILOGUE

24 *December* 1952
1 Rue du Château
Le Crotoy, France

Nature's gift for Christmas was snow on the sand and blazing pine logs on the hearth.

Kat reclined, her eyes drifting in sleep as she snuggled in the crook of a settee beneath the cottage bedroom window. A book lay butterflied on the swell of her middle, and their shepherd, Maddie, was draped in blissful sleep over her ankles. Kat had managed to get lost in this view of the coast most days now, feeling the tiny kicks in her middle and maintaining the oh-so-dear glances of a tentative Gérard, who seemed to watch her like she was a ticking bomb set to explode instead of a content mother-to-be.

Knuckles rapped the bedroom door. "You awake?"

She looked up. *"Hmm?"*

Gérard popped his head in with a tea towel slung over his shoulder and a look of dread painted upon his face. "I hate to ask you for help, but I don't think I can manage the circus much longer."

"You want me to step in on cooking Christmas dinner . . . when Julia Child is in our kitchen? Are you completely mad?"

With a light groan Gérard stepped in and closed their bedroom door behind. He swept over to kneel beside her, offering a rub behind Maddie's ears when the pup stirred with a sleepy yawn, and set

Kat's book aside to rest his hand on her belly after. "Maybe. How are you two?"

"We're tired and hungry. But happy. You?"

"The same," he said, though he shook his head. "Even though Paul and Valens have hidden themselves in the library, I assume to debate the merits of fine French wine and the reach of the Iron Curtain across the globe. They'll be in there for hours. Meanwhile, Julia dropped a leg of lamb on our kitchen floor and she's trying to put it back on the silver platter for Christmas dinner. She said something about if that ever happens, just serve it because who'd know otherwise?"

It was easy to laugh, knowing of their French chef friend's penchant for life and vitality—and fearless improvisation—when in the kitchen. "I warned you. Julia does that. She rather favors a casual air and flamboyance when she cooks. It's all about passion for her, never propriety. That's what makes her so good."

"Oui, but your mother is about to have a fit. And I'd almost rather go back to a war than have to manage those two personalities in the same kitchen. At this point I'd rather they just burned it down. And we'll sneak away to Paris where they can't find us."

Placing a hand over his, she allowed the smile in her heart to find its way to her lips. "Cheri, look at me. I'm as big as this cottage. I don't think I'll be sneaking off with you anytime soon. No matter how much I might want to."

The bell rang, the chime at the cottage front door alerting them to the addition of saviors to their number. Perhaps Christmas dinner would not be so fraught with wild abandon if another chef could step in and calm icy waters in the meal preparation.

"They're here." Kat anchored her hands on the cushion behind her back, bracing herself to try to stand. Maddie stirred and leapt down to the floor as Gérard braced an arm under her elbow.

"Finally. Gavin can keep an eye on Luc and Rosie. And with the kids occupied, I'm certain Manon will step in and have the chaos in the kitchen sorted in no time. So that means I can hide in here with you."

"But it's our home. We should go and greet our—" Kat groaned, trying to stand, and found that her imbalance sent her straight back to the cushion with a *thud*.

"You can greet our guests later. We should stay here for as long as you need to catch your breath. Or to stand comfortably. And I intend to be a pillar until then, if you want one."

The memory of one night in their Paris flat came back as Kat tried again, and Gérard held her up. It brought a smile to her heart to recall when she'd once brought a banana tart into their study, with two forks instead of one. And he'd finally shared something of himself with Kat—something true and lasting. How sweet that one decision seemed now, for stepping into that room had changed so many moments that had come after it.

"Do you know the moment I fell in love with you?"

"Let's hope it was at first sight, like it was for me." He ticked his brow a touch, giving her a look that said he was half curious yet half knowing. "But if not, I'd wager it's a day other than when you sat behind the desk in my room behind a heap of passports and with a pistol pointed in my general direction. Remind me to warn any double agents I meet never to cross paths with you."

"Lucky for you, I'd already seen the real Gérard Fontaine long before that. I think my heart already knew what my eyes had yet to see. That you are a man of courage. And honor. And strength. One who never made me feel I should have to hide in the shadows. Even if that's what I was supposed to do during the war. I look back now at all the uncertainty and the pain and the loss that nearly finished us both, and I'm not sorry. Not if we're standing here now."

"So? When was it you realized you loved your husband, Mrs. Fontaine? Yesterday or this morning?"

"That night we shared the dessert, but with two forks. It's when I realized I no longer wanted to walk separate roads. And I only want one now. Here with you. At our home, and with the beloveds in our French kitchen."

The sound of Julia's high-pitched laughter rolled in from the other room, and the clink of toasting glasses and joyful voices permeated beyond the door. Maddie tiptoed around their legs, dancing in circles as Gérard pressed a kiss to Kat's temple.

"They're waiting for us," she whispered, wanting to stay there with him a bit longer.

"They are. Even though I know that doesn't change anything. If there's only one fork left, you're still going to have to fight me for it."

He smiled back, for they both knew Kat was allowing him to guide her to the door. And at the same time, what it took for her to surrender her will and trust enough to lean on someone else for a change.

"Oh, Mr. Fontaine, I dearly hope so."

Snow dotted the skies outside the window. Winter danced on the wind that battered the harbor and covered their world in a blanket of white as they laced fingers and sat down to the warmth of a Christmas table surrounded by family, French chefs, and beloved friends.

~ *La Fin* ~

# AUTHOR'S NOTE

W *here do your story ideas come from?"*
It's the question this author is asked most. And the answer? That's a little more nuanced.

I didn't come to know Julia Child through her cookbooks or the wildly successful *The French Chef* TV show until I was in my early forties. By then she'd been a figure of my imagination all my life—the tall, uniquely voiced, and enigmatic chef who'd once been parodied (hilariously by Dan Aykroyd) on *Saturday Night Live*, who was played in flawless style by actress Meryl Streep in the 2009 film *Julie & Julia*, and from the worn volume of *Mastering the Art of French Cooking* that sat on the shelf in my mother's kitchen for all the years of my youth.

By the time I was contemplating my next novel, I hadn't a clue what (or about whom) I wanted to write. Until, in her characteristic style, Julia Child blasted onto the scene of my life and took a front row seat. And though this novel is a work of fiction—and I've taken creative liberties to imagine Kat's experiences in the OSS and crossing paths with Julia Child in 1950s Paris—it is inspired by the life of the remarkable chef who brought French cuisine into the kitchens of American housewives for generations.

I learned about Julia Child's onetime "spy" past from a podcast, in which I was shocked to learn her backstory of having worked for the Office of Strategic Services (OSS)—the precursor to the modern CIA—to collect intelligence and aid the Allies' subversive efforts during World War II. Though she'd note in her posthumous 2006 memoir, *My Life in France*, that her plan upon graduating from Smith College in 1934 "was to become a famous woman novelist," Julia found herself in Washington, DC, and once America entered World War II in late 1941, she sought to join up.

Having been rejected by the army and navy for her height (standing tall at six foot two), Julia later joined the United States' first official intelligence agency as a research assistant in the Secret Intelligence division of the OSS in December 1942. Though she was never credited with actual spy work in the field, the CIA's declassification of certain wartime documents in 1981 showed that intelligence officer Julia Child was assigned some of the more interesting aspects of subversive work, including the experimental development of shark repellant.

The OSS also offered Julia the opportunity to travel the world, including to Kunming, China, and Ceylon (present-day Sri Lanka), where she served as chief of the OSS Registry and crossed paths with fellow OSS agent and artist Paul Child, who would later become her lifelong companion. It was her husband Paul's work with the United States Information Service (USIS) at the Parisian embassy that brought the couple to the country that would forever capture her heart. Of their first lunch in France in 1948, Julia noted, "It was the most exciting meal of my life."

Imagining Julia before she was "Julia Child" gave this novel the flavor I'd hoped, to see her as a graduate of Le Cordon Bleu, a mentor and passionate instructor in French cooking, and a friend to an imagined former-OSS agent who was wrestling with the shadows of her own past experiences in the war.

The characters of Kat Harris Fontaine and French chef Manon Altier Harris emerged as constructs from real female spies who'd worked for the American OSS, the British Special Operations Executive (SOE), and the French Resistance during World War II. They include names such as Nancy Wake, Violette Szabo, Noor Inayat Khan (the first female wireless operator in occupied Europe), jazz entertainer Josephine Baker, and Virgina Hall, the latter whom the Gestapo dubbed "the most dangerous of all Allied spies." It was the ingenuity and resourcefulness of these women whose contributions to history cannot be understated and who, alongside Julia Child, formed the vision for the heroic female-led cast in this story.

Keen students of history may notice familiar names in this novel, including writers Ernest Hemingway, F. Scott Fitzgerald, John Steinbeck, James Joyce, and Sylvia Plath; famed Shakespeare and Company bookshop owner Sylvia Beach; OSS chief from 1942 to 1954, William Joseph "Wild Bill" Donovan; Château du Broutel owners Le Marquis and La Marquise de Longvilliers (the latter who bravely lectured Reich officers who'd occupied their home against nailing holes in the château walls); and French cooking instructors Simone "Simca" Beck and Louisette Bertholle, who, alongside Julia Child, imagined what would become the staple cookbook of French cuisine: *Mastering the Art of French Cooking* (1961). In addition, the modern-day Paris eatery, Le Comptoir des Saints-Pères, is the location for the first genuine meal Kat and Gèrard share that sparks their love story in the post-war storyline. Tourists and locals will note this is the same address as its predecessor mentioned in this story, the famed Michaud's.

While this story took twists and turns that even its author did not expect, the heartbeat of this novel became imagining the northern coast of war-torn France with Gavin and Manon, exploring the streets of postwar Paris with Gérard and Kat, and cooking with L'Ecole des Trois Gourmandes in Julia and Paul Child's famed flat, Roo de Loo.

Where do story ideas come from?

From life, friend.

From the flavorful, remarkable, and beautiful lives we live.

—Kristy

# ACKNOWLEDGMENTS

Like Julia, I am fortunate to have beloved friends and family and brilliant colleagues in my life. It is to them I say thank you.

To editors Becky Monds and Julee Schwarzburg: Your guiding hands, laser-sharp instincts, and passion for storytelling breathed life into this book. I couldn't have done it without you. To Rachelle Gardner: You're the Julia of my life! A constant friend, brilliant mentor, and a fearless trailblazer for women everywhere. I'm humbled to be counted among your friends. To my beloved family, Jeremy, Brady, Carson, and Colt; Rick, Lindy, and Jenny; and to dear friends, Katherine, Sarah, Maggie, Jodi, and Marti: You all have my heart. You *are* my heart. And you're the reason life is beautiful. I'm so glad I get to live it with you. To Tiffany Phillips and the remarkable team at Wild Geese Bookshop, and to the entire community in Franklin, Indiana: Thank you is never enough for adopting this fellow Hoosier into your brilliant and beautiful reading family. Every time we're together, it feels like coming home. Until we meet again!

And to you, dear reader friend: *Thank you.* I am in constant awe that you would give of your time to turn pages of my books. That you spent time with and loved these characters is my greatest wish—and I hope (just as I have) you've left this reading experience hungry for all the beauty life has to offer. May we partake with wild abandon.

As Julia would say at the end of each episode of *The French Chef*: "Bon appétit!"

# ADDITIONAL READING

Child, Julia, and Louisette Bertholle. *Mastering the Art of French Cooking.* New York: Knopf, 1961.

Child, Julia, and Avis Devoto. *As Always, Julia: Food, Friendship and the Making of a Masterpiece.* Edited by Joan Reardon. New York: Houghton Mifflin Harcourt, 2010.

Child, Julia, and Alex Prud'homme. *My Life in France.* New York: Anchor Books, 2006.

Hemingway, Ernest. *A Moveable Feast.* New York: Scribner, 1964.

Johnson, Paula J. *Julia Child's Kitchen.* New York: Abrams, 2024.

Karnow, Stanley. *Paris in the Fifties.* New York: Times Books, 1997.

O'Donnell, Patrick. *Operatives, Spies, and Saboteurs: The Unknown Story of the Men and Women of World War II's OSS.* New York: Free Press, 2004.

Pratt, Katie, and Alex Prud'homme. *France Is a Feast: The Photographic Journey of Paul and Julia Child.* New York: Thames & Hudson, 2017.

Purnell, Sonia. *A Woman of No Importance: The Untold Story of the American Spy Who Helped Win World War II.* New York: Penguin, 2019.

Rose, Sarah. *D-Day Girls: The Spies Who Armed the Resistance, Sabotaged the Nazis, and Helped Win World War II.* Reprint ed. New York: Crown, 2020.

Spitz, Bob. *Dearie: The Remarkable Life of Julia Child.* New York: Knopf, 2013.

# DISCUSSION QUESTIONS

1. In the beginning of the novel, the war-torn world of Northern France is shown in vivid contrast to postwar Paris. How do the characters navigate the reality of their worlds before, during, and after World War II? What were the moments that impacted each the most?

2. Family is a constant theme woven throughout the novel—both the beauty in relationships that stay strong and loving, and in the pain of loss, grief, or relationships that break down. How are Kat and Gérard, Manon and Gavin able to heal from the trauma of their pasts but still move forward in healthy relationships?

3. Julia Child becomes the glue that binds Kat's past experiences in the OSS during World War II to her postwar life in Paris. How do Kat's interactions with Julia pave the way for her to ultimately find out what happened to her brother? How did Julia's influence impact Kat's ability to trust others again—including to reconcile with Gérard?

4. The novel presents themes of women battling the stereotypes of their culture at the time in which they lived. How do characters Manon, Kat, Mimi, Julia, the cooking class, and even Geneviève Sullivan (Kat's maman) overcome the constraints on women in

the 1940s and 1950s? How does each find ways to thrive in her world?

5. Despite the upheaval in her life in postwar Paris, Kat finds an unexpected haven when she returns to the kitchen. How does the Paris cooking class allow Kat to revisit the darkness of her past but still help her imagine a brighter future? Does the exploration of hobbies and interests—new or old—have the ability to impact our lives?

6. The heartbeat of the story is Julia Child and her love of French cuisine. How has Julia Child's legacy impacted our world? What memories do you have of Julia Child—either as the TV show personality, the cookbook author, or as the former OSS agent during World War II?

# ABOUT THE AUTHOR

*Author Photo © Whitney Neal Studios*

Kristy Cambron is a vintage-inspired storyteller writing from the space where beauty, art, and history intersect. She's a Christy Award–winning author of historical fiction, including her bestselling novels, *The Butterfly and the Violin* and *The Paris Dressmaker*. Her work has been named to *Cosmopolitan* Best Historical Fiction Novels, *Publishers Weekly* Religion & Spirituality TOP 10, *Library Journal*'s Best Books, and she received a Christy Award for her novel *The Painted Castle*. Her work has been featured at *Once Upon a Book Club Box*, *Frolic*, *Book Club Girl*, *BookBub*, *Country Woman* magazine, and *(in)Courage*. She holds a degree in art history/research writing and spent fifteen years in education and leadership development for a Fortune 100 corporation before stepping away to pursue her passion for storytelling. Kristy lives in Indiana with her husband and three basketball-loving sons, where she can probably be bribed with a peppermint mocha latte and a good read.

Find her online at kristycambron.com
Facebook: @KCambronAuthor
Threads: @kristycambron
Instagram: @kristycambron
BookBub: @KristyCambron